Madison Lane stabbed a finger
in his chest. "I am not a Grinch,
and I am not trying to kill Christmas."

Sheriff Gage McBride couldn't believe he'd actually felt sorry for her, felt like kissing that luscious mouth. Wrapping his hand around her delicate wrist, he removed her finger from his chest. "Lady, you might not give a damn about this town, but I do. And from where I'm standing, you've done a pretty good job destroying both it and the holiday."

"Hey, this is not my fault. I had no choice but to—"

"Yeah, try telling that to the folks waiting for you in the town hall. You're real good with numbers, Ms. Lane." He went to take hold of her arm. "Let's see how you do when you have to look those people in the eye and explain—"

Glaring at him, she pushed his hand away. "I'm not going anywhere, especially with you. I don't like you, Sheriff McBride."

"Good, since I'm not particularly fond of you either, Ms. Lane. But the citizens of Christmas deserve some answers." He hauled her from the SUV. "Sorry, Ms. Grinch, but you're coming with me." •

The Trouble *with* Christmas

Debbie Mason

FOREVER

NEW YORK   BOSTON

Copyright © 2013 by Debbie Mazzuca
Excerpt from *Christmas in July* copyright © 2013 by Debbie Mazzuca

Forever
Hachette Book Group
237 Park Avenue
New York, NY 10017

www.HachetteBookGroup.com

Printed in the United States of America

First Edition: September 2013
10 9 8 7 6 5 4 3 2 1

OPM

Forever is an imprint of Grand Central Publishing.
The Forever name and logo are trademarks of Hachette Book Group, Inc.

The Hachette Speakers Bureau provides a wide range of authors for speaking events. To find out more, go to www.hachettespeakersbureau .com or call (866) 376-6591.

The publisher is not responsible for websites (or their content) that are not owned by the publisher.

ATTENTION CORPORATIONS AND ORGANIZATIONS:
Most HACHETTE BOOK GROUP books are available at quantity discounts with bulk purchase for educational, business, or sales promotional use. For information, please call or write:

Special Markets Department, Hachette Book Group
237 Park Avenue, New York, NY 10017
Telephone: 1-800-222-6747 Fax: 1-800-477-5925

To my granddaughter, Lily, who makes every day feel like Christmas. This one's for you, sweetpea.

Acknowledgments

My heartfelt thanks to Alex Logan. I couldn't have asked for a better, more dedicated editor. Your insightful suggestions have greatly improved this story. A big thank-you to copy editor Mark Steven Long for making the book so much better. To art director Diane Luger and her team, thanks so much for the fantastic cover. Many thanks to my agent, Pamela Harty, for your expert advice and all your efforts on my behalf. Much gratitude and love to my daughter, Jess, for still loving this story after reading it at least twenty times. Thank you to my writer friends, Allison Van Diepen, Lucy Farago, and Teresa Wilde, for your support and advice. To my critique partner, Vanessa Kelly, thank you for being so generous with your time and talent. And most of all, I'd like to thank my husband and children for always being there to encourage, support, and love me. I am truly blessed.

The Trouble
with Christmas

Chapter One

If Madison had a gun, she'd shoot out the sound system pumping "Jingle Bells" through her office speakers. Instead, she bit off Rudolph's chocolate head and pointed a finger at the brightly colored, foil-wrapped Santa on her desk. "You're next, big guy."

It was only November 29, and she was already sick to death of the nauseating carols hijacking the radio stations, the migraine-inducing Christmas lights that used up enough energy to power a small country, and don't get her started on the crowds—people running around buying presents they couldn't afford, racking up credit card debt that would make them want to jump off the Brooklyn Bridge come January.

Her attitude was probably the reason why her assistant decided today was a double-chocolate day. She'd worked with Madison at the resort developer Hartwell Enterprises for the last five years and knew the over-the-top holiday hoopla made Madison...cranky. She didn't know why, no one did, and Madison planned to keep it that way. To keep the past exactly where it belonged, in the past.

No *Boo hoo, woe is me* for Madison Lane. She was a "dust yourself off, pick yourself up by the bootstraps" kind of gal. And that was exactly what she'd done ten years ago. At eighteen, she'd kicked off the dirt of the small Southern town she'd grown up in and never looked back. Moved to the big city where no one knew your name, cared where you came from, or who your parents were.

She loved her life in New York. She had the best boss, the best job, and two of the most amazing best friends. Yep, her world was...almost perfect. And as soon as she figured out a way to get rid of her boss's nephew, Harrison Hartwell the Third, with his fake tan and fake British accent, it would be perfect. Six months ago, playing the family card, Harrison had slithered past her defenses. But now she saw him for what he was: a slick freeloader who wanted her job.

Her job was safe. The guy was an idiot. He'd tried to steamroll a resort development deal with the small town of Christmas, Colorado, past her—an investment that would have bankrupted Joe, her boss. But four days ago, as VP of finance, she'd presented a twenty-page argument against the deal. Her report, along with Joe's respect for her opinion, had paid off, and the negotiations ended.

Take that, Harrison, she thought, biting off Rudolph's leg.

The alarm on her watch beeped, ending her five-minute endorphin-releasing therapy. Wrapping up the half-eaten chocolate reindeer, she tucked him in the drawer along with Santa and got back to work on the budget she was presenting this afternoon. Thanks to the elimination of the deal with Christmas, Hartwell's financial future looked a whole lot brighter. She'd been practically giddy when she deleted the town from the budget. And it had nothing to do with her dislike of small towns or the holiday it was named after. She never let emotions interfere with business.

She frowned when a high priority e-mail from her best friend, Vivian Westfield, a reporter for the online *Daily News*, popped up on her screen requesting an immediate Skype conference call with their mutual best friend, Skylar Davis, a trust-fund baby who was in Belize, presumably saving the world again.

Madison had met Skye and Vivi on their first day of college, and they'd been inseparable ever since. With her father dead ten years now, not that he'd been much of a father, her friends were the closest thing to family Madison had.

She logged in and waited for the connection, trying not to worry about the reason for the call. They knew how she felt about taking personal time at work. Then again, that had never stopped them in the past. As far as they were concerned, especially Skye, Madison was always at work.

And that, Madison decided, was probably the reason for the ASAP call—her Thanksgiving no-show. Vivi had ratted her out. But Madison had a good reason for skipping the holiday. She'd been working on her report to end the negotiations with Christmas. Now that she thought about it, Vivi hadn't sounded overly upset when she'd bailed on her.

Vivi popped up on the left side of the screen, sitting on her couch and looking disgustingly gorgeous for a 9:00 a.m. call in a black tank top, her long, chocolate-brown hair falling over her shoulders as she leaned closer, narrowing her eyes at Madison. "You okay?" she asked in her raspy voice that left men panting at her feet.

Madison frowned, wondering why she asked, then realized it was probably because of all the hours she'd had been putting in at work. "Great, better than great, actually. Just going over the budget one last time, and next year's bonus looks like a sure..." She trailed off when her best friend winced.

"What's with the face?" Madison asked, pushing her black-framed glasses to the top of her head. She didn't need glasses. She'd started wearing them when she realized men thought with her blonde hair, blue eyes, and ridiculously curvy body that she was a bimbo. She wasn't. She was smart. "And speaking of faces," she said, taking a closer look, "there's something about yours. You look different. Kind of glowy and... Wow, you look happy."

Vivi blushed. Weird. Vivi never blushed.

And then, obviously as a means of distracting Madison, she said, "You look different, too. What's with the lipstick? You never wear lipstick."

She didn't. Her lips were full enough without drawing attention to them. She hadn't worn lipstick since junior high, when the senior boys told her all the disgusting things they'd like her to do with her mouth. She'd known it was because they thought she was like her mother, but knowing that hadn't made it any easier.

She touched the tip of her tongue to her upper lip. Chocolate. Taking a tissue from the box on the corner of her desk, she wiped her mouth.

"Better. Brown's not your color."

Okay, Vivi'd distracted her long enough, but before

Madison could question her about the wincing thing, and the blushing, Skye appeared in the upper right of her screen. Her butterscotch-blonde, curly hair more wild than usual, she looked like Malibu Barbie sitting cross-legged in a "Save the Planet" T-shirt on a bed surrounded by mosquito netting.

"Are you okay?" Skye asked, her eyes filled with concern.

"Y'all are making me nervous. What…" Madison's mouth fell open as a half-naked man with incredible arms, broad shoulders, and a sculpted chest walked behind Vivi's green couch. Vivi tipped her head back and followed him out of view, devouring him with her eyes.

"Move your screen! Follow that man," Skye demanded.

"Sweet baby Jesus. Who. Is. That?" Madison tugged on the black turtleneck beneath her boxy blazer.

Eyes sparkling, face flushed, Vivi…giggled. Madison gaped at her. Vivi "Kick-Ass" Westfield did not giggle. The body sauntered back into view, holding a container of milk in one hand while his other hand caressed Vivi's shoulder. A champagne-colored Stetson lowered to the side of her face as the large hand left her shoulder and reached for the screen. Their best friend disappeared from view. They heard a man's deep, sexy laugh and Vivi's breathy moan.

"Hey, not fair," Skye complained.

Nope, it wasn't. Whenever Madison mourned her almost nonexistent love life, she comforted herself with the knowledge that her workaholic friend Vivi didn't have one, either. They lived vicariously through Skye. But even Skye would be considered a nun by today's standards.

Vivi reappeared on the screen, hiking up the strap of her tank top and smoothing her hair.

"Spill," Madison said. "How...where...when?" The *why* she knew—the man's body was to die for.

Skye cleared her throat. Vivi's moony smile faded. "Right. Okay. Maddie," Vivi began, but that's as far as she got.

"Sweetie," Skye leaned forward, "we have something to tell you. Just remember, this too shall pass."

Vivi sighed, crossing her arms.

"Bad things happen to good people," spouted Skye, who flitted through life like a butterfly wearing rose-colored glasses. "It always looks darker before the sun comes out. When a door shuts, a—"

"Enough already, we don't have all day," Vivi interrupted her. "Maddie—"

"Wait." Skye held up a hand. "Take a minute and breathe, Maddie, slow and deep. Find your happy place."

"I'm in my happy place. Tell me already." Madison's left eye began to twitch.

Vivi held up the front page of the *New York Times*, pointing out the headline: The Grinch Who Killed Christmas.

"Way to go, Grinch," Madison murmured, her gaze dropping to the woman in the picture. She leaned in to get a better look. Her heart flip-flopped in her chest. "Is that me? That can't be me."

Skye tilted her head. "I know. You've got those serial killer's eyes going on, but it *is* you, sweetie. Sorry."

"But I-I am not a Grinch, and I didn't kill Christmas."

"You kinda are," Skye said.

"Skye," Vivi muttered, then redirected her attention to Madison. "It's because of the resort in Christmas, Colorado, Maddie. They're blaming you for killing the deal and the town. They've got letters from old people and four-year-olds saying it was because of your report Hartwell didn't go through with the resort."

"How would they know that? No one called me for a comment."

"Harrison spoke on behalf of Hartwell."

Madison groaned. "What did he say?"

"Um, here, I'll put it up to the screen."

Scanning the article, Madison stabbed the monitor when she came to Harrison's name and quote. "Harrison," she growled her nemesis's name. "I can't believe he questioned my numbers, and to the press! My facts are accurate. I quadruple-checked my projections. If we went through with this deal, we'd have gone under." Stupid small towns and the small-minded people who lived in them. They'd ruined her life once, and she was not about to let them ruin it again. "I'll sue. They'll have to print a retraction."

"If you say the deal won't fly, it won't. But honestly, there's not much you can do about this. They're putting a spin on the facts, but you are the one who compiled the report, even if Joe signed off on it. Harrison hung you out to dry," Vivi said.

"So I just have to sit by while they tear my reputation to shreds on the front page of the *Times*?"

"Yeah, you do. And I hate to tell you, Maddie, but with Christmas less than a month away, a headline like this is going to sell a lot of papers."

And that was her biggest concern, because Joe didn't like conflict or negative publicity. If Santa really did exist, he'd be her boss. Unlike Madison, Joe was a people pleaser and had come close to bankrupting the destination firm before she'd come on board. If he read the letters from the little kids and old people, he'd waver. He'd question her report, and Harrison would have the ammunition he needed to reopen the deal.

That was not going to happen, not on her watch.

"What are you going to do?" Skye asked.

"Once I've reamed out Harrison for talking to the press, I have to reassure Joe that the negative publicity will have no impact on us whatsoever, and that I stand by the numbers in my report."

"If you need me, I'll be on the next plane out of here," Skye offered.

"And if I can think of an angle to counter this in the *Daily News*, I will," Vivi promised.

"Thanks. I love you guys, but I'll be fine," Madison said past the fist-sized lump of gratitude in her throat. She really did have the best friends in the world.

"Group hug, it's time for a group hug." Skye waved her hands.

At home was okay, but at the office, no way. "I'm not doing a group hug. Someone might walk in, and thanks to the *Times*, I already look like an idiot." And that was bothering her more than she let on.

At the disappointed look in Skye's eyes, Madison gave in, wrapping her arms around the monitor. "Vivi, Hot Bod is welcome to join us." They laughed and made kissy noises before saying good-bye.

A throat cleared. "Ms. Lane, what are you doing?" Harrison "the Snake" Hartwell asked.

Heat suffused Madison's cheeks. "Um, I have a bad connection. Wire's probably loose." She patted her hands along the back of the monitor.

"It's wireless."

She ignored him, sat poker straight in her chair, and lowered her glasses onto her nose. She decided not to say a word about the paper tucked under his arm. She wouldn't give him the satisfaction of thinking the article had gotten to her. "What can I do for you, Harrison?"

"My uncle wants to meet with you in the conference room. Have you seen the *Times* this morning?" he asked in his faux British accent.

She looked him right in his shifty dark eyes. "Of course I have."

"And you're not concerned?"

"Why would I be? It's nothing more than a piece of sensationalist crap. Everyone will have forgotten about it by tomorrow." She hoped.

"I don't think my uncle agrees with you, nor do I. As I see it, the only way to combat the negative publicity is to reopen the deal with Christmas."

Over her dead body. She hit the key to print off her revised budget and the previous one with the resort included. Organizing the papers into a neat pile, she rose from her chair, striding past Harrison.

She walked into the boardroom where her boss stood by the window, his gray suit hanging on his too-thin frame. "Joe." He turned, his face lined with worry, his eyes tired.

Her heart pinched. He didn't need this right now. He had enough dealing with Martha, his wife of fifty-five years, who'd been diagnosed with lung cancer not long before Harrison had come on board. Madison had begun to believe that was the reason Joe had hired his nephew in the first place. He wasn't thinking clearly. And she wasn't about to let Harrison take advantage of his vulnerability.

"Don't worry, Joe," she said, coming to stand beside him. "No one's going to pay any attention to this."

"It doesn't look that way to me, Madison." He tapped the glass. On the sidewalk below, at least twenty protestors marched in a circle, waving Grinch signs that called for a boycott of Hartwell Enterprises. She couldn't believe it. With everything going on in the world, people came out to protest *this*? The paper had only been out a couple of hours. How...

Her gaze shot to Harrison, who gave her a got-you smile.

*   *   *

Madison gritted her teeth as the midmorning sun glared off the snow-covered mountains and the GPS cheerfully informed her she was going in the wrong direction. She wasn't. The problem was the town of Christmas was off the grid. She'd been lucky to find a map that showed it actually existed. And Harrison had the nerve to insinuate her visitor projections were too low? Like hell they were; no one would be able to find the place.

As the number of protesters grew yesterday, she'd practically had to tackle Joe to stop him from picking up the phone and reopening negotiations. He'd only relented once Madison had offered, as a last-ditch resort, to go to Christmas and turn the public relations nightmare around. She hadn't figured out exactly how to do that, but she would. Hartwell Enterprises' survival depended on her.

Harrison had pulled out all the stops in his campaign to be sent in her place. He'd gone from charming to butt-kissing to whining in a New York minute. But three hours later, Joe had conceded that Madison was the best one to convey her findings to the people of Christmas. Of course, she was to do so in such a way that they would understand the decision was in everyone's best interest.

Which meant she was supposed to charm and cajole the citizens of Christmas and kiss a baby or two—so not her strong suit. But she'd suck it up and get the job done. Otherwise, she might not have one.

She'd flown out on the red-eye, arriving early this morning at the Denver airport, wasting an hour trying to locate the car and driver Harrison offered to arrange for her. Only to find out it had never been ordered. She should've known better. Harrison was probably sitting in her office dreaming of her demise, which was highly likely given her limited driving experience and the hairpin curve she'd just rounded in the rented SUV.

The man in the car behind her blasted his horn as he sped by. If she wasn't terrified of letting go of the wheel, she would've flipped him the bird. She needed something to calm her nerves. She slowed down to turn up the radio when "Independent Women" by Destiny's Child came on.

Madison loved to sing, even though her friends encouraged her not to. No matter what they said, she didn't believe she sounded that bad. Her confidence returned as she belted out the empowering lyrics. The town of Christmas wouldn't know what hit them. She'd have them eating out of her hand in no time once she expounded on the evils of bringing corporate America to their sleepy little town.

She glanced at the clock on the dashboard. She'd been on the road for over three hours. According to the map, she should be approaching the turnoff to Christmas right about now. Perfect. There it was. If the meeting went as planned, she'd be back on the road by 2:00, which meant the most hair-raising part of her drive would still be in daylight.

Her breath caught as she made the turn. The town, nestled in a valley surrounded by mountains, looked like it belonged in a snow globe. Sunlight sparkled on snow-laden evergreens and danced off the pastel-painted wooden buildings in the distance. It was postcard perfect and exactly the ammunition Madison needed to convince the town that Hartwell Enterprises had done them a favor by backing out of the deal.

She'd focus on the town's positive attributes and not the negatives that had made the case against them. Like this road, she thought, her good mood evaporating as her tires spun out beneath her. She slowed to a crawl, a white-knuckled grip on the wheel. Three-quarters of the way down the treacherous hill, as she was about to release the breath she'd been holding, a movement to her right caught her attention. A deer leaped from the woods, darting in front of her. She braked hard, the car fishtailing as she slid along the road. From behind a cluster of evergreens at the side of the road, a twelve-foot Santa holding a "Welcome to Christmas" sign seemingly sprang out in front of her like a giant jack-in-the-box.

Madison screamed. Her foot mistakenly jumped to the gas instead of the brake. She watched in slow-motion horror as the car kept moving and crashed into the sign. Santa loomed, teetered, then fell on the hood, his maniacal, smiling face leering at her through the cracked windshield.

Her last thought before the airbag slammed into her face was that she'd finally succeeded in killing Santa.

Chapter Two

Sheriff Gage McBride stood in the doorway of the old town hall, scanning the familiar faces in the standing-room-only crowd for the one person who could turn the law-abiding citizens of Christmas into a teeth-gnashing mob in ten seconds flat.

His great-aunt Nell.

Gage loved his aunt. She'd stepped in when his wife left him eight years ago with a nine-month-old and a four-year-old to raise on his own. But it didn't mean he was blind to her faults.

"Where's your riot gear?" Ethan O'Connor, the mayor of Christmas, asked as he came up beside him.

A reluctant smile tugged the corner of Gage's mouth at his best friend's question. "I figure once I find out where Nell's sitting, I'll park myself where she can see me, and we'll be good."

Ethan snorted. "Yeah, right. And I can tell you exactly

where she is." He leaned past the door, pointing toward the front of the room. "Front row center. She ambushed me as soon as I arrived at the office this morning. Gave me a headache with her suggestions as to how we can change Ms. Lane's mind, then browbeat me until I let her in an hour before we opened the doors."

Gage groaned. "Are you nuts? You know better than to leave her on her own for that long. She's probably built a bomb and stashed it under the podium."

He wasn't kidding. His aunt had been an engineer at the mine before it folded forty years ago. At times, Gage questioned his sanity for having his daughters, Annie and Lily, spend so much time with her. But they loved Nell as much as she loved them, and deep down he knew she'd never knowingly put them in danger. It was the *unknowingly* part he wasn't too sure about. In the end, he went with the lesser of two evils. It was either let Nell look after his daughters when he was at work or one of the single women who vied for the position of Mrs. McBride Number Two.

"She wasn't alone. Ted and Fred were with her," Ethan added.

"Aw, hell, there's no stopping her with those two egging her on." Today had *shitshow* written all over it. Gage studied his friend. "You don't honestly believe this meeting is going to affect Hartwell's decision, do you?"

A pained expression on his face, Ethan glanced into the room filled with people who saw the resort as the last hope for their town's survival. "I wish I did. But no, I'm a realist. Ms. Lane's report didn't leave much room for optimism."

Gage had read the twenty or so pages crammed with graphs, statistics, and projections, along with a damning summary that listed the many reasons why his town didn't make the grade. He got the impression the woman who'd produced the report cared more about numbers than people. Cold and uncompromising, with no thought as to what her decision meant to the citizens of Christmas.

"So why's she coming?"

Ethan shrugged. "Not sure. When Hartwell called to set up the meeting yesterday, he said she'd explain why they decided not to go through with the deal. Interesting thing, though. I heard from his nephew a couple of hours ago. He intimated that we shouldn't give up. As far as he's concerned, the deal isn't over. But I don't think we can pin our hopes on him. It's his uncle's company, and Ms. Lane apparently has the old man's ear. From what Joe Hartwell said, he stands by her report. She's supposedly brilliant and has never steered him wrong in the past."

"Don't let Nell catch wind of the nephew's opinion. She'll never be able to let this go if she hears what he said."

"Nell hasn't given up, not by a long shot. She has this idea in her head that if she can convince Ms. Lane to stay in town for a few days, she'll fall in love with Christmas. Or better yet, one of us, and then the deal will be as good as done."

Gage rolled his eyes. "The woman is delusional."

"I don't know. Ms. Lane *is* a beautiful woman."

He gave his friend a you've-lost-it look. "Yeah, and the belladonna is a beautiful flower. But be my guest, buddy. Take one for the team."

"Maybe I will. Lately I've been too busy to get out of town." Ethan ran a frustrated hand through his hair. "It's been so long I'm beginning to feel like a monk."

Unfortunately, Gage knew how he felt. Like Ethan, he

was careful not to scratch his itch in his own backyard. In a town the size of Christmas, it wouldn't be long before the gossip reached his daughters' ears. If he wanted a relationship, that would be different, but he didn't. He had enough on his plate raising his two girls. Especially Annie, who at twelve, was making him feel a hell of lot older than his thirty-six years.

Ms. Lane's picture from the *Times* came to mind: blonde hair scraped back from a cold, emotionless face; thick glasses resting on a condescending blade of a nose above lips pinched thin in disdain. "Good luck with that. The woman looks about as passionate as a block of ice."

"I like a challenge." Ethan winked then grinned. "You might want to make your escape now. Here comes the I Want to Marry Sheriff McBride Fan Club."

"Gage. Yoo-hoo," a chorus of feminine voices hollered from behind him.

"Too late," Ethan chuckled, as Gage looked over his shoulder.

He forced a smile for the three women barreling toward him. If you went by what they were wearing, the town hall meeting seemed to be the highlight of their social calendar. Their winter jackets were open to show off tight sweaters paired with short skirts and high-heeled leather boots. He prayed Annie wouldn't get a load of their getups. The black Goth look she now sported had nearly given him heart failure, but it was better than her wearing skirts that barely covered her butt.

"Oh, Gage, I'm so glad you're all right. I heard you nearly went through the ice rescuing those boys last night." Brandi squeezed his leather-clad arm.

Hailey grabbed his hand. "Dr. Trainer was singing

your praises when he dropped by the diner this morning. Those boys are lucky you were a paramedic before you joined the force."

Heat climbed Gage's face. He'd have to have a word with Matt, the doctor who'd taken over for Gage's dad while he was away on vacation. "That's nice of Doc to say, but I was—"

"Now, don't you be hiding your light under a rock—"

"Bushel, Holly, it's a bushel," Hailey corrected her twin sister, rolling her heavily made-up eyes.

"I know that," Holly snapped, then turned a megawatt smile on Gage. "Don't you go trying to deny it, Gage McBride, you're a hero. I baked your favorite chocolate cake for you."

Brandi frowned. "His favorite is lemon cake, isn't it, Gage?"

"No, he likes—" Hailey began.

Ethan intervened. "Ladies, I'm sure Sheriff McBride would love anything you make for him, but you might want to get in there and grab a seat before there's none to be had."

The trio promised to drop off their baked goods later that night, then took Ethan's advice, sashaying their way into the hall.

"You're my hero," Ethan said in a perfect falsetto, fluttering his lashes.

Gage shoved his hands in his jeans pockets, scowling at his friend. "You think it's funny, but you don't have to deal with Annie's death glares when they stop by under the pretext of dropping off food."

"Still having problems with her?"

"She got suspended for fighting two days ago. Nell

tried to make me feel better by telling me she was just like Annie at her age." As if he didn't have enough to worry about.

Ethan laughed then sobered. "Do you think Annie's fighting has anything to do with Sheena not showing up for Thanksgiving?"

"On top of the problems she's having at school, it didn't help." He was still furious at his ex for bailing a day before the holiday. But he shouldn't have been surprised. Sheena was notorious for not keeping her promises. Her no-shows didn't bother Lily, who'd only been nine months old when Sheena left, but they were tough on Annie. He'd hoped his ex-wife would grow up and not be so self-absorbed, but given her star status in the country music scene, he didn't see that happening any time soon.

"Did you talk to Sheena about Christmas?"

"She says she'll be here, but I'm not holding my breath." The noise level in the hall ratcheted up a notch. "I better get in there."

"I'll see you in a few minutes."

Gage caught the underlying weariness in his friend's voice and turned back. After Ethan's father suffered a fatal heart attack, the town had begged Ethan, an ADA in Denver, to replace him as mayor. Deacon O'Connor had left big shoes to fill, and right about now, Gage figured Ethan must be feeling like he hadn't done a very good job filling them. All because of Madison Lane. Gage couldn't help but resent the woman for putting the look of defeat in his best friend's eyes.

"Don't sweat it, buddy. We'll figure something out. We'll get the development committee back up and running. Put Aunt Nell in charge."

"Don't mention that to Nell until we get Ms. Lane the hell out of Dodge. She's liable to think kidnapping the woman and holding her for ransom would be a good way to fill the coffers."

Given his impression of Ms. Lane, Gage said, "I doubt anyone would pay to get her back."

His radio crackled to life. "Sheriff . . . Sheriff McBride, we've got a problem."

"What's up, Ray?"

"You know that lady from Hartwell we're expecting? Well, she crashed into our welcome sign, and then, Santa, he kinda fell on top of her."

"Is she injured?" Gage asked as he moved toward the doors.

"Her face is a little beat up. Would've been worse if she hadn't been going so slow. You should've seen her, Sheriff. She was practically crawling down the road. I was thinking about ticketing her just before that deer ran out in front of her."

There was another crackle from the radio, and an outraged female voice came on.

"Me? You were going to give *me* a ticket? You people are crazy. Who for the love of God had the brilliant idea to have Santa leap out of the woods at unsuspecting drivers? I should sue. Look at that face. I'm going to have nightmares."

"Ma'am, it's Santa . . ."

Gage lowered his radio. "She really is a Grinch."

"No, ma'am, that's police property. Give it back."

"Who is this?" the woman demanded in a haughty tone of voice.

Ethan punched him in the arm. Gage rolled his eyes and waved him off. "Sheriff McBride, ma'am. Now—"

"Y'all seem to think this Grinch business is very funny. But I don't. You people have ruined my reputation and..." She sniffed.

Gage sighed. He was a sucker for a crying woman. And while Madison Lane might be responsible for stealing the hopes and dreams of his friends and family, she'd been hurt. Besides that, she had a point. He'd been against the vehicle-activated Santa for the very reason Ms. Lane had pointed out. Only he'd been overruled. Again.

He shoved his personal feelings aside. "Calm down, Ms. Lane. Everything's going to be all right."

"Calm. You expect me to be calm? Your stupid Santa broke my nose!"

"Ray," he said loud enough for his deputy to hear him, "wrap her in a blanket, but don't move her. I'll be there in a minute." He shut off the radio and scrubbed his face. "If I didn't want to tie up the ambulance, I'd call them and send Jill," he muttered, referring to his other deputy. "I'm not sure I can keep from strangling that woman."

"Go be a hero. Maybe she'll join your fan club."

He shuddered at the thought. "No thanks. I don't want her. You can have her."

"Good idea. These days my fan club consists of women who come with their own oxygen tanks."

As Gage got in his Suburban, he figured Ms. Lane was lucky they only had the one reporter in town and he was sitting in the town hall, or tomorrow's headline would read: The Grinch Who Killed Santa.

*   *   *

Not so lucky after all, Gage thought a few minutes later, as three separate sets of news crews from Denver scrambled from their white vans. Gage took in the damage to Ms. Lane's SUV and radioed Jill, requesting her presence at the town hall to handle the press. He caught a glimpse of a pale face through disheveled blonde hair, oversized sunglasses resting on a red nose.

He got off the radio, flicked on the siren and lights, and leaned on his horn. Six men and three women leaped out of his way as he angled the Suburban between them and Ms. Lane's vehicle. Grabbing the first aid kit from the back seat, he slammed the door. "Don't even think about it," he said as they lunged forward. "Ray, get them out of here."

"Come on, Sheriff, give us a break," one of the men yelled.

"Deputy, if they're not gone from here in two minutes, ticket them." Gage rounded the back end of the SUV. Ms. Lane didn't turn his way as he approached the open door. It looked as if her eyes were closed behind the sunglasses.

"How are you doing?" he asked.

"I'll be on the front pages again, won't I? They're going to say I killed Santa. Joe…" She dabbed at her nose while slowly turning her head to face him.

Carefully, he removed her sunglasses. She blinked up at him. And all he could think was the picture in the *Times* had done Madison Lane an injustice. Despite her red nose and puffy lips, or maybe because of them, she bore no resemblance to the woman in the photo. She was younger than he'd expected, her features sweetly feminine. She looked delicate and vulnerable, and all his protective instincts came roaring to the surface.

He shook off the disconcerting reaction. "It would be easier for me to check you out if you bring your legs around," he said, his voice unexpectedly rough.

She blinked again then drew her denim-blue eyes from his face to the airbag. "Oh, I...okay."

He lifted the deflated bag from her lap while she swung long legs clad in slim black pants over the side, setting her practical black leather boots on the running board.

"No problem moving your legs, no pain anywhere?" he asked, as he set the first aid kit beside her feet.

"No. I didn't hurt anything other than my nose and mouth." She touched her bee-stung lips. Her gaze shot to his. "Oh, God, they feel..." She grabbed the visor and angled it to study her face. "I look like one of those women whose plastic surgery went wrong."

He fought back a smile. "I doubt anyone will notice. The swelling should go down in a day or so."

She was too busy examining her mouth to respond, or so he thought until she pinned him with a disbelieving stare. "I have Kewpie-doll lips, and you don't think anyone will notice?"

He had to get her to stop talking about her lips so he could stop staring at them. Because right now they looked pretty damn tempting, and he couldn't help thinking what it would feel like to kiss her pouty mouth.

Ignoring her question, he said, "From the way you're moving your head around, I take it you have no pain in your neck?" At a screech of tires, he dragged his gaze from hers as one of the news vans sped by. Ray, leaning against the second van, was chatting up one of the female reporters. "Deputy, what part of 'Move them out' didn't you understand?"

"Right, Sheriff, I'm on it," Ray said with a two-finger salute.

"Thank you for not letting them take a picture of me,"

Ms. Lane murmured, glancing in the direction of the reporters.

"Just doing my job." Gage gently clasped her jaw and, with two fingers, nudged her chin up to check her pupils for signs of a concussion. He frowned. "You didn't get the bruise on the bridge of your nose from your run-in with Santa. It's at least a day old."

Her lips flattened—as much as they could given how swollen they were. She winced before saying, "No, I didn't. Because of the lies you people had printed about me yesterday, there were protesters outside my office swinging their stupid Grinch signs. One hit me and broke my glasses." She stabbed a finger in his chest. "I am not a Grinch, and I am not trying to kill Christmas."

He couldn't believe he'd actually felt sorry for her and felt like kissing that mouth.

Wrapping his hand around her wrist, he removed her finger from his chest. "Lady, you might not give a damn about this town, but I do. And from where I'm standing, you've done a pretty good job destroying both it and the holiday. Did you give any thought to holding off delivering the death blow until after Christmas?"

She gave him an offended look. "I did not destroy your town or the holiday. And it wasn't—"

"Really? It's a little less than a month before Christmas, and with your slick report and its fancy charts and statistics, you've stolen this town's hope for the future. So you tell me, what kind of holiday are we going to have with *that* hanging over our heads?" He grabbed the first aid kit and started to walk away before he gave in to the urge to shake her.

"Hey, this is not my fault. I had no choice but to—"

He turned to look at her. "Yeah, try telling that to the folks waiting for you in the town hall. You're real good with numbers, Ms. Lane. Let's see how you do when you have to look those people in the eye and explain—"

She scowled at him. "I'm not going to explain anything to anyone. I'm not going to stick around so a bunch of small-minded bullies can make me their punching bag. I've already suffered a broken nose because of—"

"Your nose isn't broken, and your mouth looks a hell of a lot better than it did in that stick-up-your-ass picture of you in the paper."

Her jaw dropped. She made a furious noise in her throat, slammed the door, and revved the engine.

Gage lurched forward at the same time as the SUV. He wrenched the door open. "What the hell are you thinking?" he said, leaning across her to grab the key from the ignition. He jabbed his finger at the wooden Santa. "He could've come through the windshield, and you would've had a lot more to worry about than a sore nose and swollen mouth."

She'd gone pale, her bottom lip quivering. "I-I thought I had it in reverse."

"Don't even think about crying."

She sniffed.

No way was he going to feel sorry for her. "I mean it. You brought this on yourself. Now come on." He moved to take hold of her arm.

She jerked away. "I'm not going anywhere, especially with you. I don't like you, Sheriff McBride."

"Good, since I'm not particularly fond of you either, Ms. Lane. Now, there are about two hundred people who have spent the last hour waiting for you. You owe them the courtesy of at least showing up."

She leaned back against the headrest and shook her head. "I have a headache, and my nose hurts."

Gage hardened his heart. After all, she wasn't *really* hurt. "Too bad. You should've thought about that before you decided to run over Santa."

"Give me my keys," she demanded through clenched teeth.

Screw it. The citizens of Christmas deserved some answers. He hauled her from the SUV.

"Sorry, Ms. Grinch, but you're coming with me."

Chapter Three

Madison's shocked gaze went from the big hand clamped on her wrist to the broad leather-clad shoulders of the Neanderthal who dragged her through the snow behind him. She tried to wrench her hand free. "I am so going to sue you," she said when he tightened his grip.

Just her luck, the reporters weren't there to witness the brutality of Christmas's finest. And to think a few moments ago, when she'd gotten a good look at her rescuer with his dark, wind-tousled hair and winter-green eyes, she'd thought him very fine indeed. Combined with his strong, masculine jaw and the shallow dent in his chin, he'd looked as though he'd stepped off a billboard and for a couple of seconds, she wouldn't have minded if he'd walked off with her.

Until he opened his damn mouth.

He stopped abruptly and turned. She bumped into his unyielding, six-foot-plus frame. Wrapping his hands around her upper arms, he brought his face within inches of hers.

"I'm going to make you a deal, Ms. Lane. You're going to go into that town hall meeting and pretend like you have a heart, like you care what your decision has cost these people—"

"You jerk. Of course I have a—"

He placed a finger lightly on her mouth, cutting off her protest. His inflexible gaze dropping to her lips, he lowered his hand. "Keep quiet until I'm finished."

She pried his fingers from her arm. "Maybe the women around here put up with your manhandling and bully tactics, but I won't."

His gaze narrowed. "If you want to get out of here today, you'll keep your Kewpie-doll lips closed and listen to me."

Her eyes widened. "I can't believe you just—"

Ignoring her, which he seemed to have a talent for, he said, "You're going to figure out a way to make the citizens of Christmas feel as though the best thing that could've happened to them is that this deal fell through. And since you're supposed to be so damn smart, it should be easy for you."

"For your information, that is exactly what I plan on doing."

He cocked a dark brow. "Really? Yet not two minutes ago you told me you weren't going to the meeting."

"So sue me. I was mad, and you made me madder. I just want to get this over with."

He studied her for a long moment then nodded. "You and me both. I'll take you into town and call a tow truck for your SUV. There doesn't appear to be much damage."

He scrutinized the vehicle before returning his attention to her. "Do you need anything out of it for the meeting?"

"Yes, my purse, briefcase, and portfolio."

He nodded then placed a hand at her elbow, guiding her toward his Suburban—a white Suburban with a picture of Santa on the door. Following the direction of her gaze, he said in a smartass tone of voice, "I hope he won't give you nightmares."

"He won't, but you will."

Dammit. Why had she said that? She blew out an exasperated breath, placed her foot on the running board, and heaved herself onto the black leather seat.

He stood in the open door, hands planted on the roof of the Suburban. "I've never had a woman tell me I gave her nightmares before, but plenty have told me I played a prominent role in their dreams."

Her gaze drifted up his lean, muscled body to his gorgeous face. She struggled to put a look of derision on hers. "Seriously? I can't imagine why."

The corner of his mouth curved.

Her head was beginning to pound, and she sank into the soft leather, closing her eyes.

"Ray, bring me the first aid kit. It should be to the left of your feet."

Madison opened one eye and caught the sheriff studying her before he met his deputy, who handed him the first aid kit. After a brief conversation, McBride returned to her side. He fiddled with the lever at the base of her seat while keeping one hand on the headrest, carefully easing her into a more comfortable position. Withdrawing a bottle of water from the backseat, he twisted off the cap and handed it to her.

Instead of taking a drink, she gently pressed the cold plastic to her throbbing lips.

"Here." He drew her hand from the bottle, placing two white pills in her palm.

She eyed them suspiciously. "I won't be much use to you if I'm dead."

His gaze glinted with what appeared to be amusement. "They're ibuprofen."

Popping the pills in her mouth, she took a deep swallow of the water. "Thanks, but don't think I'm going to forgive you now that you're being nice."

"Just doing my job, Ms. Lane," he said, as he closed her door. Retrieving her things from the deputy, McBride circled the Suburban. He opened the driver-side door, handing Madison her purse before tossing her briefcase and portfolio in the back.

As he slid behind the wheel, she removed the pins from what was left of the knot at her nape. She retrieved a brush from her purse to set her hair to rights.

"Put your belt on," he said, as he checked over his shoulder.

She did as he asked, then drew the brush through her tangled hair. She felt the weight of his gaze upon her and tried to ignore the heated flutter in the pit of her stomach. For some reason, sitting in the close confines of a vehicle with his large body brushing up against hers felt intimate.

It was all Vivi and Hot Bod's fault. Her friend's recent hook-up had Madison thinking about how long it had been since a man had his hands on her, big hands with long, broad fingers. Hands like Sheriff McBride's.

She gave her hair a sharp tug to change the direction of

her thoughts. Gathering it in a low ponytail, she twisted it into a knot and stuck the pins back in.

"*Why* would you do that?" he asked, his tone gruff.

She shifted, turning to stare at him, but he'd returned his gaze to the road. "Are you asking why I put my hair in a bun?"

He grunted. "Yeah."

That had to be the oddest question a man had ever asked her.

"Because it looks professional." Pulling down the visor to ensure that it did, she caught sight of her lips and groaned. The cold water hadn't made a difference.

He shook his head. "I don't know what you're getting so worked up about. Only thing people around here care about is what's coming out of your mouth, not what it looks like."

She pushed the visor up. "You haven't spent a lot of time in small towns, Sheriff McBride, if you think this"— she circled her face with a finger—"isn't going to garner comments and speculation."

Her stomach heaved at the thought. The torment she'd been put through as a kid came back to taunt her. God, she hated small towns. She closed her eyes and took a calming breath.

"I've lived here all my life, Ms. Lane," he replied. "Like my father and his father before him. So I do know what I'm talking about."

For some reason, the fact he was a small-town boy disappointed her. It shouldn't have. It wasn't like she was going to see him again after today, as if she even wanted to, no matter how gorgeous he was. But it bothered her to think he was like the people she'd grown up with.

They drove past a row of quaint shops with swags of garland hung over gaily painted doors. Antique streetlamps festooned with wreaths and bright red bows lined the snow-dusted sidewalk. A cheerful, welcoming street in a town that thought she'd destroyed it. She sighed. She wanted to put the town of Christmas and the memories it was stirring up far behind her.

She cleared the emotion from her throat. "Are we almost there?"

"Yeah, next street over." His observant eyes roamed her face. "Look, why don't I call the mayor? He can reschedule the meeting until tomorrow. You can take a room and get a good night's sleep."

"Thanks, I appreciate the thought, but I'm booked on a red-eye out of Denver tonight." He stiffened beside her. His reaction surprised her. She didn't think that she'd sounded ungrateful.

"I really do appreciate the offer . . ." Following his gaze, she groaned when she spotted the reporters crowded on the sidewalk outside a two-story wood building.

"I'll take you around the back."

She carefully slipped her sunglasses on. "No, let's just get this over with."

He slanted her a look then shrugged. "Suit yourself." Bringing the Suburban to a stop, he unsnapped his seat belt. "Don't get out until I come around to your side."

As oddly attractive as his protective manner was, she didn't want him to think she was a wimp. "I can handle the press, Sheriff McBride."

"Just do as I say, Ms. Lane. There's going to be a lot of pushing and shoving to get at you. Your face doesn't need to take another hit." Muttering something about stubborn

women under his breath, he pulled her briefcase and portfolio from the backseat. Closing the door, he came around
to her side.

A female deputy with chin-length brown hair shoul-
dered her way to Madison's other side.

"Glad you finally made it, Sheriff," the woman said.
"Crowd inside is getting about as restless as this bunch."

"Just what I wanted to hear," Sheriff McBride said, as
he expertly maneuvered Madison through the reporters
shouting their questions. He held the door open with one
hand while nudging her inside with the other. "Ray should
be by in a couple of minutes to give you a hand, Jill."

With a brisk nod and a resentful look in Madison's
direction, the woman took up her position in front of the
doors.

"Real friendly deputy you have there, Sheriff," Madison said, stepping away from him.

"Jill works for me part-time while helping out her sister-
in-law at the bakery. Her brother's MIA in Afghanistan.
They're going through a tough time. Your decision to tor-
pedo the resort just made it a whole lot tougher."

She shoved her sunglasses on top of her head. "If
you're trying to make me feel guilty, it won't work." But
it did, and she resented him for that. It wasn't like she'd
taken pleasure in killing the deal. It wasn't personal. Why
couldn't they understand that?

A man who'd been speaking to a group of people just
inside the doors broke away and walked toward her. With
his tawny blond hair and tailored charcoal-black suit, he
looked like he'd be more at home in the big city than in
this sleepy little Colorado town.

"Welcome to Christmas, Ms. Lane. I'm Ethan O'Connor,

the mayor." His movie-star smile dimmed when his gaze dropped to her mouth, but he quickly recovered and motioned to her portfolio and briefcase. "Why don't I take these for you?"

"Thank you," she said, catching a glimpse inside the packed room. Her fingers tightened reflexively around the handles of her portfolio. The hall had gone silent as one by one heads turned in their direction. She knew she'd be facing a tough crowd, but she hadn't been prepared for the rabid hostility she saw in their eyes. She was suddenly glad of the protective presence of the intimidating male at her back.

"I've got them," McBride said from behind her, relieving her of her bags before she could protest.

Mayor O'Connor raised a brow. His eyes flicked from her to the sheriff, a slight smile curving his lips.

What was that about?

Madison mentally shrugged, then followed the mayor into the hall. The whispers and snickers and neighbors nudging one another as she walked into the room felt all too familiar. Her stomach cramped and her chest tightened. It felt like someone was holding a pillow over her face. They were the same nervous reactions she'd suffered for months after the accident that had claimed the life of her mother and the man she'd been having an affair with—a man from a prominent and well-respected family.

Unlike hers.

In the beginning, the town's anger hadn't been confined to whispers and snickers like that of the citizens of Christmas. The townspeople had been aggressive in their condemnation, and friends of the dead man's children had made life miserable for Madison. They never let her forget who she was and where she'd come from.

She stiffened her spine as she walked to the front of the room. She wasn't that shamed little girl anymore, and she'd be damned if she'd let the people of Christmas make her feel like she was.

"Put Ms. Lane's things over here, Gage." The mayor indicated an empty chair at the end of the long wooden table where four men and a woman sat. "Ms. Lane, I can take your coat for you," he offered, stepping toward her.

She handed him her coat. "I'll set up my charts while you go ahead with the introduction, Mr. O'Connor."

The mayor smothered a cough, which sounded suspiciously like a laugh, with his hand. "I think it's safe to say, Ms. Lane, you don't need any introduction. The floor's yours."

A moment or two to prepare herself would've been nice. It wasn't like she hadn't given a speech before—she had, numerous times—but not to a crowd who considered her the enemy.

Madison took her place behind the podium. Wrestling the microphone into position, she opened her mouth to address the residents of Christmas.

"Would you get a load of those lips," an older woman in the front row said in an overloud whisper. She looked like everyone's ideal of the perfect grandmother, if you discounted the flaming red streak in her softly curled white hair. Her red sweater sported Rudolph, his nose blinking on and off. Flashing candy cane earrings dangled from her ears, casting her lined face in a pink glow.

Self-consciously, Madison's hand went to her mouth. "I—" she began.

"What was that you said, Nell?" An older man, wearing a red plaid shirt, angled his whiskered chin at the woman beside him.

No way was Madison going to give this Nell person a chance to repeat her embarrassing comment. "Hello. I'm Madison Lane. I've been asked—"

"Turn your hearing aid up, Ted. I said, get a load of those lips."

"Nell." The sheriff's deep voice interrupted the low snorts of laughter. From where he sat against the wall, he glowered at the woman.

The old lady shrugged. "I'm just sayin'."

Madison cleared her throat, determined not to let the woman get to her. "Mr. Hartwell thought it would be helpful for y'all to see the process behind our decision." Dammit, when she got nervous, the Southern drawl she'd worked so hard to get rid of leaked out. She cleared her throat again.

"Ethan, for pity's sake, give the girl a glass of water," said the woman who was fast becoming Madison's least favorite person in the room.

The mayor half-rose from his chair, hand poised over the plastic pitcher. "Ms. Lane?"

She shook her head. "No, I'm good. Thank you. As I was saying—"

"Just get to the point, girlie. Why the Sam Hill did Hartwell renege on our deal? That nice young man Harrison told us it was as good as done."

Madison didn't know who she wanted to strangle more, the old lady or the Snake. "I'm sorry, I didn't get your name..."

"McBride, Nell McBride."

Madison shot an accusatory look at Gage McBride. Of course she'd be related to *him*. A wry grimace crooked his lips, and he lifted a broad shoulder. She returned her attention to his loud-mouthed relative.

"Ms. McBride, I'm sorry if Harrison's unthinking remarks have left you feeling as though you've been misled. That was never our intention. We at Hartwell Enterprises take pride in the fact we are the premier developer of destination resorts in North America. And we didn't earn the designation by operating in anything less than good faith with our communities. There is a very strict protocol that must be adhered to before we can sign off on an offer to purchase and develop. If you allow me to show you, I have parsed the report into more easily understandable terms. I—"

"Is she saying we're stupid, Nell?" asked an older man wearing a green plaid shirt, his white hair military short.

Nell McBride nodded, her candy canes madly swinging. "Yep, I think that's exactly what she said, Fred."

Up and down the rows, angry muttering broke out.

Alarm flashed through Madison. She'd barely started, and already she was losing them. She held up her hand. "No, that is not what I said. Not at all. I've simply parsed the data that is most relevant to your community and concerns."

"Go ahead, get on with your parsing business." Nell McBride waved her fingers at the easels.

Madison took a calming breath, then set her pointer on the first line of the graph. Her tension eased as she explained the data. She took comfort in the numbers, in the knowledge that at least in this, no one could question her motives. It was based on logic, not emotions. Moving on to the comparative analysis she'd conducted on the town of Christmas, she highlighted the salient points.

An hour into her presentation, she heard a noise every public speaker dreads—someone was snoring. Loudly. She raised her voice and soldiered on as she'd learned to do in previous presentations when this happened to her. Although it was incomprehensible to Madison, there was always one person in the audience who found the information she imparted somewhat...dry. Then, one after another, the citizens of Christmas joined in a rousing snore fest. Without turning, Madison knew who the ringleader was.

"Knock it off," the sheriff ordered in his deep, authoritative voice.

She looked over to offer her thanks. Her mouth dropped. There was no mistaking the look of a newly awakened man—the red imprint of a hand on the sheriff's sun-bronzed face, his heavy-lidded eyes. Rising to his feet, he avoided meeting her offended stare. "I said that's enough."

The mayor came up beside Madison, placing a hand on her shoulder. "Sorry about that," he murmured, then addressed the now-silent audience. "Ms. Lane took time out of her busy schedule to speak with us, and I expect you to be courteous. If she has no objection, we'll move on to the question segment." He raised a brow, awaiting her agreement.

She nodded, wondering if she could ask him to kick Nell McBride and the gruesome twosome out.

The mayor disengaged the mic and led her to the empty

chair beside him. She sat down with a sigh of relief, then Nell McBride stood up. Madison groaned.

"I saw you nodding off, Ethan O'Connor, so get down off your high horse, sonny."

Madison narrowed her gaze on the mayor who shifted self-consciously in his chair. He cleared his throat. "You have a question, Nell?"

"Sure she does. Give her hell, Nellie," the old guy on Nell McBride's right said, then Fred or Ted or whoever the hell he was added his two cents. "Yeah, give the city slicker the what-for, Nell."

The head elf nodded to her posse before narrowing her shrewd gaze on Madison. "You and I both know the only reason you're here is to do damage control. You don't give a Sam Hill about our town, but you do care about your company's reputation."

Madison was not about to let this woman ride rough-shod over her. "Ms. McBride, Hartwell Enterprises has an exemplary reputation, and that piece of sensational-ism the *Times* printed will soon be yesterday's news. Both parties had until November 24 to withdraw their offers, and after careful consideration, unfortunately we had to withdraw ours."

When Nell McBride opened her mouth to object, Mad-ison quickly held up a hand. It was time for a change in tactics. "Have any of you considered what a development of this size will do to your community?"

"Yeah, our kids won't have to move away to get jobs," a man yelled from the back row. Several people echoed their agreement.

"I can't deny that, but are you willing to pay the price? I haven't had the opportunity to spend any time here, but it's obviously a beautiful town, quiet and family oriented. If the project we'd envisioned had passed, that would no longer be the case. A resort of the size we planned would attract upwards of three million visitors a year." Hartwell needed the resort to draw at least three million visitors a year to be viable, and given the town's out-of-the-way location, it wouldn't have. "Your crime rate would increase exponentially. I noticed your lovely shops on Main Street, and while initially you would see your business increase, have you thought of what will happen when the competition moves into town?

"And believe me, it will. Noise levels, traffic levels will all increase. Christmas as you know it will no longer exist." The audience fell into a contemplative silence. Several people nodded at their neighbors. Finally, she'd gotten through to them.

"Christmas isn't going to exist at all," Nell McBride said, "if our young people move out of town and the folks with businesses have no one to sell their goods to, now is it? Tell Joe Hartwell to give us an extension. Give us another few weeks to come up with a solution to the problems you were going on about."

"I'm sorry, Ms. McBride, that's impossible. Perhaps if there was a chance the state would approve the proposed bypass, we may, and I stress *may*, reconsider our stance."

"We have faith in our mayor. If you give him some time, he'll get the state to come around on the bypass. Harrison Hartwell saw the potential in our little town. When he was here, he said we were going to be the jewel in the Hartwell crown. Since you're the one who wrote the report that put the nail in our coffin, you owe us the opportunity to show you what we have to offer. Spend a few days here, and you'll see what your boss saw in our town."

"Harrison is not my boss, Ms. McBride. I'm his," Madison said, forcing her lips to curve. "As for Mr. O'Connor making headway on the bypass, I'm sorry to say I don't share your optimism. Not in this economy. And I'm afraid a few days in Christmas is unlikely to affect my decision."

The older woman's chin jutted out. "Then stay longer."

"I'm sorry, I can't. I have a meeting scheduled first thing Monday morning."

"Have another town to kill, do you?"

Madison's fingers tightened painfully around the microphone. "That's actually not part of my job description, Ms. McBride, but I do have a job to do. You can believe it or not, but I'm sorry that in this particular instance, it resulted in us not going ahead with the project."

A man stood up at the back of the room. With his snow-white hair and beard, he looked like Santa Claus. Except he wasn't dressed in red, he was dressed in furs. "Name's Coulter Dane. Just wanted to be sure you people no longer hold an option on my land."

Madison recognized the name. One of the Danes had approached Harrison with the deal. The family owned the majority of the property Hartwell had been going to purchase.

"No we don't, Mr. Dane. You should be receiving a letter from our lawyers any day now to that effect. I'll reconfirm when and how it's being sent and get that information to you first thing tomorrow."

"That'll be fine. I was just confused seeing as how Harrison Hartwell called me up this morning to tell me I'd be receiving a check for the agreed-upon amount within a week or so."

Unable to conceal her shock, Madison's mouth dropped open. What the hell was Harrison up to? The way he was undermining her, it was no wonder these people thought they had a chance of reopening negotiations.

"I'm terribly sorry for the confusion, Mr. Dane, but I have not authorized a check for the purchase of your property, nor will I be." Thank God the fact a big fat check wasn't coming his way didn't seem to bother the man. If anything, he looked relieved.

Everyone turned as a lanky, twenty-something kid burst into the hall. "Hey, did you hear? The reporters are saying the lady from New York ran over Santa."

The crowd gaped at Madison with accusing eyes. Half the front row rose angrily to their feet, Nell McBride among them. "So killing Christmas wasn't enough for you. You had to go and kill Santa, too," she shouted.

Madison's frustration got the better of her, and she snapped, "For God's sake, it's a stupid sign, and I didn't run over it on purpose. I hit Santa when I swerved to miss Rudolph."

"*Stupid?* Who do you think you are calling my sign stupid?" Nell McBride barked.

All at once, people began to shout their derogatory opinions of Madison and Hartwell Enterprises. Chairs toppled to the floor as the angry residents of Christmas jumped to their feet.

Sheriff McBride strode to the front of the room. His eyes meeting hers, he gave a disappointed shake of his head before turning on the angry mob. "Settle down!"

He actually thought this was her fault? Okay, she'd had enough. Thanks to his relative and Harrison's meddling, there was nothing Madison could say that would change their minds. Retrieving her coat and bags, she pushed back her chair and came to her feet.

"Were not finished here. You—" Nell McBride began before the sheriff cut her off.

"It's over, Nell. Let's go." Once he'd ushered the furious citizens of Christmas to the doors, the sheriff made his way back to her. He handed her a set of keys. "The body shop couldn't have your vehicle repaired before tomorrow. Someone will return it to the rental company for you. They got you a replacement. It's the black SUV parked at the back of the building." He lifted his chin to the door behind them. "I'll go out front and tell them she's in a meeting with you, Ethan. That'll give her time to get away before they realize she's gone. Ms. Lane, it's been... interesting. Just do me a favor and try not to hit anything on your way out of Christmas."

Smartass. She plastered a fake smile on her face. "As long as you don't have any elves jumping out of the woods waving good-bye signs, I should be good."

Just when she thought she couldn't wait to see the last of his too-gorgeous face, he flashed a sexy grin and winked. Then, with a nod to the mayor, he strode from the hall, closing the doors behind him.

Mayor O'Connor's cell rang as she said good-bye to him at the back door. "I'm fine. Take your call," she said, heading to the SUV.

He scanned the lot that was empty save for the two unoccupied vehicles beside hers, then nodded, answering his cell. Lifting his hand in farewell, he closed the door.

Madison caught a flash of color to her left as she slid behind the wheel of the SUV. Concerned she might be risking life and limb by sticking around, she turned the key in the ignition. Her cell rang. She was tempted to let it go to voice mail until she saw who it was.

"Madison, how did the meeting go?"

Her hands strangled the wheel. "No thanks to you, I got out of there alive. What were you thinking, Harrison? You had those people convinced there was actually a possibility this deal could be pushed through." At the sound of voices coming from the side of the building, Madison did a quick shoulder check, about to pull out.

"As far as I'm concerned, you're being overly cautious, and I feel a full review is in order before we let go of this property."

"You are not in a position to demand a review. But I am in a position to demand you write a letter of apology to this town and explain to them you were not authorized to make the promises that you did," she said, as she backed up.

A loud bang, then another, rocked the SUV. She slammed on the brakes, jerking her gaze to the rearview mirror. Ted and Fred pointed at her, shouting, "You killed Nell!"

"Oh, God, no...no," Madison cried. Heart in her throat, she jammed the gear into Park, then fought with the door handle. Her hand shook so badly she couldn't get it open.

"What was that?"

"Shut up, just shut up. This is all your fault," she yelled over the loud buzzing in her head. Using both hands, she managed to open the door and stumble from the

SUV. The two older men were yelling at her as a crowd began to form, but all she could see was Nell McBride, her earrings flashing, stretched out on the snow-covered ground with her eyes closed, hands neatly folded on her chest.

Chapter Four

Gage scanned the thinning crowd outside the town hall for his aunt, half-expecting to find her lined up with the two dozen citizens of Christmas waiting to give the reporters their next sound bite. At that moment, Brandi, Holly, and Hailey were giving them both an eyeful and an earful.

He winced. If Ms. Lane thought the press had done a number on her reputation before, he wouldn't want to be around when she caught the late-night news. She didn't deserve what they were saying about her. She'd just been doing her job. And if today was any indication, she was damn good at it. Her presentation could have used a little work, though. She'd practically put him to sleep. He gave his head an amused shake. He couldn't recall ever meeting a woman that enthralled with numbers.

A rap on the glass doors behind him drew his attention. Ethan motioned him inside.

Gage radioed his deputies who were across the street

directing traffic. "Keep 'em moving. I need a word with the mayor."

"That's one experience I'd rather not repeat," Ethan said, once Gage joined him inside.

"You and me both." He glanced at the hall's closed doors. "She get away okay?"

"Yeah, but don't worry, I've got her contact information." Ethan grinned, fishing a business card from the inside pocket of his jacket.

Gage frowned. "What would I want that for?"

Flipping the cream-colored card between his fingers, Ethan shrugged. "If you're not interested, I think I'll—"

"Give it to me." Gage took the card. "I'll have to get in touch with her about her insurance," he said in an attempt to wipe the knowing smile from his friend's face.

"Sure you do." Ethan laughed, then nodded at the reporters. "I doubt this was the publicity Hartwell had in mind when he sent Ms. Lane here."

Absently, Gage rubbed his thumb over the gold-embossed lettering. "I should have…What now?" he muttered as the crowd stampeded past the doors with the reporters in hot pursuit.

His radio crackled to life. "Sheriff…Sheriff McBride, ah, we have a problem."

"What the hell's going on, Ray?" He tried to make himself heard over the shouting in the background. "I can't hear shit." He took off after the crowd with Ethan on his heels. As Gage closed in on them, his heart about stopped. Once again, he pushed through an angry mob calling for Madison Lane's head.

"Everyone back off. Give me some room." Over the

heads of the crowd, he spotted his aunt and Ms. Lane lying on the ground. Ray was kneeling between them.

"Holy shit," Ethan groaned behind him.

He got that right. Gage shut down his emotions as he made his way toward them.

"They're alive, Sheriff. Nell's unconscious. Ms. Lane fainted, but she seems to be coming around," Ray quickly reassured him.

"No thanks to that there city slicker. She ran over Nell on purpose. Arrest her!" Fred demanded, firing up the crowd.

"Quiet!" Gage ordered as he took in his aunt's unnaturally peaceful pose and Ms. Lane, who pushed herself into a sitting position. "You call for the ambulance?" Gage nudged Ray out of the way, taking his place between his aunt and Ms. Lane.

His deputy came to his feet. "Yep, they're on their way."

"Don't try to stand up just yet," Gage said to Ms. Lane. He crouched beside her, resting a hand on her shoulder as his gaze swept over his aunt, whose eyeballs jittered behind her lids. He quickly reviewed the scene and came to the conclusion...it was a setup. He drilled a hard look at Fred and Ted.

"Hey, it wasn't us. It was her." They pointed at Ms. Lane, who took one look at Nell and appeared ready to faint, again. Gage wrapped an arm around her, drawing her to his side.

"Ray, start taking witness statements. Ethan, Jill, clear the perimeter for the ambulance. You okay?" he asked Ms. Lane before withdrawing his arm. She nodded. He leaned over to check Nell's pulse, strong and steady, then began to examine her for broken bones.

"What the Sam Hill do you think you're doing, Gage McBride?" His aunt slapped his hands away. Then, as though realizing she didn't sound like she was at death's door, she brought a hand to her brow and moaned. "What happened? Where am I?"

Ms. Lane clutched his arm. "She's alive. Oh, thank God, she's alive."

"Oh, yeah, she's alive, all right," he muttered with a frustrated shake of his head.

Nell lowered her hand from her brow, clear blue eyes narrowing on Gage before she said, "No thanks to you, girlie. Where's your cuffs, Gage? Read her her rights and throw her in jail. She tried to kill me."

Ms. Lane's panicked gaze shot from him to his aunt. "No…no, you have to believe me. I didn't mean to hit you. I didn't see you."

Gage gave her arm a reassuring squeeze. "Calm down. We'll get to the bottom of this." He brought his mouth to his aunt's ear. "You better think this through before you take it too far. She damn well didn't hit you on purpose if she hit you at all."

Nell snapped her eyes closed, letting loose a pitiful moan.

Ms. Lane buried her face in her hands. "I'm sorry. I'm so sorry. I didn't mean—"

"Don't say another word," Gage warned as Rick Dane, owner of the town's newspaper, managed to evade Jill before Ethan corralled him.

Siren blaring, the ambulance came down Main Street, drowning out the questions the reporters shouted. "Ethan," Gage yelled, waving over his best friend as he helped Ms. Lane to her feet.

Angling his body, he blocked her from the reporters' line of sight. "Take her to the station. I'll meet you there shortly," he said once Ethan reached his side. Between them, they got her into Ethan's Escalade.

As Gage fastened her seat belt, he felt her body tremble beneath his hand and cursed his aunt. She'd gone too far this time.

Ms. Lane cleared her throat. "Do I need a lawyer?"

And that was the question of the day. Gage wondered how long it would take to break his aunt and decided he'd be better off focusing his efforts on Fred and Ted. "We'll talk about it when I get to the station."

"You get those statements?" Gage asked Ray once they were safely away.

"Yeah, no one other than Fred and Ted saw anything."

Figures. "Help Jill clear everyone out of here. Then head over to the hospital and—" The beeping of the ambulance backing into the lot stopped Gage from adding anything else. Fred and Ted made sympathetic noises while Gage helped the paramedics load Nell onto the stretcher. She kept her eyes closed, adding a wince or groan of pain every so often. Even though Gage was pretty damn sure she was faking it, he leaned over and kissed her peppermint-scented cheek. "They'll take good care of you, Aunt Nell. I'll be there once I look after things here," he promised.

She cracked one eye open and gave him a sweetly innocent smile. And when had Nell ever been innocent or, for that matter, sweet? Why the hell did his dad have to be on vacation now? He was the only one who could make his aunt see reason. "Ray, don't let Nell out of your sight," Gage warned his deputy. "And keep an eye on those two."

He gestured to Ted and Fred who were shuffling toward their lime-green pickup.

With nothing left to see, the crowd began to disperse. Gage ignored the reporters' questions—he'd deal with them later—and examined the back of the SUV. No sign of impact, just like he expected. The distance from the imprint Nell's body left in the snow and the SUV validated his suspicions that it was a setup. Now he just had to prove it.

*   *   *

From where he stood in the small kitchen at the station, Gage leaned back to check on Ms. Lane, who sat in his office across the hall with a phone pressed to her ear.

"What a mess. How are you going to deal with it?" Ethan asked him.

"Kill Nell," Gage muttered, only half-joking. He shook out a packet of sugar and poured it into the cup of coffee he'd prepared for Ms. Lane.

Ethan looked at him over the rim of his mug. "You're positive Nell set this up?"

Gage raised a brow.

"Yeah, I know, it's Nell." Ethan set his mug on the poinsettia-decorated tablecloth. "If my mother hadn't distracted me with her phone call, none of this would've happened."

Gage held back a frustrated *Damn straight*. He understood why Ethan had taken the call. As tight-fisted as Liz O'Connor was, it had to be something important for her to make a ship-to-shore call. "Everything all right?"

"Yeah, guess who's in the cabin beside hers?"

No way. "Dad and Karen are on the same ship as Liz?" His father's on-again, off-again girlfriend had surprised him with a Caribbean cruise. Who his father dated was his own business, but Gage wasn't overly fond of the aggressive, thirty-something emergency room nurse. He thought his father and Liz were perfect for each other. Before the deaths of Ethan's father and Gage's mother, the couples had been the best of friends. Like Ethan, Gage figured that was the problem.

Ethan nodded then grinned. "Karen made a big production of it. She accused Mom of stalking Paul."

Gage shook his head, tossing the empty sugar packet in the garbage. "I hope Dad didn't let her get away with it."

"Karen's too smart to show her true colors when Paul's around. Mom took care of her, though. She told Karen that Paul was too old for her, and she had her sights set on a much younger man. The ship's doctor."

"Good for her." Gage laughed. Maybe the thought of Liz with someone else would give his father the kick in the ass he needed.

Ethan glanced at his watch. "I have to take off. Call me as soon as you have word on Nell. We can only hold off the press for so long."

Gage nodded, and with the cup of coffee in hand, entered his office. Ms. Lane, who'd just ended her call, looked up. Her eyes were red-rimmed, her face chalk white. Gage hadn't had a chance to speak with her yet to alleviate some of the fear shadowing her vivid blue eyes.

He handed her the cup of coffee. "Drink this—you'll feel better once you do."

Murmuring her thanks, she cupped the mug with her hands. "Am I going to be charged with attempted murder?" she asked, a quaver in her voice.

His aunt had a lot to answer for. "No, at most it will be

a charge of reckless driving," he said, as he shrugged out of his jacket and hung it beside hers on the wooden coat stand. He moved around to the front of his desk, weighing out how much he should tell her before either his aunt, or Fred and Ted, confirmed his suspicions.

"Call on line one, Sheriff," his dispatcher, Susie, yelled from the front desk.

Gage pressed the orange flashing button before picking up the receiver. "McBride here."

"Sheriff McBride, this is Joe Hartwell. What's all this about my employee being involved in an accident? Our phones haven't stopped ringing. First I hear she took out Santa." From his tone of voice, you could tell that one was a head-scratcher. "And now they're saying she hit an elderly woman...intentionally."

"Hello, Mr. Hartwell." Gage had assumed she'd been talking to her boss, but apparently not. She groaned and sank lower in her chair. He figured he could ease her worry and Hartwell's at the same time. "I'm still waiting for an update on Ms. McBride's condition, but—"

"That's the victim? Any relation to you?"

"Yes, as it happens, she's my great-aunt." Not that the connection gave him any pleasure at the moment. "As far as Nell being a victim...the jury's still out on that."

Ms. Lane straightened in her chair, brow furrowed.

"I'm not sure I understand what you're trying to say, Sheriff McBride," Joe Hartwell said slowly.

Gage gave Hartwell the same story he'd give the press if his suspicions proved correct. His aunt had fallen on the ice. Ted and Fred, given their age and diminished eyesight and the fact they were worked up from the meeting and not thinking clearly, had assumed the SUV had hit their friend. What Gage didn't tell Hartwell and Ms. Lane, who was now giving him the benefit of her full attention, was that he figured while she'd been distracted by a phone call, Nell lay on the ground a safe distance from the SUV and her partners in crime pounded the back end of the vehicle once she was in position.

It would serve the three of them right if he charged them with public mischief, or worse.

Ms. Lane narrowed her eyes on him. Oh, yeah, smart as she was, he figured she'd just about put the pieces together. And from the look on her face, she was not amused. He didn't blame her.

"Doc's on line two, Sheriff," Susie called out, as Gage wrapped up his explanation.

"Can you hold for a minute, Mr. Hartwell? I have Nell's doctor on the other line." At Hartwell's agreement, Gage leaned back and pressed the button.

"Hey, Matt, how's Nell?"

"Hang on a minute, Gage." There was a muffled exchange in the background, then Matt came back on the line, blowing out an exasperated breath. Gage didn't blame him. Dealing with his aunt could drive a sane man crazy. "Sorry, Nell decided I needed a refresher on what constitutes doctor-patient confidentiality."

"I bet she did," Gage muttered, more certain than ever his instincts hadn't failed him. "Let me guess—other than being certifiable, she's fine."

At Ms. Lane's gasp, Gage winced. He shouldn't have said that out loud.

"Are you telling me she purposely set out—"

Ms. Lane looked ready to give him a piece of her mind, and having been on the receiving end earlier, Gage figured he wouldn't be able to hear Matt if she did. He raised a hand to cut her off.

Matt laughed then sobered. "Actually, she has a stress fracture of her tibia."

Gage frowned. There had to be some other explanation. From the placement of Nell's body, any injury would've been sustained on the left side. "Which leg?"

"Right."

"Any other injuries or bruising consistent with being hit by an SUV?"

"No, and as I'm sure you're aware, a stress fracture in a woman of Nell's age and activity level isn't unusual. I've put her in an air cast. She'll be out of commission for at least twelve weeks."

"I bet that went over well," he said, imagining his aunt's reaction.

"Surprisingly, it did. Ted and Fred offered to help, but I got the distinct impression she had someone else in mind. Good luck, Gage. I think you're about to get yourself a roommate. Let me know if you need me to make a house call."

Gage scrubbed a hand over his face. He knew exactly how his aunt's mind worked—scary thought—and she'd made it pretty clear at the town hall meeting she wanted Ms. Lane to remain in town. And if he wasn't mistaken, that was exactly who Nell's intended roommate was.

He didn't plan on letting that happen. Madison Lane had caused more trouble in the last couple of hours than he'd had to deal with in over a year. He didn't want to think about what would happen if she stuck around for a few more days.

Chapter Five

Madison's left eye began to twitch. And if Sheriff McBride didn't clue her in on his aunt's condition, Madison's eye wouldn't be the only thing twitching. Trying to read his expression wasn't helpful. She kept getting distracted by the movement of his lips. She gave her head a slight shake, concentrating on what was coming out of his mouth instead and realized he'd ended his conversation with the doctor.

"What did he—"

"Your boss is on hold. Might as well do this all at once." He leaned across his desk to bring Joe back on the line.

Her hands fisted nervously in her lap. She didn't like the hard edge in his voice or what his comment seemed to imply. No, he believed her. He didn't think she set out to purposely run over his aunt. But the thought he might have changed his mind caused a rush of prickly heat to weaken her arms and legs. She felt faint. The same reaction she'd had upon seeing Nell McBride lying dead in the snow.

Only she hadn't been dead. And judging from the sheriff's comments, his crazy aunt had tried to set her up. His voice broke through her ping-ponging emotions.

"Mr. Hartwell, I'm going to put you on speaker." He raised a brow, seeking her agreement.

She nodded. It wasn't as if she could put off speaking to Joe. Instead of calling him after the mayor had brought her to the station, she'd first called Skye and then Vivi to talk her off the ledge. She'd needed their reassurance and support, not something Joe would've offered. Even though it appeared she wasn't going to be charged with attempted murder, probably hadn't even hit the schemer, Madison's PR attempt had failed miserably. And blaming Harrison for the debacle, no matter that it was true, probably wouldn't fly. Harrison was family and she wasn't.

"Madison, are you all right?"

"I'm fine, just a little shaky." She released the breath she'd been holding. Joe sounded more concerned than angry. The sheriff gave her a slow and thorough once-over, and her cheeks warmed in response to the intense perusal of those winter-green eyes. Thankfully, her boss recaptured his attention before he noticed her reaction.

"How's your aunt, Sheriff?"

"She has a stress fracture of her tibia."

Madison groaned, and her stomach heaved.

"I'm sorry to hear that. Given her injury, is it still your opinion that this was an accident and the accusations a misunderstanding?"

"Yes." He held Madison's gaze as he spoke. "As far as

I'm concerned, no charges will be brought against Ms. Lane."

She relaxed in the chair for the first time since she'd entered his office and smiled her thanks. He smiled back. A heady rush of heat enveloped her in response to the slow, sexy curve of his oh-so-kissable lips. It was a good thing she didn't plan on staying in town; the man would be dangerous to her professionalism.

"I'm glad to hear that, but I'm going to be frank with you, Sheriff. While you were on the phone with the doctor, I spoke to my legal team. We're already fielding calls from the media asking for a comment on this latest incident. Compounded with the negative publicity we received yesterday, this is turning into a bit of a nightmare for us. And I imagine your town's opinion of Hartwell Enterprises has now been further damaged, hasn't it?"

Madison stiffened. Joe might as well come out and blame the entire fiasco on her. "Joe, I—"

"Please, Madison, let the man speak," Joe interrupted her.

She gritted her teeth.

Sheriff McBride rubbed a hand over his beard-shadowed jaw, avoiding her gaze. "I'd say that's an accurate assessment."

"Would it also be accurate to say that your aunt's opinion carries substantial weight in the community?"

Madison snorted. The sheriff raised a brow. *Certifiable,* she mouthed, repeating his earlier comment.

The corner of his mouth quirked as though he fought back a grin. His amusement might have been contagious if she wasn't so damn mad.

"Yes. Nell's very involved in the community. She's chaired practically every committee in town."

Yeah, like the one that trashed my reputation, Madison thought.

"As I understand it, your aunt, along with a good number of the citizens of Christmas, want Madison to remain a few days to experience all that your town has to offer."

She knew exactly where Joe was headed, and there was no way in hell she was staying. "In hopes of changing my...*our* minds, Joe, which we both know isn't going to happen. Not to mention the budget meeting we've already pushed back. We can't afford to—"

"Madison, you don't seem to realize the amount of negative publicity this has generated," Joe cut her off sharply. And there it was again, the implication that the mess was entirely of her doing.

She scowled at the sheriff. If he hadn't dragged her to that meeting, none of this would've happened. Okay, maybe that was a stretch, but indirectly it was his fault. The crazy old lady was his aunt. Arms crossed over his broad chest, he cocked his head. She held his gaze, refusing to back down.

Caught up in their staring match, she didn't realize Joe had continued speaking until she heard him say, "I would think a week should be enough to satisfy your aunt, don't you, Sheriff?"

Panic shot through her, and she gave a frantic shake of her head. "No," she croaked at the same time the sheriff cautiously said, "Yes." He gave her a what-could-I-say look, then shrugged.

"Good, that settles it. Madison will remain in Christmas for a week. Hopefully that will appease the town.

They'll realize we value their opinions and are responsive to their concerns. I'm sure it will generate the goodwill which we so desperately need at the moment."

And if he believed that, he was as delusional as Nell McBride. "Joe, I really can't take a week off. I have—"

"Nothing is as important as turning this around, Madison. Harrison can present your budget. It's not as if you're out of contact should something arise that requires your attention."

"Harrison?" Her voice cracked on a horrified note.

The sheriff gave her an odd look. Easy for him—it wasn't his life on a collision course with disaster.

"Yes. This will be a good opportunity for him to step up to the plate," Joe said firmly.

A good opportunity for him to step into my job, more likely.

"Thank you for your time, Sheriff," Joe continued. "I'd appreciate it if you keep me updated and inform me once the allegations against Madison have been put to rest. Madison, we'll speak later."

She groaned, dropping her face in her palms. Large hands took hold of hers and drew them from her face.

"Come on, it's not that bad."

She looked down at the hands that held hers, the tanned, long, broad fingers that smoothed over her knuckles. She imagined hands like that could offer much more than comfort to some lucky woman. Her thoughts brought her up short, and she reminded herself where she was and exactly whose fault that was.

She raised her gaze to his. "Seriously, it's not that *bad*? Thanks to your aunt, my reputation is in the toilet. My boss is blaming this entire disaster on me. And while I'm stuck in this godforsaken town, his nephew is moving into my office, moving into my life, and all because your aunt set me up!"

From where he crouched in front of her, the sheriff slowly came to his feet. "No one said anything about a setup. It was—"

"Please, I'm not stupid. She's a menace and should be locked in a padded cell."

"Look, I understand you're upset, but—"

"Upset? Upset doesn't cover what I'm feeling at the moment." She couldn't believe this was happening to her. Joe trusted her. She'd proven herself time and time again. Good Lord, she practically lived and breathed Hartwell Enterprises. And now because of these people, he was questioning her abilities, blaming her for everything that had taken place. No, with Harrison and the press hounding him, Joe wasn't thinking clearly. It hadn't helped that she'd been on speakerphone, either. She had to talk to him privately.

He needed to see that there was no benefit in having her placate a woman who had no interest in being placated. Nell McBride wanted a Hartwell resort built in her town, and nothing was going to stop her from getting what she wanted. The back of Madison's neck tingled.

"Uh, Sheriff McBride, has your aunt ever spent time in prison?"

His lips twitched as though he fought back a laugh. "No, Ms. Lane. And while I admit she's a bit of a rabble-rouser, she's not dangerous."

"You're only saying that because she's your aunt. She hasn't sicced a mob on you or tried to have you charged with attempted murder, has she?"

He grimaced. "I know it seems like she's out to get you, but she's just very protective of this town. Emotions are running high at the moment. You have to look at it from their perspective. In their eyes a Hartwell resort was the answer to their prayers, and no offense, but you took that away from them."

"You shouldn't make excuses for her, and she sure as hell shouldn't be rewarded for pulling a stunt like this by getting exactly what she wants. Which is me remaining in Christmas for a few days. If she gets away with this, she's only going to get worse."

"You're not telling me anything I don't already know, Ms. Lane. After all, she is my aunt. Rest assured, if I find out she set you up, she'll face the consequences."

"No *if* about it—she set me up. And the more I think about Joe's solution, the less I like it. If you don't mind, I could use a little privacy. I'm going to call my boss back."

"Sure." He pushed himself off the desk and reached for the half-full cup of coffee she'd placed on the blue carpet beneath her chair. "I'll get you another one."

"Thanks," she said, waiting for Joe to pick up.

"Madison, please don't tell me something else has happened. I don't think my heart can take any more bad news," her boss's weary voice came over the line.

What about me? She was the one being framed for attempted murder. But Joe's comment about his heart had her swallowing her snappy comeback. "No, nothing new or dire to report. But I'm concerned, Joe. I don't think it's a good idea for us to give in to their demands. We both know it's not going to have any impact on our decision whatsoever."

A tired sigh came over the line. "*I* realize that, Madison, but...well, Harrison feels strongly about this property, and the lawyers agree that perhaps we should reevaluate our stance."

"Numbers don't lie, Joe." *Unlike your nephew,* she almost snipped.

"Look, Madison, we live in a litigious society, and they're concerned there may be grounds for a lawsuit here."

"The only one with grounds for a lawsuit is me. I've been assaulted by a twelve-foot Santa, threatened by a mob, and set up by an old lady who makes Hannibal Lecter look sane."

Nothing followed but silence. For a moment she thought she'd lost the connection. Then Joe came back on, a defeated heaviness in his voice. "I wasn't going to tell you this, but I think you have the right to know. If only so you understand how important it is to fix this. I've been advised by the head of legal that our best course of action, should a lawsuit be filed over this, is to fire you."

Madison's heart dropped to her feet. "You can't be serious?" But why was she surprised? Tom, the head of legal, was the Snake's BFF. And since Harrison had called her as soon as she left the meeting, she'd already figured out that someone from town was feeding him information. He must've been doing the happy dance when he heard about the accident. The first call he would've made was to Tom, looking for a way to use it against her. It seemed that he'd found one.

"I'm afraid so. Because you've been the target of most of the negative publicity—and, as far as the legal department is concerned, the cause of it—they believe your firing would work to our benefit. I—"

"So they're going to throw me under the bus? Make me the scapegoat?"

"You know I'll do everything I can to protect you, so put it out of your mind. Nell McBride is the answer, Madison. Focus your energy on her. If we generate enough goodwill, they'll think twice about hitting us with a lawsuit. I'm depending on you to get the job done. You've never let me down before. Please don't let me down now." The phone cut out for a second. "I have another call coming in. We'll talk later."

Madison stared blindly at her phone. And here she'd thought her day couldn't get worse.

There was a light tap on the door. Sheriff McBride walked in with a cup of coffee. Closing the door behind him, he looked at her and frowned. "You don't look so good. What happened?"

Just what a woman wanted to hear from a man whose hotness was off the charts. A man whose aunt she had to win over if she wanted to keep her job. She'd do it, but if it came down to it and they fired her, she'd slap Hartwell Enterprises with a lawsuit so fast it would make their heads spin. She sighed. No, she wouldn't. She couldn't do that to Joe.

"Gee, thanks. You wouldn't look so good, either, if you had the day I have." But he probably would.

He placed the mug on his desk, then crouched in front of her.

"W-what are you doing?" she stammered when he brought his hands to her head.

"I didn't finish checking you over earlier, and then you fainted in the parking lot." He wove his fingers through her hair, gently probing her scalp.

She didn't faint. She'd slid gracefully to the ground when her legs gave out. At least that was how she chose to remember it. But with his touch causing a heated tremor to spiral through her body, she couldn't form a coherent rebuttal and said, "Oh." Her eyes fluttered closed as she swallowed a groan of pleasure, only to blink open when he removed the pins from her hair.

"Why are you doing that?"

"I don't like your bun." He grinned, placing the pins in her palm as he searched her eyes. "No bumps, and you don't appear to have a concussion."

She was tempted to tell him he was wrong and he should check again. Instead, she said, "Woo-hoo, lucky me," and slid the pins into the pocket of her blazer.

"How's your neck...any pain?" he asked, as he gently prodded from the base of her skull to the base of her neck.

Her response came out a breathy moan. Mortified, she closed her eyes. "No, no pain." When he drew his hands away and stood up, she wished she'd lied.

Moving behind her, he gathered her hair in one hand to arrange it over her shoulder. Then those talented fingers of his went to work on her tense muscles. She groaned her appreciation, bending her head to give him better access, instantly regretting the body-concealing layers of clothing she favored. Just this once, she wished she had on something slinky and revealing so she could feel his hands on her bare skin.

"Does it hurt when you bend your head like that?"

"No," she murmured, hoping that was the right answer and he wouldn't stop.

"Sit up straight." He guided her into position. "Now

show me how far you can turn your head to the left. To the right," he said once she'd complied with his first directive. "Your range of motion is pretty limited. Once you get to the lodge, put some ice on it at ten-minute intervals."

For a moment, the reminder of where she'd be spending the next week diminished the enjoyment of his expert attention. But even her resentment over the situation couldn't compete with the toe-curling pleasure of his touch.

"Or you could just keep doing what you're doing," she suggested hopefully.

He laughed, low and deep. But she wasn't kidding. The man should give up law enforcement and become a masseuse. He'd make a fortune.

"Much longer and I'll make it worse, not better, Ms. Lane."

"Since you've practically had me moaning in your hands, I think we know each other well enough to be on a first-name..." She caught her bottom lip between her teeth, wincing at the bite of pain. She hadn't realized how provocative that sounded until it came out of her mouth.

"No 'practically' about it, *Madison*, you were definitely moaning," he said, sounding amused.

She glanced up at him. His gaze dropped to her mouth, and he appeared about to say something when there was a commotion on the other side of the door. At the sound of a familiar voice demanding to see the sheriff, Madison groaned. "It's her, isn't it?"

"Don't worry." He gave her shoulder a reassuring squeeze. "I'll handle Nell."

"You're my hero, Sheriff McBride," she said with a

trace of sarcasm, angry once again at the position his aunt had put her in.

He winked. "Gage. And that's what all the girls say."

"I'm sure they do," she muttered, as he went to open the door, trying to ignore the twinge of jealousy his remark evoked. For a moment there, she'd actually thought his protective manner, his concern, his comforting touch, had been for her and her alone. She should've known better. He was just doing his job. Too bad he was so damn good at it.

Digging the pins from her pocket, she had her hair in a bun before he ushered his aunt into the room. Without a mirror, she knew it wasn't perfect, but it helped to don her professional persona, to feel more in control of the situation.

Nell McBride thumped into the room on crutches. Madison moved to the chair closest to the dark-paneled wall, stifling a groan at the sight of the gruesome two-some who followed Nell into the office. Gage glanced at Madison and frowned, giving his head a slight shake as he went to take a seat behind his desk. Self-consciously, her hand went to her hair.

"Stop with your fussing." Nell McBride waved her friends off as they went to settle her into the chair.

Her candy cane earrings no longer flashed. And without the soft pink glow lighting her skin, the woman looked older than she had earlier. Pain appeared to have deepened her lines. But after what Nell McBride had put her through, Madison ignored the sympathetic twinge in her chest.

The older woman's gaze narrowed on Madison before she swung her attention to her nephew. "Why isn't she in a cell?"

Madison ignored her and shot Gage a look that made her expectations clear: *Take care of this or else.* "Or else" what, she wasn't sure, but she was not about to let Nell McBride get away with blackmail. That was it exactly. Blackmail, and blackmail was illegal. Right, and thanks to Joe, the woman was going to be rewarded instead of punished.

Just as Madison was sure her silent message was clear to him, so was his to her. *Keep quiet and let me handle this,* his cool gaze seemed to say.

Gage looked at his aunt. "The reason Ms. Lane is not in a cell is because she has not, and will not, be charged with anything." He lifted his gaze to Fred and Ted who sputtered their outrage behind Nell.

"There is no evidence to suggest this was anything other than an accident. Yours, Nell. You slipped on the ice, and"—he looked directly at the two men again—"Fred and Ted, in their panic and confusion, overreacted and made *false* accusations against Ms. Lane." When Nell protested, Gage listed a number of charges: public mischief, blackmail, extortion, and the penalties that accompanied them.

Ted and Fred leaned forward and whispered to Nell. While the older woman conferred with her friends, Gage printed off two documents, sliding them, along with a pen, across the desk.

Madison leaned forward and retrieved her copy of what she assumed was the *accident* report. She scowled at the paper in her hand. A sidelong glance at Nell revealed a similar expression.

"Even if it was an accident, and I'm not sayin' it was, it's still her fault."

Madison gave her a you-can't-be-serious look. But of course she was. The woman was insane. "*How* do you figure that?"

"You destroyed my sign and my town. If you want me to sign this, I want compensation for my pain and suffering."

Fred and Ted nodded their agreement.

"Pain and suffering..." Madison's voice cracked as it raised an octave. She pressed a finger to her twitching eye. "You set me up, and *you* want compensation?"

"I didn't set you up, and I have two witnesses who will back me while you have no one."

"That's enough, Nell. She doesn't need witnesses. The evidence proves, without a doubt, that she was not involved with your *accident*."

"My broken leg says otherwise."

Gage blew out a frustrated breath. "It's a stress fracture, and no it doesn't. Just sign the damn papers."

She gave a stubborn shake of her head. "No, I want compensation."

Madison couldn't let it go any further, not with the threat of a lawsuit and Joe's directive echoing in her head. "Ms. McBride, my boss, Joe Hartwell, has requested that I remain in Christmas for a—" she had a hard time getting the word out "—week." And shuddered once she did. Gage pressed his lips together as though trying not to laugh. She narrowed her eyes on him before continuing, "During that time, I will..."

Before Madison had a chance to finish, Nell McBride signed the release form, then handed it to her nephew. "Good, let's get going. Can you drive standard?"

Madison blinked. "Excuse me?"

"Standard, a stick shift."

"God, no." She could barely drive an automatic, but she wasn't about to admit that to Nell McBride.

The older woman sighed. "I'll have to teach you, then. Come on. Get your things. We're leaving now."

"I appreciate the offer, Ms. McBride, but I can find my own way to the lodge. Thank you."

"Lodge? You're not staying at the lodge. You're staying with me."

Like hell she was. Even Joe wouldn't expect her to move in with the woman. "No, I wouldn't want to put you out. You have to rest your leg."

"I know, that's why you're staying with me. No matter how you slice it, it's your fault I hurt my leg, so you'll take care of the things I can't. It's called restorative justice. Isn't that right, Gage? Just the sort of thing those reporters would want to tell their readers about. Good publicity for Hartwell, don't you think?" Nell grinned. Without waiting for her nephew's reply, or Madison's, she shuffled out the door, then stopped and looked over her shoulder. "Get a move on, girlie."

Rising slowly from her chair, Madison shoved the paper into Gage's hand. "I am going to kill Joe, and then I'm going to kill Harrison, slowly and painfully, and then I'm going to kill your aunt," she muttered through clenched teeth.

"It's not a good idea to utter death threats in my presence, Madison. I might have to arrest you."

"This is not the least bit funny," she said, noting the amusement in his eyes.

He held up his hands. "I'm not laughing, honest."

"Where the Sam Hill is she?" the older woman's voice came from out in the hall.

Madison grabbed her coat and marched out of the sheriff's office to the sound of his laughter. He was gorgeous and crazy, as crazy as his aunt, as crazy as everyone in this damn town.

Chapter Six

The driver behind Madison impatiently honked his horn when she stalled the red pickup for a third time at the stop sign.

Beside her, Nell shook her head. "No wonder you took out Santa. Good thing Fred and Ted whacked the back end of your SUV or you really would have—"

As the car lurched forward, Madison gave an aggravated shake of her head. "So you really did try and set me up." Half an hour into what Nell assured her should've been a ten-minute drive, they were now on a first-name basis. It had been at Madison's suggestion. She was tired of being referred to as "girlie."

"No, that's not what I said." She sighed, her attention riveted on the Victorian-style homes inching past the window as they crawled down the road. "I love this town, g—Madison, and there's nothing I wouldn't do to save it." Nell shifted, giving her a probing look. "Haven't you ever loved something or someone so much you'd do everything in your power to protect them?"

Telling Nell the truth, that she was protecting Joe and now, it seemed, her job, wasn't something her boss would want her to share. "Yes, I have."

"So you've got a boyfriend?"

"Nope." She caught the speculative gleam in Nell's eyes. "And I don't want one."

"How come? A girl like you…" She trailed off as something out the window caught her attention. "Here we are, second house on the right." She pointed to a two-story, mint-green Victorian.

Madison turned into the long driveway, relieved to escape Nell's interrogation.

"Careful when you…" Nell grimaced as Madison ground the gears putting the truck into Park. "All I can say is Earl better hurry up and get your SUV repaired."

Closing the door on Nell's comment, she came around to the other side. "Your home is lovely," Madison said, as she retrieved the crutches from the back seat.

"Not when you compare it to Stella and Ed's," Nell grumbled when Madison helped her out of the truck. Once Nell got settled on her crutches, she shot a sour look at the white Victorian beside hers. Big red bows decorated every window, and a family of wooden reindeer graced the front lawn. "I'm always the first one to have their decorations up, but this year I was just so busy…"

Madison put a hand on her hip. "Busy in your campaign to ruin my reputation, was that what you were about to say?" she asked, her tone sharp. She might be softening toward Nell as she came to understand what made the older woman tick, but it didn't mean she'd entirely forgiven her. She had a fairly good idea, given Nell's reputation as the town's matriarch, who'd been responsible for the letters that were published in the *Times*. "I must say, the four-year-olds in this town have an excellent command of the English language, not to mention impressive penmanship, or should I say, *crayonmanship*."

Nell didn't bother hiding her grin, but before she responded, a yellow school bus chugged up the street and came to a lurching stop two houses down. A young girl in dark, baggy clothing and black high tops disembarked. She slung a messenger bag over her shoulder, impatiently shaking her black, unkempt, shoulder-length hair.

"Hurry up, Lily," she yelled into the bus.

Nell sighed. "She's in one of her moods. I don't know what's gotten into that girl these days. Annie, don't you be hollering at your sister like that."

A little girl in a pink snowsuit with bunny earmuffs jumped off the last step with a grin. If that was Lily, she didn't appear the least bit bothered by her sister's surly disposition. Before Madison had a chance to ask after the girls' identities, Lily sprinted across the adjoining snow-covered lawns, a worried look on her face. "Auntie, what happened to your foot?"

Madison crossed her arms, daring the older woman to say she'd run over her.

Nell chuckled. "Auntie slipped on some ice, is all. I'll be as good as new in no time."

The little girl's shoulders drooped. "But we were supposed to put up the lights today, 'member? You promised."

"Don't worry, sweetpea. Auntie Nell never breaks a promise." She patted Lily's head, then glanced at Madison. "Say hello to Ms. Lane. She's Auntie's little helper."

A sinking feeling came over Madison at Nell's introduction, but she managed a smile for Lily, whose freckled nose wrinkled when she giggled. "She's not little, Auntie." She smiled up at Madison. "Hi, Ms. Lane."

"Hi, Lily. It's nice to meet you."

"Annie, get a move on. It's freezing out here," Nell hollered at the girl, who was being teased by the three boys who'd gotten off the bus after Lily.

"Yeah, Goth Girl, better get inside before you catch cold," one of the boys jeered.

"Leave my sister alone!" Lily yelled.

Just as Annie went to walk away, an embarrassed flush working its way up her face, the tallest of the boys drew back his arm and drilled a snowball at her.

She went to duck, but the snowball hit the side of her face. Madison winced as a memory of the taunts and bullying she'd endured growing up walloped her at the same time. They hadn't called *her* Goth Girl; she'd been the home wrecker's daughter, the ho's daughter, and trailer trash. Furious on the young girl's behalf, Madison wasn't thinking when she strode across the lawn. Scooping up two fistfuls of snow, she packed them into a hard ball then fired it at the boy who hit Annie. She missed his head. The snowball glanced off his shoulder instead. Sharing a shocked look, the boys hightailed it down the street.

Madison grimaced as the anger and memories faded. Good Lord, what had she been thinking? She was lucky she hadn't really hit the kid, or some parent would be hauling her in for assault. Once in one day was enough, thank you very much.

She ignored Nell's startled expression and walked over to Annie. "Assholes," the young girl snarled.

Madison saw the hurt and embarrassment in her heavily made-up eyes, the tremble of her purple-glossed lips, and gently brushed the snow from the young girl's hair. "Guys are such jerks, aren't they?"

Annie lifted her gaze to hers. "Yeah."

Madison sucked in a surprised gasp. Beneath the pancake makeup, the girl was beautiful, as beautiful as the man she was a carbon copy of. With those winter-green eyes, inky-black hair, and the shallow dent in her chin, there was no doubt in Madison's mind that Gage McBride was Annie's father.

Her stomach lurched. She'd been flirting with a married man, imagining him kissing her, fantasizing about his hands on her naked flesh. She was no better than her mother, she thought in disgust. It took a moment for her to calm herself— it wasn't as if she'd known he was married. But he did, and that hadn't stopped him from flirting with *her*, touching *her*. She was right. Guys were jerks, especially Gage McBride.

"Thanks, you know…" Annie notched her chin in the direction the boys had fled.

Madison shook off her anger and winked. "Us girls have to stick together."

Annie gave her a shy smile as they walked up the driveway. "I'm Annie."

"Nice to meet you, Annie. I'm Madison." She kept an eye on Nell, whom Lily was helping up the three steps to the white wraparound porch.

"Are you a friend of my aunt's?"

Friend? That'd be pushing it. But at least she no longer wanted to strangle the woman. "I'm staying with Nell for a few days to help out."

"Cool. Do you live around here?"

"No, I'm from New York."

"Wow, sick."

Madison frowned. "You don't like big cities?"

Annie grinned. "No, *sick* means, like, 'way cool.' I wish I lived in New York. I hate small towns."

A girl after my own heart. She could get to like this kid. "Me too," she said, giving the plastic Santa hanging from a hook on the white door the evil eye when he *ho ho, ho, ho*'d as she turned the knob. She walked inside and froze. Christmas tchotchkes covered every available flat surface in the living room to her right, where Lily happily danced around pressing buttons and turning knobs, filling the air with the teeth-grinding cacophony of Christmas music.

"I'm in Christmas hell," Madison muttered.

Annie looked up. Dammit, she'd said that out loud. And it wasn't something she should be saying in front of a kid who, given who her aunt was and where she lived, probably still believed in Santa and loved the holiday.

Annie grinned. "You don't like Christmas, either?"

Madison was trying to think up an excuse for her reaction when she realized Annie had said *either.* "No," she whispered. "You don't like Christmas?"

Annie shook her head. "I hate it. My family calls me the Grinch."

"They call me that, too," she grumbled, thinking of Gage when he'd hauled her from the SUV.

Annie smiled. "Sick."

"Yeah, sick." Madison laughed. Maybe with Annie around, being at Nell's wouldn't be so bad. She'd just have to avoid Annie's father.

"Madison," Nell called out from the plastic-covered red couch. "There are extra mitts and hats in the hall closet behind you. The boxes of lights are in the spare bedroom."

"Boxes of lights?" Madison asked, as the sinking feeling from earlier returned.

"Yay, lights! We're putting up the Christmas lights!" Lily hopped up and down, her long chestnut-colored ponytail bouncing behind her.

Annie sighed. "Lily lo-o-oves Christmas."

"I can see that." And no matter how tired she was, how the thought of putting up lights was about as welcome as having a tooth pulled without Novocain, Madison couldn't disappoint the little girl.

Nell waved a piece of paper at Madison. "Here's a diagram for you to follow."

Madison had a sudden vision of herself as Chevy Chase in *Christmas Vacation*, a movie Skye forced her to watch every year.

"Once I've had a nap, I'll be out to check up on you," Nell warned.

She narrowed her eyes on the older woman. She didn't look so good. Madison toed off her boots. "Nell, where's your bedroom? I'll get you a blanket and pillow."

With Annie and Lily's help, she settled Nell on the couch with her foot propped on a pillow and a cup of tea within easy reach. It had taken some convincing, but Nell finally conceded to let Madison exchange the plastic covering for a sheet. By the time they'd hauled the boxes from the spare bedroom, Nell was snoring to the strains of "Silent Night."

*   *   *

Gage pulled out of the station's parking lot while he spoke to Ethan on the phone. "There's no love lost between Nell and Ms. Lane, that's for sure. Maybe you can't reach them because they've strangled each other," Ethan said.

"Har har, you're a real comedian."

"That's a thought. If I lose the next election, I'll give it a shot."

"Not going to happen. You're doing a great job. Everyone thinks so."

"If Harrison Hartwell can be believed, they will."

Gage braked at the light. "What are you talking about?"

"I just got off the phone with him five minutes ago. There's going to be a full review next week. He's confident they'll be putting forward a new offer."

Gage didn't like what he was hearing. Madison believed Harrison Hartwell was after her job. It seemed pretty convenient she wasn't going to be around while they did their so-called review.

"I don't know about that guy, Ethan. Joe Hartwell didn't indicate anything of the kind this afternoon. I could be wrong, but it seems to me Madison's here to calm the waters, nothing more."

But maybe there was something more. She'd been upset after her private conversation with Hartwell. She didn't come out and say anything, but the shock in her eyes and pale face had given her away. He hadn't liked how Hartwell had spoken to her when he'd been on speaker, and after her reaction to that last call, Gage had been more than a little irritated with the man.

He wondered, not for the first time, what it was about her that fired up his protective instincts. It went beyond simple appreciation of her beauty; he liked her, liked the way her mind worked, and her sharp wit. He pushed the thought aside. His girls were enough to deal with. Not that he had any intention of starting anything with Madison. It wasn't like she was going to be in town for long. Good thing, he thought.

"Harrison asked that I keep it confidential, so this one stays between you and me, okay?"

"Yeah, sure." Oddly enough, Gage felt disloyal to Madison making the promise. There was no denying she knew what she was talking about. She'd presented a pretty convincing case against the resort being built. But if Hartwell wasn't smart enough to listen to her, that was between the two of them. Gage's first loyalty belonged to his friends and family, all of whom wanted the deal to go through.

He turned onto Nell's street and spotted Madison up on a ladder. Annie was handing her a strand of lights while Lily pointed out where they should go. Christmas lights were hung haphazardly off the porch railings and around the window frames. He started to laugh. Madison didn't have a clue what she was doing.

"What's so funny?" Ethan asked.

"You know how Nell always wins first prize for best-lit house?"

"Yeah."

"This year, she won't." The Suburban's headlights lit up the house, and he saw the ladder shift. "I gotta go. Madison's going to kill herself." He was out the door and across the lawn just in time to keep her from falling off the ladder. Unfortunately, it was his hand on her butt that held her in place. Madison glared down at him.

He slid his hands to her waist and lifted her off. Setting her down in front of him, he lunged for the teetering ladder. Once he'd wedged it securely against the wall, he turned and noticed what was on her head. "Nice hat," he said, trying not to laugh at the hot pink, bunny-eared hat she wore.

Her left eye twitched, her smile more a baring of teeth. "Lily picked it out for me."

"Daddy!" His youngest hurled herself at his legs. "You saved Maddie."

"He's a regular hero," Madison said with a curl of her still-swollen lip.

Gage frowned. He didn't understand what the problem was. They'd gotten along well enough at the station. She sure as hell hadn't minded his hands on her then. And if he was honest, he'd liked having them on her. He'd only wished that there'd been less clothes between them. Which he realized now was a mistake on so many levels.

Madison dropped her gaze to the strand of tangled lights in her hands. Gage figured that must be the reason for her mood. She was stuck entertaining his kids while forced to live with Nell for a week.

"Hey, sweetpea." He lifted Lily into his arms and received a smacking kiss for his effort. "Having fun?"

"Yeah!" She nodded as he put her down and turned to his oldest.

"What about you, Annie? You have a good day?" He walked on eggshells around his eldest lately, never knowing what would set her off.

Today she looked like she might answer him, but Lily beat her to it. "Trent and his friends were being mean to her, but Maddie fixed them." Lily beamed at Madison, who shared a smile with his daughters.

Gage stared at Annie. He hadn't seen her smile like that in a long time. He'd tried everything he could think of to coax one out of her, and in just a couple of hours Madison had succeeded where he'd failed.

"What?" Annie's smile faded, a defensive note in her voice.

"Nothing, just surprised to see you wearing a hat." He covered his reaction, gesturing to the black knit cap on her head. Also true, he could never get her to wear one.

She shrugged then looked at Madison, who was studying the paper Lily had shoved into her hands. "Maddie made me put it on."

At that moment, he couldn't help feeling a little resentful toward the woman.

Madison glanced up. "If I have to wear one, so do you. At least you got to pick yours." She made a face, then smiled when Lily looked up at her.

Annie laughed.

What the hell had happened to his daughter? "So, what went on with Trent and his friends?" he asked, hoping he'd find his answer there.

Annie's expression shuttered. Typical.

"They were calling Annie names, and Trent threw a snowball at her. He hit her right in the face," Lily said angrily then grinned up at Madison. "Maddie threw one back at them, and they ran away."

Gage's jaw dropped. "You threw a snowball at a... kid?" Did the woman have no sense? For chrissakes, she could be charged with assault. He blew out an exasperated breath. He'd known from the beginning she'd be trouble.

She shrugged. "I didn't really hit him. Besides, he deserved it. He's a jerk." She nailed him with a look that said not only was Trent a jerk, so was he.

"Yeah, Daddy, he's a jerk."

Madison grimaced. "Okay, ladies, let's get this show on the road. Nell's not going to be very happy with..." Her voice trailed off as the strand of lights that had been strung around the dining room window clattered to the ground. "Dammit. It took me a frigging hour to get them up there." Hands on her hips, she scowled at the window.

Eyes wide, Lily looked up at Gage. "Maddie said a swear," she whispered. Annie burst out laughing.

Gage scrubbed a hand over his mouth to hide his grin. "It's getting late. How about we pack up for the night and you can come over to help Madison tomorrow?"

"Can we stay for dinner with Maddie and Auntie, Daddy? Can we? Can we?" Lily tugged on his hand, jumping up and down.

"I don't know, Lily. Aunt Nell needs her rest." And he got the impression Madison wouldn't be happy if he stuck around.

"Aunt Nell won't mind, Dad. There's lots of food. The neighbors keep dropping it off." Annie pointed to the pile of foil-wrapped dishes on the porch. Gage couldn't believe it. Annie actually wanted to stay for dinner. That was a first. Typically she couldn't wait to get home to shut herself in her room.

"I guess. Madison, that okay with you?"

"Sure. Whatever," she muttered, picking up the lights.

Annie shot a confused glance at Madison, then said slowly, "Come on, Lily. Let's pick out what we want for dinner."

"Yeah. See if there's mac and cheese, Annie," Lily said, as they ran toward the porch.

Gage started shoving the lights inside a box. "Look,

if you don't want us to stay for dinner, just say so." Her bitchy attitude was pissing him off.

She looked up from where she dug a strand from the snow. "I told you, whatever. But you should probably let your wife know you're staying for dinner. She might be expecting you."

"My wife?" he asked.

"You know, the mother of your children. The woman you promised to love and cherish."

"Oh, her." He shook his head at the dirty look she shot him. "I'm divorced, Madison. Have been for quite a few years. Sheena, the girls' mother and my ex-wife, lives in Nashville."

"Sorry. I didn't know." She came slowly to her feet, brushing the snow from her knees before taking a step back to survey the house. "It probably is a good idea if you stick around. I might need backup when Nell gets a look at the lights."

"They're not so bad," he lied.

She arched a brow.

"Okay, they're pretty bad." He smiled. She gave him a heart-stopping one in return.

What the hell had just happened? Had she been angry because she thought he was married?

Nah, couldn't be.

Chapter Seven

The ringing of Madison's BlackBerry jolted her awake. Groggily, she patted the bedside table. "Hello," she rasped.

"Whoa." Vivi's throaty laugh came over the line. "No need for the sexy, come-hither voice. It's just me."

Vivi had the bedroom voice, not her. But if Madison's voice had a sexy vibe going on this morning, it was all Gage McBride's fault. Thanks to the number of times she'd bumped up against his leanly muscled body as they did dishes in the close confines of Nell's kitchen last night, he'd played a prominent role in her dreams.

Propping the pillows behind her, Madison cleared her throat. "No, that would be my just-woke-up voice."

"*You* just woke up?" Vivi's voice dropped to a surprised whisper. "Do you have a man in your bed?"

Not literally. But if Gage was as good in real life as he was in her dreams, Madison really, really wished she did.

"No, I don't have a man in my bed." Her response came out a little testy, but hey, it didn't seem fair that she was the only one not getting any.

"Since it's ten in the morning and you never sleep past six, I can't think of any other reason for you to be there. Unless...you're not sick, are you?"

"No, I'm—"

"*Depressed*. I knew it. Damn reporters. I promise, Maddie, in a day or so no one will remember you."

She didn't bother to remind Vivi that she was a *damn reporter*, too, or that Madison didn't do depressed, ever. Then she realized there was only one reason for her friend to think she was. "How bad is it?"

"Umm, bad. On a brighter note, you made CNN."

Madison closed her eyes and groaned.

"No, listen to me. The statements from both Christmas's mayor and sheriff are playing in your favor. The national media is beginning to lose interest." Vivi paused, the tapping of keys coming from her end.

"Are you on your computer?"

"Yeah, and the local media should be...Maddie, please tell me they've superimposed your head on this woman, and you didn't drill a snowball at a kid!"

Madison thumped her head against the pillows in frustration. "How did they get a picture of that? I didn't see any reporters." She tossed back the covers, suppressing a shiver as the cool air kissed her bare skin. And there was *a lot* of bare skin. She'd found the pink lace nightie in the chest of drawers in her bedroom. For an older woman, Nell had interesting taste in lingerie.

Madison wrapped an arm around her waist and began to pace, smacking her foot on the corner of the metal bed frame. She cursed under her breath, hopping on one foot to rub her throbbing toe.

"What happened?"

"I stubbed my toe."

"Stop pacing," Vivi said with a characteristic lack of sympathy. Madison's need to pace while on the phone drove her best friend nuts. "Maddie, what were you thinking?"

"Um, he threw one first?"

"You're not in high school. You can't go around—"

"I know, but they were...I know." She sighed, unable to defend her actions. Vivi was right. It had been stupid and immature.

"Hang on...Well, today's your lucky day. You should buy a lottery ticket."

She heard the smile in Vivi's voice, and a glimmer of hope stirred to life inside her. "Why? What happened?"

"The online version of the *Christmas Chronicle* has posted a retraction..."

Madison stood frozen to the hardwood floor, waiting anxiously for Vivi to continue. "Okay, not a retraction per se, but they're no longer painting you as the villain in the story. It says here that a couple of local boys were bullying the sheriff's daughter, and you were defending her. The kid's mother...Hey, she can't say that!"

"What? What did she say?"

"Nothing. It doesn't matter. Just be thankful someone's got your back. If your luck holds out and you don't do anything else stupid, this should die down pretty quick."

"Hey, I...Okay, you're right. I'll keep a low profile for the rest of my stay." Easy enough, Madison thought, as she carefully made her way to the window. She leaned over to pull on the blind to let some light into the room. The shade rolled up with a loud thwack. A pair of wide eyes in a grizzled face stared in at her. She screamed. Nell's friend—Ted or Fred, she wasn't sure which—did, too.

Gaping at her, the strand of Christmas lights he held fell from his hands. "What are you trying to do, give me a heart attack? Put on some damn clothes!" he yelled at her through the closed window. The ladder he stood upon wobbled. His eyes rounded.

"Oh, shit," Madison croaked.

"Maddie, what's going on?"

"I'll call you back." She tossed her phone on the bed. "Hang on, TedFred, I'll help you."

She tried to open the window, but it was stuck. Dropping to her knees to get a better grip, she gritted her teeth and pushed. The window jerked open, a gush of pine-scented air lowering the temperature of the room at least twenty degrees. As she raised it higher, the edge of the frame caught on the ladder, pushing it off the side of the house. Madison and TedFred screamed. She lunged, hanging halfway out the window to grab the top rung with one hand while fisting her other hand in his army-green parka. She pulled him toward her, catching sight of Gage sprinting across the snow-covered lawn with Lily and Annie on his heels. The older man's sidekick, his mouth hanging open, held on to the ladder at the base while Madison struggled to drag both TedFred and the ladder toward her.

Beneath them, Gage took over. The ladder bounced into place against the house. Both Madison and TedFred sagged in relief.

"Ted, you okay to come down, or are you going to

climb through the window?" Gage called up, his voice a gravelly rasp.

The older man's gaze dropped from Madison's face. "Down. I'm coming down," he croaked.

Madison released his jacket to give his arm a reassuring pat. "Don't worry, Ted. You'll be fine. I'll keep ahold of the ladder up here."

"No! Get out of the damn window!" the three men yelled at her, none of them looking at her face.

She followed their gazes to where her breasts were practically falling out of the nightie, her nipples standing at attention. She groaned, ducking down, her cheeks on fire.

So much for keeping a low profile.

*   *   *

Propped against the counter in Nell's kitchen, Gage listened to his messages. So much for his day off. As soon as the weekend edition of the *Chronicle* hit the streets, he'd been inundated with calls from angry citizens. He didn't know who frustrated him more: Madison, who threw the snowball in the first place; or Rick Dane, who managed to snap the picture and put it on today's front page. It was a tie.

An image of Madison in her barely-there lingerie came to mind. Blew his mind, more likely. He never would've guessed that beneath her conservative clothes lay the body of a centerfold. Casting a surreptitious glance in his aunt's direction, he decided if he didn't want to embarrass himself, he'd best get that particular vision out of his head. Not that it would be easy. Madison had been fully clothed last night, and after brushing up against her in his aunt's kitchen about a hundred times, he hadn't been able to get her out of his head. Yesterday he'd teased her about the role he played in women's dreams. Well, last night, she'd played a prominent role in his.

Sitting at the kitchen table with her foot propped on a chair, Nell scowled at the newspaper in front of her. She grunted, then returned her attention to her iPad.

"You okay?"

Involved in what he assumed was a game of Angry Birds, she waved off his question. "Fine."

He didn't buy it. She was too pale for his liking. Setting his BlackBerry on the Formica countertop, Gage gently wrapped his fingers around her toes, checking their temperature and color.

She shifted in her chair. "Stop playing with my toes."

"Don't get testy. I'm just making sure your cast isn't too tight."

She put down her iPad, crossing her arms over her chest. "See, you don't trust that new doc, either. Too damn young, if you ask me. I don't know what your father was thinking, letting him take over his patients while he's away. He never should've gone on that cruise."

"Matt's a great doctor, and he's the same age as me. And it's about time Dad took a vacation." Gage might wish his father had gone on the cruise with anyone other than Karen, but he was glad he'd gotten away. His father hadn't taken a holiday since Gage's mother died nine years ago.

"I know that. It's just too bad he's taking it with Karen." Her mouth quirked in a grin as a mischievous glint lit her eyes. "Bet Miss Snooty-Pants won't be too happy to find out Liz is on board."

"How did you know that?" Liz hadn't even known

which ship she was going to be on when she left. She'd won the cruise a couple of weeks ago. No one had believed the call had been legit until the airline ticket arrived two days later.

Gage took in Nell's self-satisfied smile and shook his head. "It was you, wasn't it?"

She shrugged. "So what if it was? Someone had to step in. You and Ethan weren't making any headway. Liz and Paul are letting misplaced loyalty stand in the way of their happiness. They're not getting any younger, you know."

Gage agreed with her, but he didn't like that once again his aunt had manipulated things to get her way, no matter how well intentioned.

"I'd like nothing better than to see Dad with Liz. But you can't keep interfering in people's lives like this, Nell. Look what happened with Madison."

"What? No harm was done, and now we have a chance to change her mind." She tapped her finger on the paper. "I don't know what the Sam Hill possessed Rick to run this story. Embarrassing Madison isn't the way to win her over." Nell had a lot of nerve calling Rick out after what she'd pulled on Madison, but he didn't bother pointing that out. She wouldn't listen. "He has as much to gain from changing her mind as anyone does."

In that, she was right. Rick stood to make a pretty penny if the deal went through.

His aunt picked up the *Chronicle* and winced. "Not very photogenic, is she?"

He took the paper and scanned the story that promised to give him a headache by day's end. "No. She looks a little scary." Scary wasn't how she'd looked earlier. More like smokin' hot.

"Thanks," Madison said drily from behind him. "Let me see that."

Her fingers brushed his as she tugged the *Chronicle* from his hand. She wouldn't meet his eyes, and he wondered if she felt the same jolt of awareness he had from that brief touch. Either that or she was embarrassed about earlier. Unable to help himself, his eyes took a slow tour of her black-on-black ensemble, searching for some sign of the incredible body he now knew she possessed.

Not even a hint.

He dragged his gaze back to her face, to that unflattering thing she did with her hair. Gage couldn't figure her out. Most women tried to make the most of their assets, but she did the exact opposite.

Muttering something about small towns under her breath, she tossed the paper onto the table and turned her attention to his aunt. "Sorry, Nell, I slept in. Can I get you something to eat?"

"Ted made me breakfast before he and Fred went out to put up the lights." Nell's voice shook with restrained laughter.

Hands on her hips, Madison scowled at her. "It's not funny. And FYI, it's not my nightie. I didn't have any clothes with me and borrowed it from *you*."

Nell's brow furrowed then cleared. "You got into Lily's drawer. Her mother gives her all her castoffs to play dress-up with. I would've given you a pair of PJs if you asked. And if Rick was out and about this morning, you're going to wish you had."

"Who's Rick?" Madison's gaze went from him to his aunt.

"He owns the *Chronicle* and—"

"Oh, God, he's the one who took my picture yesterday," she interrupted Gage, the color draining from her face. "What if—"

"Don't worry about it. I didn't see him, but—"

"I didn't see him yesterday, either, yet he was there."

"You didn't let me finish. I'll call him and take care of it." Hopefully Rick hadn't been anywhere near Nell's this morning. Because if he got a picture of Madison hanging out that window, Gage would have a hard time convincing him not to print it, and every red-blooded male within a hundred miles would land on Nell's doorstep hoping to catch a glimpse of her. The thought irritated the hell out of Gage. A reaction he didn't want to think about.

"How can—"

"I'll take care of it," he repeated firmly, catching the speculative gleam in his aunt's eyes as she listened to their exchange. He shot her a don't-even-think-about-it look.

She grinned then said to Madison, "Don't worry about Rick. I'll handle him. I already gave him a piece of my mind this morning. Can't call yourself a journalist if you don't give both sides of the story, I told him."

"It was you? You told him I threw the snowball because the boys were bullying Annie?"

At the sound of a muffled sob, the three of them turned. Annie stood in the doorway, a telling sheen in her eyes. "You told him they were bullying me? I-It's in the paper?"

Nell's brow furrowed. "Yes, now they'll—"

"Annie," Gage called out, as she took off up the stairs. He went to go after her, but Madison stopped him with a hand on his arm. "Let me. It's my fault."

He hesitated, then gave a tight nod. He didn't like to

admit it, but Madison would probably have more luck getting Annie to open up than he would.

Lily came into the kitchen. "Why's Annie crying?"

"It's okay, sweetpea. Take off your jacket and go watch cartoons. Annie'll be down in a few minutes."

She glanced up the stairs. "Maddie will make her feel better. Annie likes her."

From the look on Madison's face when she came down fifteen minutes later, she hadn't fared much better than Gage would have.

In response to his raised brow, she shrugged. "I don't know if I was much help. She's not crying anymore, but she won't come downstairs. She says she's not going to school on Monday."

"That's nothing new, but thanks for trying." Even though a part of him blamed Madison for the mess, he appreciated that she'd taken the time to talk to his daughter.

Nell frowned. "I don't know what she's so upset about. Those boys won't bother her now that it's out in the open."

"I wish that were true, Nell, but more than likely it'll make it worse," Madison said quietly.

Gage glanced at her. There was something in her voice, in her expression, that said she spoke from experience. He was tempted to ask her about it when a shrill whistle distracted him. Probably a good thing, he thought, as he turned to take the kettle off the stove. Because the more he learned about Madison Lane, the more he liked her.

"Nell, I need to pick up some clothes to get me through the next few days. Since Gage and the girls are here to look after you, I thought I'd go now. I won't be long."

Gage set a cup of tea in front of his aunt. "I have to

put in a couple of hours at the station, but the girls will be here." He didn't add that the only reason he had to go in was because once again Madison had the citizens of Christmas up in arms. He figured she felt bad enough.

"I'm not an invalid, you know. I can look after myself."

Madison gave her a pointed look. Gage grinned, waiting for his aunt to start backpedaling.

"For an hour or two. I'm good for an hour or two." Nell avoided looking at Madison and grabbed a pen. "While you're out, there's a few things I need from the store. We're going to make gingerbread for the church bazaar today."

Nell's little helper narrowed her eyes, obviously thinking through the implications of that piece of news. "I can pick up whatever you need and drop it off before I go shopping. That way you and the girls can start baking right away."

Good try, Gage thought, covering his laugh with a cough.

Baby blues narrowed on him.

"It'll wait until you get back." Nell rubbed her shoulder. "You'll be the one doing the baking. My bursitis is acting up."

Alarm shot over Madison's face. "I don't know how to bake."

"I guess I'll have to teach you then, won't I?"

Madison sent Gage a pleading look.

"Lily and Annie are pretty good in the kitchen. Maybe they'll give you a hand" was the best he could do.

"Thanks," she muttered.

Nell waved the list at Gage. "You'd better drive Madison. I don't trust her with my truck."

Madison opened her mouth, then shut it.

"Sure," Gage shoved the list in his pocket, "but I'll be at the station for a while."

"There's enough shops on Main Street to keep Madison busy. It'll give her an opportunity to get to know the shopkeepers." His aunt grinned. "Maybe you ought to take her to Naughty and Nice first."

"Naughty and Nice?" Madison asked.

"Come on." Gage nudged her out of the kitchen before his aunt could tease her further.

"I don't know why you had to tell her about the nightie," Madison said in a disgruntled whisper.

"I didn't. Ted did. He was afraid he was having a heart attack and came in for an aspirin." Gage didn't blame him. Gage had thought he was having one, too.

She shook her head then cast a worried glance up the stairs. "Do you think Annie will be all right?"

"Yeah, she'll be fine. Lily," he called into the living room, where his youngest lay on the area carpet in front of the television. Absorbed in her cartoon, she didn't answer. He walked over and crouched beside her. "Daddy's gotta go to work. You look after Aunt Nell, okay? Give Annie a few minutes then get her to come watch TV with you."

"Um-hmm." She nodded, eyes glued on *Dora the Explorer.* He kissed the top of her head, giving her ponytail a gentle tug. "Call me if you need me. Ted and Fred are out front."

Madison watched him, an odd expression on her face. He cocked his head. "What's up?"

"You're a good dad. Annie and Lily are lucky to have you."

"Thanks," he said, as he opened the door, "but I'm the lucky one. They're great kids." It wasn't always easy being a single parent, but Gage wouldn't trade his life for anyone else's.

Fred and Ted made their way up the porch steps, stopping short when they saw Madison. The three of them tried to look anywhere but at each other.

Gage held back a laugh. "You two planning on sticking around for a bit? I'm taking Madison downtown, and I've got to go to the station."

"We'll be here for at least another hour or so. We have to put Nell's lights to rights," Fred said, shooting an accusing look at Madison.

"I didn't do that bad a job," she muttered under her breath as she walked past them.

"You sure as hell did. Poor Nellie would've had a stroke if she saw the mess you made."

Madison turned on the bottom step. "Hey, I thought you were supposed to be deaf."

"That'd be Ted." Fred jerked his thumb at the man standing beside him.

"Yeah, that'd be me." Ted tapped his hearing aid. "You nearly blew out my eardrums screaming like you did."

A put-upon expression on her face, she said, "I saved you from falling off the ladder. You should be thanking me."

"Thanking you? It was your fault I nearly fell in the first place. Standing in your window naked like you were, you about gave me heart failure."

"I was not *naked*," she said, as her face flushed.

"Pretty damn near, you were."

"All right, that's enough," Gage said. "Boys, do me a favor and keep an eye on Nell and the girls."

"I was not naked," Madison grumbled, stomping toward the Suburban.

He didn't think she expected an answer from him, but obviously she did as she leaned against the hood, jerking her thumb in Ted and Fred's direction. "You were there. Tell them."

Gage rubbed a hand along his jaw then turned to the two men standing on the porch. "Ted, Fred, she didn't have a lot of clothes on, but she did have clothes on."

"Real helpful." She scowled at him as he held open the door.

"That one's trouble, Gage. You better keep an eye on her," Ted said.

Before Gage closed the door, Madison leaned past him. "I am not trouble, and I do not need a babysitter."

"Yes, you are. You need a keeper."

Gage closed the door on her response.

"None of this is my fault, you know," she said, as soon as he got behind the wheel. "Nell set me up, those boys were tormenting Annie, and I *saved* Ted."

She was right about Nell, and damned if he was going to bring up her hanging out the window half-naked again. "Yeah," he said, starting the engine, "you only nailed a kid with a snowball."

She turned to look out the window. "I barely hit him."

"And that's what I'm going to tell everyone who's calling for you to be charged with assault. Including Trent's mother, Brandi."

"Maybe Trent's mother should be more concerned that her son is bullying a young girl and making her life miserable than getting bent out of shape about a teensy tiny snowball that grazed her son's shoulder."

Gage frowned. "Is that what Annie told you? I thought yesterday was an isolated incident."

"No, from what I got out of her, this has been going on for several months."

His fingers tightened on the steering wheel. If what Madison said was true, it went a long way in explaining the changes he'd noticed in Annie. "I don't get it. What is it about you? You've known Annie for less than twenty-four hours, and she tells you things I've been trying to pry out of her for the last few months."

Madison shifted in her seat, searching his face. "And that makes you angry, hurts your feelings?"

"I'm not a damn girl." He blew out a frustrated breath. "All right, sure. Maybe you can tell me why my daughter confides in a stranger and not her father?"

"Let's just say we found out we have some things in common. As for her not telling you, she's a smart kid and probably has a pretty good idea how you'd react. Having her dad, who just happens to be the sheriff, confront those boys would be pretty embarrassing for a twelve-year-old girl."

He turned onto Main Street, casting her a sidelong glance. "So how'd you get so smart? I know you're single and don't have kids of your own." Once Nell had found out the name of the woman who'd put together the report for Hartwell, she'd done a little investigating on her own. She'd been happy—maybe too happy—to report Madison's single status to Gage and Ethan.

"Surprising as it may be, I was one once."

Gage grinned. "You know what I mean. I can't imagine someone like you was ever bullied."

"No? Then you'd be wrong." There was no amusement in her eyes now.

Something about her made him want to push and find out what had caused the light to go out of her eyes. "Let me guess—the girls were jealous because you were beautiful and stole all the boys' attention."

"Wrong again, Sheriff. I know you think there's nothing better than living in a small town, but when you don't fit in, or God forbid you're from the wrong side of the tracks and have a father who's a drunk and a mother..." Her lips flattened.

And the puzzle that was Madison Lane started to click into place. Some of her reactions and comments began to make sense. He pulled in front of Naughty and Nice, then turned off the engine. Her eyes met his, and his chest tightened at the pain he saw reflected there. "Just like people, not all towns are the same, Madison." Unable to help himself, he lightly brushed her hair back from her face. Fighting an urge to tug those silky strands from their unflattering confines, he curled his fingers into his palm.

"Sorry to break it to you, Sheriff, but so far Christmas hasn't given me much reason to change my opinion of small towns."

Considering what she'd had to deal with in the last twenty-four hours, he understood why. "Give us a chance. We might just surprise you."

Aw, hell, that sounded like he wanted her to give *him* a chance. And maybe for a minute there he had, but only for a minute. That is, until she nervously ran the tip of her tongue over her upper lip. Not the Kewpie-doll mouth from the day before; now her lips looked delectably full and kissable.

As if she could read his thoughts, she jerked her gaze from his, angling her head to get a better look at the window display. "Umm, I'm not sure this is the right store for me," she said slowly.

"I don't know," Gage said, taking in the scantily clad mannequin. "Looks a bit like what you had on this morning, only in red."

She swung her gaze back to him. "None of you are going to let me forget that, are you?"

"Nope, probably not." He knew he sure as hell wouldn't be able to. "Give me your phone. I'll put my number in. That way you can call when you're finished shopping, and I'll pick you up."

"Thanks, but it might take me a while. I'll walk back to Nell's."

"You're forgetting you have a date with some gingerbread men."

She sighed and handed over her phone.

"Now remember," he said once he'd finished entering the number, "if anyone ticks you off, you call me. No nailing them with a snowball."

"I'm a big girl, Sheriff. I can take care of myself," she said, as she got out of the Suburban. "Besides, I plan on keeping a low profile from now on."

Chapter Eight

Madison focused on the store window in front of her, afraid that if she looked back, she wouldn't be able to resist the urge to climb into the Suburban and throw herself into Gage's arms, letting him take away that small ache—the one that crept up on her whenever she took a trip down memory lane.

He was getting to her. Dammit. Physical attraction was one thing—and she was attracted, all right. She'd have to be dead not to be. But beyond his gorgeous looks and panty-melting voice, the man was the real deal.

She heard him pull away from the curb and, unable to help herself, looked over her shoulder to watch him drive down the snow-dusted, cobblestone street. One week, she reminded herself, only one week, and she'd be back in the city, enjoying the comfort of anonymity.

She opened the red door, refusing to think about the fact that being comforted by Gage would be much more satisfying. As she took in the glitz and glamour of the clothes lining the racks, her first thought was: keeping a low profile while being outfitted by Naughty and Nice would be next to impossible.

A heavily accented voice called out, "I will be right with you." Madison turned to see a woman wiggling her way beneath the red satin drapery that formed the backdrop to the window display.

"No problem. I'll just look around."

There was nothing small town about Naughty and Nice, with its white marble floors, white leather lounge chairs, and poinsettia trees standing sentry at the fitting room entrance. It was as upscale as any Fifth Avenue boutique. Not that Madison shopped in upscale boutiques. She could afford to, but she preferred to save her money rather than spend it. Skye and Vivi had been known to call her cheap on occasion, but Madison liked to think of herself as fiscally responsible. If she didn't have at least a year's salary sitting in her accounts, she broke out in hives.

Madison hadn't made it more than two feet into the store when the woman behind the curtain let loose a string of incomprehensible words.

"Sophia, watch your mouth," a petite strawberry blonde said, as she walked beneath a plastered archway that connected two stores. And if the delectable scent perfuming the air was anything to go by, the other shop sold chocolate.

Madison's stomach rumbled loud enough for the woman approaching her to hear.

Wearing a brown apron with sparkling pink writing that read "Sugar and Spice," the woman grinned.

"Today's sample." She offered a crystal platter laden with chocolates.

The curtain rustled, and another string of what Madison thought might be Spanish blistered the air.

"Sophia, you have a customer." The woman smiled an apology. "Don't be shy, take one."

Madison put a hand on her stomach. "I couldn't. I haven't eaten breakfast yet."

"So I heard." She chuckled. "Chocolate's the breakfast of champions, don't you know?"

Of course she did. "Thanks." Madison chose a chocolate cup with an intricate white lace design on top. Taking a bite, she closed her eyes and hummed her appreciation. "I've never tasted anything this good. I-It's..."

"Orgasmic?"

Madison nodded enthusiastically. "That's it exactly. I'll take a dozen before I leave." The woman laughed. "No, I'm serious." Who needed a man when you had chocolate this good? Unless the man was Gage McBride...At the thought, she helped herself to another.

When she opened her eyes after devouring the second, equally delicious chocolate, the most beautiful woman Madison had seen outside of a magazine stood before her. She had a waterfall of long, dark hair, her exotic features enhanced by warm mocha skin.

"I stabbed myself," the woman whined.

"You're such a baby, Sophia. Let me see." The chocolate lady handed off the platter to Madison, then pulled the woman's finger from her mouth. "It's a...*pinprick*."

"Yes, but it hurts," Sophia pouted.

With a roll of her eyes, the other woman turned to Madison. "Sorry, I should've introduced myself. I'm

Autumn Dane. I own Sugar and Spice." She pointed in the direction of the shop on the other side of the archway before retrieving the crystal platter from Madison. "And this is Sophia Dane. She owns Naughty and Nice."

"Yes, she is the nice in naughty, and I am the spice in sugar." Sophia let loose a throaty laugh.

Madison looked from one woman to the other. "Sisters?"

Autumn laughed. "Sisters-in-law."

"Are you married to the Danes who own the ski hill and lodge?" Madison asked tentatively. If they were, keeping her identity to herself might be best. Coulter Dane hadn't seemed to mind that the resort deal had gone south, but she didn't think his great-grandsons and great-nephew would be as understanding. Madison had heard that it was Rick Dane, his great-nephew, who'd first approached Hartwell, but she'd never had any dealings with the man.

"Yes, but my husband, Bryce, he died two years ago. It was very sad." Sophia sniffed. "And Logan, the ass, he divorced Autumn."

"I'm sorry. I—"

Autumn patted Sophia's arm. "I'm sure Ms. Lane didn't come in to hear our life story."

So much for keeping her identity a secret. "I didn't realize you knew who I am."

Sophia recovered quickly, her deep laugh booming through the shop. "Yes, you are the Grinch lady. The one the town hates."

"Sophia," Autumn groaned. "Don't mind her," she said to Madison.

Hands on her hips, Sophia rounded on her sister-in-law. "What? That is what they call her." She turned to Madison. "Do not worry. They hate me when I come to town, but now they lo-o-ove me." Her smile faded as her dark eyes narrowed, her nose wrinkling in distaste. "Why do you dress like this?"

"Sophia," Autumn muttered, then gave Madison an apologetic shrug.

"I . . . well, it's practical for work, and—"

"No, no more practical. I will make you beautiful." She flicked Madison's black coat with a long red fingernail.

Autumn gave a resigned shake of her head and walked away to place the platter on a glass counter.

"Um, I don't need beautiful. Just maybe—" Madison shot a desperate look at the racks "—jeans . . . jeans and a couple of sweaters."

"I will dress you. I know what I am doing. I was a model." Taking her firmly by the hand, Sophia dragged Madison to the far end of the store. Madison shot a desperate look over her shoulder at Autumn.

Autumn grinned. *Miss January,* she mouthed.

An hour later, Madison stood in a fitting room overflowing with clothes. As she pulled a red knit dress over her head, she struggled to retain her balance in a pair of black leather thigh-high boots with five-inch needle-thin heels.

"Sophia, I don't know why I'm trying this on." Madison raised her voice to be heard through the fitting room door. "I'm not going to need a dress while I'm here."

"Yes, you do. You are coming to the Penalty Box with us on Friday night. Let me see the dress."

Madison didn't bother to argue. She'd quickly learned the Latina beauty talked right over you if you tried. Unaccustomed to wearing heels, Madison wobbled out of the fitting room. She promptly lost her balance and clung to the door.

Sophia, who sat on a white leather chaise filing her nails, looked up and tipped her head back. "Autumn!" she yelled, before returning her attention to Madison. "Come here."

"I don't think I can, not without falling."

With languid grace, Sophia rose from the chaise and came to Madison, prying her fingers from the door. "Walk like this." Hips swaying, Sophia sashayed across the marble floor.

"If I walk like that, I'll fall on my butt."

The door chime cut Sophia off mid-laugh. She waved at the tiny gnome of a woman who entered the store.

"Teach Maddie to walk in her boots while I look after Mrs. Tate," Sophia said to Autumn, who'd come up the steps from her shop.

"Wow, you look amazing, Maddie."

"Yes, and she is wearing that dress when she comes out with us Friday night," Sophia yelled from the front of the store.

"That's great. I'm so glad you're coming with us," Autumn said warmly.

"I wish I could, but I'm leaving Friday morning." Madison enjoyed hanging out with the two women, but that didn't mean she wanted to stay in Christmas any longer than she had to. Thoughts of what her to-do list would look like when she returned to work was giving her hives. And worrying about what Harrison was up to while she was away wasn't helping.

"Why don't you stay for an extra day or two? We'll—" Autumn began when a shrill voice from the direction of Sugar and Spice cut her off.

"Autumn, where are you? I need chocolate. Now," a woman's strident voice demanded.

"Maddie, get in the fitting room." Autumn gave her a push. "Be right with you, Brandi."

A sinking feeling came over Madison. "Autumn, Brandi wouldn't be—"

As heels clattered up the stairs, Autumn gave a panicked gasp and went to shove Madison through the fitting room door.

"What are...What is *she* doing here?" a woman with bleached-blonde hair demanded, glaring at Madison.

"Sophia, I can't believe you allowed her in your shop after what she did to Trent," another woman, this one with a cap of spiky black hair, said as she marched to the blonde's side.

"Enough, Hailey," Sophia called out, heading in their direction.

"Ignore them," Autumn said under her breath before she walked over to the two women, taking them by the arms.

"Let me go." The blonde pushed Autumn's hand from her arm, glowering at Madison. "Who the hell do you think you are, picking on my kid? You want to pick on someone, pick on someone your own size."

Perfect. Just as Madison had suspected, the belligerent blonde was Trent's mother. The only way to defuse the situation was to apologize. "Look, I'm sorry—"

"No, I will take care of them," Sophia cut Madison off and stared down the two women. "Sugar and Spice is that way." She pointed. "Get your chocolate fix. You need it."

Brandi snapped her gaze to Sophia. "I swear, Sophia, if you take her side over ours, you'll regret it."

Madison wasn't about to let Sophia suffer on her account. "Hey, don't threaten her. You have a problem with me, that's fine, but leave—"

"Is that right. Whatcha going to do about it?" Brandi shook off Sophia's hand and took a step in Madison's direction.

Well acquainted with small-town bullies, Madison figured the faster she got out of Sophia's shop the better, for everybody. Holding on to a naked mannequin for support, she leaned over to unzip the boots.

"Yeah, show us what you got. You're not looking so tough now," the dark-haired Hailey jeered.

Autumn threw up her hands. "Oh, come on, ladies. This is—"

Sidestepping Sophia, Brandi bumped into the mannequin. The arm Madison was holding on to broke off in her hand. She stumbled. Her arms windmilling as she struggled to remain upright, the mannequin's hand clipped Brandi's shoulder. Hard.

"Oh, shit," Madison gasped, as she fell back against the wall. "Sorry, I—"

"You hit me!" Brandi cried, reaching for her.

"*Hija de puta*, it was an accident. Do not touch my friend." Sophia inserted herself between Madison and Brandi. Planting both hands on Brandi's chest, she shoved her back.

Brandi lost her balance. Cursing at Sophia, she grabbed her hand as she went down. The two women ended up sprawled on the slippery, marble floor.

Hailey hip-checked Autumn out of the way and reached for her friend.

"Stop that! You're going to—" Madison winced when the two women ended up falling on top of Sophia and

Brandi on the floor. She bit her lip to hold back a nervous laugh as she leaned over to help Autumn up.

"You think it's funny, do you?" Brandi muttered, and with an outthrust foot, she brought Madison to the ground. In a tangled heap of arms and legs, the women fought to free themselves amidst a chorus of grunts, groans, and curses.

"Say cheese, ladies."

Madison looked over her shoulder, blinking into a camera's flash. She rubbed her eyes, trying to clear away the spots.

"No more pictures, Dane," a familiar voice ordered.

"Hey, what happened to freedom of the press? Never mind, I've got a great one right here. Perfect for the next edition of the *Chronicle*."

Madison frowned. Rick Dane was the owner of the *Chronicle*? That made no sense at all. Wouldn't the man who'd initiated the resort deal be doing his best to kiss up to her? *Not when you keep providing him with pictures guaranteed to boost his readership*, she thought with a mental eye roll.

A large, warm hand closed over Madison's, hauling her from the pile of flailing arms and legs. Gage set her on her feet in front of him. She swayed, grabbing hold of his jacket, the leather cold beneath her fingers. Unlike the rest of him. Both the heat of his body and his clean outdoor scent enveloped her, causing a shiver of awareness to curl up her spine. No doubt about it, the man was seriously hot, and seriously ticked off, if the look he skewered her with was anything to go by.

"This"—he jerked his chin at the women still on the floor—"is your idea of low profile?"

His deputy offered Sophia and Autumn a hand up, while the other two women appeared to be waiting for Gage to help them off the floor. Either he didn't hear them calling out to him or was too annoyed with Madison to care, because right now all that testosterone-laden attention was focused solely on her.

"No way, you're not blaming me for this. It's not my fault. It's theirs." She pointed at Hailey and Brandi, who probably figured Gage was too busy giving her hell to lend them a hand and were finally pulling each other to their feet.

"Right. I forgot. It's never your fault." His hand at her waist tightened, his voice deceptively calm. "I can't leave you alone for more than five minutes without you stirring up trouble."

"An hour, at least." She hadn't realized she'd moved closer until she felt his chest against hers, his thighs brushing hers.

Someone cleared their throat. Someone chuckled. And a couple of someones . . . growled.

Good Lord, what was she thinking? *She* wasn't; her hormones were. Releasing her hold on Gage's jacket, Madison gave his broad chest a grateful pat. "Thanks. I think I have my balance now." As soon as she took a wobbly step back, the mean girls moved in.

Hailey shoved her out of the way. Luckily for Madison, Sophia and Autumn each grabbed an arm. Winter-green eyes took a slow trip from the top of Madison's head to the tip of her leather-shod feet before returning to Brandi and Hailey. "All right, quiet." Gage's command ended the women's name calling.

"Maddie did nothing. They were pushing, and yelling, and pushing, and—"

Gage held up a hand to interrupt Sophia. "I think I got it. Thanks."

Hands on their hips, Brandi and Hailey angrily protested, trying once again to lay the blame on Madison.

"That's not…I didn't…" Madison gave up. She didn't know if Gage heard her or not, although every time she tried to add her two cents, and failed, the corner of his mouth twitched.

Thankfully Sophia, who was louder than Madison and the other women combined, had her back. Only problem was, the more agitated Sophia became, the less you understood her.

"Hey. Hello." Madison waved her hands. "Since none of you are interested in my version of the event, I'm going to change now," she said loudly, not that it did her any good. She took mincing steps to the fitting room, arms extended to keep her balance.

She heard a low laugh and glanced over her shoulder, meeting Gage's amused gaze. *You're trouble,* he mouthed.

No, Madison thought when she went all warm and gooey inside, *I'm in trouble.*

*   *   *

Gage rubbed the knotted muscles at the back of his neck, wondering what the hell had happened to his quiet and peaceful town. Then the answer walked out of the dressing room buried under a pile of clothes.

At the sight of Madison's practical black boots and conservative black pants, the knots in his shoulders released. It hadn't been easy keeping his mind on the job with her pressed up against him looking like sex on a stick in that siren red dress, with her thick hair all messy and loose.

She dumped the pile of clothes on the counter, blowing a strand of hair off her face. Gage decided she should wear it in a bun all the time, unless she was alone with him. *Geezus, did I really just think that?* He scrubbed a hand over his face. He needed to get a grip.

Sophia told whoever she was on the phone with that she'd give them details later and hung up. "Good. You are taking everything," she said to Madison.

"Ah, no, I thought I'd..."

Ten minutes later, they were still weeding their way through the clothes. Madison would demur, and Sophia would insist, and another item would end up on the to-buy pile. But when Sophia held up *the* dress and said, "Yes," Gage said, "No."

The two women swivelled their heads to stare at him. He shrugged. "She's not going to need a dress while she's here."

Sophia waved him off. "She looked gorgeous. She's going to wear that dress to the Penalty Box Friday night."

Over his dead body she was. "She'll be back in New York by Friday."

Madison raised a brow. "Anxious to get rid of me, Sheriff?"

While part of him—the stupid part—wanted to shout *Hell no*, the sane part wanted to yell a resounding *Hell yes*. But something in her eyes held him back. It was as if his reaction had hurt her feelings. "Hey, you're the one who doesn't want to be here. Unless you've changed your mind?"

She averted her gaze from his. "No, of course I haven't. Why would I?"

Yeah, and that was what he wondered.

In the end, the dress, along with the damn boots and

half the clothes on the counter, ended up in four—yeah, four—pink Naughty and Nice bags. And naughty was exactly what Madison would look like kitted out in her new wardrobe. He should've taken her to Hardy's, where the only thing remotely sexy was long thermal underwear, but on Madison it would be.

"All right, let me have it," she said, once she was settled in the Suburban with two boxes of chocolates on her lap.

"Let you have what?" he asked as he backed out of the parking space.

"The lecture. You know, the one where you tell me it's all my fault that Brandi and her psycho friend attacked us and we ended up rolling around on the floor like every man's fantasy."

He grinned. "I think you had too many clothes on to qualify for that. And no, I'm not holding you to blame for what went on, but—"

"There's always a *but* with you," she muttered.

"With you, there seems to be. Look, I read the two of them the riot act. They won't be bothering you again."

"Is that all? If they'd pulled a stunt like that in New York, they would've been hauled off to jail and charged with assault."

"Yeah, and so would have you for nailing a kid with a snowball."

"It grazed his shoulder. Not like the one he drilled Annie with."

"I've dealt with him. Just like I've spent half the day dealing with the fallout over this. And don't get me started on what I had to deal with yesterday, thanks to you."

"Well, excuse me for ruining your day. But for the record, yesterday is on Nell, not me." She dug inside the Sugar and Spice box and pulled out a chocolate. "I hate small towns," she said with feeling, then popped the candy in her mouth.

"Yeah, well, I'm pretty sure the feeling is mutual." Aw, hell, he shouldn't have let her comment get under his skin. If he wasn't so damn tired, it wouldn't have. He'd had the week from hell dealing with Annie after Sheena's Thanksgiving no-show, and this week hadn't been much better.

"Sorry," he apologized. "That was uncalled for."

"Don't worry about it. I'm used to it." She turned to look out the window, but not before he saw a flicker of hurt in her eyes.

Way to go, McBride.

He felt like he'd kicked a puppy. Pulling into the grocery store parking lot, he turned off the engine. "Hey." He cupped her chin, drawing her gaze to his. "You just have to give them a chance to get to know you. Sophia and Autumn like you. Annie and Lily think you're great. Even Nell likes you."

She angled her head. "You forgot to include yourself in that long list, Sheriff. Don't you like me?"

Oh, yeah, he liked her just fine. Probably more than was wise. And he was pretty sure his self-imposed celibacy played a part in the attraction. At least he hoped that was the case.

She smiled, and he started to laugh.

"What?"

He tapped his front tooth. "You have chocolate on your teeth."

She ran the tip of her tongue over her pearly whites then bared them for his inspection. "Better?"

He smiled. "You're good to go. Come on." He unbuckled his seat belt, anxious to get out of the close confines of the truck before he did something stupid like kiss that sweet mouth of hers. "Nell won't be happy if we come back without her baking supplies."

"I saw a bakery back there." She pointed down the road. "I'll just go buy the gingerbread cookies from them. Nell shouldn't be baking in her condition."

She looked so pleased with her solution that Gage almost didn't have the heart to burst her bubble. Almost. He kind of got a kick out of watching how she reacted when things didn't go exactly the way she wanted. "You're kidding, right? Nell's gingerbread is a big draw at the Christmas bazaar. She's not going to let a little thing like a stress fracture and bursitis hold her back."

"Maybe you weren't listening earlier, but Nell said *I'll* be the one making the gingerbread, and I don't know how to bake, at all."

"Sorry, but we're big on tradition here in Christmas, and Nell's gingerbread is tradition. You'll just have to learn."

"Fine." She shoved her door open. "How hard can it be to make a dozen cookies?"

Gage waited until she met him at the front of the truck to drop the bomb. "Fifteen dozen."

She froze. "What?"

"Fifteen dozen gingerbread men. Women, too." He grinned at her horrified expression. "And in case you're wondering, the Christmas bazaar is tomorrow. But cheer up. Nell's a good teacher. Who knows, maybe you'll be able to win over the citizens of Christmas with your baking."

Chapter Nine

Madison's gingerbread might not be winning over the citizens of Christmas, but from the leering looks the three older men at the nearby table were sending her way, the cranberry-wrap sweater she'd bought at Sophia's was.

At the sight of Nell crutching her way across the crowded church hall, Madison groaned. Nell had been scoping out the competition, and her expression didn't bode well. "We're in trouble," the older woman said, slightly breathless upon reaching their table. "Word's gotten out that my gingerbread isn't up to snuff, and they're buying my neighbor Stella's instead."

"I warned you I didn't know how to bake." Madison held up a cookie to inspect it. "But I think they look pretty darn good." After the hours she'd spent slaving away in the overheated, ginger-scented kitchen yesterday, Madison had developed a newfound respect for bakers and... Nell. She might be a cantankerous schemer, but the woman had a big heart and cared deeply for her family and town. Madison thought about her own hometown, and she wondered if things would've turned out differently for her if someone like Nell had lived there. No, Nell probably would've run them out of town after her mother's first affair.

At that happy thought, Madison returned her attention to Nell, who waved off her earlier comment. "I'm always the first to sell out, and we have an hour to go. If we don't start moving these cookies, Stella's going to beat me."

"We wouldn't want that to happen, now would we?"

Nell appeared oblivious to Madison's sarcasm. "Darn right we wouldn't." She glanced in the direction of the three leering men and grinned. "I'll be right back."

There was a mischievous twinkle in the older woman's eyes as she took off at a determined hop. "Nell...Nell, what are you up to?"

She ignored her, stopping at the lady five tables down. Earlier on a break, grudgingly granted by Nell, Madison had purchased two gorgeous handmade quilts from the woman for Skye and Vivi. Madison's insistence that she pay fair-market value, instead of the pittance the woman had asked for, put the quilt lady firmly in the I-like-Madison camp.

A somewhat exclusive camp at the moment, Madison admitted, but with Nell no longer rousing the rabble, she hoped to grow beyond her current seven members by the end of the day. Lucky for her, Gage's fan club wasn't in attendance.

Madison replaced the scowl that the thoughts of the women evoked with a smile for Lily, who skipped toward the table with three of her friends in tow. Since Annie refused to attend the bazaar, and Gage wasn't comfortable leaving Annie alone, Nell volunteered to bring Lily so she didn't miss out on the fun. And Madison had to admit that not only did the kids appear to be enjoying themselves, so did the adults.

A lot of work had gone into making the hall festive. Santa competed with the Three Wise Men for space on the stark white walls with glittery gold garlands swagged above them. The attendees sat at tables covered in white linens, a poinsettia on each, devouring party sandwiches made by the one committee Madison thanked God Nell wasn't on. Christmas music and holiday excitement filled the hall and would've been contagious if one were into that sort of thing—which, of course, Madison wasn't.

"Are you girls having fun?" she asked, as Lily and her friends approached the table.

All four of them answered at the same time, telling her exactly how much fun they were having. As the chatter died down, one of Lily's friends, who wore a big red bow in her dark hair, piped up, "Are you Lily's daddy's girl-friend?"

Madison blinked in surprise. "No, Lily's daddy and I are just friends." From the disappointed dip of Lily's shoulders, it wasn't the answer the little girl had wanted to hear.

"Lily said you were." Red-bow Girl plopped her hands on her small hips and turned to Lily. "You lied."

Madison sighed. Young or old, girls were all the same. They'd turn on you in a heartbeat. Growing up, Madison had only two friends she could count on. But even they'd abandoned her after the fallout from the Christmas Eve accident.

"Lily didn't lie. I'm a girl, and I'm her daddy's friend." Madison smiled brightly, retrieving her purse from under the table. She pulled out two five-dollar bills, depositing one in the cash box.

"There, you can each have a cookie, and Lily will buy you a cup of hot chocolate to go with it."

They looked at one another and wrinkled their noses. "It's okay. We'll just get the hot chocolate. Thanks." Lily reached for the fiver.

Madison held the bill above her head. "You have to take a cookie if you want the cash." One way or another, Madison was getting rid of the gingerbread. She wasn't about to let Nell blame her for their lackluster sales.

"But Fred said he almost broke a tooth when he ate his." Lily's friends nodded in agreement.

"That's 'cause Fred wears dentures. They're not as strong as real teeth." Madison handed each of them a cookie. Surreptitiously, she tapped a gingerbread man against the table leg and decided Fred might have a point. "Dunk them in your hot chocolate first," she added. The last thing she needed was to be blamed for a bunch of toothless eight-year olds.

"I like your daddy's girlfriend. She's nice," one of the girls said, as they started to walk away.

"I like her too," Lily said. "When they get married, I'm going to be the flower girl."

Madison closed her eyes on a groan. She needed to have a heart-to-heart with Lily. From what Nell said, Sheena McBride had no time for her daughters. Probably the reason the little girl was intent on finding a replacement. How the woman could abandon a man like Gage and daughters like Lily and Annie was beyond Madison.

The thought that Lily liked her enough to consider her stepmother material left Madison with a warm, fuzzy feeling. But she knew better than to encourage the little girl's fantasy. The last thing Madison needed was for Gage to hear about it. Not that she hadn't entertained a fantasy or two about the man, but none of them involved wedding bells.

"Here you go." Nell tossed an apron across the table at her.

Madison caught the frilly white fabric and frowned. She held it out in front of her. Pink lips covered the apron, and pink letters exhorted the reader to "Kiss the Cook." A sinking feeling, one she was becoming familiar with when it came to Nell, settled in the pit of Madison's stomach.

"Get a kiss with your cookie, boys. Come on, kisses and cookies. One dollar for a kiss and a cookie." The woman sounded like a barker at a sideshow.

"Here they come." Nell made her way around the table. "Watch out for Bill," she warned, tying the apron at Madison's waist. "He's third in line, and he might try to slip you the tongue."

"I'm going to strangle you," Madison said through clenched teeth.

Nell laughed. "Pucker up, girlie."

*   *   *

Since they'd sold out and Stella hadn't, Nell had been in a particularly cheerful mood as they left the bazaar. She seemed surprised that Madison wasn't. Especially since, according to Nell, Madison had won over the male geriatric population of Christmas. Madison still wanted to strangle Nell for turning their table into a kissing booth, but the older woman was right. Joe would probably be thrilled with the progress she'd made today.

With Ted and Fred coming to dinner, Nell insisted she be dropped off first—which worked out well for Madison. She didn't want an audience when she had her chat with the little matchmaker bouncing in the back seat singing "Santa Claus Is Coming to Town" at the top of her lungs.

Bless her heart.

With the slushy condition of the roads, Madison decided to hold off the conversation until they were safely parked in Gage's driveway. They traveled across town at a snail's pace, and her shoulders dropped from around her ears when she finally turned onto Gage's street. Gorgeous stone bungalows sat on heavily forested lots, with the mountains providing an impressive backdrop. As Madison had learned, the McBrides were one of Christmas's founding families, and Gage and his brothers had inherited a good chunk of land.

A white Explorer turned into the driveway ahead of her. "For God's sake, do I have 'Kick me' written on my butt?" she muttered upon seeing Brandi and Hailey get out of the SUV, each of the women carrying what looked like a cake.

Madison felt a tug on her arm and looked down to see Lily's small hand, fingers wiggling.

"Hold on a minute. I'll give you my contribution to the swear jar," Madison said, as she parked beside the other vehicle. At the rate she was going, she'd probably pay for Lily's college education before the week was out. Gage and his daughters had stuck around for her first two attempts at baking yesterday. She'd unconsciously voiced her frustration in front of them, several times.

Madison leaned over to retrieve the container of not-good-enough-to-sell gingerbread that Nell had insisted she drop off at Gage's. Or more precisely, given the two women now knocking on his door, Lily would be delivering to her father while Madison hightailed it out of there.

She shifted in her seat. "Lily, I—"

The little girl was out the back door before she could finish. Madison was about to bang her head against the steering wheel in frustration when Gage opened the front door. Sweet baby Jesus, it should be illegal for a man to look that good in a pair of jeans. She touched the side of her mouth to make sure she wasn't drooling.

Tearing up the two steps, Lily almost took out the two women waving a white... "Oh, no," Madison groaned and shot a desperate look to the empty backseat. Lily'd taken the apron. Now she'd regale her father with tales about the kissing booth.

Which she obviously did since Gage laughed, motioning Madison over. Brandi and Hailey turned to glare at her.

Clutching the cookie container to her chest, Madison slung her purse over her shoulder and got out of the truck. By the time she walked up the steps, Hailey and Brandi were already inside.

"Not a word," she warned Gage.

He held up his hands. "I was just going to ask how it went."

"Fine. We sold out. Stella didn't. Nell's happy." The corner of his mouth twitched. She sighed. "Don't believe anything your daughter tells you. She's on a sugar high."

"So you didn't kiss hundreds of men?"

"Go ahead and laugh. I know you want to." Opening her purse, Madison retrieved a dollar bill, then handed it to him. "For Lily's swear jar."

"Just one?" He grinned.

She rolled her eyes, about to give him the container of cookies when Annie appeared at the door. "Hey, Annie, how—"

Annie hauled her into the house before she could finish. "I'm glad Dad invited you to dinner, Maddie. Maybe you can help me with my math homework after we eat," she said in an overloud voice.

Madison glanced back at Gage.

He shrugged.

"Sure, sounds good," she murmured, as they walked into a huge kitchen with its top-of-the-line stainless steel appliances.

Brandi and Hailey stood at the island—their perfect cakes sitting on the black granite countertop—and did their best to ignore Madison's presence.

Brandi fluttered her fake lashes at Gage. "I was just telling Annie that I wanted to invite the three of you to dinner at my place tonight. I thought it'd give the kids a chance to work out their differences before school tomorrow. That boy needs a man's influence, Gage, and you're the only one he'll listen to. I swear he worships the ground you walk on," she gushed, then shot an eat-shit-and-die look at Madison. "But it seems you already have plans for the night."

Talk about laying it on thick, Madison thought. At least she now knew what Annie was up to.

Gage rested a hand on Annie's shoulder. "I appreciate the thought, Brandi, but the kids will work it out."

Annie ducked from under his hand, mumbling something about homework as she left the kitchen.

"I guess they'll have to, won't they?" Brandi said with a tight smile.

"Seeing as how you have plans, we'll go now. We'd promised to bake your favorite cakes the other day, and with everything going on we didn't get a chance until now. But I'm sure ours can't compete with Ms. Lane's," Hailey said with a snide smile for Madison. "What did you bring?"

Madison tightened her hold on the cookie container. No way she was letting them get a look at her contribution to dessert. "It's nothing. Really."

"Oh, don't be modest," Hailey said. Before Madison had time to react, the woman jerked the container from her hands.

Hailey opened the lid and blinked. Brandi leaned over, looked inside, and snorted a laugh.

Gage took out a gingerbread woman. The one Madison had added red horns to, along with some white icing on its right leg. He looked at Madison and started to laugh—a laugh that curled around her, enveloping her in its warmth. She shrugged, smiling up at him.

Lily skipped into the kitchen wearing the "Kiss the Cook" apron. "Daddy, do you have dentures?" she asked just as Gage went to take a bite of the cookie.

He frowned. "No, why?"

"'Cause Maddie said only people with dentures will break their teeth."

Slowly, he lowered the cookie. "Good to know."

"Well, Gage, it looks like you'll be eating our desserts after all." Brandi smirked. "Holly's going to drop hers by later," she added. The two women pushed past Madison on their way out, and Gage winked as he escorted them to the door. Probably proud of her for holding her temper and not giving them the finger, Madison thought. He should be.

"Aren't you going to take your coat off?" Lily asked, as she plunked a container of milk on the counter.

"Oh, right." Madison started to shrug out of her coat.

Gage came back into the kitchen, and Lily ran out. "Annie, you can come out now. They're gone."

Moving in behind Madison, Gage helped her with her coat. She startled when he leaned closer, sniffing her hair. "You smell like you showered in gingerbread," he said, his breath warming her ear.

"Bite me," she croaked.

His low laugh ruffled her hair. "I might just do that. I really, really like gingerbread."

At that moment, so did Madison.

*   *   *

Gage entered his dark and quiet house. Shrugging out of his jacket, he hooked it on the back of a chair while snagging a gingerbread cookie off a plate. He took an oversized bite, then remembered Lily's warning. Chewing carefully, he went in search of Madison.

Through the bank of windows in his living room, the full moon lit a path to the woman asleep on his leather couch. He set the half-eaten cookie on the fireplace mantel.

His daughters had been thrilled when Madison had offered to stay with them until he got back from work. Their reaction, he knew, wouldn't have been the same if one of the single women from town had volunteered.

And while he'd been more than happy to accept Madison's offer at the time, seeing her sleep-tousled hair shining like a beacon in the moonlight had him rethinking his decision.

Only one woman had ever slept at his place—his ex-wife, and that was for the sake of his daughters. Sheena's visits were infrequent and brief, and he'd never been able to say no to Annie when she begged for her mother to stay. Now the two of them seemed to take the arrangement for granted. Even if he wanted to, Gage doubted he could change it without having a battle on his hands.

He glanced at his watch. It was after midnight, and Madison looked to be in a deep sleep, her chest rising and falling beneath the green throw. He felt bad for having to wake her, but there was no way in hell he'd get any sleep with her under the same roof. He'd had a hard enough time keeping his hands off her earlier. If his daughters hadn't been in the next room when she said, "Bite me," he would have. And having her here when Lily woke up would be asking for trouble. His youngest had gotten it in her head that Madison was his girlfriend and if she wasn't, she should be. Gage, along with Madison and most especially Annie, had tried to shoot down her suggestion. That was one complication he didn't need.

Nudging the coffee table out of the way, he crouched beside her. "Madison." When she didn't respond, he put his hand on her shoulder and gave her a gentle shake.

"Umm," she murmured with a slight curve of her lips.

He fought the urge to trace her lush mouth with the tip of his finger and quietly said her name instead. She wriggled closer, nuzzling her face into his shirt. He swallowed a groan as the blood rushed from his head, his stomach muscles tightening in response to her warm breath heating his skin through the fabric.

"Madison." His voice came out a strangled rasp.

The nuzzling stopped. Slowly, she drew back to look up at him. "Oh, God," she groaned. "S-Sorry, I was having a...dream." She ducked her head and pushed herself upright. The light from the moon revealed the pink flush coloring her chest and cheeks.

He drew his hand from her shoulder while he retained a semblance of self-control and came to his feet. "Not a problem. Must've been a good dream. Too bad I had to wake you up," he teased, in hopes of covering his own reaction.

She grimaced, removing the throw from her shoulders to reveal the sweater he'd wanted to unwrap from the moment he'd removed her coat earlier. It had taken everything he had not to touch her then. And since he had a pretty good idea what lay beneath that sweater, he'd been grateful for the emergency call that came in forty minutes after her arrival.

He realized she was talking to him and drew his wandering eyes back to her face. "Sorry, what was that?"

She gave him a questioning look as she came to her feet. "I asked how your night went."

To prevent himself from doing something stupid like tugging her into his arms, he shoved his hands in his jeans pockets. "Quiet once we got the accident cleared out."

"I hope nobody was hurt." She leaned over to place the throw on the back of the couch, her sweater rising up to reveal her shapely behind. The black leggings she wore didn't leave much to the imagination, although his was now working overtime. She glanced at him over her shoulder.

He cleared his throat. "Uh, no, nobody injured. Can't

say the same for the vehicles, though." He did a mental eye roll, but figured it didn't matter what he said as long as he kept talking and stopped staring. "How were the girls? Annie give you any trouble?"

She smiled and shook her head, the movement drawing his attention to her hair. She looked like she'd spent the night making love instead of asleep on his couch. "No, not at all. Both she and Lily were great."

"Good, that's good to hear. Ah, you might want to—" he motioned to her head as they walked to the front hall "—put your hair in that bun thingy you do." He'd been wrong at Sophia's. Even alone with him, Madison needed to wear her hair confined in a bun.

She stared at him. "I don't know what it is with you and my hair, but your daughters and I had a makeover session tonight. They told me I should wear it down, not up."

"What do they know? They're twelve and eight," he muttered, then realized what she'd said. "Please tell me you didn't dye Annie's hair in this little makeover session of yours. She's been after me to let her color it purple."

"No, just a couple of green lowlights... very tasteful."

"You're joking, right?"

"I am." Her smile faded as her expression turned serious. "I'm sorry your wife isn't able to spend more time with Annie and Lily. I think Annie really misses having her around. Girls her age need their mothers..."

She stopped talking. He imagined his angry expression was the reason, and he was angry. He worked his ass off trying to be both mother and father to Annie and Lily and didn't know where Madison got off telling him he was doing a lousy job of it.

"A few hours in my daughters' company doesn't make

you an expert, Madison. You don't know what you're talking about."

Her eyes widened, and she caught her bottom lip between her teeth. "I'm sorry. It's none of my business."

"You're damn right it's not."

In an instant, her expression went from apologetic to ticked. She stalked to the front hall closet, opening the door to grab her coat and boots.

He shoved his hand through his hair. She might've pissed him off with her observation, but she'd done him a favor by staying with his girls. "Look, Madison," he began, reaching for her coat to help her put it on.

She jerked away from him. "I've got it."

His cell rang. He checked caller ID. Great. "Hang on a sec, Madison. I have to take this."

Ignoring him, she shoved her feet into her boots and opened the front door.

"Give me a minute, Sheena," he said to his ex-wife, and called out to Madison, who was storming to her vehicle, "Take it easy out there. The roads are icy." She slammed the truck's door on his warning.

"Aw, hell," he said when she squealed out of his driveway. As he watched her taillights fade in the distance, he brought the phone to his ear. "What's up, Sheena?"

Half an hour later, Gage finally got off the phone with his ex-wife. They'd spent the last five minutes talking about her plans for Christmas and their daughters, the first twenty-five about her career. While half-listening to Sheena's hysterical rant about her throat problem and its impact on her music career, he'd been playing over his conversation with Madison in his head.

He'd overreacted. Her comment had been directed at

Sheena, not him. He knew he was a little thin-skinned when it came to his parenting skills, and he knew why. At times, Gage questioned whether he was doing a good job raising his daughters on his own. Scrubbing his hand over his face, he called Madison.

"Hello," she said, her voice husky.

"Hey, sorry, did I wake you?"

"No."

"I just wanted to be sure you got to Nell's okay and to—"

"I did. Thanks." She hung up.

Gage stared at the phone. That went well.

Chapter Ten

Madison bit into a sugar cookie and savored a moment of peace and quiet. After the two hours she'd spent with Nell and her friends this morning, she figured she deserved a break.

"Madison," Nell hollered from the living room. "We're waiting on our tea and cookies."

Madison rolled her eyes, popped the rest of the cookie in her mouth, and for the third time that morning set the Santa teapot on the silver tray alongside a platter of sugar cookies.

Nell held up her teacup as soon as Madison entered the room. When four more sets of arthritic fingers raised their cups, she bit her tongue to hold back a curse.

"You're a dear," Mrs. Tate gushed.

With a strained smile, Madison poured tea into the older woman's cup. If not for Mrs. Tate, neither the police nor Rick Dane would've caught wind of the free-for-all at Sophia's, and

Madison's picture wouldn't once again be gracing the front page of the *Chronicle*. To hear Mrs. Tate tell it, she'd saved Madison from a whupping at Brandi and Hailey's hands.

Bless her heart.

Earlier that morning, Vivi had voiced her disappointment with Madison, while Skye thought the new photo was an improvement over the one in the *Times*. Since Madison had been on her hands and knees with her butt in the air in the *Chronicle*'s latest photo, she didn't take much comfort in Skye's observation. Madison figured she had grounds to sue—there was no way her butt was as big as the one on the *Chronicle*'s front page.

Once she'd filled everyone's cup, she set the tray on the coffee table, then slowly backed out of the room.

"Madison, get over here and sit down. We haven't gone over the schedule of events you'll be participating in yet." Nell patted the chair beside her, waving what appeared to be a very long list in Madison's direction.

"Yeah, you're gonna want to have a seat for this, that's for damn sure," Ted said under his breath as Madison walked by.

She caught the sympathetic tone in Ted's voice and nervously took her seat. If Ted felt sorry for her, she really didn't want to see that list. Reluctantly, she took the paper from Nell. Her mouth fell open. Nell wanted her to be an elf in the Santa Claus parade. Madison expelled a relieved breath when she noted the date of the event.

"You know, Nell, I would *love* to take part in the parade—" Ted and Fred's snorts cut her off. She gave them a look then continued. "—but I'm only here until this Friday, so I'm afraid I won't be able to be Santa's little helper." *Thank you, baby Jesus.* "And I—"

She was about to continue listing the events she couldn't take part in when Nell interrupted her. "I knew you wouldn't want to miss out on all the Christmas fun we have planned, so…" Madison narrowed her eyes on the older woman, whose knowing smirk gave her away. "I got in touch with your boss, Mr. Hartwell, this morning. He thought your staying in Christmas for another couple of weeks was an excellent idea."

Madison's heart did a nosedive. There was no way…"You talked to Joe?"

"No, your other boss. Harrison Hartwell. He—"

Madison forced a benign expression onto her face. "He's not my boss. And while I—"

"Well, that's just wonderful." Mrs Tate clapped her hands, as if Madison hadn't been about to say something.

"It is. It really is." Nell's neighbor Stella beamed. "That'll give you more time to form a positive opinion of our town, Madison."

Oh, she'd formed an opinion all right, and at that moment it was far from positive.

"Um-hmm, she sure will. And none of those silly little problems like that new road will matter anymore." Mrs. Tate smiled at Madison over the rim of her teacup.

Yeah, like a new road's a little problem, Madison thought with a mental eye roll.

"You're so right, ladies, and it gives us a chance to get to know Madison better." Nell patted Madison's jeans-clad leg a little harder than necessary. "I can't tell you how much I appreciate having her here with me. She's a god-send. And as you all know, I haven't been too happy about how Hartwell has treated our town, but I tell you, thanks to Madison, my opinion of them is improving by the day."

Madison gaped at the woman. It was as though she'd been listening in on her conversation with Joe that day at the station.

Stella nodded. "Mine too, Nell. I said that exact same thing to my bridge club last night. Hartwell is a company that cares, that's what I said."

"You're so right, Stella. And I'll be sure to let my quilting club girls know you've changed your opinion about Hartwell when we meet tonight, Nell." Mrs. Tate nodded like a bobblehead doll.

A smug smile on her face, Nell waggled her brows at Madison. Dammit! The woman should write a book on the art of manipulation. And with this show of support and a promise of more to come, Madison was well and truly manipulated. But staying in Christmas longer than the end of the week was out of the question, no matter what Harrison said. If she'd helped change Mrs. Tate and Stella's opinion of Hartwell to that degree in just three days, imagine what she could do when they spread the word, and she had four misstep-free days to work with.

"That does my heart good to hear, ladies." Madison patted Nell's knee as enthusiastically as she'd patted hers. "But, if you'll excuse me for a moment, I have a couple of calls to make."

"Don't forget your list. You'll probably want to put the dates in your calendar. There's quite a few of them." Nell grinned.

"Right." Madison faked a smile as she took the paper, fighting the urge to crumple the list and lob it at Nell's head.

As Madison speed-walked through the kitchen, she

glanced down at the purple sweater she wore. It would have to do. She didn't want Nell to overhear her conversation, and the only place she felt certain of privacy was outside. Spotting a pair of boots at the back door, she shoved her feet in them and snuck out. The crisp mountain air whistled through the trees and instantly cooled her boiling blood. Good thing, since she wanted to be calm and collected when she spoke to Joe.

With her phone at her ear, she ducked around the side of the house. "Hey, Joe, it's Madison," she said as soon as the line picked up.

"Madison, it's Harrison. How are you?" he asked in that smarmy voice of his. He made her skin crawl.

She'd deal with him later. "Put me on with Joe, please," she said curtly.

"I'm sorry, he isn't taking any calls. He's dealing with a family emergency at the moment."

"Has something happened to Martha?" She steeled herself for his response.

"It's a private matter, Madison. A family matter." One, he seemed to say, that had nothing to do with her. But before Harrison had come on the scene, it would have.

She struggled to keep the emotion from her voice. She wouldn't give him the satisfaction of knowing how much his jibe hurt. "When he has a moment, it's important I speak with him."

"It'll be some time before he's able to get back to you. If there's a problem, you'd better talk to me."

A gust of wind rattled the shutters on the window above her head, and she gritted her teeth to keep them from chattering. "Okay, let's cut to the chase. I know

you've led Nell McBride to believe I'm at their disposal
for however long my presence is required, but as per Joe's
directive, I'm leaving Christmas first thing Friday morning. So you better call Nell and clear up the misunderstanding ASAP."

"Sorry, no can do. Maybe if you hadn't hit a kid with
a snowball and ended up in a brawl with the women of
Christmas, my uncle and Hartwell's lawyers wouldn't feel
it necessary for you to remain beyond Friday, but you did."

Okay, admittedly, it looked kind of bad from their perspective, but she wasn't about to let Harrison know that.
And she had a feeling there was more to them keeping her
in Christmas. "What's going on? Why are you so determined to keep me here?"

In the background, she heard someone's urgent whisper and Harrison's muffled response before he came back
on the line. "Other than you creating a publicity nightmare for Hartwell, nothing's going on. It's my uncle and
the company lawyers who are insisting you remain in
Christmas, not me."

"Am I on speakerphone, Harrison?"

She heard a distinctive click. "Ah, no, you're not."

"Yes, I was, and you might as well put me back on so
Tom doesn't miss a word of our conversation," she said,
referring to the head of legal and Harrison's BFF.

"Paranoid much?" he muttered. Then the phone
clicked again.

She wouldn't waste her breath responding to his comment. "Just so the two of you are aware, I might've ended
up in the paper a couple of times, but I'm making headway
here. In fact, just this morning several people told me how
much Hartwell has risen in their estimation, and that's due

to my efforts, not yours." Not really. But she wasn't about to tell them it was due to Nell's efforts and not her own.

"I'm glad you're doing what you can to rectify the matter, since you're the one who created the mess in the first place. But until the company lawyers are confident a lawsuit won't be filed, you *will* remain in Christmas."

She opened her mouth to respond when someone pulled into Nell's driveway. She peeked around the corner of the house and groaned. Gage. She didn't want to deal with him now.

She'd made a fool of herself last night. Her cheeks warmed at the memory of waking up from the erotic dream he'd starred in to find herself nose deep in his shirt, her lips pressed to what felt like an impressive six-pack. And to make her night complete, he'd acted like a jerk when all she'd tried to do was talk to him about Annie. She shook off the thought that maybe his daughter wasn't the only one who missed Sheena McBride and returned her attention to Harrison.

"You know what, I'm pretty sure this isn't part of my job description and—"

His gusty sigh cut her off. "Look, Madison, my uncle's going through a difficult time. Aunt Martha's been hospitalized, and it's not looking good. We need to keep his life as stress-free as possible right now. You know how much Hartwell's reputation means to him, and for some reason, he believes you can change the town's opinion of us. We've managed to keep your latest debacle from him, so if you care at all about my uncle, you'll remain in Christmas for a couple of weeks and turn this thing around."

Maybe she'd been wrong about Harrison. He sounded as upset as she was. "Okay, I'll take care of it. Please let

Joe and Martha know I'm thinking about them." Her voice broke a little at the thought of how much Joe loved his wife. Madison didn't know how he'd go on without her. She cleared her throat. "If anything...Just let me know if..."

"Of course. I'm late for a meeting, so if there's nothing else, I'll let you go."

"The budget, have—"

"With everything going on, we've pushed the meeting back. I really do have to go, Madison."

She swallowed her objection to the meeting's delay. For Joe's sake, she had to suck it up and find a way to work with Harrison. "Sure, fine."

As she closed off, she heard the crunch of snow and huddled closer to the wall, struggling to contain her emotions. Dammit, she would not cry.

                    *   *   *

Gage walked to the side of Nell's house where, unless he was imagining it, he'd seen a flash of purple and a familiar head of blonde hair. Nope, not his imagination. Madison stood with her back to him, her arms wrapped around her coatless body, a pair of...men's boots on her feet. He frowned. "Madison, you okay?"

She put up a hand, warning him off. "I'm fine." Her voice was muffled.

"You don't look fine to me. Come on, it's freezing out here. Let's get you inside." He rested his hands on her shoulders and felt her bone-deep shiver.

She shook her head. "Can't. Not yet."

Shrugging out of his jacket, he draped it over her shoulders before turning her to face him. She kept her head bowed, her phone and a crumpled piece of paper clutched in her hand. Her nose was bright pink, and if he wasn't mistaken, she was trying not to cry.

He took her icy hand in his. "If you won't go in the house, we'll sit in the truck and get you warmed up."

Once he had her settled, he started the engine, jacking the heat to high. He rested his arm along the back of the seat. "Want to talk about it?"

"Not really." She closed her eyes, leaning against the headrest.

He gently brushed the strands of hair from her cheek, his fingers skimming over her soft skin. "Need me to beat someone up for you?"

She cracked one eye open, a slight smile wavering on her lips. "I can think of a couple people."

After last night, he figured he was one of them. "Don't worry, I've already beaten myself up." Taking her hand, he gave a slight tug to get her to look at him. She turned her head, opening her eyes.

"I'm sorry I overreacted last night. I guess the chip on my shoulder is bigger than I realized."

"I was only trying to help."

"I know." He studied the small hand in his, rubbing his thumb over her knuckles. "It's just that as the girls get older, I feel like I'm in over my head. I'm not always sure I'm handling things the way I should."

She gently squeezed his fingers. "You are. And for the record, it wasn't *your* parenting skills I was questioning."

He smiled. "Thanks, and thanks for what you did for Annie. She looks incredible."

She straightened, shifting to face him. "You didn't make a big deal about it, did you?"

"No, I played it cool. But it was tough not to react."

"Wow, I'm impressed." She smiled. "You did good, Sheriff."

"Yeah, well, Lily did the zip-it thing behind Annie's back." He drew two fingers across his lips. "You want to share your secret and tell me how you managed to convince Annie to get rid of the makeup and fix her hair?"

"She's wearing makeup, just not as much as she used to. I showed her how to apply it with a light touch instead of painting it on, and her hair just needed to be shaped. I used to cut my own when I was her age, so it was easy enough to fix. It's actually Lily who deserves all the credit. She's the one who suggested we do makeovers, and I swear she knew exactly what she was up to. She got that same look in her eyes that Nell does when she's up to something."

"Great, just what I wanted to hear. And speaking of my aunt, did she do something to upset you? You looked—"

"I wasn't upset."

He lightly tapped her nose. "Careful, it's going to grow."

She sighed and tugged her hand from his. Shoving her phone between her thighs, she took the crumpled paper and smoothed it on her knee before handing it to him. He scanned a list of duties with Madison's name written beside each one, struggling not to laugh when his gaze hit the middle of the page. "You're going to be an elf in the Santa Claus parade?"

"I'm glad you think it's funny." She leaned toward him, stabbing the page with her finger. "Check out the dates."

He didn't need to. The parade was the same time every year. He frowned. "But you'll be gone by then. How...Oh."

"Yeah, oh. Nell made a call to Hartwell this morning and got the go-ahead for me to stick around. Seems my picture in the paper wasn't exactly the press they'd been hoping for. They figure I've managed to damage Hartwell's reputation further, not repair it."

"That's not true. Plenty of people stopped me this morning to tell me what a good sport you were at the church bazaar, and not just the men who got a kiss." Although some of the old-timers declared they were now in love with her, several women from the ladies' auxiliary had stopped him when he grabbed a coffee at the bakery to tell him how Madison had pitched in with the setup and cleanup. "If you want me to, I'll give your boss a call."

"Thanks. I appreciate the offer, but with Harrison calling the shots, it won't make a difference."

"Why's that?" he asked, trying to ignore the part of him that was glad she'd be around for a while longer.

"Joe's wife is in the hospital. Harrison's been left in charge." She shrugged as though it didn't bother her, but it was obvious it did.

"You're worried about something. What is it?" A wedge of guilt lodged in his chest, and he was tempted to tell her about his conversation with Ethan. But he couldn't go back on his word.

"Joe. I would've liked to be there for him. But it'll be okay. He's got his family."

"You're close?"

She nodded, looking at the hand she rubbed along her thigh. "I've always thought of him like a father, but I'm beginning to realize it was probably one-sided. Harrison's his family, not me." Her gaze flitted to his, her cheeks pink. "Pretty lame, huh?"

"No, not at all." There was something about her that got to him. Beneath her tough façade, there was a soft and vulnerable woman. "Don't you have family of your own?"

"No, but my friends Vivi and Skye are like sisters. They're my family."

"When did you lose your parents?"

"My mother died when I was twelve, and my father died when I was eighteen." She shook her head. "Don't... don't feel sorry for me."

His sympathy must've shown on his face, and he did feel sorry for her. But there was something else, something about... "That's what you meant last night when you were talking about girls Annie's age needing a mother. You were—"

She leaned over, covering his mouth with her hand. "Don't try to analyze me."

"I'm not," he murmured into her sweet-smelling palm. He lifted his gaze to hers. "Have you been baking? You smell like sugar cookies."

"Ah, no." She tried to pull her hand back.

He firmed his grip, then placed a soft kiss on the center of her palm. Her eyes darkened, the hurt he'd seen there moments ago turning to heat. "Tastes like sugar cookies to me," he said gruffly. The look on her beautiful face urged him on, and his kisses grew hotter, hungrier.

A needy whimper escaped from her parted lips and shot straight to his groin, shutting down the voice of caution in his head—the warning that if he kissed those pouty lips nothing would ever be the same. He slid his free hand around her waist, tugging her closer, drawing a finger into his mouth.

"Oh, God," she moaned, her eyelids fluttering closed.

He kissed the tip of each finger then brought his mouth to her ear. "You sure you weren't baking today?"

She shook her head, curling a hand around his neck, drawing him closer. "No, I ate one, maybe two," she murmured, turning her face so that his mouth slid across her cheek to her lips.

"Geezus, you're sweet," he said just before he covered her mouth with his. And instead of worrying that he was kissing a woman, a woman he had no business kissing—in his aunt's driveway—all he could think was he finally had the mouth he'd fantasized about since the first day they'd met. Framing her face with his hands, he took advantage of her parted lips and delved inside her mouth. She melted against him, caressing his tongue with hers, tangling her fingers in his hair. He took the kiss deeper, losing himself to the wild mating of their mouths.

He heard a dull thump, wondered if it was his heart, wondered if he'd survive the fiery heat of desire and lust she'd ignited in him.

"What the hell are you two doing in there?" a muffled voice came through the driver-side window.

Madison jerked back, her eyes wide and glassy, her lips wet and kiss swollen.

Gage leaned his head against the seat, dragging in a ragged breath before he lowered the steam-fogged window. "Talking. We're just talking," he said to the older man staring in at them.

Ted raised a bushy, gray brow. "Is that what they're calling it these days?" He jerked his chin toward an embarrassed-looking Madison. "She stole Fred's boots. He won't press charges if she gives them back."

Gage glanced at her feet, then shook his head. "She'll be in in a minute." He went to raise the window, but Ted stopped him with a hand on the glass.

The older man looked at Madison. "You all right?"

She blinked, her gaze flitting from Gage to Ted. "Yeah, I'm good. Thanks for asking."

Ted grunted. "You better be getting yourself inside now. Nell's worried about you."

"Oh, I…sorry." She shrugged out of Gage's jacket. "Thanks for the, ah, thanks for listening." She didn't meet his eyes as she handed him his jacket.

"Anytime," he said, but she'd already closed the door. Ted followed her up Nell's driveway, shooting a hard stare at Gage over his shoulder as if to say, *What the hell were you thinking?* Gage wondered the same thing. He thanked God that it'd been Ted who found them and not Nell.

As Gage tugged on his jacket, the scent of Madison and sugar cookies enveloped him. He'd never be able to look at a sugar cookie again, not without thinking of her and how she'd felt in his arms, how her soft lips felt under his. There was no help for it. He'd have to avoid being alone with her, being in the same room with her—because next time he wouldn't be able to stop at just one kiss.

Chapter Eleven

Madison needed a caffeine infusion. She'd spent the last two hours in the church hall putting twenty kids through their paces, half of whom, like Annie, acted as if they'd been given a detention without access to their computers and video games instead of performing in the annual Christmas pageant.

But the kids weren't the problem. Toward the end of practice, with a little humor and cajoling, she got them on board. Her rendition of "The Little Drummer Boy" seemed to break the ice. She had no idea what they found so hilarious about her performance, but hey, whatever worked.

No, her problem was with Nell, and her failure to disclose the names of the two women who were helping Madison with the pageant—Hailey and Holly. Hailey acted like a four-star general putting her troops through their paces. While Holly seemed to think they were taking the show on the road—next stop Broadway—and spent at least an hour going over the motivations for each part, from baby Jesus to the cow.

Madison parked just down from the Sugar Plum Bakery on Main Street and trudged through the heavy, wet snow that was falling fast and furious from the low-gray sky. Ducking beneath the bakery's purple-and-white-striped awning, she hid behind the wreath to peek in the front window, checking out who manned the counter. If it was Jill, Madison would have to survive the confrontation with Nell without the benefit of caffeine and sugar.

After a somewhat tension-filled first meeting, thanks to Jill, Gage's deputy, who blamed her for dashing their hopes of increased business from the resort, Madison struck up a friendship with Grace.

Behind the counter, the willowy blonde waved her in. Madison sighed. The cloak-and-dagger routine was obviously not her forte. Since coming to town, Madison had discovered there was quite a bit she wasn't good at, and the confidence she'd spent years developing had plummeted. One more reason for her to quickly convince the citizens of Christmas that she was one of the good guys, and they'd survive without a Hartwell resort.

She opened the door to a warm gush of cupcake-scented air and holiday music. Oddly enough, the carols no longer set her teeth on edge like they used to. She supposed being surrounded by people who loved the holiday, like Nell and Lily, made it hard not to get caught up in the hoopla of the season. Like a bad cold, it was contagious.

Or maybe the new memories were easing the pain of the old ones. The memory of that long-ago Christmas Eve where she'd sat on the church steps waiting for her mother—while carols were being sung behind the closed doors—no longer evoked the same stomach-churning emotion it once did.

She stepped inside the shop, where groups of teens congregated around the tables, chattering four decibels above normal while inhaling cupcakes and coffee.

"You're safe." Grace grinned as she slid a tray of Santa cupcakes onto the glass shelf. "Jill's working at the station today."

"I wasn't—" Madison started to protest, but gave up the pretense at Grace's you-don't-fool-me look. She shrugged. "Jill doesn't like me very much."

Grace grimaced. "I didn't think you noticed."

"It's a little hard not to. I think she spat in my coffee yesterday."

"She did not." Grace laughed, shaking her head.

Madison smiled. It was good to see Grace laugh, to see the tension lines around her mouth and eyes erased, if only for a few minutes. Unwittingly, she'd added to Grace's stress by cancelling the negotiations with Christmas. And even though she knew she'd made the right decision, Madison couldn't help feeling a little guilty. She glanced at the teenagers taking up eight of the ten tables. "Looks like you're busy despite the snow."

"Weather doesn't bother them. They've been coming in every day after school since I opened. Good thing they do." She tried to cover the worry Madison heard in her voice with a smile. "Do you want your usual?"

"Grace, are you okay?" Stupid question, of course she wasn't. Her husband had been MIA for almost a year, his Black Hawk shot down over the mountains of Afghanistan, and she was running a business while caring for her young son—a business that appeared to depend on the teenage population of Christmas.

"Tired, that's all. I've been putting off doing the books and decided to tackle them last night. Jack used to..." She lowered her eyes, but not before Madison saw the shimmer of tears.

Worried the woman she'd come to admire was close to the breaking point, she intervened, "Why don't you let me do your books for you?"

"I can't afford to—"

Madison stopped her with a wave of her hand. "You'd be doing me a favor."

Grace gave her a disbelieving look. "You can't be serious."

Madison waggled her brows. "Oh, but I am. What can I say—I'm weird that way." It was true. She looked forward to doing the books. At least it was something she did well.

"Well, if you're positive you don't mind..." Grace said, as she dug beneath the cash register. She plunked a ledger, checkbook, and manila envelope stuffed full of receipts onto the counter. "Sorry, I know I should've converted to a computerized accounting system a long time ago, but I'm not much of a techie."

Madison was surprised, too, but covered her reaction. "No problem."

"Um, are you ordering?" a freckle-faced teenager asked from behind her.

"Go ahead." Madison moved aside so the girl and her giggly friend could place their orders. While they did, she perused the trays of baked goods in the glass case. One of the cakes on the bottom shelf caught her eye. She bent down to get a better look. Madison knew from firsthand experience that Grace's cupcakes and cookies were to die for, but this cake was a work of art. A small, pink Victorian house, complete with stained-glass windows and decorated for the holidays with realistic-looking colored lights, sat on a cake iced to look like snow.

When the two girls walked away with their Santa cupcakes and cinnamon-scented coffee, Madison tapped a finger on the glass. "Grace, this cake is incredible. It's not edible, is it?"

Grace leaned over the counter. "Of course you can eat it. It's my sugar plum cake. I love making them, but they're labor intensive, and I haven't had a lot of time lately." She smiled wistfully at the cake. "That one's a special order for Mrs. Rich. I tuck a note in a chocolate sugar plum with an appropriate wish for the occasion and hide it in the cake. Autumn makes the sugar plums for me. They're pretty popular for engagements, but I've had to cut back."

Madison looked from Grace to the cake, and instead of visions of sugar plums dancing in her head, she saw dollar signs. She dug her BlackBerry from her purse and handed it to Grace. "I want a list of all the ingredients as well as the amount of time it takes you to make your cake."

Grace wrinkled her nose. "I'm sorry, Maddie. I can't. It's a secret family recipe passed on from Jack's grandmother. I'm not allowed to—"

"No," Madison interrupted her. "I don't want the recipe. In fact, I want you to promise not to share it with anyone. If this cake tastes even half as good as it looks, I think it might be the answer to your cash flow problems."

"Really?" Grace said, looking like she'd had the rug pulled out from under her so many times she was afraid to hold out hope.

"Let me do a cost analysis and some market research first, but yes—" The ringing of the phone cut Madison off.

"Hold that thought." Grace held up a finger and answered the call. The excited flush that pinked her cheeks only seconds ago drained away as she listened to whoever was on the other end. "I'll be right there." She fumbled the receiver.

"What's wrong?" Madison rounded the counter and took the phone from Grace's hand, replacing it in the cradle.

"Jack...it's Jack Junior." She turned in a circle as if she didn't know what to do. "He fell out of his crib and hit his head."

"It's going to be all right." Madison put a hand on Grace's shoulder. "Who can I call?"

"I don't...If something happens to my baby, Maddie, I—"

"You listen to me, Grace Flaherty, Jack Junior will be fine. Kids have hard heads. They fall out of their cribs all the time. I used to babysit for a little boy, and I swear he fell out of his bed every night. I just heard the other day he's going to be a brain surgeon." It was an out-and-out lie, but Madison would say anything to wipe the fear from Grace's eyes.

Grace gave a jerky nod and swallowed hard. "You're right." She hurried through the doors to the kitchen, returning seconds later with her coat. She glanced from the clock to the teenagers as Madison helped her put it on. "I hate to ask, Maddie, but can you stay until Jill gets here?"

"Of course. Hey, guys, would one of you be able to drive Mrs. Flaherty home?" Madison handed Grace her purse and shushed her objection. "You're too upset to drive."

Two boys stood up. "Sure."

Madison took a twenty from her wallet and offered it to them.

With an offended look, they shook their heads. "No, thanks. Come on, Mrs. Flaherty, we'll get you home to little Jack."

"I hope Jack Junior's going to be okay. I babysit for Mrs. Flaherty when she gets stuck," the freckle-faced teenager from earlier said, her expression worried as she stood with Madison at the window watching the boys settle Grace in their car.

Madison gave her arm a reassuring pat. "I'm sure he'll be just fine." Nice kids, she thought. It was obvious they cared about Grace and Jack Junior. Madison supposed that was one benefit to living in a small town: everyone looked out for one another. At least in Christmas they did.

She walked to the back, replacing her coat with an apron, then pulled her hair into a ponytail. Madison wasn't worried about holding down the fort. She had plenty of experience. After her father had been fired for drinking on the job, Mavis, her mother's old boss at the local diner, had taken pity on Madison. Even though she was underage, Mavis had given her a job, paying her under the table. Madison had started out as a dishwasher, slowly working her way up to assistant manager. It'd been years since she'd thought about the cigar-smoking Mavis Wilson. She found herself smiling at the memory. Her old boss and Nell were a lot alike.

After filling several orders, Madison realized two things. One, Grace needed to increase her prices, and two, Madison didn't have a clue how to use the computerized cash register. If she had to guess, she'd bet it was the dangerously handsome man in the photo tacked to the wall, a yellow ribbon pinned to the frame, who'd ordered the high-tech model. Madison found the key in a drawer beneath the register and jotted down each item sold while handing back change.

Once the customers were taken care of, she turned her attention to Grace's books. Caught up in organizing the receipts, she didn't realize there was someone at the counter until she heard the impatient tapping of a foot. She glanced up with an apologetic smile. "Sorry. What can I get for you?"

An older woman with a cap of steel-wool hair looked down her narrow nose at Madison. Without returning her smile, she said, "I'm here to pick up my order." She pointed a finger weighed down by a huge diamond at the sugar plum cake. The ring probably cost as much as Grace made in a year, maybe two.

Finally, she thought, she'd be ringing in a decent sale. Withdrawing the cake from the shelf, Madison looked for the price.

She didn't find a sticker and set the cake on the counter. "I'm sorry. Grace had an emergency at home. I'm not sure how much to charge you. I'll just—"

"Charge me?" the woman said in a snippy tone of voice. "There's no charge. Grace never—"

Grace, Grace, Grace, what am I going to do with you?

The woman was too kind for her own good. But Madison wasn't, and she had no intention of letting the old bat take advantage of Grace. She cut her off. "I'm sure you misunderstood."

"I most certainly did not." She reached for the cake, but Madison was quicker. She picked it up and stepped back from the counter. In a performance that even Holly would be impressed with, Madison widened her eyes and gave her a dumb-blonde look. "Silly me, there's the sticker." She added a girlish giggle.

Madison had never been a giggly teenager, so she was impressed with how much she sounded like the girls Grace had served earlier. Actually, she'd never had a chance to be a teenager at all. "That'll be sixty-five dollars. Please." She gave the older woman a simpering smile—genius.

"What?!"

Heads swiveled in their direction.

"I know, can you believe it? In New York, this cake would cost, like wow, I don't know, at least triple that. I'll box it up for you." Madison grabbed the white card-board from the shelf, turned her back on the woman, and hummed along with the carol playing on the radio as she made up the box.

"This is an outrage. Grace never charges me. I'm not—"

Madison ignored her. "A real steal, I tell you, with the amount of time it takes Grace to make one of these cakes. Will that be cash or charge?" She turned with the boxed cake in hand. But instead of facing down the woman's outraged glare, she looked into the cool, winter-green gaze of Gage McBride.

And cool, she thought, described their interactions of late. He'd barely said more than five words to her when he picked up Annie and Lily at Nell's. It was as though he couldn't bear to be in the same room with her. Today he hadn't even bothered to pick up the girls from pageant practice. He'd sent his father, Paul McBride, instead.

Maybe Gage wished that mind-blowing kiss they'd shared had never happened. Madison wished she felt the same way, but she didn't. She'd been kissed before—she was a workaholic, not dead—but never had a kiss left her weak-kneed and wanting so much more.

The corner of his perfect lips twitched. Madison's eyes jerked from the mouth she'd been staring at to his amused gaze. Her cheeks heated at the realization she'd been salivating over him and he knew it.

"Sheriff, I'm so glad you're here," Mrs. Rich said. "This...this woman is holding my cake hostage. She's trying to make me pay for it."

Madison got rid of the simper and snapped, "Maybe they do things differently around here, but where I come from, when a person provides a service or product, you pay for it." She was partly furious at the woman for trying to rip off Grace and partly embarrassed because she'd acted like a love-struck teenager in front of Gage.

"Well, I never—"

"I'm sure Ms. Lane—" Gage went to intercede.

Madison cut him off. "You never what...pay?"

From behind the furious old bat, Gage drew a finger across the lips Madison had spent way too much time fantasizing about and stepped up to the counter. The smell of freshly laundered clothes wafted past her nose as he did. He reached for the box, his cold fingers brushing hers. A drop of water fell from the damp hair slicked back from his face, splashing onto the cardboard. She kept her gaze glued to the spot, afraid that if she looked into his eyes he'd see the spark of desire his touch ignited.

He ignored her muttered protest when he tugged the box from her hands, turning to give it to Mrs. Rich.

"Thank you, Sheriff." She pinned Madison with a just-you-wait look. "Grace will hear about this." Then, like the queen of all she sees, she swept from the bakery.

"I hope she chokes on the sugar plum," Madison muttered, as she bent down to retrieve four twenties from her purse. She stuffed them in the cash register drawer.

Gage rubbed his beard-shadowed jaw, his gaze flicking from the door to the teenagers crowded around the tables, then back to Madison. "That was one of Grace's sugar plum cakes?"

"Yes. You should've arrested that woman instead of handing it over." Dear Lord, why did he have to be so damn gorgeous? It was difficult to think with him standing so close, looking all manly and…wet. And judging by his father, Gage would be just as handsome when he was in his sixties.

"Mrs. Rich heads up one of the women's committees in town. Grace probably donated the cake for a Christmas raffle."

"She can't afford to donate a cake, especially one that takes her so much time to make, and she knows it. But she's a people pleaser, just like Joe, and can't say no," Madison grumbled.

"And you're not…a people pleaser?"

"I can't believe you even asked me that." She snorted a laugh. "No, more like a people pisser-offer, don't you think?"

His gaze roamed her face. "No, not always you're not."

Flustered by the warmth in his eyes and the way his gaze drifted to her mouth, she said, "I-I should call Grace. Jack Junior…"

"That's why I'm here. Grace wanted me to check on

you and to let you know that Jack, other than the egg sprouting from his forehead, is fine."

Madison blinked to get rid of the moisture welling in her eyes. It wasn't like her to be so emotional, but the thought of Grace and everything she was dealing with got to her. "Good, that's good to hear. Thanks for letting me know. Grace... Why are you looking at me like that?"

"You don't fool me." He smiled, leaning closer. "You, Madison Lane, are a marshmallow."

"I am not." She was tough. In her world, it didn't pay to be a pushover. She took pride in the fact she was known as a ballbuster and pit bull. She'd worked hard to cultivate the image. So to be compared to a marshmallow, well, that was just insulting. Jenny Mae Lane, Madison's mother, had been sweet and gullible, a real people pleaser. And look what that got her.

*   *   *

From her offended tone of voice, Gage figured it wasn't what she wanted to hear. Too bad, it was true. He had her number now. For all her uptight, don't-mess-with-me attitude, underneath there was a big-hearted woman who cared more than she let on. He might not always agree with how she showed it, like the way she stood up for Grace with Mrs. Rich just now or how she went about protecting Annie, but damned if it didn't turn him on.

If he had only himself to think about, Gage wouldn't have hesitated to act on his attraction. But he was responsible for two impressionable young girls. And as much as his youngest believed Madison was perfect girlfriend material, he knew better. As soon as she got the green light from her boss, she'd be out of there.

When her beautiful blue eyes met his, he thought how staying away from her was easier said than done. Especially when he remembered their kiss, and how that small taste of her, the feel of her in his arms, left him wanting a hell of a lot more.

Yeah, it was time to leave. But before he could make his escape, a meaty hand landed on his shoulder. "Hey, Sheriff."

Gage turned to the heavily bearded bear of a man standing behind him. "Harlan," he said, nodding at the plow parked in front of the bakery. "You boys are going to have a long night."

Harlan waggled a toothpick between his teeth. "Tell me 'bout it." He nudged the bill of his John Deere cap with his finger. "Hey there, sweetheart."

Gage grimaced, pretty sure the endearment wouldn't go over well. When Madison's left eye began to twitch, he prepared to intervene. Harlan handed her a long list, and she…smiled. A little forced, but it was a smile nonetheless. She scanned the list, glanced over her shoulder at the menu board, and said, "That'll be thirty-eight dollars and fifty-eight cents, Mr. Harlan."

Harlan scratched his head, looked at Gage, who looked at Madison. Her cheeks flushed. "I just wanted to make sure, you know, after Mrs. Rich…" She shrugged then drew a tray of cupcakes from the glass case.

Gage leaned across the counter. "I know you're trying to help Grace, but you can't just pull a number out of your head. You have to ring the order through."

She frowned. "What are you talking about? That's the total."

With an exasperated shake of his head, he rounded the counter. "I'll take care of it, Harlan."

Madison rolled her eyes, handed Gage the list, then went back to filling the order.

At the appreciative hum coming from Harlan's direction, Gage turned. The man rested his elbows on the counter, watching Madison, who had her back to them, softly worn denim cradling her shapely behind.

"How's the wife doing, Harlan?" Gage asked, slapping the piece of paper on the counter. "Read off the list to me."

Harlan chuckled. "No law against lookin', is there?"

Gage ignored him and punched in the order. He looked at the total, then checked the list against the items he'd punched in to be sure.

"Thirty-eight fifty-eight," he said, wondering why he was surprised she'd been right.

Harlan pulled his wallet from his back pocket. "It's like she has a freakin' computer in her head."

"I know." And for some reason Gage found that sexy, hot as hell. It turned him on as much as her centerfold body.

Madison nudged him out of the way and placed two trays of coffee on the counter. She glanced up. "What?"

"Nothing," he muttered, taking the two twenties from Harlan. He didn't want to know how she did it. If she started to explain, it would be complicated and long-winded, just like her presentation her first day in town. And then he'd have to kiss her just to shut her up, and he knew exactly what that would get him...trouble, and lots of it.

He ignored her soft, feminine scent, the brush of her arm against his, and handed Harlan his change. "I'll help you out with your order," he offered, picking up the trays of coffee.

"Appreciate it." Harlan winked at Madison, who piled three boxes into his arms. "Thanks, sweetheart."

Gage battled the wind to get the door open. They were in for a good one. "Madison." She glanced up, a guilty expression on her face, a chocolate cupcake in her hand. "Were you going to eat that?" he asked.

"No, I was just fixing the icing." She picked up a knife, pretending to smooth the top of the cupcake. She sent the candy-coated Santa flying. She scowled at Gage. "Are you just going to stand there grinning like a fool or do you have something to say?"

Yeah, he was a fool—a fool for her—and that's why he had to leave. "I have to head out. The storm's kicking up. If you're nervous to drive, ask Jill to take you home when she comes in to close."

Chapter Twelve

Madison leaned against Nell's front door as she tugged on the black cowboy boots with red stitching that Sophia had grudgingly allowed her to exchange for the leather thigh-high pair.

Nell, who sat at the kitchen table playing cards with Fred and Ted, shifted in her chair and gave Madison the once-over. "Make sure you have your house key now. I don't want you waking me up in the middle of the night to let you in."

She managed not to roll her eyes, barely. They'd been over Nell's going-out-on-the-town list three times already.

"You have pin money? Those bank machines break down all the time, you know."

"I do, yes," Madison said, resigned that once again they were going to go through the list in its entirety. But in an odd way, it felt kind of nice to have Nell looking out for her. Probably because when she was growing up no one ever had.

"What about your phone?"

Looking up from his cards, Ted shook his head. "You're turning into a regular mother hen, Nell. Leave the girl be." Ever since the day he'd interrupted Madison and Gage's steamy kiss, Ted had become her champion.

Nell grunted. "A girl can't be too careful these days. Not everyone who goes to the Penalty Box is from town, you know."

Probably a good thing they weren't, because while Nell, Ted, and Fred seemed to be in the I-like-Madison camp these days, the majority weren't.

Both Fred and Ted looked up at that. "Sawyer runs a tight ship, but if anyone gives you trouble, just give me and Fred a call. We'll come get you."

Aw, that's so sweet. The three of them were growing on her.

Nell glanced at Ted then returned her narrow-eyed inspection to Madison. "I'm going to give Gage a call. I'd feel better if—"

"No." Madison blurted out. "I'll be fine. Honestly."

After yesterday, the last person she wanted Nell to call was Gage. Once again, Madison had made a fool of herself with the man. She'd practically drooled over him. Good Lord, she'd never behaved this way with the strait-laced accountants and bankers she dated. None of them ever made her lose her head like Gage did. She knew why—she was too comfortable with him, too attracted to him, and it was making her stupid. For someone who took pride in her brainpower, that was just annoying, and she had to put a stop to it.

The bleat of a horn interrupted her thoughts. Opening the door, she smiled. "I'll see you guys later."

"Don't be late. Behave. Be careful." She wasn't sure which one said what, but she felt a warm rush of affection for the three of them. "I won't, and ditto on the I will."

Five minutes later, Sophia drove the candy-apple-red Expedition through the streets of Christmas like she was in the qualifying round of the Indy 500. Blissfully unaware she was giving her passengers heart failure, she continued with her story about the customer from hell. "Today she comes back to return the dress. She says she did not wear it, but it has stains, right here." Lifting her arm, she pointed out where the stains were with her finger and sailed through the stop sign.

"Hands...hands on the wheel," Madison yelped from the backseat.

"Slow down! You ran the stop sign."

"I did not," Sophia said to Autumn, then looked over her shoulder at Madison. "You are as uptight as she is."

Before Madison could protest, the tires hit a ridge of snow and swerved. "Eyes on the road!" Madison and Autumn yelled at the same time.

"Uptight old ladies," Sophia muttered, but thankfully returned her hands to the wheel, her eyes to the road.

She wasn't an uptight old lady, was she? "Just because I'm cautious doesn't mean I'm uptight."

Sophia snorted. "Hah, you are wound so tight, your head, I am surprised it does not pop off."

"Sophia!" Autumn turned. "Don't listen to her, Maddie."

"You are just like her, Autumn. The two of you have no idea how to have fun."

"I know how to have fun," Madison protested. She

always had a good time with Skye and Vivi when they went out. Not that they'd gone out very often in the past year—Madison's fault, not theirs.

"Prove it. Do not worry what anyone thinks of you tonight. Just enjoy yourself," Sophia challenged.

"You're on. I'll do it," Madison said with a decisive nod.

"Uh, I don't know if that's a good idea, Maddie. You need to win over the citizens of Christmas, not—"

Cutting Autumn off with a dramatic slash of her hand, Sophia held Madison's gaze in the rearview mirror. "Do not listen to her. You do what I say, and you will win... Oh-oh."

*   *   *

Autumn ushered Madison across the wood-planked floor of the rustic bar to a table beside the dance floor.

Madison collapsed in the chair. "I need a drink."

"Me too," Autumn agreed, taking the seat beside her. "I never should've let Sophia drive. We're going to need some help digging out of that snowbank."

Madison shrugged out of her coat. "No kidding." At the opposite side of the room, Sophia was wrapped around a blond Adonis who manned the bar. "Who's she flirting with?"

"Sawyer Anderson. He owns the Penalty Box. He retired as captain of the Colorado Flurries a couple of years ago." At Madison's blank look, Autumn shook her head. "They're a professional hockey team. You better not let Sawyer find out you didn't know who they were."

"I don't have time to watch much TV," she said, which sounded lame, even to her. She sighed. Maybe Sophia and Skye had a point; she didn't do much else other than work. Something that became more obvious the longer she stayed in Christmas.

Well, tonight she'd prove both women wrong and have fun.

"Ready to order?" Autumn asked.

"Sounds good to me." It did, until Madison saw who their server was. "Make that a double," she muttered when Brandi, wearing a tight black-and-white-striped jersey and short black skirt, approached their table.

Autumn grimaced. "Hey, Brandi. How's it going?"

The other woman's red-glossed lips curled as she gave Madison an up-and-down look. One that made Madison feel like a wad of gum stuck under her clunky heels. "Been better. What can I getcha?" she asked, slapping a bowl of pretzels in the middle of the table.

"Oh, I don't know. What do you recommend?" Autumn asked.

Brandi's gaze cut to Madison. "Sawyer created a drink in honor of Ms. Lane here. Why don't you go with that?"

"Aw, that's so nice. I'll have one of those. Maddie?" Autumn gave her a see-everyone-likes-you smile.

Madison knew better. "Sure," she said in a resigned voice.

"Two Grinches coming up," Brandi said with a smirk.

"Don't worry about it," Madison said when Autumn opened her mouth to call after the woman.

Sophia flounced to their table, waving an annoyed hand at the crowd belly-upped to the bar. "Look at them. They are watching the game, and Sawyer, he says no karaoke until it is over."

Madison brightened. "Karaoke? I love karaoke."

"Sawyer, another one for karaoke," Sophia yelled

across the room. When his only reaction was an amused shake of his head, Sophia solicited the customers at the neighboring tables to champion her cause.

With a finger, Sawyer nudged up the bill of his cap. "Behave, or you're going in the box."

"The box?" Madison asked.

"The penalty box." Sophia pointed to the left of the jukebox, where a white bench sat, enclosed by white-and-black-painted boards with an electronic clock affixed above. "He puts you in there if you cause trouble."

"It's like a time-out for adults. Sophia spends a lot of time in there." Autumn gave her friend a pointed look.

"For what?" Madison asked.

"Excessive flirtation." Autumn said drily.

Sophia made a face. "I do not flirt. I am just friendly. You should..." She caught sight of the two women entering the bar—Grace and Jill—and waved them over. But they were waylaid by Sawyer, who came out from behind the bar to greet them.

Both women looked tired when they eventually wove their way to the table and took a seat. After her son's fall yesterday, Madison imagined it had taken some convincing on Sophia's part to get Grace to join them. And knowing how Jill felt about Madison, Sophia must've had to do some arm twisting to get her to come along. Jill had grudgingly thanked Madison when she arrived to lock up the bakery yesterday, then reverted to her taciturn self. Madison had braved the storm and driven herself to Nell's.

Brandi delivered Madison and Autumn's drinks to the table—two martini glasses filled to the brim with a foamy lime-green concoction topped with a green cherry. Brandi patted Grace's shoulder. "Nice to see you out. How are you doin'?"

So, not always a bitch.

Grace smiled. "Good, I'm good, Brandi. You?"

"Give me a week or two, and I'll be great. When is it exactly that you're leaving, Ms. Lane?"

Nope, she's a bitch. "Oh, didn't you hear, Brandi? The citizens of Christmas are so friendly I've decided to stick around. I'm looking at the house that's up for sale just down from yours." Madison smiled sweetly.

The women at the table, along with Brandi, gaped at her. *Geez, don't they get sarcasm?* "Kidding," she said.

Brandi rolled her eyes then turned to the other women. "What can I get you ladies?"

"I'll take one of those." Sophia pointed at Madison's drink. Jill and Grace ordered the same.

"Three Grinches coming up."

Sophia's narrowed gaze followed Brandi across the dance floor.

"Did she say what I think she did?" Grace asked.

"Yep." Madison raised her glass. "Named after yours truly." She took a sip. A little sour, but not bad. She figured after a couple more their jibe wouldn't sting quite so much.

Jill bit her lip as though trying not to laugh.

Sophia sighed. "Mine was the Gold Digger." She shared a commiserating smile with Madison, bumped her shoulder against hers then grinned. "We'll order mine after we drink yours."

"Sounds good to me." Madison laughed. "Let's get this party started, ladies."

"Oh, no," Autumn groaned. "Don't encourage her, Maddie."

"Don't be a spoilsport, Autumn. If Sophia and Maddie want to cut loose a bit, they should. God knows someone deserves to have a little fun," Grace said, then glanced around the table. "Sorry, I..."

Jill put an arm around her sister-in-law's shoulders. "You have nothing to apologize for. If anyone deserves to sound bitter, it's you."

Grace groaned. "I did sound bitter, didn't I? I don't—"

Jill interrupted her sister-in-law, shooting Madison a censorious look. "The bank called to set up a meeting for Monday."

Grace squared her shoulders. "It'll be okay."

It wouldn't be. While going over the books last night, Madison had been surprised the bank hadn't called sooner. "Don't worry about it tonight, Grace. I'll go with you to the meeting on Monday."

"Really? So the numbers aren't as bad as I thought?" Grace asked, exchanging a hopeful glance with her sister-in-law.

No, they were bad, probably worse than Grace even realized. She hadn't seen the profit-and-loss projection for the next year like Madison had. She chose her next words carefully. "Look, I deal with stuff like this all the time. Let me worry about the bank and enjoy yourself tonight. We'll get together on Sunday and go over the idea I mentioned to you yesterday."

If the bank wouldn't get on board for the expansion loan based on Madison's prospectus, she'd already decided to invest. And not because she felt guilty. Madison never allowed her personal feelings to come into play where money was involved. Her analysis of the market validated her belief that Grace's sugar plum cakes would be a hit.

For the first time since she'd met her, Jill gave Madison a genuine smile.

"Thank you, Maddie. You don't know how much…" Grace's eyes filled, and she shrugged helplessly. "Sorry," she said once she got her emotions under control. "Sometimes it's just so hard."

They all reached for Grace's hand at the same time. Sophia cleared her throat, slapping her palms on the table. "Time for karaoke. Come on, ladies." Pumping her arms, she encouraged them to join her in a we-want-karaoke chant.

Behind the bar, Sawyer shook his head and laughed. The dark-haired man seated in front of him swiveled on the high-backed stool to face them, his lips curved in a smug smile. Madison's stomach did a little dip at the sight of Rick Dane and his trusty camera. She shrugged it off. After all, it wasn't like she planned on doing anything that would land her on the front page of the *Chronicle*.

*   *   *

The first person Gage saw upon entering the crowded bar was Madison, sitting in the penalty box with Sophia. The minutes ticking down on the clock over their heads indicated they'd been given a major. *What the hell did she do now?* was the first thought that popped into his head. Followed closely by *Geezus, she looks hot in that dress.* On any other woman, the simple red-knit number wouldn't be what you called provocative, but on Madison with her bombshell curves, she was a wet dream come to life, at least his. Her hair fell to her shoulders in that sexy, mussed-up way that drove him nuts. She laughed, her beautiful face glowing, and a warm tingly sensation raced through him. He forced himself to walk in the opposite direction.

He should've refused to meet Ethan here. But his father had gotten it into his head that Gage didn't get out enough. Paul McBride ordered him to go and have some fun at the Penalty Box, and he took Annie and Lily for the night. Gage knew it wasn't a coincidence that his father had just hung up from Nell when he'd made the suggestion. After meeting Madison while picking up the girls from choir practice yesterday, his father had obviously decided to try his hand at matchmaking. He was as bad as Nell.

Gage glanced at the clock. Just enough time to hear what Ethan had to say and get out of there. Heading for the table at the far corner of the bar, Gage said hello to several people while pretending not to see the others who flagged him down. If he acknowledged them all, he'd never get out of there.

"What did she do now?" he asked, as he pulled out a chair.

Ethan looked up from his BlackBerry. "Hello to you, too."

Gage flipped him off.

With a knowing grin, Ethan finally relented. "She and Sophia were singing karaoke."

"And?"

"She can't sing, and she doesn't like to share."

Gage relaxed. That didn't sound so bad. His gaze strayed once more to Madison, who was gesturing with her hands as she spoke—she'd obviously been spending way too much time with Sophia. When Madison's dress slipped off her shoulder, revealing creamy-white skin and a red bra strap, Gage swallowed a groan. He dragged his attention back to Ethan. "Any reason in particular we had to meet here?"

"My mother. She wouldn't let up until I promised to come. I don't know what's gotten into her. Ever since she's come home, all I hear is how it's about time I found myself a nice girl to settle down with."

"She have anyone in particular in mind?" Gage's hand balled into a fist on his thigh.

He knew who was stirring up the matchmaking pot, but the thought that his best friend would make a move on Madison bugged the hell out of him.

"Madison." Ethan's smile faded. "Hey, don't look at me like that. It's not like I planned on making a move on her, but I thought you might be interested in knowing Nell's up to her old tricks."

"I'd already figured it out. She's got Dad playing matchmaker, too. You'd think getting our parents together would be enough to keep her occupied."

"If she's been talking to my mother, which we know she has, she's probably given up on them. Liz is furious with Paul."

Gage frowned. "Why, what's up?"

"You know how they came home early because of an outbreak of flu on board ship?"

Gage nodded.

"Well, from what my mother tells me, it was not the epidemic Paul made it out to be. He strong-armed her into coming home. Went on about her weak heart, asked her how her children would feel if something happened to her while she was away."

"Since when does Liz have a weak heart? I didn't think her mitral valve prolapse was that serious."

"It's not. And once she got home, my mother found out there was only one case of flu and the cruise continued."

Gage imagined Karen must be as furious as Liz. "He's paranoid. If anyone he cares about so much as gets a scratch, he goes to the worst-case scenario." Gage grinned. "You thinking what I'm thinking?"

"Yep, there's hope for them yet, as long as we can get my mom to speak to him after this. Right now, the odds are against it."

The timer on the penalty box buzzed. Time to leave. To be on the safe side, Gage was taking Ethan with him. "Let's go to my place for a beer and watch the game. Dad took the girls for the night." He saw Madison clamber out of the box, her dress riding high on her well-toned thighs, and he lurched to his feet.

Ethan frowned, then followed the direction of his gaze and grinned. "You've got it bad."

Gage ignored him, tracking Madison's movement across the dance floor. She did a sexy little bump and grind with Sophia then took her seat at the table where Grace, Jill, and Autumn sat. His best friend was right. He had it bad.

Ethan gave his head a slight shake. "That...was hot."

It was, and Gage couldn't take his eyes off her or get his feet to move. Brandi walked over, handing him a beer he hadn't ordered. "You better keep an eye on your girlfriend. They've moved on to Candy Cane shooters." She nodded at the five girly drinks—each a frothy white liquid with a line of red swirled through the center—on her tray. "Rick has his camera at the ready."

That got his feet moving—in the wrong damn direction. Brandi's reference to Madison as his girlfriend should've sent him for the door, but all he could think of was how upset she'd been when Hartwell forced her to remain in Christmas after her last stint on the front page of the *Chronicle*. He wove his way through the tables to stand behind her chair.

"Hey, Gage." The four other women waved their fingers at him and grinned.

Geezus, they're looped.

Madison tipped her head back, smiling up at him. "Sheriff."

The sexy curve of her full lips and the slumberous look in her eyes sent a fierce jolt of desire through him. It took a minute to untie his tongue. "Ladies." He looked down at Madison. "It's time for you to go."

Her head snapped up. "Whoa—" she pressed two fingers to her temple "—a little dizzy there." She turned to face him. "Why? Is something wrong with Nell?"

He considered lying to her, but saw the worried look in her eyes and couldn't do it. "No, I just—"

"Oh, good," she said. He lost her attention as soon as Brandi set the shooters on the table. "I've got it." Madison waved off Sophia, who was digging around in a purse the size of a suitcase. "Thanks." She gave Brandi a wide smile, thrusting a wad of bills in her hand.

"She's a good tipper. I'll give her that." Fighting back a grin, Brandi walked away.

"Bottoms up, ladies," Madison said. The five of them tossed back their drinks, polishing them off in a single gulp. Eyes watering, they gasped for breath between manic giggles.

Ethan came up beside him. The women smiled at him, wearing matching milk mustaches. "They're blitzed," he said under his breath, as he returned their finger waves.

"Ya think?"

Out of the corner of his eye, Gage spotted Rick, camera in hand, leaning on the jukebox. "Okay, ladies, it's time to call it a—" Before Gage could finish, "Girls Just Want to Have Fun" blasted out of the speakers. The five women squealed, jumping from their chairs to head for the dance floor. Sophia dragged Ethan along with her.

Gage took hold of Madison's hand. "Oh, no, you don't. I'm taking you home."

She frowned. "I can't leave now. I'm having fun. Sophia said I was uptight and…" She shook her hand free, placing it on her hip. "You said the same thing about me when we first met."

What he'd said was she looked like she had a stick up her ass—not actually her, but the picture of her in the *Times*. "No, I didn't. Come on, let's—"

She tilted her head. "You know what, Sheriff? I think you're the one who's uptight." She grabbed his hand. "But don't worry, I'll loosen you up. You're in good hands."

That was what worried him. It'd taken everything he had to control his body's reaction while watching her on the dance floor. So getting up close and personal with an attentive audience, one of whom had a camera, was the last place he wanted to be. "Madison, trust me, this isn't a good idea. Let me take you home."

The music changed. "Woo-hoo, conga!" She grabbed his hands, placed them on her hips and started wiggling her way to the dance floor while clapping her hands over her head.

Other than tossing her over his shoulder, it looked like he was stuck. But if he kept his eyes glued to Ethan's head—four couples down—instead of Madison's butt, and ignored the feel of her hips swaying beneath his hands, he'd be good. He was just starting to relax when the line circled the dance floor for the second time and they passed the jukebox. Rick smirked, then pressed a button.

Gage groaned as a slow, sexy beat pulsed through the speakers. They had to leave...now. "Madison."

She turned. The adorable loopy smile on her face faltered when he took a step back. "I can't..." he began, but then two men came into his line of sight, waiting expectantly for him to move on so they could move in on Madison. To his left, Rick lifted his camera.

To hell with it. Gage tugged her into his arms.

*   *   *

"Stay put," Gage warned Sophia, buckling her into the backseat of Ethan's Escalade. It was hard enough to understand Sophia sober, let alone when she was half-cut, but he took a shot. "I don't care if you're going to hurl. You're not sitting up front. Use your purse."

"Easy for you to say," Ethan grumbled, shutting the door on a blast of Spanish. "Why the hell did you make them eat before we left?"

"To sober them up." It'd seemed like a good idea at the time.

Ethan snorted. "Right." He looked at the women laughing hysterically in his Escalade and sighed. "Explain to me again why I have to drive all four of them home, and you only have to take Madison," he said, as he walked around to the driver's side.

Gage looked over to where the woman in question stood under the soft glow of the streetlamp, catching snowflakes on the tip of her tongue, and wondered the same damn thing. He was an idiot. "They live closer to you than me."

"Like I'm buying that." Ethan shook his head, opening the driver's-side door to Sophia's unintelligible rant. He lifted his eyes to Gage. "You owe me."

"I'll shovel out Jill's place tomorrow." As friends of Jack, he and Ethan shared the responsibility of looking out for his family.

"Almost makes it worth driving Sophia home. Almost," Ethan repeated when she yelled at him. " 'Night, Madison. Gage."

" 'Night. Drive safe." Madison bent over to wave good-bye to her friends as Ethan pulled away from the curb.

"You have a good time tonight?" Gage asked, as they headed for his truck.

"Great time. You?"

"Yeah, you ladies were very entertaining." He frowned, halting her forward motion with a hand to her arm. "You're as bad as Annie. You're going to catch a cold." Tugging her coat closed, he began to do up the buttons while trying to ignore the voluptuous curves his fingers brushed against as he did.

"I'm hot."

"Yeah, you are," he said without thinking.

She put a hand on his chest. "So are you."

He shook his head. "I promised myself I was going to stay away from you."

She searched his face. "Why?"

Seeing the hurt look in her eyes, he walked her backward to the alley between the bar and hardware store. "Because you make me want to do this." He lowered his head and kissed her like he'd wanted to all night. She tasted like candy canes, her lips soft and pliant, opening for him on a needy exhalation.

"But I like when you kiss me," she murmured against his mouth, wrapping her arms around his waist.

"Yeah, so do I." She felt good snuggled up against him, like somehow they fit. A dangerous thought, a thought that should have him backing away.

It did.

He broke the kiss, then lowered his forehead to hers, listening to the soft rasp of their breath, a car in the distance, the dull throb of music and voices from the bar. The door to the Penalty Box opened, a shaft of light illuminating the sidewalk. He turned, blocking her from sight. A man and woman laughed as they walked by. He released the breath he'd been holding. It wasn't Rick.

"It's getting late. I'd better get you home before Nell starts to worry." He placed a hand at her back.

She slanted him a look as they crossed the road. "I'm a big girl, Sheriff. If you're not interested, just say so."

That was one of the many things he liked about her, Madison didn't pull any punches. She was open and honest. And maybe it was time he was honest with her.

He opened the passenger-side door and helped her inside. She tugged on the seat belt. He cupped her chin, raising her gaze to his, then kissed her hard and fast. "I'm interested."

"But?"

He tucked a silky strand of hair behind her ear. "I don't get involved with women from town. With my job, I'm under the microscope enough as it is, and I've got Annie and Lily to think about. I don't want them hurt or confused or to have to listen to a lot of crap about their dad.

I dealt with enough of that when Sheena left us. If it was just me, trust me, you wouldn't be going home to Nell's tonight."

"You're a good dad, Sheriff." She gave him a half smile. "I guess we'll have to settle for just being friends then."

Friends with Madison? A woman he couldn't be within a hundred feet of without wanting to kiss her, to take her to his bed? Maybe once she was back in New York they could be friends.

Chapter Thirteen

Madison plunked herself down on a chair at the back of the empty church hall, releasing a weary sigh. Looping her foot around the leg of the chair in front of her, she turned it around to put up her feet. She smiled, feeling pretty pleased with herself.

Even though pageant practice wasn't for another two hours, she'd used it as an excuse to escape the citizens of Christmas who'd descended on the warehouse armed with drills, hammers, paintbrushes, and chainsaws to work on the floats for the Santa Claus parade. They were like an army of elves—elves with ADHD—and a head elf, Nell, with attitude. Madison figured they were as glad to see her go as she was to leave.

She supposed she couldn't blame them. But it wasn't as if she'd blown the fuse box on purpose or that she'd intentionally painted Santa's house the wrong color. Maybe she shouldn't have articulated her negative feelings about

Christmas so loudly. At the time, it'd seemed like a better option than the curse words that popped into her head after she'd hammered her finger instead of the nail.

So much for peace and quiet, she thought when her cell phone went off. She dug around in her purse, wincing when her wounded digit came into contact with her phone. "Hey, Skye," she said around her finger.

"Maddie? There's something wrong with the connection."

"Sorry." Madison took her finger out of her mouth and blew on the discolored nail. "What's up?"

"Have you talked to Vivi lately?"

"Uh, yeah, why?" She'd drunk-dialed Vivi from the Penalty Box last night, passing her around the table to introduce her to her new friends.

"There's something going on with her. It sounds like the guy she's been seeing pulled a Danny," Skye said, referring to Vivi's college boyfriend who'd ended their year-long relationship without an explanation. "She's acting like it's no big deal, like it was just an extended one-night stand, but I know it meant more to her than that. Vivi doesn't do one-night stands."

It'd been pretty obvious to Madison during their Skype conversation that Vivi had fallen head over heels for Hot Bod, so she didn't buy that she wasn't upset, either. Besides that, none of them did one-night stands. If the guy wasn't relationship worthy, they walked away. Only now it looked like this time the guy had done the walking.

Sort of like Gage. He was relationship worthy. But he'd made it clear last night that he wasn't interested in one, at least not with her.

She'd had an odd feeling of déjà vu when he kissed her in the alley, like somehow they were meant to be. When he held her in his arms, they seemed like a perfect fit, which made it hard to let go of the idea they might have a future together. She pushed away the thought she might've found the one, only to have to let him go.

"Maddie?"

"Sorry. You're right. I'll give Vivi a call tonight, see if I can get her to open up."

"You know how hardheaded she is. It'd be easier to get her to open up face-to-face. Are you going home soon?"

"Not for at least another week. Nell has this long list of events I have to take part in, and I have a meeting with the bank manager on Monday, and then there's the pageant I'm working on. I don't want to disappoint them." She startled, thinking about what she'd just said and how she hadn't mentioned Hartwell, not once. When, she wondered, did the citizens of Christmas become more important to her than the job she was sent here to do? "What about you?" she asked before Skye commented on her telling response.

"No, I have a meeting—"

Behind Madison, a throat cleared. She swiveled in the chair. Annie and Lily stood beside their grandfather. "Hey, Skye," she cut off her best friend. "I've gotta go. I'll call you once I talk to Vivi."

Disconnecting from Skye, Madison stood up. "You guys are early." Not that she minded. She enjoyed spending time with Gage's daughters.

"Oh." Paul McBride glanced around the empty hall. "Nell called to say you changed the practice time."

Madison sighed inwardly. She should've known she

couldn't put anything past Nell. At the sound of stampeding feet coming from the other side of the door, it appeared the Christmas hotline was alive and well. The church hall began to fill. Madison made a show of looking at her watch, then tapped the face. "Would you look at that, my watch stopped." It wasn't as if she could tell them Nell had figured out she lied about having to get to the church hall for practice... fibbed. *Lying* seemed a little harsh.

"Maddie, what happened to your finger?" Lily asked, scrunching her turned-up nose.

"It had a run-in with a hammer."

Dr. McBride and Annie leaned in for a closer look. Gage's father took Madison's hand in his, gently bending her wounded digit. "It's not broken, but you'll probably lose your nail." He looked up with a smile. "You'll have to get Gage to teach you how to use a hammer. He's very good with his hands."

He wasn't insinuating what she thought he was, was he? She narrowed her eyes, catching the twinkle in his. Oh God, yes, he was. Faintly horrified, she mumbled, "Good to know."

Time to make a break for it, she decided, then noticed Annie's under-the-lashes glance at the four girls forming a tight-knit circle on the far side of the room. They were a clique Madison had pegged as the in crowd the first day of practice. And it was clear Annie didn't belong. In Madison's opinion, that wasn't a bad thing. But she knew what it was like being on the outside looking in, and her heart ached for Annie.

Another little girl took a step in the direction of the four girls. They gave her an up-and-down look then turned their backs. Like Annie, she didn't make the grade. Madison wanted to shake them, but had a better idea. "Sara." Madison waved her over. "You know Annie, don't you?"

Head bowed, Annie shifted uncomfortably. Madison moved in beside her and gave her a gentle nudge.

"Hi," Annie mumbled. Sara, a shy smile on her sweetly rounded face, returned the greeting.

Madison handed each of them a clipboard and pen. "I need you and Annie to help me out." The It Girls looked on with interest, sidling closer. "Find out what part everyone is interested in trying out for and write them down for me. We need two copies. Don't worry if you have more than one name per part. We'll figure it out later."

"We can help too, Ms. Lane." The leader of the pack, tall with perfect teeth and shiny blonde hair, offered.

Madison smiled. "Thanks, sweetie, but we're good. If there's a part you're interested in, just let Annie and Sara know." The girls crowded around them.

Lily crooked her finger. Madison bent down. "Make Annie be Mary. She has the bestest voice," Lily whispered in her ear.

Since Annie had stood in the back row during practice, Madison didn't know if she could sing or not. "I'll see what I can do."

"Okay. Can I be a lamb?"

Madison straightened, then ruffled Lily's hair. "You'd make a great lamb. Tell Annie and Sara to put your name down."

"If I get the part, you'll have to make my costume. Daddy doesn't know how to sew," Lily said, as she skipped off.

Good Lord, neither did she. Madison called after her,

"Lily, maybe you should be a shepherd instead. They're really cool." And all she'd need was a sheet.

Lily shook her head and gave an excited wiggle, rubbing her hands up and down her arms. "I want to be a lamb with a soft, furry costume."

Madison groaned. Gage's father laughed and patted her arm. "Nell will give you a hand." His gaze followed his granddaughters, then returned to Madison. "Annie and Lily are crazy about you. You're all they ever talk about these days. I can see why."

"The feeling's mutual. They're great kids."

"Yes, they are. And my son's a wonderful father. But it's only since you've been around that Annie's come out of her shell. I think she needed a woman's influence."

"Gage is a great dad," Madison said, ignoring the last part. She had Paul McBride's number now, and there was no way he was drawing her down that road. It had a lot of hairpin curves, and she wasn't a very good driver.

"He'd make a great husband, too." He gave her a pointed look, one she couldn't ignore.

"Doctor McBride, you are as bad as your aunt."

He laughed, then glanced at the woman who entered the hall. His mouth pulled in a wary grimace when she shot him a disdainful look. "Never met a woman who could hold a grudge as long as Liz O'Connor," he grumbled.

Madison had heard all about the stunt Dr. McBride had pulled and didn't exactly blame Ethan's mother for being upset with him.

Madison had met Liz O'Connor at the warehouse this morning. And like Paul McBride, she looked nowhere near her age. Her toffee-colored hair was cut in a youthful style that fell to her shoulders, framing her striking, oval face.

Coming to stand by Madison, Liz ignored Dr. McBride and handed Madison the garment bag. "You forgot your costume."

"Thanks." Madison forced a smile. She'd been hoping no one would notice she'd left it behind.

"Hello, Liz. You're looking well."

She lifted her chin. "That would be because I am well, Paul. Healthy as a horse, despite you trying to make me feel otherwise."

He blew out a frustrated breath. "I was looking out for you, that's all. And whether you want to admit it or not, you have MVP and that puts you at—"

She raised a silencing hand. "No, I don't want to hear it. I'm an adult and quite capable of looking out for myself."

"Yeah, well, I made a promise to my best friend to take care of you, and I plan to keep it whether you want me to or not."

"Is that right. Well, I made a promise to my best friend to take care of you and the boys, and I don't see you listening to me."

Madison broke their silent standoff. "Thanks for the costume. I should go—"

Liz drew her gaze from Gage's dad. "I'm pretty sure it'll need to be adjusted. You might want to try it on a few days before the parade so I have time to make the alterations." She tapped her chin. "You know what, I have a better idea. Ethan's coming for dinner Wednesday night. Why don't you join us, and I can take care of the alterations then?" She flashed a smug smile at Dr. McBride, who narrowed his eyes at her.

From Gage's father's earlier comments and the ones Liz had made at the warehouse, Madison had a good idea what the two of them were up to. And the last thing she wanted to do was encourage them. But the thought that she could talk Liz into helping with Lily's costume had her weighing out the pros and cons. The pros won. "Sure, sounds great. Now, if you'll excuse me, I have to round up the kids for practice."

She managed two steps before Paul stopped her in her tracks. "Madison, I'm having my annual skating party next Sunday. We'd love for you to join us. Gage and the girls will be there, of course."

"I, uh, don't know how to skate. Maybe—"

He waved off her excuse. "Don't worry about it. Gage is a great skater. He'll teach you."

Of course he was. But Madison didn't have an athletic bone in her body. From the determined look on his face, Dr. McBride was not going to give up easily, so she did. "Sounds like fun, look forward to it."

She went to walk away. Ethan's mother opened her mouth. No doubt to issue another invitation.

"Madison. Madison Lane!" She never thought she'd be glad to hear that voice calling her name, but she was. She met Hailey halfway, looping her arm through hers.

Hailey jerked back in surprise. "What's wrong with you? And why didn't you tell Holly and me you were starting practice early?"

"Long story." Madison glanced back to see Liz and Paul in a heated exchange. She decided then and there to join forces with Nell. She needed to get Paul and Liz focused on each other, instead of on Madison and their sons. And that was when she knew the citizens of

Christmas had gotten to her. They'd sucked her into their madness.

* * *

Gage headed for the church hall to catch the tail end of the practice. When his father volunteered to drop off and pick up the girls today, Gage had gone to the station to catch up on some paperwork. But his father called him ten minutes ago to beg off on pickup duty due to a sudden onset of the flu. If his father had anything, it was a case of matchmakingitis, and it appeared to be catching.

"What are you doing here?" he asked Ethan, who stood outside the closed doors to the church hall. Ethan held up a green garment bag.

"My mother gave Madison the wrong elf costume. I'm here to do an exchange." With a pained expression on his face, Ethan angled his chin at the closed doors. "What are they doing in there? It sounds like they're strangling a cat."

Gage winced when he recognized the voice. Madison had sung along with the music last night, only she'd been quieter, and he'd been distracted by the feel of her curvy body. He must've been in a lust-induced coma not to realize just how god-awful she actually sounded.

"It's Madison. Why don't you leave the costume with me? I'll see that she gets it." He went to take the bag from Ethan, but his best friend tightened his grip.

"It's okay. I've got it."

Gage let go of the bag, about to ask Ethan what the hell he was up to when Hailey burst through the doors. Madison warbled a high note. Hailey cringed. Shutting the doors, she leaned against them. "Don't say a word. I need total silence." She closed her eyes.

After a couple seconds of deep breathing, Hailey turned to Gage. "Arrest her."

He didn't need to ask who she referred to. "For what?"

"Are you deaf? For disturbing the peace, that's what. I think she's tone-deaf. It's the only explanation. She actually thinks she has a great voice." She sighed. "It's sort of sad. I kinda feel sorry for her."

"Did you tell her?" Ethan asked.

"No, I couldn't. She looks like she's having a religious experience or something. Her face lights up, and she gets this big smile on her face." Hailey shook her head. "You tell her."

"Uh, no way. You tell her," Ethan said to Gage.

The last thing Gage wanted to do was hurt Madison's feelings, but he didn't like the idea of people talking about her behind her back. "Maybe the kids will tell her."

"Nope, they think she's hilarious. They love her." Hailey pressed her ear to the door. "Thank God, she's stopped."

Then, from behind the closed doors, came a voice so pure and sweet it sent chills down Gage's spine. The three of them reached for the door at the same time and crowded into the church hall. Madison stood in front of the stage, nodding, hands raised, clearly encouraging whoever was singing. The angelic voice rose, crystal clear and powerful. Madison shifted, and Gage drew in a shocked breath.

It was Annie.

"Oh, my, God, she's incredible," Hailey whispered.

"Holy hell," Ethan breathed.

Gage couldn't speak. All he could do was stare at his beautiful little girl.

Annie hit the last note then self-consciously looked

down at her feet. There wasn't a sound in the room. Gage started to clap, breaking the spell his daughter had cast over them. When everyone joined in, Annie flashed a shy smile before being swallowed up by an admiring crowd.

Madison looked over her shoulder. Their eyes met and held, a telling sheen in hers. They shared a smile. His was one of gratitude. If not for Madison, Annie wouldn't have found her voice, found the courage to sing today. And there was something else, an emotion so strong it scared the hell out of him.

Ethan leaned into him. "You're in trouble, buddy."

"More than you know." And it wasn't Annie he referred to. At that moment, Gage was imagining what his life would be like with Madison in it.

Lily broke away from the group of kids that surrounded her sister and ran to Gage. "Daddy, Maddie said Annie gets to be Mary in the Christmas pageant. She's going to be a star just like…" Her face crumpled, and her narrow shoulders slumped.

He crouched in front of her. "What's wrong, sweetpea?"

Her bottom lip trembled. "I don't want Annie to move away like Mommy did. I don't want her to leave us. Don't let her go away, Daddy."

He stood up with Lily in his arms and held her tight. "She's not going anywhere." But Madison was. She'd never be satisfied with life in a small town, and he'd never let his daughters get attached to someone who'd up and walk away. Not again. They'd been through enough.

What the hell had he been thinking?

Chapter Fourteen

The last place Gage wanted to be was sitting across from Madison in the red-vinyl booth at the Rocky Mountain Diner with his daughters hanging on her every word. It felt a little too close to the fantasy family he'd envisioned only a short time ago. But aside from being flat-out rude, there'd been nothing he could do when Lily and Annie asked her to join them after practice.

He dragged his gaze from their smiling faces to focus on a menu that hadn't changed since Holly and Hailey's parents had started up the diner forty years ago. Madison and his daughter's easy laughter was more difficult to ignore. He released a thankful sigh when Holly arrived at the table to take their orders.

"Hi, Gage, girls, *Ms. Lane.*" Holly looked at Annie. "I heard about your performance today. I'm sorry I missed it, but *someone* changed the time without telling me."

Madison opened her mouth as if to explain, then

simply said, "Sorry." She drew a piece of paper from her purse and handed it to Holly. "I e-mailed you a list of who's playing who, but here's a hard copy."

Lily leaned across Madison. "I'm a lamb. Maddie's going to make my costume for me."

"Really?" Holly smirked. "I can't wait to see it."

Neither could Gage. Madison might be a lot of things, but Suzy Homemaker she was not.

"Yeah, it's going to be all soft and furry...like this." Lily rubbed the arm of Madison's pink fuzzy sweater, drawing Gage's attention to the glittery snowflakes winking at him from her incredible chest.

As if he wasn't having a hard enough time keeping his eyes off her. He took Lily's hand and placed it on the table. "Time to order."

Madison arched a brow. He ignored her.

One of the girls from practice approached the table. "Annie, you want to sit with us?" She pointed to a table where a group of girls and a couple of boys sat.

Annie looked at him. "Can I, Dad?"

His gaze narrowed on the boys. He was about to say no when a foot lightly kicked his. He looked up.

Yes, Madison mouthed, nodding.

He scowled at her, but knew she was right. "Okay. Fine."

Holly, who'd been taking it all in, grinned. "You want your usual, Annie? I'll just add it to your dad's bill."

"'Kay, thanks," Annie said, then trailed after her friend.

Lily went to scramble after her sister. Madison held her back. "Hey, where are you going?"

Arms crossed, Lily pouted. "I wanna go sit with Annie. Can I, Daddy?"

Great idea. Lily'd make the perfect chaperone. He was about to say yes, when once again Madison tapped his foot.

With a subtle shake of her head, she pulled a piece of paper and a pen from her purse. "I'm not sure I know exactly what you want your costume to look like, Lily. Why don't you draw me a picture?"

"She's good," Holly murmured.

Gage sighed. She was.

His youngest looked like she was about to acquiesce when a boy stood on his chair and waved at her. "Lily, wanna sit with me?" he yelled across the diner.

Gage groaned. He always knew he'd have to deal with boys sooner or later, but he'd prefer later, like when his daughters were forty.

"Can I, Daddy? Can I?" Lily bounced in her seat.

Madison fought back a smile. "They've just moved to town," she said. "Billy's a cow. He's harmless."

"He's a what?"

"A cow. In the pageant."

Lily ducked under the table to come out the other side. "I'll have my usual, Holly. Just put it on Daddy's bill."

"God, she's cute," Holly said, watching as Lily introduced herself to the boy's parents. One of the other waitresses signaled that Holly had a phone call. "Sorry, I'll be right back."

"Stop looking at Billy like that. You're going to terrify the poor kid," Madison said.

"Good," Gage muttered, then returned his attention to Madison, who was biting the inside of her cheek. "It's not funny."

"It kind of is. But don't worry, Daddy, your girls will be fine." She reached over and patted his hand.

He frowned and turned his hand over to clasp hers. "What happened to your finger?"

"Your aunt."

"Nell did this to you?" Absently, he stroked her delicate hand with his thumb, trying not to think about how it felt like it belonged in his. "Madison?"

She blinked and drew her gaze from their joined hands. "Oh, right. Nell and my finger. Okay, so I might've been the one who hit it with the hammer, but indirectly, it's her fault. If she hadn't insisted I work on the floats, it wouldn't have happened."

Gage shook his head and laughed. "That's the kind of logic Nell uses. I think you've been spending too much time with my aunt, Ms. Lane."

"Yeah, me too," she said, a smile in her voice.

Holly came back to the table and glanced pointedly at their entwined fingers.

"Everything okay?" he asked as he disengaged his hand from Madison's. He knew from experience that Holly and Hailey didn't allow personal calls at the diner unless there was an emergency.

"Steve's in town. He ran into Trent and a bunch of his friends in here. No surprise, Steve had been drinking. He was trying to bum money off Trent. I got him out of here, but the kids started to tease Trent about his father being a drunk and it got out of hand. Trent was pretty upset when he took off. I called Brandi to give her a heads-up. You'll probably be hearing from her. He hasn't come home yet."

Someone had screwed up. Gage was supposed to be informed the minute Steve got out of jail. His cell rang.

Madison placed their orders while Gage tried to calm Brandi down on the phone. As soon as he disconnected, he put a call into the station, then one to the parole officer assigned to Steve. By the time he got off the phone, their orders had arrived.

"Sorry about that," he said.

She frowned, putting down her BlackBerry. "Why? You had things you needed to take care of."

He shouldn't be surprised by Madison's easy acceptance of his inattention, but it was a nice change. The women he'd dated in the past weren't as understanding when their evenings were interrupted. Then again, he and Madison weren't on a date.

"Yeah, I did." He tucked into his burger.

"You were great with Brandi. I'm sure she felt better after talking to you." Madison pushed a piece of lettuce around the plate with her fork.

He studied her, wiping his mouth with the napkin. "Hey." He nudged her foot with his. "You okay?"

She nodded, resting her fork on the edge of the plate. "Just not hungry." She sounded tired and a little sad.

He reached across the table, nudging her chin up with his knuckle. Her gaze flitted away from his, as if she were afraid he'd see more than she wanted him to. He pulled his hand back. "What is it?"

"I didn't know." She shrugged helplessly. "I didn't know he'd been bullied. God, I'm no better than they are. No wonder his mother went off on me."

"You were standing up for Annie," he reminded her. Holly, who was wiping down the table beside theirs, avidly listened to their conversation. He warned her off with a look, one she pretended not to see.

"No, I wasn't. Don't make excuses for me. I was getting back at all the kids who bullied me, the ones who never let me forget my father was a drunk and my mother..." She closed her eyes and blew out a breath before opening them again. "Don't you see, Gage? I hit a kid who was just like me." She was quiet a minute then her gaze jerked to his. "His dad won't hurt Trent if he finds him, will he?"

He hated to see her beating herself up like this. She didn't deserve it. "If I thought he would, do you think I'd be sitting here? Look, Trent's good at hiding out until things quiet down. And Steve was never physically abusive. Verbally, yes, but never physically...at least not with Trent."

"It still hurts, you know, the verbal abuse. It leaves a mark that never really goes away."

He wanted to hold her, kiss away the haunted look in her eyes, but settled for taking her hand instead. "Your dad was verbally abusive?"

She nodded. "My mom got the worst of it, and no one ever stopped him." She gave Gage a soft smile, an emotion in her eyes he couldn't read. "But you've been there for Brandi and Trent all along. You're a good man, Gage McBride."

He shifted, uncomfortable with her praise. "It wasn't only me looking out for them. I just made sure I was there to nail his sorry ass when I had the chance."

"I wish someone like you had been looking out for me and my mother." She glanced out the window, then drew her hand from his.

"So do I." In his job, Gage had seen firsthand the damage an abusive parent could do. It made him sick to think about what Madison had suffered as a little girl.

Picking up her purse and jacket, she slid along the bench.

"Where are you going?"

"It's getting dark out." She stood, shrugging into her jacket. "I thought I'd drive around, see if can find Trent."

"He'll go home, Madison. He always does. He's done this before."

"They don't always go home, you know. Sometimes they do something stupid, and they never go home again."

He didn't like it. Her voice was distant, as if she was caught up in the past.

"Madison—"

She held up a hand, her gaze moving over his face like a caress. "I need to try. Thanks for inviting me to dinner with you and the girls. Say good-bye to them for me."

He glanced to where Annie shyly talked with her friends while digging into a chocolate sundae, to Lily who was still eating her pizza. There was no way he could leave. He watched in frustration as Madison walked away. She opened the door and turned up her collar against the cold wind blowing her hair back from her beautiful, sad face.

Holly approached the table. He raised a brow. With a sheepish look, she slid into the booth. "Sorry, I didn't mean to eavesdrop." Propping an elbow on the table, she rested her chin in her hand. "We're as bad as the people who bullied her in that stupid town she grew up in. We should've known better." She rubbed her cheek with her hand. "I think we misjudged her. But you didn't, did you?"

He didn't want to lump himself in with the rest of them, but in the beginning, he had misjudged her. "Yeah, we did. Everyone did. But in our defense, she doesn't always make it easy not to."

She didn't. When Madison first arrived in town, her defense mechanisms were so deeply entrenched no one would've believed that underneath her take-no-prisoners attitude was a warm, caring woman with a heart of gold. It might've been better—for him—if she'd left her defenses in place.

A customer waved Holly over. She stood and studied him. "You really like her, don't you?"

"I do. She's become a good friend."

Holly pulled a face. "Friend?"

No, but that was all they could be."Yeah, don't read anything more into it." And he'd try to do the same.

* * *

For the last two hours, Madison had looked for Trent in the places she'd gone to when things got bad at home. She'd tried the playground, the church, the library, but there was no sign of him.

Her phone buzzed. Gage. "Did you find him?" she asked.

"No, but Steve's in custody. They picked him up on a DUI twenty minutes ago in the next county. From what they got out of him, he didn't see Trent after he left the diner."

She pulled alongside the curb just down from an old-fashioned lamppost. "Do you think he's telling the truth?"

"Yeah, I do." His deep voice was confident and reassuring. "I called some of Trent's friends. One of the girls saw him hanging around the hardware store a couple of hours ago. Where are you?"

Snow blew from the trees on a gust of wind. She leaned forward to read the sign. "The corner of Aspen and Mountain Ridge Road."

"Okay. I'm going to head out as soon as my dad gets here. You sound beat. Why don't you head home?"

She was tired. And Gage probably had a better idea where to look for Trent than she did. "You'll call me, right, if you find him?"

"*When* I find him, I'll call you."

She laughed. "Cocky much?"

"Confident." She heard the smile in his voice. "It's nice to hear you laugh. I was worried about you," he said.

"Sorry, I didn't mean to get so emotional. I guess Trent's situation hit too close to home."

"You don't need to apologize, not to me. When you talked about someone not being able to go back home, was that you?"

She really had run off at the mouth. "No, my mother."

"Will you tell me about her?"

She wanted to, and that surprised her. But maybe it shouldn't have. From the beginning, there'd been something about Gage that made it easy for her to open up. And now, sitting alone in the dark, she felt less self-conscious, like she was in a confessional.

It'd been Mavis, her boss at the diner, who'd sat Madison down the day she turned sixteen to tell her about her mother. She'd always wondered if it'd been because Mavis had worried Madison would turn out the same.

"My mother was sweet and incredibly naïve. My father wasn't. He was a mean drunk. He felt like life had done him wrong and took it out on my mother, both physically and verbally. When I was six, he put her in the hospital. She wanted to leave him, but didn't see how she could. She didn't have much of a support system. Only Mavis, her boss, and the men who came to the diner and gave her the attention she craved. It was a small town. People talked. They made her out to be the town tramp. She was an easy target, pretty and from the wrong side of town. Her boss told me there was only one man before Mitch, but in the end he went back to his wife.

"My mother thought Mitch was different. I never met him, but I don't think it speaks well of a man who'd leave his wife and three kids on Christmas Eve. Anyway, my mother woke me up on the morning of the twenty-fourth to tell me they were getting married. I don't think I'd ever seen her so happy.

"They didn't want to tip off my father or Mitch's wife and were leaving that night after they'd finished their shifts. Mitch's father-in-law owned the mill in town. Mitch and my dad worked for him. I was to wait for them on the front steps of the church. I waited, but they never came. My father arrived just as the service let out. He was fall-down drunk and told me my mother got what she deserved. They'd gone off the road and hit a tree. They died instantly." She took a moment to swallow the emotions welling upside her. "So there you have it, Sheriff, my sorry tale."

"Don't, don't try and make light of it." His voice was rough and edgy. "It got worse, didn't it, after your mother died?"

She rubbed the steering wheel. "It did. Everyone blamed her for what happened to Mitch. Since she wasn't around, they took their anger out on me. And not surprisingly I guess, given the circumstances, my father was fired from the mill a few months later. His drinking got worse. And when he was drunk, he'd confuse me with my mother."

"Did he—"

"No." She shook her head. "No. If it got really bad, I'd go stay with Ruby. She lived in the trailer next door to ours." Madison started. She'd forgotten about Ruby.

A weighted silence filled the SUV. "Gage?"

"I'm here, sweetheart."

She smiled. The endearment left her feeling warm and fuzzy inside, cared for and protected.

"So no one did anything to stop him? There was no one looking out for you?"

"A few months ago, I would've said no. But since I've been in Christmas, I've remembered things differently. Like just now. I'd forgotten about Ruby and how she always seemed to be there when I needed her. Ruby and Mavis, they tried to help."

"Not goddamn hard enough. What the hell was wrong with those people? You were the same age as Annie."

"I guess not all towns are filled with nosy, interfering people like the ones who live here," she teased in hopes of lightening the mood.

"I'd take Christmas over the town you lived in any day."

"Me too." It was true—she would.

"Hang on. In here, Dad." Gage came back on the line. "Dad says hi, and I'm supposed to remind you about the skating party. What skating party is he talking about?"

Madison laughed, welcoming the release. "The one he says you have every year. You know what your dad and Mrs. O'Connor are up to, don't you?"

He sighed. "Yeah. And if it's bothering you, just say the word, and I'll put a stop to it."

"No, it's fine. They're harmless."

"Harmless? That's debatable. So, are you going to tell

me who's in the lead?" he asked, as though he, too, realized she needed the normalcy, the lightness.

"No contest, Sheriff. There's only one man in the running...you." She wasn't teasing anymore. It was true.

"Good answer. I wouldn't want to beat up my best friend."

"You wouldn't beat up Ethan over a woman."

"Depends on who the woman is. For you, I would."

"I wish..." She couldn't finish, couldn't tell him how much she wished things were different.

"So do I," he said quietly.

"It'd never work, you know."

"I know. You hate small towns."

"Right." Not so much anymore, not Christmas at least. "And long-distance relationships don't work."

"That's been my experience. And you love your job."

"I do, and so do you. And my tendency to attract negative press wouldn't be good for an elected official."

"Yeah, trouble seems to have a way of landing on your doorstep, Ms. Lane. And I do need to keep my job."

"Yes, you do, for Annie and Lily's sake." She thought about the two girls. Annie with her incredible voice. The pleasure Madison got out of watching her slowly come into her own. And Lily with her boundless energy and sunny disposition, who never failed to make Madison smile. "I really like your daughters."

"They really like you, too. So do I."

What she wouldn't give to have him with her now, to have him hold her in his arms.

"That wouldn't be a good idea. I wouldn't be able to let you go."

"How did you know what I was thinking?"

"Easy. I was thinking the same thing."

It was on the tip of her tongue to suggest they give whatever this was between them a chance when she spotted a boy, tall and lanky, coming down the road from the warehouse. "Gage, I think I see Trent." She turned on the engine and pulled away from the curb. Trent got caught in her high beams. "It's him."

"Okay, I'll be right there."

"Would you mind if I picked him up? I'd like a chance to talk to him."

"Sure. I'll call Brandi. Let her know you'll be bringing him home."

"Thanks. And Gage, thanks for listening."

"No need to thank me. I'm glad you trusted me enough to tell me."

She did trust him. He made her feel safe. "Have a good night."

"You too. Good luck with Trent."

She'd need it. As she lowered the passenger-side window, Trent eyed her suspiciously, a belligerent jut to his chin. But no matter how tough he pretended to be, she recognized the look in his eyes. She should. She'd seen it often enough looking back at her in the mirror.

"Hey, Trent. I'm Madison Lane, a friend of Sheriff McBride's. Hop in. I'll give you a lift home."

His upper lip curled. "I know who you are. You're the psycho who nailed me with the snowball."

Madison decided to save the apology. "Yeah, and you're the kid who hit Annie in the face with one. Come on, it's cold out, and it's getting late." She held up her hands. "No snowballs."

He stole a quick glance over his shoulder then

nodded. Opening the back door, he tossed his knapsack inside.

"Why don't you sit up front? You'll warm up faster." And it'd be easier for her to talk to him.

He eyed her warily.

"Here—" she held up her phone "—call Sheriff McBride. He'll vouch for me."

Shooting another look over his shoulder, he shook his head. "No, it's okay." He shut the back door, then climbed in the front seat.

As he went to pull the seat belt over his shoulder, she noticed his hand. "Oh, my God, Trent, you're hurt! You're bleeding." She reached for his hand.

He jerked it away from her. "It's not blood. It's paint, just paint." From his reaction, she must've looked as panicked as she felt.

He scrubbed his hand on his jeans.

"Okay, that's good." Her pulse slowed to a normal rhythm, and she put the SUV in gear. "What were you painting?"

His gaze shifted from her to the window. "Umm, a sled. I was painting a sled at my friend's house."

"There must be some pretty good hills around here for you to go sliding on," she said in an attempt to keep the conversation going.

He rolled his eyes. "A sled isn't a toboggan. It's a Ski-Doo."

Okay then. "You should've called your mom to let her know where you were, Trent. A lot of people were worried about you."

"There was nothin' to be worried about. They're just a bunch of busybodies."

Madison smiled. "They are. But you know what? I wish I'd had as many people looking out for me when I was growing up as you do."

"Yeah, right. You don't know what it's like."

"I think I do." She hesitated, not sure how to broach the subject. But she wanted to let him know he wasn't alone. "I, ah, heard about what happened in the diner today... with your dad. I'm sorry your friends gave you a hard time."

He shrugged. "It's not a big deal. My dad's a loser."

"You're handling it better than I did. My dad was like yours. He used to embarrass me something awful. And he didn't care who was around when he did."

The rhythmic swish of the wipers filled the silence as Trent stared out the window.

She'd just decided he wasn't ready to open up to her when he shifted in his seat. "Did the kids make fun of you?"

She nodded. "Every single day until I left that town." They'd gone way beyond making fun of her, but that wasn't something Trent needed to hear.

"What did you do?"

"Nothing. And I should have."

"Like what?"

"Stand up for myself. Not let them see how scared I was, and face them down." She showed him her best don't-mess-with-me face.

"Scary." He gave her a crooked smile. "That's how you looked when you threw the snowball at me."

Madison winced and shook her head. "I'm sorry, Trent. I shouldn't have done that." She glanced at him. "Forgive me?"

"I guess. I shouldn't have thrown one at Annie, either," he admitted sheepishly.

"No, you shouldn't have. The thing is, Trent, when you've been bullied, you've got to be careful not to become one. You have to remember how it feels and not do that to someone else. Annie's a really great girl. I bet if you apologized to her, you two could become friends."

He ducked his head, his cheeks flushed. "Maybe," he mumbled.

There was something about his reaction that made Madison think Trent might've been trying to get Annie's attention. Not exactly the smartest way to go about it, but then again, boys weren't always smart when dealing with girls they liked. And not just little boys—big boys, too.

"And, Trent, when I say stand up for yourself, I don't mean getting physical. If someone hurts you or you're afraid they're going to, you need to tell someone."

"I can't tell my mom. She might...she's kinda overprotective. Maybe I could tell you or Sheriff McBride?"

She held back a smile at his comment about Brandi. And while Madison wasn't surprised he'd thought of Gage, she was surprised and touched that he thought of her. "Sheriff McBride is a great choice. I'm not sure how much longer I'll be in town, but while I am, you can call me anytime."

She pulled in front of the tidy white bungalow with its blue Christmas lights blinking on and off. Brandi stood, arms crossed, at the open door with a frown on her face. "You better get going. Your mom's waiting for you. And, Trent, remember, your father has the problem, not you." She took a business card from her purse and handed it to him. "Call my cell number."

He pocketed the card and smiled shyly. "Thanks, Ms. Lane."

He was a sweet boy. With everyone looking out for him, he'd be okay. One more person couldn't hurt, she thought, as she leaned across the seat. "Hey, Trent, we need a tall guy like you to play Joseph in the Christmas pageant. Interested? Annie's playing Mary." Good Lord, she was getting as bad as Nell.

He lifted a shoulder. "Maybe."

"Trent, get in here. I'm freezing," his mother yelled.

"Next practice is Wednesday night. If you need a ride, give me a call."

"Okay. Thanks."

Brandi responded to Madison's wave with a reluctant one of her own. Now that she knew about Brandi's husband, her eat-shit-and-die attitude didn't bother Madison as much as it did before.

She turned up the radio, humming along with an upbeat tune. It felt like a heavy burden had been lifted from her shoulders. Confession, it seemed, really was good for the soul. Or maybe it was just the man she'd confessed to.

Chapter Fifteen

Madison hummed along with the carol playing on the radio. Her good mood from the night before continued as she drove down the road on her way to drop Nell off at the warehouse. At the end of the street, the sun peeked through the snow-frosted trees on the mountain ridge, casting the town in a soft, welcoming glow.

"It's going to be a gorgeous day." She smiled at Nell and got a sour look in return.

"What the Sam Hill's wrong with you?" the older woman said. "You're acting like you got into my hooch."

Hooch? Madison shook her head and laughed. "Forget about it, Nell. Nothing you say can ruin my good mood today."

Tugging a piece of paper from the pocket of her plaid jacket, Nell shot her a wanna-bet look. "I'm giving you another chance on Santa's float. Here's the list of paint colors you're *supposed* to use."

Madison sighed. Nell'd managed to ruin her good mood in under five seconds. She held up her finger, wiggled it and faked a yelp. "Sorry, I don't think I'm up to it."

"You've got a bruised fingernail while I've got a broken—"

"Stress fracture."

Nell grunted. "Same difference. And *I* managed to put in a full day yesterday. Most of which I spent fixing your screwups. While you sat in a corner pouting and sucking on your finger before you made your escape."

"I wasn't pouting. And if I'm such a screwup, why do you want me there?"

"You weren't that bad. Everyone else had their family with…" She trailed off, then lifted a shoulder.

So. As much as Nell was growing on Madison, it appeared she was growing on Nell, too. She patted the older woman's arm. "Okay, I'll help. But only for a couple of hours. I have to meet with G—someone later."

Nell rolled her eyes. "I don't understand why you want to keep what you're doing for Grace a secret."

"How…never mind." Madison should've known it was next to impossible to keep anything quiet in Christmas. "We're only at the early stages. Until I talk to the bank manager tomorrow, nothing is for certain."

"Even if nothing comes of it, it's a nice thing you're doing for Grace. Shows you have a heart. Folks around here are beginning to realize you've had their best interest in mind all along. Mr. Hartwell will probably be calling you any day now. I just hope he lets you stick around for a while longer. It's late in the game to be looking for another elf," Nell said, her voice gruff.

A fist-sized ball of guilt lodged in Madison's chest.

It was a lie. She hadn't come here with the town's best interest in mind. Everything she'd said and done had been in the best interest of Joe and Hartwell. She was about to confess as much to Nell when she realized while that might have been true in the beginning, it wasn't true now.

She cared what happened to Gage and his girls, to Nell, to Ted and Fred, to Grace, to all of them, really. And Madison wanted Christmas to stay just the way it was.

"You're right. I do have the town's best interest at heart. You don't need a Hartwell resort to turn Christmas around. The other business owners in town are just like Grace. None of them have explored all the options available to expand their customer bases and decrease costs. I can show them how. It'll take time, but in the end it'll be better for everyone."

"That's all well and good, but I don't see how anything can come of your ideas if you don't plan on sticking around."

Sticking around wasn't an option for Madison. She couldn't give up the security her job at Hartwell provided. The money and benefits package were great, and she'd worked too hard to get where she was to give it all up. After being told for so long that she'd never amount to anything, never knowing if there'd be enough money for food growing up, the thought of being unemployed, or underemployed, set off a tsunami of panic in her stomach. And no matter how much Madison had come to care for the people in town, namely Gage, she couldn't live in a fishbowl.

"I can consult from New York." With her workload at Hartwell, she'd be stretched thin, but it wasn't like she had any other demands on her time. If she was in a relationship, it might be a problem, but she wasn't. Probably wouldn't be for a very long time if she compared every man she met to Gage. "I'm sure I can schedule..." She trailed off, realizing she no longer held Nell's attention.

The older woman was focused on the people milling around outside the warehouse. As Madison pulled into an empty space in the parking lot, she spotted Mrs. Tate and Stella. Both women were crying.

"What the Sam Hill is going on here? They're carrying on like someone died."

Nell wasn't exaggerating. Something had clearly happened to upset the citizens of Christmas. Madison could only be thankful it didn't have anything to do with her. As soon as she put the SUV in Park, Nell was out the door. Now that she no longer required crutches, she was hard to keep up with. Tracking Nell's progress, Madison scrambled from the SUV. She grabbed her purse and locked the doors. Ted and Fred broke from the crowd and rushed over to Nell.

"Ms. Lane." She turned to see Rick Dane, an almost gleeful expression on his hound-dog face, approach her. Unlike Rick, the men and women who followed after him looked angry and confused.

Dear Lord, what now?

Ted moved in front of Rick. "You leave the girl be, Dane. You're not the law. Gage is on his way."

Without looking at Madison, Nell jerked her thumb. "Get in the SUV. Now."

Surely they weren't up in arms over yesterday. "Is there something I can do for you, Mr. Dane?"

"Madison!" Fred, Ted, and Nell rounded on her.

She held up a silencing hand. She needed to know what was going on.

"Sure is, Ms. Lane. You can tell us why you were hanging around the warehouse last night."

"I wasn't…" She was about to deny the charge, then realized she'd been parked down the street from the warehouse while she spoke to Gage. "Not that it's any of your business, but I'd pulled over to talk on the phone. What's this about?"

"Funny, that's what we want to know. You made your opinion about us and our parade pretty clear yesterday, but did you have to go so far as to destroy the floats?"

"I didn't destroy the floats! I painted Santa's house brown. Nothing I did yesterday was on purpose." No one listened to her. They were too busy hurling accusations as they crowded closer.

Nell, beating a hasty retreat, stumbled.

"Hey, back off," Madison warned, sounding a lot tougher than she felt. She moved protectively in front of Nell and dug in her purse for the item Mr. Hardy of Hardy's Mountain Equipment Co-op told her no city girl should be without. "Take a step back, and no one gets hurt."

*   *   *

Gage had an unwelcome sense of déjà vu as he pulled into the warehouse parking lot. Once again the citizens of Christmas were calling for Madison's head. Only this time she was on her feet and holding them off with…a can of bear spray.

Heads swiveled in his direction when he slammed the door of the Suburban. The crowd parted like the Red Sea as he strode toward Madison. "About time," she murmured with a shaky smile.

He cocked a brow and wrapped his fingers around her wrist, removing the can. "Bear spray?"

She shrugged, her gaze flitting from the crowd back to him. "I don't know what's going on—"

"You ruined our floats! That's what's going on," several people yelled.

"How could you, Ms. Lane? Nell trusted you. We all did," Nell's neighbor Stella cried.

Madison looked stricken, eyes wide in her pale face. She didn't deserve this. He shoved the can in his jacket pocket before he gave in to the urge to get off a few shots at Dane. Once Gage put the allegations against Madison to rest, he had a few questions for Rick. He'd been the one to report the vandalism, laying the blame on Madison. And that alone put him at the top of Gage's suspect list. Because from the moment Madison had arrived in town, Dane had done his best to sabotage her efforts to win over the citizens of Christmas. Granted, in the beginning, she'd made it easy for him.

"Gage, I don't know what they're talking about. I thought Santa's house was supposed to be brown. I didn't—"

Sirens blared as his deputies squealed into the parking lot. "Don't worry. We'll get everything straightened out," Gage tried to reassure her. "But it's not just Santa's house they're talking about."

"What do you mean? I thought..." Her gaze shot to the warehouse, and she started forward.

He reached for her arm. "Hang on." He waved Jill and Ray over. "Let me..."

Madison broke away from him, skirting the crowd. He groaned in frustration. He wanted to pick her up, toss her over his shoulder, and get her the hell out of there. "If anyone of you saw or heard anything, see my deputies." At least twenty people converged on Jill and Ray. "That goes for you too, Dane."

Rick followed Madison's progress and smirked. "Always glad to do my duty as a concerned citizen." He ambled into line.

Concerned citizen, my ass. Shit disturber, more likely.

Gage caught up with Madison just as she reached the entrance to the warehouse. Staring through the open doors, she released a horrified gasp. "Oh. My. God."

He silently echoed her sentiments. It was worse than he expected. The words "I hate Christmas" were splattered in red paint across every float. Besides the graffiti, each of the holiday displays on the flatbeds had been damaged. Gage doubted there'd be time to repair them for the parade.

"Why would he..." She bit her lip, casting a furtive look Gage's way.

"Who, Madison? Who did this?"

She cleared her throat. "I don't know what you're talking about. I didn't say anything."

"There's about twenty people here who think I should arrest you right now for this, so don't lie to me."

She glanced behind her, then back at him, a resigned look in her eyes. "I guess you'll have to arrest me then."

"For chrissakes, Madison, you—"

"Sheriff McBride, seeing as how you're romantically involved with the suspect, don't you think it'd be best if your deputies question her?" Rick called out as he walked toward them, a handful of men at his back.

"Not that it's any of your business, Dane, but Ms. Lane and I are not romantically involved." Technically, it was true. But after their conversation last night, he'd wondered if he was a fool to give up on them so easily. To not give whatever it was between them—and there was definitely something between them—a shot.

"As the ones who put you in office, we might disagree with you there, Sheriff."

The men with Dane nodded their agreement, while several people in line were more vocal in their assent. It took Gage aback. Not once in his three years as sheriff had his integrity been questioned. Madison tensed beside him. He wondered if she was remembering their conversation of last night. Because this was exactly what they'd been talking about. Proof they'd been right not to take their attraction further.

He needed to shut Dane up. "Ms. Lane is not a suspect. As she was in the area last night, it is possible she may have seen something without being aware of it. She's agreed to come to the station—" he gave her a don't-even-think-about-it look when she opened her mouth to disagree with him "—and give her statement. This area is off-limits while my deputies process the scene. I suggest you all go about your business until we can let you back in."

Madison stood quietly beside him as he answered questions about the time line of the investigation.

When the crowd started to break up, he returned his attention to her. "You can…Madison." He followed her gaze to where Nell stood talking to Jill and tried again. "Madison."

She looked up at him, blinking the moisture from her eyes. He wanted to shake her and hold her in his arms at the same time. "I'm not letting you take the fall for this. Just tell me who did it."

"I can't believe they think I did," she said, a hitch in

her voice as she once again looked at Nell. With his hand at the small of her back, he nudged her along.

Rick fell in step beside them.

"Dane, don't you have somewhere you need to be?"

He held up his camera. "I want a shot when you search her vehicle. You are planning on searching it, aren't you?"

No, he hadn't been. But to prove to Dane his suspicions were unfounded, Gage held out his hand for Madison's keys.

She appeared ready to cooperate, then her gaze shot to the SUV. She closed her eyes for a brief moment then opened them to give him a look that would've shriveled a lesser man. "Unless you happen to have a warrant in your possession, Sheriff, you will not be searching my vehicle."

*   *   *

Twenty minutes later, they arrived at the station. Without Dane and his camera in his face, Gage hoped to make Madison see reason. "Do you want a coffee?" he asked before he shut his office door.

"No, thank you," she said woodenly.

At least she was speaking to him. But unless he figured out who she was protecting... He mentally slapped his head. He'd been so intent on protecting Madison, he hadn't thought through the evidence. She'd been down the street from the warehouse when she'd spotted Trent. A few hours earlier, the kid had been seen at the hardware store, probably loading up on red spray paint. Of all the misguided, stupid, idiotic, incredibly selfless things to do—she was protecting Trent. She both amazed and infuriated him.

If only the press who'd dubbed her "the woman without a heart" knew her like he did. But he had to make her realize the consequences of her action, to protect her from herself.

"Look." He crouched in front of her and took her hands in his. "I know why you think you need to protect Trent, honey." Her shocked gaze jerked to his. He didn't know what shocked her more, the endearment that slipped so easily from his lips or that he'd figured out who'd vandalized the floats.

"Trent has to face up to what he's done. And you—" he squeezed her hands "—you don't deserve this. If you take the fall for Trent, you'll lose your job."

She swallowed hard, then looked him straight in the eye. "I have no idea what you're talking about."

He came slowly to his feet, taking a step back before he gave in to the urge to shake her. "You're not doing him a favor taking—" The door to his office burst open.

Nell, followed by Ted and Fred, hobbled in. The three of them glared at him, taking up their positions behind Madison.

There were times when his aunt and her partners in crime annoyed the hell out of Gage, but this wasn't one of them. How could he be mad when their show of support put that smile on Madison's face?

Nell patted Madison's shoulder. "Don't you worry, we got you a lawyer. Ethan," she hollered over her shoulder.

Ethan, somewhat sheepishly, entered his office. Gage stared his best friend down. "*You* can't defend her."

Madison released an offended gasp.

Gage winced. "Sorry, but it's a conflict of interest. He's the mayor."

Ethan scratched the back of his neck. "Technically—"

With a dismissive sweep of her hand, Nell said, "You're not going to charge Maddie. You have no evidence against her."

Gage didn't wear a badge because the money and benefits were good or because he liked the power and prestige that went along with the job. His grandfather and father had instilled in him and his brothers the desire to serve and protect, to give back. He believed in the law, and he wouldn't let his feelings for Madison get in the way of his upholding it. "You're wrong, Nell. I can and will charge her with obstruction. She's withholding evidence. She knows who is responsible for vandalizing the floats."

Ignoring their shocked expressions, he checked his watch. "I'll give you ten minutes to confer with your client."

Exactly ten minutes later, Gage entered his office, prepared to take Madison's statement. The five of them were huddled together like they were on the ten-yard line preparing for the winning handoff.

"Time's up," he said, taking a seat behind his desk. He steepled his fingers and looked at Madison, who now sat stiff-backed in front of him, the four stooges standing behind her.

"I did it," she confessed.

The breath shot out of him like he'd taken a bullet. He couldn't believe it. "You, you, you, and *you*"—he stabbed a finger at each of them in turn—"out." Madison half-rose from her chair. "Oh, no, you don't, sweetheart. Sit down." He took a pair of cuffs off his belt and slapped them on his desk.

Ethan stepped forward and nudged a paper under his nose. "Here's her signed confession." Before Gage tossed him out of his office on his ear, he quickly added, "My client suffered a moment of temporary insanity and deeply regrets her actions. She'll make full restitution and will guarantee the parade will go on as scheduled. Everyone's happy."

Gage leaned back in his chair and crossed his arms. "I'm not happy."

"Too bad. We are, and so is Ethan," Nell said. "He's the mayor, which makes him your boss. We have lots to do in the next five days, and you have paperwork to take care of, so we'll get out of your hair." Nell pulled Madison to her feet. The five of them looked anywhere but at him as they hightailed it out of his office.

*   *   *

It'd been a couple of hours since they'd cleared out of the station. Gage had expected to be fielding calls from angry citizens the entire time, at the very least from Dane. But the phone lines were unusually quiet. Gage was still angry at what they'd pulled. He didn't agree with Madison taking the rap for Trent, but he knew why she did. And it bothered him to think of her with only Nell, Ted and Fred, and possibly Ethan, his ex–best friend, helping her to repair the floats. With public opinion running high against her—again—no one else in town would lift a finger to help her.

It wouldn't look right for him to lend a hand, but that didn't mean he couldn't help in a roundabout way. He called his dad to suggest he head over to the warehouse with Annie and Lily to offer their support, but his cell kept going to voice mail. He tried to reach Brandi; one way or another he was determined Trent would make amends for what he'd done. Frustrated when he couldn't get through to her, either, he disconnected and pushed away from his desk to head to the warehouse.

When he got there, the lot was full, his deputy's vehicles blocking the entrance. Preparing for the worst, Gage parked on the street. He checked his radio—it was on— and headed for the building. Ready to do battle on Madison's behalf once again, he flung open the doors. His jaw dropped.

There were between thirty and forty people running around like a bunch of demented elves. He spotted Madison on her knees at the front of Santa's float with a paintbrush in hand. Annie, Lily, and his dad were working alongside her. Above them, Brandi and Trent were setting the reindeer to rights. As if Trent felt Gage's hard stare, he looked up. Gage did a two-finger point to his own eyes then shot a finger at Trent. The kid looked like he was going to puke. Good.

Gage's dad saw him and nudged Madison. She looked over her shoulder. Annie and Lily turned to wave. Handing off her paintbrush to Lily, Madison came to her feet. Big mistake, Gage thought, when his youngest gleefully splashed white paint onto the boards and everyone within spraying distance.

Madison walked toward him. "Hey," she said softly.

"Hey, yourself." He looked down at her and shook his head. "You're as crazy as they are, you know." And damned if he wasn't crazy about her. He supposed it was about time he did something about that.

"Yeah, I know." She laughed then sobered. "Are you still mad at me?"

"Would you care if I was?"

She nodded, her eyes searching his. "I would. I do. I

know you don't understand, Gage, but it was easier for me to take the blame than it would be for Trent. Everyone—"

"No, it wasn't," Gage interrupted her. He couldn't stand the thought of her being hurt, not after last night. "And you have a lot more on the line than he does. When Rick gets—"

"Nell went with Ted and Fred to talk to him. They seemed pretty confident they can get him not to run the story."

Of course they did. One or all of them undoubtedly had something to hold over Rick's head. They'd known him since he was in diapers.

Several people called out to her, and Gage released a frustrated sigh.

She glanced over her shoulder. "I better go see what they need."

What he needed, he realized, was time alone with her. "I want to talk about this, about Trent. Pick a night, and we'll go out. There's a restaurant...What?"

"Are you asking me on a *date*, Sheriff?

"I guess I am. There's an Italian restaurant I've wanted to check out," he said, laying odds the chances of running into anyone from town would be next to nil. It was expensive and in the next county. "How about Thursday at seven?"

She smiled up at him. "You're sure?"

"Yeah." He was sure all right; sure he'd just made either the smartest decision of his life or the stupidest, because they both knew this was more than a date. "So, do you have an extra paintbrush lying around?"

Chapter Sixteen

Gage stood behind the barricade on Main Street with Nell, Annie, and his dad waiting for the Santa Claus parade to begin. And if his aunt didn't quit talking about the difficulty she had stuffing Madison into her body-hugging elf costume, he was going to gag her.

He was frustrated enough without having that visual in his head.

Between Annie's and Lily's last-minute school projects, and an uptick in assholes who thought they could drive after indulging at their annual Christmas parties, he'd had another week from hell. And with Madison's promise to have the floats repaired in time for the parade, her pageant practices, and the business plans she was apparently writing up for the whole damn town, they'd barely seen each other. They'd made do with phone calls, texting, and the occasional face-to-face. By the time Thursday rolled around, he'd been pathetically anxious

for their date. Only Madison had begged off on account
she was worried about Nell.

He glanced at his aunt. Madison was right, her coloring was off. "Nell, are you sure you're up to this?"

"You're as bad as Maddie. Stop coddling me," she
groused, shifting her weight off her air-casted foot. Of
course she'd been too stubborn to bring her crutches.

Over her head, he met his father's concerned gaze.
Needs to sit, he mouthed.

Gage nodded. "Save my place," he said to Annie. "I'll
be right back." He had a fold-up stool in his trunk.

As he wove his way through the crowd, the *Grinch*
theme song jangled in his jacket pocket. So that's what
Madison had been up to when she'd commandeered his
phone at the warehouse this morning.

He laughed, answering his cell. "Funny girl." She was
funny and smart, a caring, sweet woman all rolled up in
a gorgeous, sexy package. "How's things in the North
Pole?"

"Funny guy." He heard the smile in her voice and
grinned like the idiot she'd turned him into. "It's freezing
and…Hey, you try and goose me one more time, Santa,
and I'm tossing your scrawny butt to the curb."

Gage rubbed a hand along his jaw. And lest he forget,
she was also tough and stubborn, and stirred up trouble
faster than his aunt. He figured his conflict-resolution
skills would come in handy if they were going to give this
relationship thing a go. He opened his mouth to tell her to
take a couple of deep breaths and picture the faces of the
little kids if she followed through with her threat, which
was entirely possible. Then he realized what'd come
before the tossing part.

"Put Santa on the phone." Gage opened his trunk while he gave the guy hell and told him what to expect if he so much as looked at Madison sideways.

She came back on the line. "Aw, bless your heart, sugar. What would I do without a big, strong man like you to protect li'l ol' me?"

He smiled, tucking the stool under his arm. "Okay, you've made your point. But the kids would be upset if they saw Santa's elf beating him up, so I suggest you keep your distance."

"Not when they get a good look at him, they won't. Seriously, Gage, I don't know where Nell found this guy. He looks like Jack Nicholson in *The Shining*, only with a rat's nest for a beard. I swear, he'll give them nightmares."

"Is that what you called me for?"

"No, just wanted to say hi. I haven't talked to you since this morning."

He'd been fighting the urge to call her himself. Ethan was right. He had it bad. "Hi."

She laughed. "Where are you watching the parade from? Are Nell, Annie, and your dad with you?"

"We're across from the station. Dad and Nell are with me, Annie too. I had to fight with her for twenty minutes to get her here." He'd been tempted to give in, but Lily would've been disappointed if her sister didn't see her in the parade.

"She can't help it. She's twelve and thinks she's supposed to be too cool for parades. I'm glad you didn't give in. Lily would've been disappointed. And in the end, so would've Annie."

For a woman who didn't have kids, Madison knew his pretty well. He enjoyed talking to her about the girls. A new experience for him, he'd never been comfortable talking about Lily and Annie with the women he'd dated in the past.

"I'll be looking for you guys. Make sure you wave so I can see you."

"From what Nell said about your costume, I won't be the only one waving."

She snorted. "I've got my coat on. I don't plan on letting anyone but you see me in this getup."

"That's my girl," he said, undeniably relieved.

"Maybe we'll play Santa and his little helper tonight." Lowering her voice to a sultry whisper, she told him exactly what Santa could do to his little helper. He dropped the stool.

Bending down to pick it up, he apologized to the woman whose foot it landed on, then said to Madison, "I wish we could get together tonight, but Dad volunteered to take a shift at the hospital. It's too late to call a babysitter now. If Nell was feeling better, I'd leave the girls with her, but I don't think that's a good idea."

"No, I just thought... never mind."

He heard the disappointment in her voice, but he wasn't comfortable having her back to his place, especially when he wouldn't be able to keep his hands off her. Lily would get her hopes up, and he didn't want her hurt if he and Madison didn't work out. And, no matter how much Annie adored Madison, if she thought there was something going on between them, that would change. In Annie's perfect world, Gage and his ex would be back together again. "Madison—"

"Gotta go, they're loading the kids on the float. Hey, Lily," she called out, a forced brightness in her voice.

"We'll talk—" The line buzzed in his ear. Gage rubbed

the back of his neck. He had to find a way to carve out time for them to be alone or they'd be over before they got started.

Ten minutes later, the parade wound its way down Main Street. Madison's suggestion they end thirty-five years of tradition and hold the parade at night had met with fierce opposition—none fiercer than Nell's. But his aunt had met her match in Madison.

And Madison had been right. It was dark enough that the floats' imperfections were hidden, and the Christmas lights gave the parade a magical feel. Going by the *ooh*s and *ahh*s from the crowd—even Annie uttered a few—the parade was a hit. He glanced at his aunt, gauging her reaction.

She frowned up at him. "Don't look so smug. I can admit when I'm wrong."

He grinned. It was ridiculous how proud he was of Madison. She was turning him into a sap.

Gage was about to suggest that his aunt should be telling Madison she was wrong and not him, when he spotted Trent in an elf costume following behind the horses with a shovel. Nell wasn't the only one who would have to admit to Madison about being wrong. Because right about now, he figured Trent would've preferred Gage's brand of justice to hers.

Annie's face lit up with a smile as she waved shyly to someone in the parade. Trent, who only a couple of seconds ago looked like he wanted to sink into the pavement, walked a little taller, waving back with a grin.

He glared at the kid. Trent ducked his head. From behind him, Gage heard his father chuckle. "They gotta grow up someday, son."

"Easy for you to say. You had boys."

"Dad." Annie tugged on his arm. "There's Maddie and Lily."

Lily and three of her friends, dressed as elves, sat in the fake snow under an artificial white tree strung with red lights, waving their fake hammers. Gage's smile faltered when Madison came into view standing a safe distance from Santa's chair.

"Where the hell—" Annie glanced at him "—*heck* is her coat?"

His aunt snorted a laugh. "I told Fred and Ted to take it from her once the parade started." She shrugged at the look Gage shot her. "What? She's covered up."

Right. And on anyone else, the long-sleeved red top buttoned up to her neck, a matching red hat perched on top of her shiny, loose hair, and a short, black skirt with a pair of red-and-black-striped leotards covering her incredibly long legs would've looked...cute. But Madison with her bombshell body looked anything but cute. She looked centerfold sexy, and he wasn't the only one who thought so.

He scowled at the three men hooting and hollering at her from the front of the crowd. "You're blocking the kids' view," he called out. "Take it to the back." They were about to argue until he flashed his badge.

His father and aunt smirked knowingly.

"Annie." Madison waved as they got closer. Smiling that wide smile of hers, she pointed to the fistful of candy canes in her hand and drew her arm back. "Catch," she shouted as she drilled them into the crowd. Everyone ducked and covered their heads. Laughing, Annie and a bunch of kids scrambled to pick the candy canes up off the ground.

Madison was directly across from him now. Her hand raised, she looked shy and vulnerable. As if unsure he'd want her to draw attention to them. He lifted his own hand, hoping somehow she'd see how he felt about her. Her smile widened, and his gut, along with his heart, clutched as if he'd taken a hairpin turn doing one-eighty.

His hand was still up in the air when the float rolled out of view. Quickly, he shoved it in his pocket.

After saying good-bye to Annie and Nell, his father put a hand on Gage's shoulder and leaned in. "I used to look at your mother the same way you look at Madison. Don't let her get away, son. Women like that are hard to find," Paul said quietly, his voice gruff with emotion.

Instead of the denial Gage was about to make, afraid it was a lie and his father would call him on it like he always did, he laid a hand over his father's. "'Night, Dad. Talk in the morning."

With long, easy strides, his father worked his way through the crowd, acknowledging friends and patients in his typical genial manner. Paul McBride was a good man, one of the best, and he deserved to be happy. Gage didn't like to think of him spending the rest of his life alone. But he didn't know if his father, after experiencing a love like he'd had with Gage's mother, would ever be able to move on with someone else.

Nell drew his attention from thoughts of his father. "Did you get a load of Santa?" she asked, rising stiffly from the stool.

He didn't, but he wasn't about to let his aunt know he hadn't been able take his eyes off Madison long enough to check him out. "He looked like Jack Nicholson in *The Shining*," he said, repeating Madison's description. "What were you thinking when you hired him?" He folded the stool and tucked it under his arm.

"It wasn't me who hired him. It was Fred. And let me tell you, I'm going to give him an earful. Good thing Madison distracted the crowd." His aunt started to follow the throng of people moving down the street in the direction of the town hall.

"I think you've had enough excitement for one night, Nell. I'm taking you home," he said firmly. Whether she'd admit it or not, there was something going on with his aunt.

"Oh, no, you're not. They're announcing who won for best-lit house, and I'm not missing that. I'll get someone else to take me if you won't," she said, her lips set in a determined line.

She would, too. "Fine, but we're not walking."

Gage didn't like to take advantage of his badge, but he made an exception tonight and pulled in front of the town hall. Ethan must have decided to do the same, as he parked beside him. Annie helped Nell off the running board, earning her a scowl and a grumpy "What the Sam Hill is wrong with you people? I'm fine."

Despite her protest, she took Annie's arm.

Ethan met him on the sidewalk. "Attendance is way up this year," he said, eyeing the long line Nell elbowed her way to the front of.

Annie shot Gage a pleading look over her shoulder. He winked and held up two fingers. "Yeah, Madison was right. Holding the parade at night was a great idea." Again he felt that surge of possessive pride.

"Stroke of genius." Ethan nodded then grinned. "But I hate to tell you, buddy, I think the real draw was your girlfriend. She looked smokin' in her elf costume. I didn't think elves were supposed to be sexy, but…" He gave a wolf whistle.

"Okay, give it a rest."

"So I was right?"

"Right about what?"

"You and Madison."

What the hell—it wasn't like Ethan would shoot off his mouth. "Yeah."

"Finally, it's about time you came to your senses."

Gage nodded, then noticed the three guys from the parade standing in line. "I'd better get in there. I'll see—"

"Hang on a minute." Ethan stopped him with a hand on his arm. "I got a call from Hartwell just before the parade started. Looks like the deal's back on." He slapped Gage on the back. "Town's going to have something to celebrate this Christmas after all. Hartwell's flying in on the morning of the twenty-fourth to sign the papers." He frowned. "What's wrong? I thought you'd be as happy about this as I am."

Gage didn't know how he felt. All he could think about was Madison's reaction to the news. "Which Hartwell are you talking about, the old man or the nephew?"

Ethan looked surprised. "Joe Hartwell's stepping down. He'll make the announcement Monday morning. Didn't Madison tell you?"

"As far as I know, she has no idea about any of this." After everything she'd done for them, they were screwing her over. And Joe Hartwell, a man she looked up to, didn't have the decency to give her a heads-up. "This is bullshit. How the hell am I supposed to break this to her?"

Ethan grimaced and nodded at the entrance doors. "You'd better figure it out fast. Here she comes."

*   *   *

Madison elbowed her way through the crowd in search of Gage. He didn't know it yet, but he was about to don a red suit and beard. There was no way she was going to allow the children of Christmas to be subjected to the lecherous lout masquerading as Santa. Not only did he have the hands of an octopus, he was drunk. She was pretty sure the eggnog he claimed to have in his flask contained more nog than egg.

Several people called out to ask where she was going. She flashed a smile. "Don't worry. I'll be right back." She spotted Nell and Annie and hurried over to them. "I need to find Gage." She tugged them out of line. "We have a problem with Santa."

Nell looked around. "Where is he?"

"In the supply closet. Believe me, it's safer that way," she said in response to Nell's shocked expression. "Fred and Ted are taking care of him now. All I need to do is find Gage. He can take Santa's place. But you need to buy us some time. The kids are getting antsy." She narrowed her eyes at Nell. "Unless you're not up to it. I can always—"

"You're all getting on my last nerve," Nell said. "Of course I'm up to it."

Annie pulled a face. "Maddie, my dad won't play Santa."

"You let me handle your daddy, sugar, and you and Nell handle the rug rats."

"This I gotta see." Nell chuckled. "Last I saw of him, he was out front with Ethan."

"Did you spot Rick Dane in the crowd, Annie?" Madison heard Nell ask as they went in opposite directions.

As someone who'd spent time on the front page of the

Chronicle, Madison felt a smidgen of sympathy for Gage, but only a smidgen. It was about time someone took the heat off her. She smiled as an image of Gage dressed as Santa popped into her head. She could think of a few things she'd like to ask Santa Gage for Christmas. Her smile faded. She'd already mentioned a couple of ideas to him, and his response hadn't been what she'd hoped for.

She hadn't thought through the consequences of dating a single father, especially a single father who put his daughters' feelings above everything else. She didn't blame him. His devotion to Lily and Annie was just one of the many things she admired about him.

He'd made it clear he wanted to keep their relationship on the down-low, but she was beginning to wonder for how long. Maybe he'd be more confident they'd make their relationship work if it wasn't for the long-distance thing. His attempt at one with Sheena had been a disaster. Obviously, since they were divorced.

Madison caught a glimpse of Gage through the glass doors. When his winter-green eyes locked with hers, all her worries faded. There was something about the way he looked at her, a softening of his expression that made her breath catch and her heart flip-flop in her chest. They could be together forty years, and she didn't think her reaction would ever change. Maybe she'd found her one-and-only after all.

Hmm, at that moment, her one-and-only looked a little nervous. She wondered if someone had tipped her hand. Fast walking—she wasn't about to let him get away—the bells on her black slippers jingled. As Gage opened the door, she hit a patch of ice. "What…oomph," he said when she plowed into him.

His hand went to her waist to steady her, and his icy fingers brushed the thin strip of bare skin between her skirt and top.

"Cold." She shivered.

With a sneaky move he'd probably perfected in his years of being sheriff, his eyes did a thorough sweep of her body—one that no one would notice but her. "Hot," he murmured, his hand tightening on her waist, his peppermint-scented breath warming her cheek. She lifted her eyes to his. He grinned, flicking the bell on her hat. "Cute."

Ethan cleared his throat. Gage's good humor instantly faded, and he set her away from him. Madison knew how Gage felt about PDA, but he was being ridiculous. It wasn't like they were making out on the street. But she didn't have time to get into it with him now.

"Hey, Ethan," she said, taking Gage by the hand. Probably something else she wasn't supposed to do, she thought grumpily, but it was the only way she knew to make sure he didn't get away. "Come on."

"Madison, I have to talk to you for a sec." Gage reached past her to open the door. He was a gentleman, she'd give him that, and in her current frame of mind that was about all she'd give him.

She tightened her hold on his hand and kept walking. "I need your help."

"Okay, but what I have to talk to you about is important."

The urgency in his voice caused her stomach to dip. She wasn't sure she wanted to hear what he had to say. The worry that he might be having second thoughts about them returned. Maybe he was beginning to realize she wasn't a fan of keeping their relationship on the down-low, wasn't particularly good at it, either.

She cut through the people in line and walked down the hall to the supply closet. Nervously moistening her lips, she checked to be sure they were alone. It'd be less painful to get it over with quickly instead of listening to Gage list all the reasons they weren't going to work out. "Are you..." She hesitated, feeling stupid, feeling like a dorky fifteen-year-old asking the captain of the football team if they were breaking up. "Are you breaking up with me?" Her Southern drawl thickened the words, making it difficult for even her to make out what she'd just said.

The corner of his mouth twitched. He glanced over his shoulder, nudging her back against the door. His gaze roamed her face, then he gently nipped her bottom lip. "No. Why would you ask?"

Relief swamped her. She tried to answer him, but with the warmth of his hard body caging her in, the words jumbled up in her head. So she looped her arms around his neck instead. "Kiss me."

"Happy to." He smiled before fitting his lips over hers. She tangled her fingers in his hair, absorbing his heat and his woodsy scent. The warm, seductive slide of his lips over hers turned fierce and hungry. He was as desperate for her, it seemed, as she was for him. She reached behind her, fumbling for the doorknob with one hand while fisting the other one in his jacket to drag him into the supply closet with her. Two minutes, she just needed two more minutes in his arms, with his mouth on hers, before she told him about Santa.

Gage backed her against the now-closed door. His leanly muscled body was the only thing keeping her from sliding to the concrete floor as the hot, openmouthed kiss they shared weakened her knees. His hands went to her waist, his fingers caressing the strip of bare skin there. "Umm, nice," he murmured against her lips, sliding his hands under her top.

"Oh, God," she moaned, as his fingers moved higher. In a passion-induced haze, she decided two minutes wasn't enough, an hour, a lifetime, wouldn't be enough. She began to undress him. Smoothing her hands over his chest, she worked her way up to push his jacket from his broad shoulders.

He lifted his head, his breathing a rough rasp against her cheek. "Honey, as much as I want you, and I really, really want you…" She kissed his throat. He stopped talking, releasing a low groan instead.

She tried to wrap her fingers around his wrists, to guide his hands lower. He took the hint and slid them to her thighs, to the hem of her skirt. "Oh, yes," she breathed, working the sleeves of his jacket over his flexed biceps, down his arms to his hands. One tug, then another, and his jacket fell to the floor at their feet. Next she went to work on the buttons of his shirt.

He put his hand over hers, stringing kisses from the corner of her mouth to her ear. "Aren't you supposed to be out there with Santa?"

"Santa's in here with me." She undid a button, kissing the warm skin she revealed.

Slowly he raised his head. Patting the wall, he found and flipped on the light. Once his eyes adjusted, he scanned the cluttered room. He took in the tidy pile of clothes in the corner with Santa's fur-trimmed jacket on top. His gaze swung back to her. "Is there something you want to tell me?"

She saw the worry in his eyes. *Good Lord, he thinks I knocked off Santa.* "Oh no, you found me out. And here I thought I'd done such a good job cleaning up all the blood."

His sheriff's face firmly in place, Gage crossed his arms.

"If you didn't look so hot making that face," she ran the tip of her finger along the shallow dent in his chin, "I'd be really annoyed with you right now. I *fired* Santa. Ted and Fred got him out of costume, dressed, and, I'm assuming, home."

"And?"

She smiled, moving into him, lifting her eyes to his as she undid another button. "Can you say, 'Ho, ho, ho'?"

He stilled her busy fingers. "No, no, no."

She rose up on her toes, fluttered her lashes against his cheek, then kissed the corner of his mouth. "Please, for me? It's only for an hour or so."

"And what's in it for me?" His voice was toe-curling deep, his eyes hot.

"Me." She pushed the sides of his shirt open, baring his sculpted chest to her enthralled gaze. "I'll be your little helper."

He kept his eyes on her as he moved away from the door, shrugging out of his shirt. "Yeah, what exactly do little helpers do?"

"Well, we help get you into your costume for one thing." She picked up Santa's jacket, drawing it over his arms, her fingers caressing his chest as she lingered over her job. "And we help you *out* of your clothes too." She reached for the button on his jeans just as the door flew open.

A camera flashed.

Rick Dane came into focus. "The ladies are going to love this issue." He grinned then turned to Madison. "Ms. Lane, do you want to comment..."

She'd give him a comment all right, but as she opened her mouth to tell him exactly what she thought of his sleazeball reporting methods, he finished, "...on Hartwell's decision to reopen the resort deal?"

Chapter Seventeen

From the guest bedroom window, Madison watched Nell's neighbor Stella shovel her driveway as Harrison confirmed the rumors of the night before.

Harrison confirmed them, not Joe.

Between handing out candy canes last night, Madison had left several urgent messages, which either her boss chose to ignore or his nephew deleted. Her shock over the news had faded several hours ago, and now all she felt was a deep sense of betrayal. She deserved a heads-up at the very least, the courtesy of a phone call from Joe.

Harrison bawled her out for calling him at home—with Nell's help she'd found his unlisted number—before nine on a Saturday morning. She'd been waiting out his angry rant for the last five minutes.

"So, as I'm sure you'll agree, it's for the best."

Huh? "Wait... what did you just say?"

He sighed. "I said, I'm sure—"

"No, before that."

"Since you seem to have such a difficult time under-standing, I'll be blunt. You're fired. Your services are no longer required. There, does that clear it up?"

"I have a contract," Madison said, her voice a strangled whisper.

"Which, if you'd read carefully, included a clause that states in the event Hartwell undergoes a change of own-ership or restructuring, your contract can be terminated. We are, and it has been." He sounded like he was taking a great deal of pleasure in delivering the news, the Snake.

Harrison had won. He'd slithered in and stolen every-thing she'd worked so hard for, everything she cared about. He was right about the clause, but no way would she let him hear her panic. "You can't fire me, Harrison. I quit. You're the last person I'd work for. You'll bankrupt Hartwell Enterprises within the year."

"We'll see who comes out on top in the end, Madison. Enjoy the unemployment line. No one's going to hire you, not after the negative publicity you've generated of late."

He was right. No one in the industry would touch her now. And she didn't put it past Harrison to slander her fur-ther. She was hurt and scared, but more than that, she was angry. "I know you set me up, Harrison. I was the only one standing between you and what you wanted—a Hartwell resort in Christmas. But guess what? This isn't over yet. I have friends here, and I won't let you destroy this town."

It was an idle threat, and she knew it. Once word spread through the town hall last night that the deal was back on the table, the citizens of Christmas couldn't contain their relief or excitement. If she didn't know how it would all turn out in the end, she would've been as happy as they were.

Harrison laughed. "Good luck with that. From what I've been told, the only one in town who doesn't want the resort built is you. Let it go, Madison. You have more important things to occupy your time than beating a dead horse. I'll expect to see you in the office first thing Monday morning. We'll take care of the paperwork then, and you can clean out your desk and hand in your phone and laptop at the same time."

Her heart jackhammered against her ribs. If it hadn't seemed real before, it did now.

"Madison?"

Struggling not to hyperventilate, she took a minute before she could get the words out. "Yes, yes, I'll be there at nine a.m. Monday morning."

"See that you are."

The line buzzed in her ear.

Breathe, she ordered herself in an effort to overcome the panic rising back up inside her. Logically she knew she could go without a paycheck for at least a year, but that didn't stop the roller-coaster ride her stomach was on. She didn't want to use up her savings. If Harrison started slandering her reputation, who knew when she'd get a job? But the real reason behind her topsy-turvy emotions was the thought that she had to leave Christmas, and Gage.

Their long-distance relationship was going to start sooner than expected. She hoped he was up for it. Last night, he'd been furious on her behalf, protective and supportive, but every so often when he wasn't bouncing someone on his knee or *ho, ho, ho*ing, he looked worried.

Worried, she imagined, what the citizens of Christmas would think of the picture Rick had taken of them in the supply closet. After everything that had happened, Madison had expected him to invite her back to his place, if only to explain to the girls about the photo, but all she got was a promise to call her later. He didn't.

Maybe he'd be glad to be rid of her, after all.

She rubbed her temples, trying to squelch her worries. Her cell rang. She checked caller ID. Finally. "Vivi, why haven't you returned any of my calls?" Now that Madison had her friend on the line, she wasn't letting her off until she found out what was going on with her. She'd deal with her own problems later. At the thought, her stomach did that topsy-turvy thing again.

"I'm calling you now. What's up?" Vivi sounded like she had something in her mouth.

"What are you eating?" When her best friend was upset, she withdrew. When she was really, really upset, she sat holed up in her apartment eating gallons of Rocky Road ice cream.

"Umm, strawberry ice cream."

Vivi hated strawberry ice cream. "I don't believe you. Skye said you're upset. She thinks..." Madison hesitated, trying to come up with a diplomatic way to say: she thinks you're upset because the guy you're in love with dumped you.

A frustrated sigh gusted over the line. "I know what she thinks. It was stupid. I was stupid. You can't fall in love in a week. It was lust, nothing more. I'm over him. All the women's magazines say you shouldn't sleep with a man until you've been together for at least three months. I should've taken their advice."

"Really, that's what they say?" she said, instead of asking Vivi when she'd started reading women's magazines. The funny thing was, Madison had unconsciously been following their advice for years. She'd been paranoid about getting involved with a guy who had a wife hidden away and, like her friends, didn't sleep with a man unless she thought they'd go the distance. Both of which took at least a few months to figure out. Probably the reason why, although she'd dated several men over the years, she'd only slept with one.

But now that she was head-over-heels-stupid in love with a man she'd known for only a few weeks, Madison took exception to the theory. "What happened?"

"I don't know. One minute everything's perfect, and then he was…gone. He never made any promises. I just thought…He told me he moves around a lot with his job and doesn't do long-distance relationships, but…"

Hot Bod sounded a lot like Gage. And an image of Madison and Vivi sitting cross-legged on her couch sharing gallons of Rocky Road ice cream popped into her head. She suddenly wished she hadn't pressed for details, but that didn't stop her from asking, "What does he do?"

"I don't know. Can you believe this is me talking? I don't know anything about the guy." She went quiet for a long beat then said, "When I didn't hear from him for a few days, I tried to look for him. I can't find him, Maddie. It's like he's a ghost."

"What possible reason—"

"I don't know." Her laugh was brittle, fragile, very un-Vivi-like, and that worried Madison. "What I do know is I'm sick to death of those three words."

"I'm coming home. I'll be there tonight or tomorrow at the latest." Madison ignored the hollowed-out feeling in her chest at the thought she was really leaving.

"If you're coming home because of me, don't. I'll be fine." She huffed out an exasperated breath. "I *am* fine, and I won't let you put your job at risk because you're worried about me."

Might as well get it over with. "I don't have a job. I quit. Actually, Harrison fired me, and then I quit." It was worse saying the words out loud. She took a slow, even breath to steady the panicked gallop of her pulse.

"Shit. I'm sorry, Maddie. I'd heard rumors Joe was stepping down, but I thought if it was true you would've heard them, too."

"You'd think, wouldn't you? I have to face it, Vivi. Just because I felt like I was more than an employee to Joe doesn't make it true." Suddenly exhausted, she lowered herself to the edge of the bed. "Keep your ear to the ground, will you? Harrison's got it in for me. I'm worried he's going to do something to make it impossible for me to find work."

"Let him try. He's an idiot. Men are idiots, and I say good riddance to them all. Who needs them, anyway? We'll both be fine. Hartwell won't last a year without you." It sounded like Vivi was talking around another spoonful of ice cream. And if eating ice cream was Vivi's endorphin-releasing therapy, she needed to try something else. Because clearly, it wasn't working.

"I'm sure you're right. I'd better go book my flight. I'll text you shortly with my arrival time."

"For someone who practically had to be blackmailed to stay in Christmas, you don't sound very enthusiastic about leaving."

"Of course I'm happy to be coming home." But aside from her best friends being there, at least Vivi, New York didn't seem much like home anymore. Christmas did. "It's just that I'll be missing the pageant, and I hate to let down the kids and Nell." She heard the tap, tap of keys.

"Umhmm." There was a smirk in Vivi's voice. "Nothing to do with Santa baby?"

Madison groaned. "Don't tell me, the weekend edition of the *Chronicle* is online?"

"Got it in one." Vivi laughed. "That man is so hot I'd almost be tempted to let him slide down my chimney if I had one and I hadn't sworn off the jerks. And for a girl who doesn't like Christmas, I'd say you've had a change of heart. Because it looks like you really like Santa. Cute costume, by the way."

"Oh, God, does it look like I like him, or that I *like* him like him? Vivi?" she said when the silence dragged on.

"Yeah, I'm here."

"What's wrong? You sound weird."

"Madison, you're not in love with him, are you?"

She heard the worry in Vivi's voice, and given her best friend's current frame of mind, decided to lie. "Don't be ridiculous. Of course I'm not. How could I be in love with the man? I've only known him for a few weeks, and we haven't... you know."

Vivi sighed. "I wish I hadn't."

Madison wished she had. But considering the state her best friend was in, maybe it was a good thing they hadn't. She heard the rattle of pots and pans from the kitchen below. "I've gotta go. Nell's up. Talk when I get home." She disconnected, relieved to end the conversation.

Her relief faded when she realized she had to break the news to Nell. Opening the bedroom door, she called down the stairs. "Give me fifteen minutes, Nell. I'll be down to get breakfast."

Twenty minutes later, the smell of bacon wafted past Madison's nose as she stood on the landing at the top of the stairs. She sighed. Just this once she'd wanted to make breakfast for Nell. The last breakfast they'd spend together for a while. Madison had a seat on the red-eye out of Denver that night. It was better this way. No long, drawn-out good-byes.

She took a step, and the stair creaked. No turning back now, she thought, forcing a smile on her face while quickly going over her speech in her head. With Nell, it was best to be prepared. Madison didn't want to think about what she'd to say to Gage.

"Good morning," she said as she entered the kitchen, her voice a little too over-the-top chipper.

"What the Sam Hill has gotten into you this morning?" Nell stood at the stove frying bacon. Her gaze flicked to Madison, taking in her ill-fitting New York suit, and a frown deepened the lines on her brow. Slowly she rested the tongs on the side of the pan, then turned off the burner. Hobbling to the kitchen table, Nell lowered herself heavily in the chair. "You're leaving."

Unable to meet her eyes, Madison self-consciously smoothed back a strand of hair that had escaped her bun. Something else that felt oddly uncomfortable rather than natural, just like her ugly suit. A heavy weight settled in her stomach, taking her carefully rehearsed speech down with it.

"I have to go." She sat in the chair across from Nell. "I, um, Harrison fired me. I've got to get back and clean out my office, start looking for a job."

Nell gave a pained grimace, then rubbed her shoulder. "It's my fault you lost your job. I never should've—"

Unable to handle Nell's guilt-ridden expression, Madison interrupted her, "No, this has been a long time coming.

Harrison has wanted me gone since the day he arrived at Hartwell. With Joe stepping down, there was no one to stop him from getting rid of me."

Nell paled, and a sheen of perspiration broke out on her forehead.

"I'll be fine, Nell. And I'll be back to visit." Madison tried to reassure her.

"What about the pageant, your plans for Grace, your plans for Christmas?" She was agitated, her expression anxious.

"Nell, the resort is going to go through. You're getting what you wanted."

"So you're giving up? You're going to let Harrison..." Groaning, she bent over and clutched her chest.

"That's not funny, Nell. Stop it. I know what you're doing, and it's not going to work this time. I can't stay."

Nell slumped forward then fell on the floor.

"Nell!" Madison rushed to her side. As she carefully turned the unconscious woman onto her back, a terrifying thought raced through Madison's mind: this time, she really had killed Nell.

Chapter Eighteen

No, she didn't kill Nell, Millie. Ms. Lane saved her."
Since Madison and Stella had been shown into the hospital waiting room twenty minutes ago, Nell's neighbor had been doing her best to spread the news of Nell's heart attack to the entire population of Christmas.

Stella had arrived in Nell's kitchen at the same time as the paramedics. Madison hadn't noticed. She'd been too busy performing CPR on Nell while frantically praying she was doing it right.

Ted and Fred, who'd arrived for their morning coffee as the ambulance pulled out of the driveway, sat on the uncomfortable molded blue chairs on either side of Madison.

She anxiously watched the bustle of activity at the nursing station across the hall. "Don't you think someone should've come to tell us how Nell is by now?"

"Nell's going to be just fine, you hear?" Ted said gruffly, patting Madison's knee.

"Sure she is. Our Nellie's a tough old gal," Fred said.

Madison wanted to believe the two men, but they hadn't seen how Nell looked lying on the kitchen floor. Madison inhaled deeply, trying to relax the viselike grip fear had on her chest.

Ethan and his mother rushed into the waiting room. Ethan, looking like an ad out of *GQ* magazine, shook Ted's and Fred's hands, then crouched in front of Madison. "How are you doing?"

"Better, now that Nell's here."

Liz patted her shoulder. "Nell's lucky you were with her and that you knew how to perform CPR."

"I hope I never have to use CPR again. I don't think I could live with myself if—" She broke off, remembering how, in her panic, her mind had blanked, and for a couple of terrifying seconds, she couldn't recall what she was supposed to do.

"You did good, girlie." Ted squeezed her knee.

"Darn right, she did," Fred added.

Madison wondered how they'd feel when they found out she was the reason Nell'd had the heart attack in the first place.

Ethan took her hand in his. "Why don't I get you a cup of tea?"

What she needed was to walk off some of the nervous energy that had her wound so tight.

Fred and Ted, stiffening on either side of her, glowered at Ethan. He rolled his eyes. "Don't get your shorts in a knot, boys. I'm not asking her out on a date, just if she wants something to drink."

"Sure you are," Ted grumbled. "Where's Gage?"

"There's a hostage situation over in Summit Ridge. Gage was called in early this morning," Ethan said, then listened with growing amusement as the two men rhymed off a list of Gage's accomplishments. They made him sound more like Superman than a small-town sheriff.

News of the hostage-taking didn't surprise Madison. She'd overheard Gage talking to one of the paramedics on the radio. And she'd fought the urge to grab the radio from the paramedic's hand to hear Gage tell her that Nell would be okay, that Madison had done everything right.

"Mr. Mayor—" Stella waved him over "—can I use your phone for a minute? My battery died."

Liz held out her hand. "Come on, Madison. We'll go down to the cafeteria. Does anyone want anything, Ted, Fred?"

Madison stood to follow Liz at the same time as a large group of women, including Nell's friend Mrs. Tate, walked in. It took another five minutes before she managed to escape their well-intentioned questions and the now-overcrowded waiting room.

Gage's father, wearing a white coat with a stethoscope around his neck, looked up from the chart he perused. At his side was a beautiful redhead in pink scrubs. The nurse gave Liz a condescending up-and-down look. Madison had never met the woman before, but from her reaction to Liz, she'd lay odds this was Dr. McBride's on-again, off-again girlfriend, Karen. They looked like they were in their on-again phase.

"Madison." Gage's father set the chart on the desk, stepping forward to take her hands in his. "I'm sorry you had to go through that this morning, but I'm very glad you were there for my aunt. If you…" He shook his head and squeezed her hands.

Liz rubbed his arm. "Nell's going to be fine, Paul." Their eyes met and held. Madison wondered if they were remembering when it had been Liz's husband and Paul's best friend who'd had the heart attack. He hadn't been fine.

Madison shuddered at the thought.

The redhead cleared her throat, loudly. "Dr. McBride… Paul." She glanced pointedly at the chart. He released Madison's hands. Liz let her own fall to her side.

"Madison, I'll wait for you in the cafeteria. Paul. Karen." With a curt nod, Liz headed for the elevators at the end of the hall.

"Liz," Dr. McBride called after her.

She stopped, gave a slight shake of her head, then glanced at him over her shoulder.

He cleared the obvious frustration from his face. "I, uh, I had to leave Annie and Lily with Gage's neighbor. I was wondering if you'd—"

"You left them with Mrs. Gunter?" Liz interrupted him, scrunching her nose.

Paul grinned, looking almost boyish. "Yeah. Would you mind staying with them for a few hours until we know what's happening with Nell?"

Her expression softened. "I'll head over now and take them back to the ranch with me. Madison—"

"No, you go ahead. Don't worry about me." Madison would have offered to look after the girls herself, but she couldn't leave the hospital until she knew Nell was going to be okay.

"Paul, there's no need to impose on Mrs. O'Connor."

Karen's patronizing tone made it sound like Liz was eighty. "I'll look after the girls. I'm finished my shift in fifteen minutes, and you know how much I love spending time with them." Gage's father looked like that was news to him. His gray eyes pleaded with Liz to intercede.

Liz held his gaze, then responded to Karen, "It's not an imposition. Annie and Lily are the closest thing to grandchildren that I have. Besides, I have to get them to try on their costumes for the pageant."

Karen waited for Paul to say something, but he busied himself making notations on the chart. She sniffed and tossed her long hair. "Fine." Grabbing the chart from his hands, she strode down the hall.

Paul winced as he watched her walk away, then returned his attention to Liz. "Thanks. Lily and Annie aren't overly fond of Karen, and they're upset about Nell. I feel better knowing they're with you, Liz." He studied her. "They won't tire you out, will they?"

Liz went toe to toe with him, twisting his stethoscope between her fingers. "Stop treating me like an invalid. There's nothing wrong with me. I might not be in my thirties like your girlfriend, but I'm not old! And for your information, there are still a lot of men out there who think fifty-nine-year-old women are hot."

"Liz, I'm sorry. I didn't mean... Who thinks you're hot?"

Madison winced. Paul McBride had just proved that even smart men could be stupid.

Liz made an annoyed sound in her throat, pivoted on her heel, and stalked to the elevators.

"I don't know what's gotten into her lately," he said, staring after her with a confused look on his face.

Madison hadn't set much store by Nell's belief there was more between Paul and Liz than friendship, but after what she'd just witnessed, she decided Nell was right.

"Dr. McBride, I'm going to get myself a cup of coffee. Would you like one?"

"I thought we'd agreed it's Paul, remember?" He gave her a tired smile. "And no on the coffee. I'm good, thanks."

She started to walk away, then hesitated. "Maybe I should wait until we hear something about Nell. We should know something soon, shouldn't we?"

"They're running her through some tests. Once we have the results, we'll have a better idea what we're dealing with. Excuse me for a moment," he said when his cell rang.

It was Gage. His father updated him on Nell's condition then handed the phone to Madison. "He wants to talk to you." Paul McBride smiled as though he'd just won Matchmaker of the Year.

Madison lifted the phone to her ear. "Hi."

"Why aren't you answering your phone? I've been trying to reach you for the last twenty minutes."

She frowned and took the phone from her jacket pocket. Her screen was blank. "Sorry, there's something wrong..." And then she realized what that something was. "Harrison must've canceled my service. I'll have to pick up another BlackBerry."

"Why would he cancel your phone?"

"As of this morning, I am no longer an employee of Hartwell Enterprises. Harrison fired me." Funny, the words didn't have quite the same earth-shattering impact as they did earlier.

"That's bullshit. He can't fire you."

"Yes, he can. He's taking over from Joe."

"I don't care if he is. Joe should damn well go to bat for you." He blew out an aggravated breath. "I'm real sorry about this, Madison. You've had one hell of a morning, haven't you? Are you okay?"

Gage was the one person she didn't have to pretend with. Walking a short ways down the hall, she turned to face the wall for some privacy. "No. But being fired is nothing compared to having Nell collapse in front of me. I've never been so scared in my life. I wasn't sure if I was doing everything I was supposed to. I wasn't sure if she was already..." Her breath caught on a sob as she struggled to contain her emotions.

"Aw, honey, I wish I could've been there for you. And you did everything right. If Nell had been alone, there's a real good chance she wouldn't have made it. Look, we're almost done here. I should be at the hospital within the hour."

She glanced down the hall to where Paul spoke to Ethan and lowered her voice, edging closer to the wall. "You don't understand. It's my fault Nell had a heart attack in the first place. I told her I was leaving tonight, and she...Gage, I thought she was faking. If I would've realized sooner that she wasn't, she wouldn't have fallen off the chair and hit her head."

"You're leaving...today?"

"I was, but I can't now, not until I know Nell is going to be all right."

"Were you planning on saying good-bye or were—"

"I don't understand you," she interrupted him. "I just told you it's my fault Nell had a heart attack, my fault she hit her head, and all you can ask is if I was planning on saying *good-bye*."

"Come on, you're a smart woman. You know you didn't cause Nell's heart attack, and given what she pulled on you after the town hall meeting, it's no surprise you'd think she was faking it. But in the end, you saved her life, Madison." His voice was tight, his words clipped.

"Why are you so mad at me? I don't get it."

"Sorry, it's been a tense couple of hours here. I'm not mad at you…I just thought you'd give me a few days' notice before you took off, that's all."

"Well, I've had a pretty crappy day, too. And after last night, I didn't think you'd care one way or the other if I was leaving." It wasn't entirely true, but she needed to hear him tell her she was wrong without asking him flat-out. She didn't want to come across as a needy, love-struck woman. She wasn't needy. Love-struck… probably.

His long, drawn-out sigh held a heavy dose of frustration. "You're kidding me, right? I was so damn hot for you I couldn't keep my hands off you. What part of me having my hands up your top and my tongue down your throat made you think I wouldn't give a damn if you took off without a word?"

"No, not then." She cleared the husky quality from her voice and tugged at her turtleneck, feeling a little warm at the memory of their steamy supply-closet encounter. "I may not be very experienced with this kind of thing, but I'd lay odds you've made out with lots of women and didn't spare them a second thought the next day."

"I'll be right with you," he said to someone in the background, then lowered his voice. "Just so we're clear on this, you're not like any of the other women I've been with. I care about you—a lot."

For the first time that day, Madison smiled, until she remembered... "But you were mad after Rick took our picture. You said you'd call, and you didn't." Okay, now she sounded needy. If she added a pout, she'd be one of those women she'd promised herself never to become.

"I was angry at Dane for refusing to delete our picture, not at you. You have to admit that photo wasn't exactly a ringing endorsement for a guy who holds public office. As for not calling, Lily got sick. By the time I settled her in for the night, it was late."

"Your dad never said anything. Is she all right?"

"Yeah, too much sugar. I've..." An angry shout came from the direction of the waiting room. "What's going on there?"

Madison glanced over her shoulder. Ethan escorted Coulter Dane from the waiting room while Gage's father tried to calm down Ted and Fred. "I have as much right to be here as they do," Mr. Dane said to Ethan as they walked toward the elevators.

She repeated the exchange to Gage. "Don't ask," he said when she started to. "It's a long story. You'll be at the hospital when I get there, right?"

"Of course. I'm not going anywhere, not until I know how Nell is."

"Good. Because once we know she's going to be okay, you and I are going to find somewhere quiet to talk and figure out where we're going with this."

"This?"

"Us." Someone called his name. "Gotta go. See you in a bit."

As Madison wondered how their conversation would play out, Matt Trainer, Dr. McSteamy's look-alike, walked over to where Nell's friends gathered in small clusters outside the jam-packed waiting room. From his expression, she tried to gauge whether the news was good or bad. She couldn't, and her stomach heaved.

"Listen up, folks. Unless you're family, I'm going to have to ask you to leave."

Everyone began to talk at once. Half of them questioned Dr. Trainer about Nell's condition, while the other half protested their ejection.

Gage's father caught Madison's eye and waved her to his side. "Go ahead, Matt."

Dr. Trainer nodded. "Nell's conscious. The next twenty-four hours are critical, but barring any unforeseen complications, I feel confident she's going to make a full recovery."

It was as if they all exhaled at once. "Thank God," Madison murmured, fighting back tears. Ted cleared his throat a couple of times, and Fred surreptitiously rubbed his eyes.

Dr. Trainer fielded questions while politely but firmly sending everyone on their way. "For the next day or so, only members of the family will be able to see Nell."

"We might not be related by blood, but we're just as much Nell's family as you are, Paul. Me and Fred are staying." The two older men took their seats, their expressions daring Dr. Trainer or Gage's father to argue.

"Get over here, Maddie." Ted patted the chair between them. "She saved Nell's life, you know," he said to Dr. Trainer, his chest puffed up with pride.

No matter how much Madison wanted to stay, she

couldn't. She'd learned her lesson with Joe and didn't plan on making the same mistake. "I think it's best if—" she began before Gage's father interrupted her.

"Ted and Fred are right. Nell would want the three of you here."

"Actually, Nell would like to see Ms. Lane," Dr. Trainer said.

Madison was anxious to see Nell, but she was also worried what would happen if she did. Oh, she knew Gage was right, knew she hadn't actually caused Nell's heart attack, but she also knew any type of stress wouldn't be good for Nell. "Are you sure? Shouldn't Dr. McBride go in first?"

Paul smiled. "Heart attack or no heart attack, my aunt is not a woman who takes kindly to people not doing as she wants."

No, she didn't, Madison thought, as she went to follow Dr. Trainer down the hall. Once they reached Nell's room, he began telling Madison what to expect. Suddenly a loud beeping came from behind the slightly ajar door as a light flashed above it. A nurse ran toward them. Dr. Trainer rushed into the room as quickly as the blood rushed from Madison's head. She leaned against the wall.

"Nell, you can't take out your tubes. I don't care if they're bugging you," Dr. Trainer said sternly.

Madison didn't know whether to laugh or cry. She laid a hand on her chest to make sure her own heart was still beating.

"No, I didn't get my degree from a Cracker Jack box, and I don't care if you want your nephew to treat you, he can't. No, neither can your great-nephew. He was a paramedic, not a doctor. No, it's not the same difference." Dr.

Trainer sounded like his patience was wearing thin. "If you don't behave, I'm sending you to Denver."

His threat must've worked because a couple of minutes later he and the nurse left the room. The nurse gave her head a bemused shake as she walked back to her desk.

"You can go in now," Dr. Trainer said.

"Nell's okay?"

"Stubborn and ornery, but yes, she's okay."

"I can hear you," Nell's gruff, albeit weak, response came from behind the door.

Dr. Trainer grinned, lowering his voice. "She's something, isn't she?"

"She sure is." Madison's smile faltered as she stepped into the room. Nell, attached to the tubes and the bleeping machines by her bed, looked tiny and frail, and every day of her seventy-six years.

Madison forced the smile back to her lips as she pulled a chair from under the window to the side of the bed. "Don't play with that. You just about gave me a heart attack," she said when Nell raised a finger to the oxygen tube in her nose.

Nell pulled a grumpy face, but did as Madison asked. "Don't even joke about having a heart attack. Believe me, they're no fun."

"Tell me about it. I was there, remember?" Madison gently pushed a strand of Nell's red-streaked hair from the bump on her forehead and winced. "I'm sorry I thought you were faking. At least I could've stopped you from falling."

"No, that's on me. If I hadn't pulled a fast one on you after the town hall meeting, you would have. I'm the one who should be apologizing. You lost your job because of me." Her eyes met Madison's. "I'm real sorry about that, Maddie. I've learned my lesson. No more interfering for me."

Somehow, Madison didn't believe her, about the interfering part, anyway. She placed her hand over Nell's, careful to avoid the narrow plastic tubing. "Harrison firing me had nothing to do with you. Like I told you, he's been trying to get rid of me from the start. Really, it's for the best. I couldn't work under him." But she would have, at least until she found another job.

"You don't like him much, do you?"

"No. I don't trust him, and I don't like the way he does business."

"Then why don't you want to stay and stop him?"

"Because, Nell, you and everyone else in town want him to build the resort." She glanced at the lines on the screen. "We shouldn't be talking about this. There's nothing I can do about it, anyway. I'm sure everything will work out." She was pretty sure it wouldn't, but Nell didn't need to hear that now.

Nell weakly waved her hand, and one of the machines beeped. Madison jumped. "What's that? Are you all right... Are you in pain? I'll get the—"

"Calm down. I feel better now than I have for the last while. It's just this thingie here." She pointed to her finger with the clip on it. "The machine squawks whenever I move my hand. Besides, we need to talk about this. It'll bug me, and that can't be good for my—"

"Oh, no you don't," Madison interrupted her. "You're not pulling that on me."

"What? It's the truth. You're smart, and if you don't think the resort will get off the ground, it won't. And there is something we can do to stop Harrison. We'll ask Ethan to put the resort to a vote. You've got some good ideas how to turn the town around. You just have to get them out there."

"I do, but I don't think I'll be able to convince anyone, at least not enough of them to win out over the resort."

"You convinced me, didn't you?"

Madison nodded and smiled. "I guess I did, didn't I?" Joe had believed all along that it was Nell who was the key to turning around the publicity nightmare. And the thought of beating Harrison at his own game held a certain amount of poetic justice. Best of all, Madison would have a chance to save Christmas…and Joe. After five years of friendship, despite how she'd been treated, she couldn't let him go broke. She knew Harrison didn't have the funds to buy Hartwell outright, and if the company went down, so would Joe.

"So, is it a deal?" From the self-satisfied look in her eyes, Nell already knew the answer.

"Yes." Madison stood up. "I guess if I'm going to do this, I'd better get busy."

"I'll call Ethan. Have him put the vote on the agenda. Harrison's flying in the morning of the twenty-fourth, so that gives us a little over a week to get enough people on our side to vote your plan in."

"Oh, no, you don't. I'm going to take care of this, not you. You're going to take it easy and get better. Ted and Fred will help me." At the doubtful look in Nell's eyes, Madison said, "Trust me, I can handle it." She tucked the sheets under Nell's chin and kissed her cheek. "You rest. I'll check on you later."

"You're not going soft on me, are you?"

"Not a chance." But as Madison left Nell's room, she thought she just might be. It was the only way to explain why she'd agreed to stay in Christmas and launch a campaign against Hartwell. She was jobless, staying in a small town where everyone knew your name and your business, and she'd never felt happier.

Chapter Nineteen

Gage stood in the hall down from Nell's room, warding off his father's probing fingers. "Dad, stop, I'm fine." A millimeter in and he wouldn't have been, but he was. And thankfully, so was everyone else.

Gage had almost talked Johnny, the guy holding a gun on the store owner and his employees, into giving up, when one of the young girls made a run for it. Johnny had panicked, aiming the gun at her, prepared to shoot. Gage dove for the girl, shielding her with his body while one of the deputies fired on Johnny. The bullet from Johnny's gun whistled past Gage's head, taking a bit of skin as it went by.

"If you won't let me check you out, at least let Matt have a look," his father said, as he leaned in to peer at Gage's forehead, straining to keep his fingers to himself. "You can never be too careful with head wounds."

Gage reined in his frustration. "Dad, it's not a head

wound. I took a look at it and so did the paramedics. I'm good to go."

"You see this?" His father tugged on a couple strands of gray hair. "This is what you and your brothers have done to me. Why couldn't the three of you find jobs where you don't get shot at every day?"

Gage didn't bother to point out that at sixty-two his father should have a head full of gray hair instead of the silver wings at his temples. "Come on, I've been shot at once in two years." His brothers, Chance and Easton, were a different story, but he wasn't going to go there now.

He suspected his father would, but instead, he looked over Gage's shoulder with a gotcha smile.

Madison's voice came from behind him. "What's going on?"

Gage turned, catching the look of concern in her eyes as she walked toward them in her shapeless black suit with her hair scraped back from her pale face. He really hated that suit. It reminded him that she planned to leave. His over-the-top reaction upon hearing the news earlier had been about as surprising as the bullet whizzing by his head.

"Nothing," he said at the same time his dad said, "Gage got shot."

Her eyes widened as she rushed to his side. "Are you all right?" She searched his face, gently touching just below the abraded skin with the tips of her fingers. "What happened there?" Before he had a chance to explain, her eyes conducted a full-body search. "Where did you get shot?"

"In the head," his father said.

Gage groaned. "For chrissakes, Dad. I wasn't shot. The bullet grazed my head, that's all." He closed his hand over hers. "I'm fine. But how are you? How's Nell?"

"I'm good, and your aunt is much better than I expected." Her gaze flitted back to his forehead then to his dad. "Is he really okay? Did you examine him?"

He gave Gage a smug look. "No, he won't let me. Maybe you can talk some sense into him."

Not going to happen. "I'm checking on Nell, and then I'm taking Madison home." He walked toward his aunt's room, shaking his head in exasperation when he heard his father outlining his concerns to Madison in graphic detail.

His frustration was replaced by an uncomfortable tightness in his chest at the sight of Nell asleep in the hospital bed. The only time he'd ever seen her this quiet and pale was when she'd faked being hit by Madison's SUV. He wished she was faking now.

As though she sensed his presence, her eyes blinked open. He went to the side of the bed, leaning over the rail to kiss her cheek. "You scared the hell of out of me, you know."

She patted his face. "I'm not going anywhere yet. I plan on being around for a good long while."

"I'm counting on it." At times she drove him crazy, but he didn't want to think what life would be like without her. "I'm going to talk to dad about you moving in with one of us once you're released."

She frowned. "Why would I do that? Maddie's staying with me."

From his earlier conversation with Madison, Gage knew she'd told his aunt she was heading back to New York. But maybe Nell had forgotten—understandable, given what she'd been through.

"Why are you looking at me like that? Don't you believe she's staying with me?"

He wanted to, and not just for his aunt's sake. He'd real-ized when Madison told him she was leaving how much he wanted her to stay. She drove him as crazy as Nell, but more in an I'm-so-hot-for-her-I-can't-think-straight kind of way. He wanted more time with her, time alone with her, time to make sure she knew what she was getting into. And thanks to today, she had something else to think about…he had a job that put his life on the line.

He glanced at the monitor as he took Nell's hand in his. "Madison was fired today. Once she knows you're okay, she's heading back to New York to look for a job."

"Why are you talking to me like I'm an idiot? I had a heart attack. I didn't lose my marbles. I know she got fired. And if you ask me, that Harrison fella is a damn fool letting her go. She's sharp as a tack, and if she says the resort's not going to fly, it isn't. What the Sam Hill is wrong with Joe Hartwell letting his nephew get rid of her?"

The line on the screen spiked. Gage was as mad as Nell at how the Hartwells had treated Madison, but before he could do anything about it, he had to calm his aunt down. "Let's not talk about this now. You need your rest."

"Well, you mark my words, they're going to regret let-ting her go now that she's working for us."

"What exactly do you mean, working for us?" Gage said slowly, not sure he wanted to know.

"Didn't Madison tell you? Me and her have a plan. We're going to turn Christmas around. We just have to get the rest of the town on board."

Aw, hell, he'd rather have ten guys taking potshots at him then deal with Madison and Nell plotting against Hartwell. The old saying "Be careful what you wish for…" came to mind.

*   *   *

"I hope you're satisfied now," Gage muttered, his hand at the small of Madison's back as they made their way from his father's office to the bank of elevators.

"You don't have to be so grumpy about it. It only took—" she glanced at her watch "—forty-five minutes for your dad to check you out." Which seemed a little excessive, even to her. Not that she'd share her opinion with Gage. It had taken ten minutes of pleading and cajoling just to get him to agree to the exam. She hadn't realized how stubborn the man could be. And until today, she hadn't realized how dangerous his job was. How if the bullet had…

"Right, forty-five minutes to check out a scrape on my head." He blew out a frustrated breath. "Ever since my mom died, he's been paranoid. If you get so much as a scratch, he's sure it's going to turn into a flesh-eating disease."

"That's sad. You should humor him."

"Believe me, in the beginning we did. But after nine years, it's wearing a little thin."

The elevator doors opened, and he nudged her inside. She waited impatiently for the doors to close. At the sight of Gage in the hall—looking big and strong in his uniform—all she'd wanted to do was run into his arms, but she knew how he felt about PDA. Finding out he'd been shot had only made it harder to hold herself back.

As the doors closed, she moved into him, wrapping her arms around his waist to rest her cheek on his chest. She listened to the steady drumbeat of his heart, breathing in his familiar scent of clean mountain air and leather. His arms went around her.

"I've wanted to do this since I saw you outside Nell's room. I need a minute, okay?"

He smiled into her hair. "Sure, anything you need. You've had a real crappy day, haven't you?"

She leaned back to look up at him. "I didn't think it could get much worse, then your dad said you were shot. Do you get shot at often?"

His chest expanded on a sigh as he set her away from him. "Not often, but it happens. Are you having second thoughts?"

It wasn't exactly the answer she'd been hoping for, but she'd rather deal with the worry than not have him in her life. He wasn't the type of man to take unnecessary risks. He was solid and dependable. And thankfully, Christmas was a small town where guys holding hostages at gunpoint wasn't an everyday occurrence. "No, I'm not having second thoughts."

"Glad to hear it." He smiled down at her as the elevator stopped, then said hello to the elderly couple who waited for them to get off. Once he'd patiently answered their questions about Nell, he'd walked Madison to the front doors of the hospital, leaving her inside while he brought the truck around.

With the arctic air whipping the snow across the parking lot, she'd appreciated his thoughtfulness, but seeing the man stomping the snow from his boots just outside the doors, now, not so much.

As Rick Dane entered the hospital, his basset-hound brown eyes fastened on her like she was a juicy rabbit. "Ms. Lane, just the person I was hoping to see."

"Mr. Dane, what can I do for you?"

He took a pad of paper and a pen from his jacket pocket. "Thought you might like to make a comment before I put my story to bed."

She glanced out the glass doors and contemplated making a run for it. She vetoed the idea when an image of her sliding across the ice-slicked blacktop on her butt came to mind. "About what?"

"The fact you were fired this morning and are no longer an employee of Hartwell Enterprises."

Her jaw dropped. How had he found out so quickly? *Harrison.* She should've realized from the beginning that Dane was his contact. No wonder the man was doing his best to make her look like an idiot in the paper. Harrison had been trying to discredit her and undermine her all along, and he'd found the perfect person to do his dirty work. But she couldn't let news of her firing become public knowledge. If it did, her chances of finding a job would be slim to none.

Dane smirked as she struggled to come up with a response, but her response hinged on Joe. In between worrying about Gage, she'd come up with a way to minimize the impact her leaving Hartwell would have on her job prospects.

And Dane was about to ruin everything.

She was counting on Joe to, at the very least, give her a letter of reference, even better, to publicly announce she'd resigned and wish her well.

In her panic, she didn't realize Gage had parked in front of the hospital and was on his way in until he opened the door and said, "Everything all right here?" With one look at what she imagined was her deer-caught-in-the-headlights expression, his eyes narrowed on Dane. "Madison, get in the truck."

There were times when Gage's overprotective, alpha-male attitude drove her nuts, but this wasn't one of them. He held the door open, and she ducked under his arm, leaving a protesting Dane behind.

A few minutes later, Gage—on his cell—strode to the Suburban. Whoever he spoke to was getting an earful. "Yeah, well maybe you should tell her that." He handed her the phone as he shut his door. "It's Hartwell," he said as though the name left a bad taste in his mouth. "Senior."

"Joe?"

"Madison, I'm so sorry. I had no idea what was going on until Sheriff McBride called me."

Funny, and not in an LOL kind of way. She'd been trying to get in touch with him for days, yet he answered Gage's call right away. With his eyes on the road, Gage pulled out of the lot. Madison stroked the backs of her fingers over the muscle that ticked in his jaw. He gave her a sidelong glance. *Thank you,* she mouthed.

He turned his head, brushing his lips over her fingers while his eyes remained focused on the road. If she hadn't already fallen for the man, the way he'd looked out for her just now would've guaranteed she did. She lowered her hand, placing it on his thigh.

"Madison?"

"Sorry, Joe. When you say you didn't know what was going on, are you referring to the reopening of the deal with Christmas or Harrison firing me?"

After several beats of silence, Joe answered, "I had some idea the deal would be reopened once I stepped down, but I had no idea Harrison planned to fire you." His voice was tight with anger. "I'll take care of it right away. As far as anyone will know, you tendered your resignation today." She noticed he didn't say he'd insist she be rehired, not that she'd accept, but it would've been nice if he'd made the offer.

"That'll be difficult to pull off, Joe, seeing as how word has already been leaked to the press here."

He cleared his throat. "I'll find out how that happened. But from what Sheriff McBride said, that's no longer an issue."

Gage laid his hand over hers, nudging it lower. *Oops.* Aggravated with Joe, she must've been rubbing Gage's leg, her hand creeping higher.

"Safer that way." He winked, then returned his attention to the slowing traffic up ahead.

She tried to ignore the heated flutter in her stomach to focus on what Joe just said. "What was that? We must have a bad connection."

Gage snorted a laugh, then choked on it when she slid her hand higher, lightly squeezing his upper thigh. Her smile faded as she realized she'd missed Joe's response, again. What was wrong with her? Here she was having what very well could be the most important conversation of her life, and she was too busy flirting with Gage to pay attention. Nothing had ever been more important to her than her job at Hartwell.

"...I'm sure it wasn't intentional. I've been distracted and not keeping up with things as I should have. When I didn't hear from you, I assumed Harrison had updated you, and you were on board with the plans."

She didn't bother asking what he'd said prior to her tuning back in; she'd heard enough. Harrison hadn't forwarded her messages. "No, he didn't. And I...Joe, I know you're going through a tough time right now, but we've worked together for five years. I think you at least owed me the courtesy of telling me you were stepping down. I shouldn't have had to hear it from a reporter."

"What do you mean you heard it from a reporter? I was going to call you yesterday, once we got Martha settled at home. But Harrison said he was afraid you'd hear about it secondhand and told you himself." Joe sounded upset and confused.

Harrison was worse than she'd thought. None of this was Joe's fault. "It's all right. I feel better knowing you'd planned to tell me yourself. And I'm happy to hear Martha will be home for Christmas."

"I don't know if she'll make it to Christmas. But she wanted to be home when..." He blew his nose.

"Oh, Joe, I'm so sorry. I wish there was something I could do." She leaned against the headrest. Gage entwined his fingers with hers.

"I'm sorry how things worked out, Madison. I'm going to miss you. I couldn't have asked for a better employee. If you'd like, I can give Ben over at Triwest a call. He's always threatening to steal you away from me."

"Thanks, I'd appreciate that. I'm going to miss you, too." She was close to tears and took a moment, swallowing hard before she said, "Take care, Joe."

"You too. And, Madison?"

"Yes."

"I've been following your exploits in the *Chronicle*." She groaned, and Joe chuckled. "You look different, more relaxed, happier. Maybe in the end this is for the best, Madison. The last few years you've buried yourself in your work. Not that I'm complaining, but life's too short not to live it."

He didn't need to tell her that, not after today. Nell and Gage were proof to her of how quickly life could change. If Nell had been alone, if the bullet had veered just a little to the left... "You're right, Joe, maybe it is for the best."

"In light of how this all played out, you may not believe me. But if I had a daughter, I'd have wanted her to be just like you." His breath hitched and so did her heart. "Do an old man a favor—enjoy your life for a change."

Her throat was tight, and it took a moment before she could speak. "I will. And Joe, give Martha my love. Please let me know..."

In the background someone called his name. "That's Martha's nurse. I have to go. Keep in touch, Madison."

"I will. Bye, Joe."

Gage gave her hand a comforting squeeze. "Tough call, huh?"

"Real tough. But I'm glad I finally got a chance to speak with him. Thanks again for making that happen." She leaned over and pressed her lips to the corner of his mouth.

He drew her close and kissed the top of her head. "Do you want to talk about it?"

"Maybe later." At the moment, she couldn't talk about Joe without crying. But she felt better knowing she was as important to him as he was to her. She was more determined to stop Harrison than ever. Joe needed to be protected.

She frowned when they turned onto Gage's street. "I thought you were taking me to Nell's."

He raised a brow. "I will if you want me to."

"No. It'd be nice to spend some time with Annie and Lily."

"How about spending time with me? The girls are having dinner with Liz. Dad's going to pick them up later."

A ray of sunshine broke through the clouds, and Madison swore she heard a choir of angels singing *Hallelujah*. She joined the chorus.

Chapter Twenty

Gage's plan to get Madison out of her clothes and into his bed as soon as they entered his house had faded with the loud rumble of her stomach and her reluctant admission that the last things she'd eaten were two candy canes the night before.

He leaned against the island, watching as she devoured the grilled cheese sandwich he'd made for her, along with half of his. Every second bite, she'd close her eyes and make this soft humming sound that drove him crazy.

She dabbed her mouth with a napkin. Finally, she was finished. Then her gaze shifted to the chocolate cake sitting on the center of the island. The one Holly had dropped off yesterday. The one he should have hidden.

"You want a piece, huh?"

She rewarded him with that wide smile he couldn't resist. "Yes, please."

Taking a knife from the drawer, he drew the cake toward

him. He made the first cut, then moved the blade over a couple of inches. "A little more," she said.

He widened the slice. "Okay?"

"Maybe just a teensy bit more." She spread her thumb and forefinger a good six inches.

Gage sighed, put the knife down and pushed the cake, platter and all, in front of her. "Have at it."

"I've had a real crappy day, you know," she said, as if to explain her need for a chocolate transfusion. She slid a piece in her mouth. Closing her eyes, she did the humming thing again.

"You're killing me." He groaned, rounding the island to stand behind her.

But she was right. She'd had a crappy day. The last thing she needed was for him to rush her into bed. She deserved a little pampering. And at least he'd get to touch her while he doled out some tender, loving care.

Smiling, she tipped her head back. "Just a couple more bites, promise."

He leaned over to kiss her chocolate-coated lips. "Take your time. We've got all day."

"Umm, I like the sound of that."

"Me too." He removed the pins from her hair, combing his fingers through the thick, soft waves and gently began to knead her scalp.

She moaned her appreciation.

He smiled, reminded of the time at the station when she'd done the same. He lowered his hands to her shoulders, massaging the rigid band with his fingers.

"Oh, God, that feels so good." She put down the fork and bowed her head. "Don't stop."

"You have too many clothes on."

"You're right, I do." She started to undo her jacket.

"I have a better idea. Come on." He took her by the hand, leading her through the living room, then down the hall to the bedrooms. Flipping on the light, he entered the first room with its over-the-top feminine décor of white leather, hot-pink satin bedding, and mirrored furniture.

"Ah, you have a real...pretty bedroom." She grimaced.

Gage laughed. "It's not my room. It's..." Maybe this wasn't such a good idea after all. He cleared his throat. "Sheena's. I thought some time in the hot tub would do you good. The dresser's packed with clothes she never wears, including bathing suits. You can take whatever you want," he rambled on as he pulled open the top drawer.

Frozen in the doorway, she stared at him. "Your wife...This is your wife's room?"

He heard the accusation in her voice and knew he had some explaining to do. Given her past, Madison would never want to be seen as the other woman in a man's life, let alone be that woman. "It's not what it looks like."

Eyes narrowed, she crossed her arms. "Really? Maybe you'd better explain what it is."

"Look." He went to her, framing her face with his hands. "Sheena stays here when she visits the girls. She doesn't get to spend a lot of time with them, and this makes it easier." On them, but not always on him. "I didn't want to disrupt their routine when they were little. This works for everyone."

When Annie and Lily were younger, he liked to be around. It wasn't that he didn't trust Sheena with the girls, she just wasn't the motherly type. He'd always worried if he wasn't there to keep an eye on things, something would happen. And the easier he made it, the less likely Sheena'd want them to visit her in Nashville.

"I bet it does," Madison muttered.

He knew her well enough to realize that unless Madison believed him, this was a deal breaker. "Trust me, there's nothing between Sheena and me." It was the truth, but not the complete truth.

There'd been that one night last February when neither he nor his ex were involved with anyone, and they'd shared a couple of bottles of wine, reminiscing about happier times. He wasn't sure which it was, reliving the old memories, the warm buzz from the wine, or if he was just lonely at the time. But whatever the reason, he'd made a mistake, a big one.

"That's not true. You have two children together and that creates a strong and *lasting* bond."

"Yeah, we do. But we've been divorced for a long time, and I don't love her. If I did, you wouldn't be here right now." That was the truth, and in his mind, all that really mattered. "I think you know me well enough by now to know I'm not a man who would cheat on his wife or someone I love."

Her blue eyes cold and assessing, Madison remained silent, which surprised and pissed him off at the same time. Shoving his hands in his pockets, he took a step back. He didn't deserve her censure. "You know what? I've had a crappy day, too. I'll be in the hot tub if you want to join me."

He strode from the room, then stopped to look back at her. "If you don't trust me, let's not take this any further. I want more from you than sex, no matter how fucking fantastic I know it would be. There's a set of spare keys on the hook in the kitchen for the Range Rover. It's in the garage. I'll send someone by to pick it up later."

Her eyes widened. Yeah, he thought, as he stalked to his bedroom, he was a guy, a horny, pissed-off guy who wanted to get laid. He shouldn't give a damn if the woman who got him hard just looking at her, just thinking about her, didn't trust him.

But he did.

*   *   *

Madison had stood in stupefied silence for a couple of minutes after Gage had delivered his trust-me-or-leave ultimatum. Once she'd recovered, well, she'd started to laugh. She put her inappropriate reaction down to a delayed form of shock. Because really, who got fired, had a woman they care about almost die in front of them, and a man they were falling for get shot at, all in one fricking day. Maybe God was trying to get her attention and thought she needed a triple whammy to get it. He'd got it all right.

And the window that opened when the door closed... felt like it was on the twenty-third floor with no safety net below. She wasn't stupid. She'd heard the message often enough from Skye, and more recently Joe. Now she had to decide if she had the guts to take the leap.

Gage made her want to. His admission he wanted more from her than just sex was most likely the cause of her earlier giddiness, because she felt the same. It wasn't fair to put her issues on him or to let them come between them. She'd overreacted because of her past. It was hers to wear, not his. He hadn't done anything wrong. She did trust him, completely.

Tightening the belt on the white, terry-cloth robe she'd

found hanging in the en suite bathroom, unsure if she'd have the nerve to take it off, Madison stepped out of the bedroom. The itsy-bitsy starred-and-striped bikini, with diamond-encrusted—she hoped to God they were fake—American flags holding the material together between her breasts and at either side of her hips, was not something Madison would've chosen for herself. She'd realized two things when she stuffed herself in the bikini. One, Gage's ex-wife was a size two, and how unfair was that? And two, the only thing she had in common with the woman was their taste in men.

Madison opened the French doors off the living room to step onto the deck. As much as the frigid, pine-scented air stole her breath, so did the view. The majestic mountains towering above the pristine snow-covered valley and spruce forest filled her with a sense of reverence. Up until that moment, she'd thought there was nothing more beautiful than the city vistas from her twenty-third-floor apartment window.

At the opposite end of the deck, a cloud of steam floated over the cedar rails. She wrapped her arms around her waist and headed in that direction. Rounding the corner, she stopped short. The winter wonderland had nothing on the man sitting in the hot tub, his dark hair slicked back from his chiseled profile. Through wisps of steam, his bare shoulders glistened, the muscles in his arm flexing as he tipped a bottle of beer to his mouth. As if someone had shocked her heart with a defibrillator, a heated jolt jagged through her.

Sweet baby Jesus.

She must've made a sound, maybe a needy moan, because he slowly turned his head. Embarrassed at being caught stunned stupid, she speed-walked the last eight feet. Before she could think about it, she shed the robe.

He spewed a mouthful of beer.

"Not a word." She grimaced at the color of the leg she lifted over the side of the tub. Whereas Gage looked like he'd been sitting on a beach for a week, she was so white she practically glowed.

"Can't talk," he choked out, setting his beer in the molded holder to help her in.

She groaned with pleasure as she slid beneath the hot, bubbling water.

Gage shook his head as though to clear it, then tugged her between his legs, pressing her back to his broad chest. She relaxed against him, absorbing the feel of being enveloped in all that glorious muscle and heat.

"I think my heart stopped," he said.

She reached back, threading her fingers in his hair to bring his face to hers. "No joking about hearts. Kiss me."

"I think I can manage that." Looking into her eyes, he fused his lips to hers.

She rested her head against his shoulder, reveling in the feel of his attentive mouth, in the thought they could stay cocooned in the warm water while the cold winds danced over the snow for however long they wanted without interruption.

Forever worked for her.

He kissed his way down the side of her neck to reach the sensitive place at her shoulder. He lingered there, tasting and nipping. She moaned, moving against him as her pent-up desire swirled higher inside her.

His arm around her waist tightened as his hand stroking her stomach stilled. "Careful," he said, his voice a muffled rumble as he kissed his way back up her neck to her ear. "We're going to take this slow and easy."

"What if I told you I want it fast and hard?"

A gust of surprised laughter warmed her ear. "Don't worry, I plan to give you exactly what you want. But right now, we're doing it my way."

She didn't want to admit it, but his take-charge attitude turned her on. She shifted in his lap, trying to bring her legs over his.

He brought both hands to her waist, widening his legs to tuck her more securely between them. "Now," he said, "why don't you sit back and relax, and I'll take care of that tension for you? But I think we should get rid of this first."

Before she had a chance to react, he'd unclipped the flag, sliding the narrow straps from her shoulders. The starred-and-striped bikini top floated along with the bubbles to the other side of the tub. "Oh," she gasped, crossing her arm over her chest.

"Honey, trust me, those scraps of material weren't hiding much of you anyway."

"It was the biggest swimsuit I could find," she grumbled. "I think your wife's anorexic."

"Ex-wife. And no, she's not." He smoothed her hair from her face, then kissed her temple. "You have nothing to be embarrassed about." Drawing her arm from her chest, he lightly stroked her breasts. "You're perfect."

She wasn't, but he made her feel like she was. She resisted the urge to cover herself by pressing her hands between her legs and taking in the scenery. A gust of wind blew two bluebirds from their perch in the evergreen beside the deck. "This is incredible. You have an amazing view."

"Yeah, I do." There was something in his voice that made her glance back. His eyes were on her, a tantalizing promise in his heated gaze.

"I'm serious."

"So am I."

"How long have you lived here?"

"Eight years. We broke ground the day we found out we were expecting Lily."

She tipped her head back. "You built this place yourself?"

"I contracted out some of it. But yeah, for the most part, I did."

"Guess your dad wasn't kidding when he said you're good with your hands. You're not just a pretty face, are you?"

"Why don't I show you just how good I am?" He kissed the sensitive place below her ear as his calloused hands worked their way through every knot in her shoulders, then moved up her neck to do the same. Slowly the tension left her body, and his fingers gentled. Instead of kneading and massaging, they now stroked and caressed.

"You're not going to sleep on me, are you?"

"Maybe." Drowsily, she lifted her arms, looping them behind his neck.

He groaned.

Her eyes blinked open, and she glanced down. Her breasts were lifted above the water, the cool air tightening her nipples. She went to lower her arms.

"Oh, no, you don't." His strong fingers wrapped around both her wrists, holding her in place. "Stay just like that, honey."

"You need to kiss me." She tilted her head to give him better access.

"Yeah, I do." He lowered his mouth to hers, his hands moving over her body in slow, mind-numbing strokes.

She needed to feel closer to him and lowered her arms. Resting a hand on his thigh, she repositioned herself on his lap. "Better," she murmured, linking her fingers behind his neck.

"Much." He put his arm around her waist, tipping her backward with the force of his insistent, hungry kiss, a wild clash of tongues and teeth as they devoured each other in a passionate frenzy. Their hands searching and touching as the desire they'd kept bottled up inside exploded.

"Now," Gage rasped, "we do it your way." He lifted her easily, rising from the water. She gasped as the cold air nipped her naked body—her completely naked body.

Eyes wide, she looked up at him. "I'm naked."

He grinned, a flash of white teeth. "No one can see you."

"What about Rick Dane?" she asked with a panicked gesture at the wide-open vista. "He could be out there with a telescopic lens."

"He wouldn't do that." But she noticed he scanned the tree line before opening the French doors that led into a masculine-looking room with a massive sleigh bed on dark wood floors, a big-screen TV suspended above a fieldstone fireplace on the opposite wall.

He pulled back the brown-suede duvet, tossing her into the middle of the cool cotton sheets. Following her down, he rested a hand on her hip as he reached across her to open the drawer of the bedside table. She snuggled against him, trying to absorb his warmth. "Maybe you could light the fire," she suggested hopefully.

Ripping open the condom wrapper with his teeth, he

grinned. "Honey, the only fire you're going to need is the one I light in you."

He was right.

*   *   *

Madison shoved her hair from her sweat-dampened face. "Oh, God, that was…great." It was better than great; it was incredible, amazing, earth-shattering. But she was afraid to wax poetic in case it only seemed that way because of her lack of experience.

He raised himself on an elbow. "That's all you got? I was thinking more on the lines of fan-freaking-tastic, incredible, earth-moving."

"Oh, good, I thought it was just me. I don't have a lot of experience so I wasn't sure you'd felt the same."

"What you do mean by not a lot?"

She probably shouldn't have blurted that out. Her cheeks warmed. "Um, eight times."

He looked like the number surprised him, which didn't surprise her. But he quickly smoothed the expression from his face and smiled. "You don't have to be embarrassed. You're almost thirty, I expected you to have been with a few men."

With an affronted huff, she said, "Times, Gage."

He rubbed his jaw. "Okay, let me get this straight. Are you saying you've only had sex eight times?" At the incredulous look in his eyes, she suddenly felt ridiculously naive and exposed.

"Yes. And you know what," she sat up, wrapping the sheet around her, "I don't think this is an appropriate conversation for us to be having. I'm going to take a shower."

She shimmied toward the end of the bed. Gage took hold of the sheet and reeled her back in. She scowled at him. "Come on, don't be mad. You can't tell me you've only had sex eight times and not expect me to be a little surprised."

"Surprised, maybe, but not shocked. You make me feel like a—"

"I'm sorry." He stroked her cheek. "I didn't mean to embarrass you. But it's obviously an issue with you, honey. I just thought it'd help if we talked about it."

"While we're on the subject, why don't we analyze your sex life too. How many women have you slept with, Mr. Sexpert?"

The corner of his mouth twitched. "Not as many as you seem to think, but it's nice to know I get expert ranking in your books."

"Since I've only been with one man, I don't... Why are you looking at me like that? I told you I only had sex..." She made an annoyed sound at the back of her throat. "You thought I slept once with eight different men, didn't you?" He rubbed his hand over his mouth. "Don't bother trying to hide it. I know you're laughing at me."

"I'm not laughing at you, honest. You're just so damn adorable when you get mad. You make me smile."

Slightly mollified, she said. "Okay. And for the record, I have very good reasons for being somewhat inexperienced. One of which is I don't do the 'friends with benefits' thing. In my opinion, women are hardwired differently than men, and we attach emotions to sex." She thought of some of the women she worked with at Hartwell. "Well, most women anyway. I met Michael when I was twenty-five. We dated for three months before we... you know."

His brow raised. "Three months?"

"Yes, it takes three months for a person to drop their masks and reveal their true selves. I don't have sex unless I feel the man is someone I want a long-term relationship with. So you can understand why, given my criteria, I haven't had a lot of experience, sexually speaking."

He rubbed his hand over his mouth again. "That's a real interesting theory you've got there, honey, but *we* haven't known each other for three months."

Dammit. When would she learn to keep her mouth shut? "I made an exception in your case," she said primly, then added, "I'm going to have my shower now."

This time, he didn't try to hide his smile. "Oh, no, you don't." He rolled her into his arms, bringing them nose-to-nose. "This is getting real interesting now. Let me guess, you can't resist a guy with a big gun." She narrowed her eyes at him, and he struggled to keep a straight face. "No? Okay, let me see—"

I fell in love with you, you big jerk. She interrupted him. "I forgot my rabbit at home and—"

"You're so full of it," he laughed. "Admit it. It was love at first sight."

"Yeah, that's it exactly," she tried for a light and teasing tone. She didn't want him to know there was an element of truth there. "And you're easy on the eyes, Sheriff."

"So are you." He smiled, holding her hair back to nuzzle her neck.

She shivered. "You can do that again."

"I will, but while you were talking to Joe, I was thinking about something and wanted to run it by you."

She angled her head. "Okay, shoot."

He hesitated, looking a bit unsure of himself, which

surprised her. Gage McBride was one of the most confident, self-assured men she'd ever met.

"I've made it pretty clear how I feel about doing the long-distance thing, so I was thinking now that you're no longer with Hartwell, you might consider relocating."

"Ah, where?" A hint of the south crept in her voice as the nerves in her stomach did a dance.

"I love that Southern drawl of yours, but you don't have to be nervous. I was just going to make you an offer. No pressure." He brought his hands to her shoulders, kneading the muscles that were beginning to tighten up again. "I don't have many contacts in New York, but I do in Denver. So do my Dad and Ethan. I'm sure between the three of us, we can come up with a list of people and make some calls for you. That is if you're interested. I know how you feel—"

She placed a finger on his lips. "Thank you. I appreciate the offer, but—"

He exhaled deeply. "It's okay. I know you love New York and aren't too crazy about hanging out in small towns. I just thought..." He shrugged.

"I might not be crazy about small towns, but I've discovered a few things in Christmas that I really, really like." She smiled up at him. "And about all that's keeping me in New York are my friends. But Skye's hardly there anymore, and Vivi, I don't know, she might be up for a change."

"So you're seriously giving it some thought?" He looked stunned. She didn't know if that was a good sign or a bad sign.

Here it goes, she thought, taking a leap of faith. "I

seriously am. Joe's putting in a word for me with one of our competitors. Ben, at Triwest, is an old friend of his and has shown some interest in me in the past. His head-quarters are in Denver." She talked slowly, enunciating the words carefully in an effort to keep her drawl at bay. It didn't work.

Gage grinned. "You're really nervous about this, aren't you?"

"Yeah. Tense, too. Maybe you could work on that for me." She smiled, but it was a little forced because she felt kind of sick to her stomach.

"Don't be scared. If things don't work out with Triwest, and we have to do the long-distance thing, we will. But it's tough, if not almost impossible, to make it work. And I want to give us a shot, a real shot." He leaned over and kissed her, swallowing her "Me too."

"Now, why don't I take care of that tension for you?"

Blissfully tension-free after Gage fulfilled his promise a couple times over, Madison curled into him. If this was how good taking a leap of faith felt, she should've done it a long time ago. But then again, she'd never been in love with a man worth taking the risk for.

Chapter Twenty-one

"Knock off the attitude, Annie," Gage said, as he pulled the Suburban into his aunt's driveway. And attitude was all he'd been getting from his oldest for the last few days. Ever since she'd caught him kissing Madison in the kitchen.

With Nell in the hospital and his dad back at work, Madison had been looking after Annie and Lily for him. Gage hadn't realized until then how much he'd missed having a woman in his life—especially a woman who made him laugh, who was great with his girls even though Annie was being a pain in the ass. And that was one of the reasons he'd taken the day off: he wanted Annie to get used to seeing him with Madison.

"We're going to have a great time," he said firmly. As he unbuckled his seat belt, he caught Annie's eye roll in the rearview mirror.

Gage shifted in his seat. "Madison's looking forward

to picking out a Christmas tree. She's never had one before." And that conversation just about broke his heart. They'd been talking about the holidays while doing the dishes last night and, with some effort on his part, he got her to open up. "You don't want to spoil her fun, do you?"

When Annie wasn't acting like a grizzly with her paw caught in a trap, she was a sweet and caring kid. He saw a hint of that in her eyes just before she shrugged and notched her chin at the lime-green pickup parked in the driveway beside him. "Why can't Ted and Fred take her?"

Because Gage wanted to.

Before he thought of a way to say that to Annie without getting her back up, Lily piped in, "Daddy, how come Maddie never had a Christmas tree?"

He went with the easy answer. "Some people don't celebrate Christmas, sweetpea."

"Lucky them," Annie muttered.

Gage didn't see it that way, not when he thought of Madison as a little girl, a little girl who'd once loved Christmas even though her dad never let her celebrate. And when her mother died on Christmas Eve, so did Madison's love for the holiday. Her time here seemed to have changed that. She'd become as much a champion of Christmas as his aunt, both the holiday and the town.

In the backseat, his daughters engaged in a heated exchange over the merits of celebrating Christmas.

"You're being a sh—" Lily cast him a sidelong glance "—poopyhead. You better be careful or Santa won't bring you any presents."

"There isn't—" Annie caught Gage's don't-even-think-about-it look "—such a word as *poopyhead*." He smiled. She smirked and added, "It's *shithead*."

"Aw, come on, you two, give me a break." He opened the glove compartment to dig out a couple of granola bars and tossed them each one. "No fighting. I won't be long."

Gage walked in to find Madison—wearing red flannel PJs with "Ho Ho Ho" imprinted on the butt—on her hands and knees in the living room. She was talking to Fred and Ted as she shuffled through reams of paper spread out on the floral-printed area rug.

The three of them looked up. "Oh, no." Her gaze shot to the cuckoo clock on the wall. "I didn't realize what time it was." She gave him a flustered smile. "Don't worry, it won't take me but a minute to get ready." Sitting back on her heels, she shoveled the papers in a folder. She came to her feet, handing off the file to Ted.

She walked to where Gage stood in the hall and stretched up on her toes. "Hi," she said, then glanced over her shoulder at Fred and Ted. Instead of the kiss she'd been about to give him, she patted the black, down-filled vest he wore over his sweater.

"Hi, yourself." He kissed her cheek, lingering as he savored the feel of her warm, soft skin.

Out of Fred and Ted's line of sight, Gage traced a finger over the buttons of her PJs. "I like your nightie better," he murmured.

"It was too cold to wear last night. But, if I had someone to keep me warm, I might be persuaded to wear it again," she whispered.

"Not fair."

Fred cleared his throat.

Gage took a step back, unable to keep the frustration from his voice. "'Morning, boys. What brings you around so early?"

Ted tapped his gnarled finger on the folder. "We're helping Maddie prepare for her presentation on Monday. She gets a half an hour and so does Hartwell. Vote's at noon."

"Vote?" Gage frowned. "When was this decided?"

"Last night," she said. "Ethan gave me the news when he drove Liz over to drop off the costumes."

It would've been nice if Ethan had given Gage a heads-up, seeing as how he'd be the one dealing with the fallout. Gage didn't know what was up with him, but his best friend seemed distracted lately.

"Good boy, that Ethan."

"Yeah, good-looking, too, just like his mother."

"Okay, you two, you're not funny," Gage said.

Madison fought back a smile.

"And you're absolutely sure he approved this?" Gage asked her. "Because there was nothing in the paper this morning, and it has to be publicized at least seventy-two hours in advance of the vote for the results to be legal." Maybe Ethan was looking for a way out after being put on the spot. Given Madison's last appearance at the town hall, Gage hoped to hell that was the case.

"Gage is right. You got a copy of this morning's paper, Maddie?" Fred asked.

"I'm sure Ethan said he'd call Rick and get the announcement in there." She frowned. "Today's edition is beside your chair, Fred. If the announcement isn't in there, can you give Ethan a call while I get changed? See what's going on?"

"Sure thing."

Distracted by the "Ho Ho Ho" on her butt as she walked away, Gage didn't bother reminding Madison he'd read the paper in its entirety, and the announcement wasn't there. He went to follow her. "It's cold out. I'll help you find—"

"Gage, Fred and I'd like a word with you," Ted called out.

"I'll be with you in a minute." After he had five alone with Madison.

In an overloud conversation, Fred and Ted started listing Ethan's many accomplishments. "Yeah, yeah, you've made your point," Gage muttered, glancing longingly after Madison before he headed for the living room. He took a seat on the couch. "What's up?"

Fred sat back in his chair and gave Ted a go-ahead nod.

"We want to know what your intentions are toward Maddie."

"You're kidding." Gage's laughter faded as their serious expressions remained firmly in place. "You're not kidding." His voice cracked.

"Nope, we're not. Maddie's got no family to look out for her, so we are."

Gage wondered what Madison would think of her self-appointed guardians. Touched, he supposed, and for that reason alone, he'd give them an answer. Only he had a hard time getting the words out. He'd always been a private person. More so after his life became fodder for the tabloids—the title song on Sheena's second album had skyrocketed to the top of the country music charts at the same time as their marriage imploded.

Ted stared him down while Fred impatiently beat a tattoo on the arm of the chair. Gage shifted uncomfortably on the couch. "What exactly do you mean by *intentions*?"

"I thought he was supposed to be smart. Graduated at the top of his class, didn't he?" Fred said to Ted.

Ted nodded. "I heard that, too. Maybe—"

"All right already," Gage cut him off. "We're dating. I care about her. She's important to me. I'd never do anything to hurt her, if that's what you're worried about."

The two men shared a look that said Gage wasn't the sharpest tool in the shed.

"Come on, give me a break. We're taking it slow. Her living in New York won't make it easy. But I told her Dad, Ethan, and I will make some calls for her, see if there might be something for her in Denver."

That perked their interest. They leaned forward in their chairs. "What'd she say?" Ted asked.

"She doesn't need our help, at least not yet. Joe Hartwell is talking to someone who might be interested in hiring her. Their home office is in Denver." He smiled, remembering their conversation, what she looked like while they were having it and what they'd been doing before and after.

The two men guffawed, then Ted said, "Okay."

"Okay? Okay, what?"

"You told us what we needed to know," Fred said.

"What did I say to make you change your minds?"

"It's not what you said." Ted grinned. "But we know now that you love her."

"I do. I mean, *I do*?" His voice jumped an octave. "What makes you say that?" It was something Gage needed to know so he could stop doing it right away. He didn't want to deal with Annie and the citizens of Christmas who might not be happy with his choice. He needed to take it slow. To get Annie used to the idea of him with Madison and not her mother. Give the folks in town a chance to know Madison better.

He worried that if news of their being together got out too soon, not only would he have to put up with a lot of crap, so would Madison. He'd been able to come up with a plausible explanation for the picture of him and Madison in the supply-closet—she'd been helping him get ready for his stint as Santa. At least Lily and Annie had bought it. But if anything else was printed about them, people would start getting suspicious. And the last thing Madison needed, given her past, was everyone ganging up on her.

"I'm ready," Madison said, putting an end to their conversation. Standing in the entrance to the living room in a pair of jeans and a blue sweater that matched her eyes, her gaze flitted to each of them. She frowned. "What's going on?"

"Nothing. We better get going, the girls are waiting." He wanted her out of there before Ted or Fred repeated their conversation.

The two men snorted, then Ted said, "You go on with Joe College. We'll get on the horn with Ethan, straighten everything out."

Madison, seemingly oblivious to his new nickname, kissed their cheeks before retrieving her coat from the hall closet.

Ted and Fred kept an eye on them as Gage helped her into a plaid jacket that looked a lot like his aunt's.

"You watch out for her, Gage. She's a city girl. They're not used to tromping through the woods."

"Fred's right," Ted agreed. "Maybe you should go on over to Charlie's. He has some mighty fine trees on the lot."

Madison held back a smile. Gage didn't have to. He wasn't smiling. "I'll take good care of her."

"Promises, promises," she murmured, wrapping a neon-green scarf around her neck.

Taking hold of either end of the scarf, he tugged her closer. "If I could get you alone for few minutes, I would."

"I wish." She sighed, shoving the hot pink, bunny-eared hat on her head.

He raised a brow at her get-up. Nothing matched, and she didn't seem to care. He flicked a bunny ear. "You're one of the most low-maintenance women I've ever met." And after living with one who wasn't, it was one more thing he appreciated about her.

"Mitts," the two men called from the living room.

"Aren't they adorable?" she laughed, following him out the door.

She was adorable. *They* were a pain in the ass.

*   *   *

An hour and a half later, Gage decided he should've listened to Ted and headed to Charlie's tree lot instead. His plan to spend an enjoyable morning with the three girls in his life had pretty much ended the moment he'd pulled out of Nell's driveway.

"Wow, that sun's deceiving. It's freezing out here." Stomping her feet, Madison blew on her purple-mittened hands. "Is anyone else cold?"

"Quit talking about it, and you'll be fine." He tried to keep the frustration from his voice, but since she'd been complaining about the cold for the last hour, it was difficult.

"Daddy, can we go now?" Lily asked, crossing and uncrossing her legs.

Before he could respond, Annie said, "Do you remember

the time Mom made snow angels with us, Lily? She played outside all day and never complained once. And it was *really* cold out."

From the look on Madison's face, Annie scored a direct hit. His oldest had spent the entire walk through the woods talking about Sheena. Madison had been a good sport. Up until now, she'd ignored the subtle digs Annie couched in praise of her mother. To hear his daughter tell it, Sheena should be crowned Mother of the Year.

Lily scrunched her nose. "I don't remember that. Maybe you're mixing Maddie up with Mommy. She made snow angels with us yesterday, 'member?"

Annie turned on her sister. "Shut up, Lily. You don't know anything."

"That's enough, Annie. All of you pick a tree. Now," Gage said through gritted teeth.

"Mom'll like that one." Annie pointed to a perfectly proportioned spruce just off the path at the same time Madison pointed to one of the scraggliest at the bottom of the hill, and said, "That one."

Annie pulled a face. "Mine's better. Yours is ugly. It won't hold the decorations."

Lily looked from her sister to Madison. "I like Maddie's tree. He looks kinda lonely and sad."

Annie's "Pick mine, Dad" sounded suspiciously like *Pick me*.

Now what was he supposed to do? His gaze shot to the Douglas fir they'd just passed. "What about that one?" He jerked his thumb at the tree.

Madison stomped over and wrenched the ax from his hand. "You take whichever one you want, but that's my tree, and I'm taking it home with me." She stalked down the hill to her butt-ugly tree and began whacking away at the trunk.

"Stay put," he said to Lily and Annie, who gaped at Madison. He walked up behind her. "Give me the ax. You're going to hurt yourself."

"No, I don't need your help." She kept her back to him, her voice husky.

She went to take another swing, and he wrapped a hand around the handle, sliding his other arm around her waist. He lowered his mouth to her ear. "I'll cut it down for you, honey."

She sagged against him. "I don't understand why Annie hates me now. What did I do wrong?"

"She doesn't hate you. She's mad at Sheena, and she's taking it out on you. Every year her mother promises to show up for Christmas and never does."

Madison sniffed. "That's horrible."

"Yeah, and this year's worse because Sheena didn't make it for Thanksgiving, either. And as much as Annie won't give up on her mother coming home for Christmas, she won't give up on the idea Sheena and I will get back together again." Madison stiffened in his arms. "It's not going to happen," he reassured her before explaining what the real problem was. "And it doesn't matter that you've given her more time and attention in these last few weeks than her mother's given her in the last eight years. Once she caught me kissing you, you became a threat to her fantasy."

Madison tipped her head back. "Because she knows I'm in love with you."

"No." He smiled. This was the first time she'd said the words out loud. "Because she knows I'm in love with you."

She turned in his arms, rising up on her toes to look over his shoulder. "I want to kiss you, but I won't."

"I always want to kiss you. But for now, until Annie gets used to the idea, we'll save it for when we're alone."

"Okay." She took a step back and pressed the ax into his hands. "I think you'd better get chopping. Lily's doing her I-gotta-go dance again."

"You know what? The three of you are a pain in the ass. Next year, we're buying our tree at Charlie's lot." He nudged her out of his way and caught the look of surprise in her eyes. "What?"

"You said next year we'll buy *our* tree at the lot."

"Yeah, and I meant it. You're the whiniest bunch of females I've ever met."

She bit her bottom lip. "It's really beautiful out here. I'm glad you brought us, even if I am freezing."

He cut down her tree with one solid whack. "Good." He rested the ax on his shoulder. "But I'm not changing my mind."

The return trip turned out better than he'd expected. Madison warmed up by dragging her Charlie Brown Christmas tree back to the truck, and a pit stop behind another tree took care of Lily. Annie seemed to sense she'd hurt Madison's feelings, and there was no more mention of Saint Sheena.

Once they reached Nell's, Gage got Madison's tree out of the trunk while she said good-bye to Annie and Lily. "I'm going to give your costumes to your dad. Don't forget to bring them with you to rehearsal. See you at three."

He carried the tree inside for her. "Why don't the four of us go to the diner after practice? Then, if my dad doesn't have any plans for the night, I'll have him stay with the girls, and we can decorate your tree together."

She opened the closet, handing him a garment bag. "That'd be nice, but you might want to check with Annie first. I think she's had enough of me for one day."

Good point. Gage didn't relish the idea of suffering through a dinner with Annie taking pot shots at Madison. If he intervened, it'd look like he was slamming her mother instead of standing up for Madison. And if Annie thought he was sticking up for Madison... Yeah, it was a lose-lose situation.

"You're probably right. I..." The words backed up in his throat at the hurt look in her eyes. He shut the door. Hooking the garment bag on the knob, he took her in his arms. "I'm sorry." He kissed her. "It'll just take time for her to get used to the idea we're together."

"Maybe if you tell Sheena what's going on, the two of you can make Annie understand it's over between you. Let her know that you've both moved on with your lives."

He rubbed the back of his neck, unsure how Madison would react to what he had to say. "Up until you, there's never been anyone I wanted to move on with."

"Hold it. I thought you said you haven't been in love with Sheena for a long time."

"I haven't, but since I also haven't been in a serious relationship since we split, Sheena thinks..."

Her eyes narrowed. "Sheena thinks what?"

He sighed. "That I'm still in love with her, and that one day we'll get back together." Madison opened her mouth. He held up a hand. "I'm not. But Sheena thinks everyone's in love with her. So in her mind, why would I be any different?"

"She's not involved with anyone?"

"No, I wish she was. But she's dedicated to her career and doesn't have time to invest in a relationship." It sounded like someone he knew—at least it used to.

"And you've never given her any reason to believe you're still in love with her?"

That he was in love with her? No. That he found her physically attractive and shared some good memories? Yes. The bedroom had been about the only place they were in sync. "No," he said slowly, wondering how much he should tell her.

"I hear a *but* there." She searched his face, and her jaw dropped. "You had sex with her!"

He put his hands on her shoulders to keep her from taking off like she appeared ready to. "It's not what—"

"When?" she snapped.

"Last Valentine's Day. It was the one and only time. We had too much to drink. And . . . it was Valentine's Day," he said, as if that explained everything. "I don't know, maybe we were both lonely. But what I do know is it was a stupid mistake. And I knew that even before Annie discovered us sleeping in the same bed the next morning."

Madison gasped. "Poor Annie—no wonder she thinks you're getting back together." A horn blasted. "You'd better go." She reached around him for the doorknob.

"No, not until you hear me out. It was just sex, Madison. Don't make more out of it than what it was."

"How can you say that? We had sex and—"

"We didn't have sex. We made love. And if you don't think there's a difference, tonight I'll show you there is." He framed her face with his hands and went to kiss her. She turned her cheek, wrapping her fingers around his wrists.

He pulled back. "You're not giving up on us, are you?"

"No, but for a smart guy, you can be a real dumbass, Sheriff. You've got to fix this. Promise me you'll talk to Annie."

Okay, that was going to be a hard promise to keep, at least for right now. "I will, but this is a tough time of year for her. Can we get through the holidays first, and then I'll talk to her?"

"Fine." She gave him a know-it-all look. "You see, this just goes to prove my theory that the 'friends with benefits' thing doesn't work."

"Yeah." He kissed her, then grabbed the garment bag and opened the door. "Just remember, you and me, we've gone way past friends."

And the thought didn't scare him anymore, not as much as losing her did.

Chapter Twenty-two

Madison was late for practice. After Gage's confession, she'd walked to the hospital to see Nell instead of driving, as a way to burn off her anger and frustration at the man. On the way home, she got caught in a snow shower that left her soaked to the skin and as frustrated as when she'd headed out.

And that was where her TMI moment with Vivi came into play. Madison should have taken a hot shower instead of calling her best friend to vent. But then again, if she hadn't ended up having to defend Gage and his relationship with his ex-wife to Vivi, Madison wouldn't have talked herself into being somewhat more understanding of his position. She couldn't say the same for Vivi. Her best friend had threatened to hop on the next plane and stage an intervention.

Madison ran into the hall. "Sorry I'm late." She shrugged out of her jacket and, along with her purse, tossed it on a chair before walking toward Hailey and

Holly, who were surrounded by kids clamoring for help with their costumes.

Hailey glanced at her sister. "It's okay. We understand." She smiled at Madison.

Madison's stomach did a belly flop. "What's wrong?" And there had to be something wrong, because Hailey never smiled, at least not at her.

"We heard the news." Hailey's head whipped around. "Billy, that's Liam's staff, not yours," she barked, then turned to Madison. "If you aren't up for practice, we totally understand. Don't we, Holly?"

"Oh, yes. Totally." Holly nodded with a sympathetic smile.

"Okay, y'all are starting to scare me. What happened? Is it Nell?" No, Nell had been fine, better than fine, when Madison left her a couple of hours ago. But if it wasn't Nell...She scanned the hall for Annie and Lily, and her pulse kicked up. "Where's Annie and Lily, has something happened to them?" Her knees buckled when the sisters grimaced.

Hailey grabbed her arm. "Jesus, don't faint on us. Holly, get her a glass of water." Hailey turned to the two boys whispering behind her. "I didn't swear, Billy. I said, 'Praise Jesus.'" She stared the little boy down until he walked away, dragging his cow costume behind him.

"Hailey, if you don't tell me what's happened, I'm going to scream."

"Keep your voice down. Lily and Annie are fine."

Holly returned with the water. Hailey took the glass from her sister. "You really don't know, do you?"

"Would one of you just—"

"Madison."

Thank God. She turned to see Gage striding toward her, his hair looking as though he'd repeatedly raked his

fingers through it. "Where have you been? I've been trying to get ahold of you for the last couple of hours," he
said, a harried expression in his eyes.

"Is it Fred and Ted? Has something happened to Fred
and Ted?" She clutched Gage's arm.

He frowned. "What are you talking about?"

She was close to losing it now. "No. One of you"—
she swept her finger over the three of them—"is going to
answer me. What. Is. Going. On?"

Gage glanced at Holly and Hailey, who stood arms
akimbo. "Oh." He rubbed the back of his neck. "Uh,
Sheena made it home for Christmas. She's here."

"Here?" Madison croaked. The three of them watched
her closely, waiting for a reaction. They weren't going to
get one. Nothing could be as bad as the scenarios she'd
been panicking about only seconds ago. "How nice for
y'all. I'm sure Annie and Lily are just thrilled to bits."

Gage rubbed her arm. "I'm sorry, honey. The girls
wanted her to come with them to rehearsal and—"

"She's *here* here?" Madison's hand went self-consciously
to the still-damp hair she'd pulled into a ponytail while talking to Vivi.

"Yeah." He looked over her head and grimaced.

Madison slowly turned…And wished she hadn't.
Sheena McBride, her beauty-pageant hair tumbling in
luxurious chestnut waves over the shoulders of her fur-
lined brown leather coat, walked toward them like she
owned the room. Her gorgeous face lit up with a teasing smile when she looked at the man standing behind
Madison. Her daughters held on to her hands, Annie
beaming up at her glamorous mother.

"You took off so fast, honey, I thought there must've

been a shooting," Sheena McBride said with a sultry twang as she closed in on them.

A distinct possibility, Madison thought, as her stomach twisted in a disappointed knot. She loved when Gage called her honey, but to hear the endearment slip so familiarly from the other woman's glossy red lips, it was obviously one the couple shared.

Lily let go of her mother's hand to take Madison's. "Mommy, this is Maddie. She's Daddy's girlfriend. They're going to get married."

"Aw, hell," Gage muttered, nudging Madison aside.

Before Gage intervened, Annie said, "That's not true, and you know it, Lily. Take it back! Mommy and Daddy—"

"Annie, that's enough," Gage said sharply.

From the expression on her face, Sheena McBride found the idea that Gage was involved with Madison laughable. Since Madison figured she looked like something the cat dragged in, she understood why.

"Funny, your daddy hasn't said anything to me about . . . Sorry, what's your name?"

Madison felt like crawling under a chair, but instead offered her hand. "Hello, Mrs. McBride. I'm Madison Lane."

Gage slanted her a censorious look. What did he expect her to call the woman?

Sheena ignored her hand and frowned. "I've heard your name before." Her eyes rounded. "You're the woman who killed the resort deal. The Grinch, isn't that what they call you?"

Holly and Hailey saved Madison from having to respond by loudly announcing, "It's time for practice. Everybody, go get your costumes on."

"Lily, Annie, get a move on. We've held everyone up long enough," Gage said with a pointed look at his ex-wife. Oblivious to the tension, Lily skipped away, but Annie hung back.

"Mom," she said, tugging her mother's hand, "you're going to stay and watch us practice, aren't you?"

Sheena gaze moved from Gage to her daughter. "I think your daddy and I have a few things to discuss, precious. Besides, I'll see the pageant on Christmas Eve."

Gage went to say something, but Annie interrupted him, "You should stay and take over the choir, Mom. Maddie has an awful voice and—"

Madison gasped, feeling like she'd been sucker punched.

"Annie," Gage ground out, "you apologize to Madison right now."

Annie flinched, ducking her head.

"Oh, Gage." Sheena wrapped an arm around Annie. "You've embarrassed her. And of course, I'll help out. We want the pageant to be a success, don't we?"

"Holly, Hailey, and Madison have it covered. And you're under doctor's orders to rest your voice."

"You're sweet to worry about me, darlin', but I'll be careful. Unless Ms. Lane isn't comfortable with my offer." Sheena raised a perfectly penciled brow.

"I'm sure the kids will be thrilled to have you lead the choir, Mrs. McBride," Madison managed to say despite the emotion clogging her throat.

"Maddie," Lily shouted, waving her costume. "I need help."

At least someone wanted her around. "Excuse me."

Gage reached for her as she went to walk away. "Madison."

She held up her hand and shook her head, unable to look at him, desperate to get away before she embarrassed herself further.

Her bottom lip started to quiver as she hurried across the room to where Lily stood. What was she so emotional about, anyway? It was just a stupid Christmas pageant. And she didn't even like Christmas. Bowing her head, she surreptitiously wiped away a tear. Hailey, crouched beside Billy, took one look at her and shot to her feet.

"With me. Now," she snapped, frog-marching Madison to the doors. "You—" she shot a finger at Gage, who looked up from the conversation he was having with Sheena and frowned at Madison "—do something useful, get Lily in her costume. I need Madison to help with… something." She grabbed her purse off a chair, shoving Madison through the doors. "In here." Hailey ducked in front of Madison. Opening the door with her hip, she pushed Madison inside the four-by-four washroom.

Hailey leaned against the door, reaching back to lock it before rummaging in her purse. She handed Madison a wad of facial tissues. "They're clean." She glanced at her watch. "Go ahead, you can cry now. But we've only got four minutes, so make it fast." Hailey took a tube of lipstick from her purse, setting it on the sink's ledge.

Madison's sob turned into a choked laugh. "It's okay. I'm not going to cry." And she wasn't going to until she realized that Hailey, who didn't like her, had saved her from making a fool of herself in front of Gage's ex-wife. A hot tear rolled down her cheek. "Nice…that was so nice of you to do for me. Thank you," she warbled.

"I'm not nice. I don't even like you, remember?"

"I know. You don't even like me, but you saved me from making a complete idiot of myself." Madison hic-cuped on a sob, trying to get ahold of herself.

Hailey's lips twitched. "I guess you've grown on me, because I kind of like you. But Miss Fancy-Ass McBride, I've never liked her. She always thought she was too good for this town."

Madison dabbed at her eyes. "You really don't like her?"

"No, I don't." Hailey eyed her. "Are you done?"

"Yeah, I feel better now. Thanks."

"Good. Splash cold water on your face." Someone knocked on the door. "Occupied," Hailey barked.

"It's me." Holly's voice came through the door.

Hailey opened it an inch. "Whatya need?"

"I want to check on Madison." She pushed her way in, tugging on her purse when it got caught on the knob. Hailey shuffled closer to the toilet. "Are you okay?" Holly asked.

At the look of concern in Holly's eyes, tears pooled in Madison's.

"Oh, come on, I just got her to stop crying. Tell her you don't like her."

Holly's brow furrowed. "But I do like her."

"Really, you like me? I like you, too." Madison nod-ded, then blew her nose.

"Thanks." Holly smiled.

"Okay, you can go back and help—" Hailey began.

Holly cut her off with a shake of her head. "Gage got the rest of the kids into their costumes. Mrs. Ellis is warming them up now. At least she's trying to, but Miss Fancy-Pants McBride keeps interfering." Holly made a face. "She said something about whipping them into shape."

"You can't be serious," Madison splashed cold water on her face. "They're just little kids. They're supposed to have fun."

Hailey scowled at her in the mirror above the sink. "Yeah, and that's why you should've said thanks but no thanks. It's not her place to waltz in here and take over."

Patting her face dry with a paper towel, Madison said, "You can't blame Sheena. Annie asked her to take over." And she couldn't blame Annie, either. She knew how much she missed her mother. Madison just wished she'd been a little more considerate of her feelings.

"What Annie did to you was downright mean. She's acting like a brat, and her father's letting her get away with it."

"It's because he feels guilty," Holly said knowingly.

"Gage doesn't have anything to feel guilty about. He's an amazing father." Madison crumpled the paper towel and tossed it in the wastebasket.

The sisters exchanged a look. "Yeah, he is," Hailey agreed, "and he'd do just about anything to ensure Annie and Lily's happiness, including sacrificing his own. So don't you find it interesting that the one thing he wouldn't do is move to Nashville? If he did, he and Sheena would still be together."

"He was worried about his dad. It hadn't been that long since his mom died. Besides, Sheena was touring and Gage had a good support system in town. Not to mention his job," Madison defended him, repeating what Nell had told her. "And he tried to make it work, but long-distance relationships aren't easy."

"She's got it bad," Hailey said to her sister.

"Yeah, I know." Holly smiled, then maneuvered herself behind Madison, tugging the elastic from her hair.

"Ouch." Madison put a hand to her head. Holly ignored her and turned on the hand dryer on the wall, shoving Madison's head under it.

"Holly," she protested.

"Shush, listen to Hailey."

Hailey bent down to look Madison in the eye, raising her voice to be heard over the dryer. "Tell me this. You're in love with Gage. Are you going to do the long-distance thing or are you going to move to Christmas?"

"Denver," Madison admitted.

"Aha, you just proved my point."

"But I'm not Sheena McBride, country singer extraordinaire. It's easier for me. I've lost my job, and the company I'm applying to is located in Denver."

"Yeah, and if it wasn't, I bet you'd still be thinking about relocating."

Madison couldn't argue her point. She would.

"And I can name you a bunch of singers bigger than Sheena McBride who don't live in Nashville. If you really love someone, you make it work. Sheena's all take. She wanted Gage, and she got him, even though she had to get pregnant to do it."

That wasn't something Madison expected to hear. "I didn't know. But Gage must've been in love with her. They got married."

"We're talking about Mr. Do-the-Right-Thing McBride here, Maddie. Of course he married her. None of us ever thought he was in love with her. Lust for sure, but not love. She's not his type. You are. But he stuck it out because he's one of the good guys. When Sheena's career took her to Nashville, he had an excuse to end the marriage. The excuse was his daughters."

"You think I'm his type?" Madison hadn't heard much after that.

Hailey rolled her eyes. "Why do you think none of us liked you? Of course you're his type."

Holly let Madison up, fluffing her now-dry hair. "Thanks," Madison said, then turned back to Hailey. "You really believe Gage was looking for an excuse to end the marriage?"

"I do, not that he'd ever admit it, even to himself. And that's why he feels guilty about the girls not having their mother around. Why Annie can play him like she does. For your sake, Maddie, I hope you can make him see that or you're in for a rough ride."

It felt like Hailey'd taken a big fat pin and stuck it in the bubble of optimism that had been expanding in Madison's chest. If today was an example of the ride she was in for, Madison didn't know if she was up for it.

"We gotta get of here." Hailey scrutinized Madison's face and grimaced. "You finish up with her hair, Holly. I'll look after her makeup."

Madison took in Hailey's heavily made-up eyes, Holly's teased beehive, and cringed inwardly. They'd been so sweet and supportive, she didn't have the heart to say thanks but no thanks.

Five minutes later, her scalp stinging, her eyes so heavy she could barely lift them, Madison forced herself to look in the mirror. *Oh. My. God.* "Wow," she said, "That's... ah...amazing."

Hailey nodded. "Looks pretty good," she said to her sister.

"It would've been better if we had more time, but you're right, Hails. She looks good. Oh, wait." Holly took a can of hair spray from her purse. Before Madison could stop her, she gave her a full hit.

"Much better," Holly gasped, choking on the fumes.

The three of them were coughing, batting away the haze, when Gage's concerned voice came through the door. "Madison, are you in there?"

Madison put a finger to her lips and shook her head. She didn't want to speak to him until she knew her emotions were completely under control. They ignored her and opened the door.

"If you make her cry again, McBride, I'll serve you premade burgers for a year." Hailey pushed past him.

"That goes for me, too," Holly said, following after her sister. Behind Gage's back, she gave Madison the thumbs-up. Madison ducked her head and tried to squeeze by him.

"Oh, no, you don't." Gage held on to her and shut the door. Once he locked it, he turned to look at her and blinked. "What the hell did they do to you?"

"They were being nice. They thought I needed some help competing with your wife."

"There's no competition. I love you just the way you are." He reached behind her to pull a paper towel from the dispenser, then dabbed at her lips and cheeks with it. "Better," he said before lowering his mouth to hers. His kiss was gentle yet thorough, leaving her gasping for air when he finally pulled back to look down at her. "Did I really make you cry?"

"No." Annie did, but she didn't want to tell him that. And after what Hailey said, she doubted it would do any good.

He lifted his hand to her face, stroking her cheek with his thumb. "But you were crying. I'm sorry Annie asked Sheena to take over. She shouldn't have done that, but you understand why she did, don't you?"

"Sure, I do. She's proud of her mother and wants to show her off. And she wants to sing for Sheena, make her mother proud of *her*. Psych 101, Sheriff, not too hard to figure out. But what's harder to understand is why *you*"— she thumped her finger on his chest—"didn't introduce me to your ex-wife as your girlfriend. And why *you* let Annie deny it without correcting her." Okay, so maybe it wasn't only Annie who hurt her feelings.

"You know what Annie's like. She just needs time to adjust to the idea…" Madison went to give her opinion on that, and he placed a finger on her lips. "All I'm asking for is a little time. And just so you know, I took Sheena aside and told her we're involved."

Madison narrowed her eyes. "What kind of 'involved'?"

"I told her you're important to me, that I care about you."

"You didn't tell her you loved me, did you?" She got her answer from the evasive look in his eyes. "Have you told *anyone* that you're in love with me?"

"What does it matter what anyone else thinks? You know I love you."

It shouldn't have mattered, but it did. She was beginning to feel like his dirty little secret, and it reminded her of her mother. It wasn't the same situation, but there were enough similarities to make her nauseous.

Her reaction must have shown on her face, because he took her in his arms, nuzzled her neck, then brought his lips to her ear. "I'll tell Ethan and my dad, how's that?"

Debbie Mason

Okay, she was being an idiot. She didn't want to pressure him into telling people about them. He was a guy; they didn't go around broadcasting their feelings. "No, you don't have to tell anyone but me." With the tip of her finger, she traced the zipper of his leather jacket. "I'm feeling a little insecure with Sheena back in town, that's all." She looked up at him, his eyes warm and tender. "It's just that she's gorgeous and this big celebrity, and she's staying with you, and you slept—"

He cut her off with a long, toe-curling kiss. Cradling her head in his hands, he tried to tunnel his fingers through her hair. They got stuck. He pulled back, making a frustrated noise in his throat. "Don't ever let them put that crap in your hair again." Gingerly, he patted the strands back in place, then kissed the tip of her nose. "I adore you, Madison Lane, and you are the only woman I want to sleep with."

Then he rubbed the back of his neck. A sure sign he was about to tell her something she wouldn't like. She braced herself.

"I know we talked about going to the diner together after practice, but Annie's made plans for a family dinner. I don't want to disappoint her. You don't mind, do you?"

She felt like a yo-yo. One minute she was up, the next down. With her hand on the door knob, she forced a smile. "Of course not."

"Great," he said with a relieved smile. "Once the girls fall asleep, I'll come over and spend the night. And when I'm finished with you, you're not going to have any reason to doubt me again. Now, if you're okay, I'll get going. Dad called and asked me to look in on Nell. I'll be back in about an hour."

"I'm glad you're checking on her. When I stopped by this afternoon, she was making plans to break herself out."

"Good to know." He followed her out of the bathroom. "See you in a bit."

She really did love the man, she thought, watching his confident, loose-limbed stride as he walked away. He looked over his shoulder, caught her ogling him and grinned. "Play nice in there."

She flipped him off. He shook his head and laughed.

The first thing Madison heard upon entering the hall was Sheena's strident demand. "Water, I need a drink of water. *Someone* get me a glass of water now."

Arms crossed, Holly and Hailey didn't move from their front-row seats. Madison glanced at Annie: her color was high, her eyes overly bright. Poor kid, she thought, she's embarrassed. "I'll get you a glass of water," Madison volunteered.

Hailey met her in the small kitchen off the hall. "The woman is a nut job. She's been snapping at everyone. Mrs. Ellis is so nervous she keeps forgetting which song she's supposed to play, and Billy started to cry when Sheena yelled at him for singing off-key." She opened a cupboard. "There's gotta be some rat poison in here somewhere."

Madison laughed. "It can't be that bad."

"Yeah? You wait and see."

Hailey was right. It was bad, but Madison was afraid to intervene. What kid would want her leading the choir when they had country star Sheena McBride? And then there was Annie...

"Again, from the top." Sheena's directive was met with muffled groans of complaint.

Madison remained in her chair, biting her tongue, when Hailey and Holly left their seats to organize the children on stage for the next number.

Brandi slid in beside her. "How you holding up?" she asked, shooting a thumbs-up to Trent. He grinned and gave her one in return.

"You there, Joseph, there will be none of that," Sheena said sharply.

"Hey, Sheena, Joseph's mine. His name is Trent, and he can give me the thumbs-up anytime he wants. Got it?"

Sheena glanced over her shoulder to where they sat twenty feet away. Probably judging how far and how fast she'd have to run if she decided to defy Brandi. "Yes, Brandi. I've got it."

"Way to go," Madison murmured.

"Gotta stand up to the bullies. Isn't that what you told my son?" She slid Madison a sidelong glance, then returned her gaze to Sheena. "She used to sing at the Penalty Box before she was discovered. Sometimes she forgets where she came from. You didn't answer my question. How you doing?"

"Fine. Why?"

She held up her phone. "Trent texted me, said you were upset. He thought you might need some backup."

Madison blinked. "You came for me?"

"Yeah. Why do you look so surprised? You're one of us now. We look after our own."

Hailey marched over. "Do not tell her you like her." She looked at Madison, then sighed and pulled another wad of tissues from her pocket.

Brandi frowned. "I thought you were supposed to be tough, a hard-ass. What happened to you?"

Madison took the tissues and sniffed. "I am. I was. And then—" she waved her hand at the little kids in their costumes, the room, and everyone in it "—you all got to me. Christmas got to me." She stifled a sob behind the tissue.

"So the Grinch has a heart after all." Brandi grinned.

Hailey stopped laughing when her sister sidled up beside her. "This isn't going to be pretty," Holly said.

"What?" Madison blew her nose.

Holly glanced at the stage, worrying her bottom lip between her teeth. "Annie's number is next."

Madison frowned. "Annie's got an incredible voice. Sheena will be busting with pride when she hears her. I was, and I'm not even her mother."

"And therein lies the problem," Brandi murmured. "Mommy dearest is not going to like the competition or comparisons."

"Yeah, Sheena never sounded half as good as Annie when she started out," Hailey said.

Unbelievably, they were right. Annie had barely started to sing when her mother stopped her, shaking her head over some imagined note her daughter didn't hit. By midpoint in the song, and at least eight reprimands later, the kids shifted uncomfortably from foot to foot. Lily was practically wringing her hands, and Trent's were balled into fists. Madison, just as upset, dug her nails into her palms, but she didn't think Annie would appreciate her interference. Unable to take it any longer, she was about to leave when Annie lifted her head. She looked directly at Madison, her eyes tear-filled and pleading.

Madison shot from the chair.

"Thank God," Brandi, Hailey, and Holly exhaled from behind her.

Clapping her hands, Madison walked toward Sheena. "Come on, guys, let's give it up for Ms. McBride. Thanks so much for all your help, Ms. McBride." She encouraged the kids to join in.

"But I'm not finished," Sheena looked around, seemingly confused.

"Yes, you are." Madison kept her voice low. "You can sit in your car or go somewhere for a coffee. I don't care what you do, but I want you out of here. Now. Practice will be over in thirty minutes. You can come back then."

Still clapping her hands, Madison walked past her. "Okay, Mrs. Ellis, we've gotta loosen these kids up. Maybe a little rock 'n' roll. What do you say, Billy?" He looked past her, shuffling his feet.

Madison turned. Sheena hadn't moved. She stood there tight-lipped and furious. "You have no right kicking me out of here. Those are my children, and their performance reflects on me. I—" She broke off as Madison strode toward her.

"You don't want to mess with me, Sheena. Nell messed with me, and I ran her over. Ask them if you don't believe me." She jerked her thumb at the three women who were struggling not to laugh as they moved toward Sheena.

"It's true. You better do as she says." Holly said, taking Sheena by the arm to lead her away.

Madison turned back to the kids, clapping and wiggling her butt. "What do you say, Billy? Can you give me a moo?" He grinned and started wiggling and mooing. "What about you, Lily?" And before long they were all laughing and getting down to Mrs. Ellis's rendition of "Great Balls of Fire." Madison caught Annie's eye and winked. Annie smiled, then started to shake it up with Trent.

Maybe they'd be okay after all.

Chapter Twenty-three

As Gage pulled into the parking lot of the Rocky Mountain Diner, he figured dealing with his ex-wife and daughter should be a piece of cake after the last hour he'd spent with his aunt. The better Nell felt, the higher the likelihood she'd follow through with her threat to check herself out of the hospital. She was riled up about the vote on Monday. Something Gage meant to talk to Madison about. He didn't need to be dealing with a riled-up citizenry at the moment—he had enough on his plate dealing with Sheena.

And the last thing he wanted was for Madison to be hurt if the vote went the way he expected it to. It'd been tough enough watching her reaction to Annie asking her mother to take over the practice. He hadn't helped. For the last eight years, his world had revolved around his daughters. And today, in trying to protect Annie, he'd hurt Madison. He hated knowing he'd made her cry.

Somehow, he had to find a way to balance her needs with his daughters.

He pressed the lock button on his keys and headed for the diner. Beneath the red-and-green glow of Christmas lights, Ethan stood on the top step of the log building with a to-go bag in one hand, texting with the other.

"Have you ever thought of tossing that thing?" Gage nodded at the phone. He knew he had.

"Only every hour or so, but then Nell would be harassing you instead of me. Never say I don't have your back, buddy." He grinned, shoving his phone in the pocket of his sheepskin jacket.

"Thanks." Stalling, Gage rested one foot on the bottom step and leaned on the banister, careful not to dislodge the pine bough. "What's Nell bugging you about now? Is she trying to talk you into breaking her out of the hospital?"

"No, she's chapping my ass over the announcement not making the paper on time, and . . . Hey, Harlan," Ethan said, making room for the other man to get by.

"Mr. Mayor." Harlan flicked the brim of his John Deere cap, a warm gush of grease-filled air and chatter following him out the door. "Mighty fine family you have, Sheriff. Better get in there before the boys make a move on your pretty wife."

Gage opened his mouth to tell him the boys were welcome to her, then closed it. Like Harlan, most of the citizens of Christmas chose to ignore the fact that Gage and Sheena were divorced. They liked the idea of having a real-life celebrity attached to one of their own and planned to keep it that way, no matter what Gage said. "Have a good night, Harlan."

"And that would be the subject of Nell's latest text," Ethan said as the other man lumbered off to his truck. "She suggested Sheena move in with me for the duration of her visit."

"Interested?" Gage asked, even though he knew his ex wasn't Ethan's type. His best friend liked his women smart, refined, and reserved—the perfect politician's wife for the career he hoped one day to pursue.

"In Sheena? Not a chance. Wish I could help you out, but the last thing I need is everyone up in arms because your ex is shacking up with me."

Gage rubbed the back of his neck. Ethan was right. And if the citizens of Christmas got wind that Gage and Madison were together while Sheena was in town, they'd make Madison's life miserable.

"She's only staying for a couple of days, right?"

"I think so." Gage hoped so, for his sake and Madison's. But Sheena had arrived with four overstuffed Louis Vuitton suitcases that said otherwise, and a crapload of anxiety about her throat condition having the potential to end her career. And what she'd do if her career was over worried him the most.

"I hate to break it to you, buddy, but Sheena being in town is going to be the least of your worries." Ethan came down the stairs. "I got a call from Harrison Hartwell while I waited for my order. He wasn't happy I'm allowing a vote on the resort. Offered to do whatever's necessary to make it go away."

"He tried to bribe you?"

"Not in so many words, but I wouldn't be surprised if he paid Rick to keep the announcement out of the paper. Dane's back is to the wall financially."

Everyone knew Rick was a month or so away from declaring bankruptcy. He'd spent the last year coming up with one get-rich-quick scheme after another—a couple this side of the law. Gage would've felt sorry for the guy if he wasn't such an asshole. But he'd been on Gage's shit list since the day he'd figured out Rick was the one who sold photos of Lily and Annie to the tabloids, along with information that was nobody's business but theirs. Dane hadn't even bothered to deny it when Gage confronted him.

"I take it the announcement got up in time or we wouldn't be having this conversation."

"Oh, yeah, Nell took care of it by posting it on the town's website and Facebook page. She's probably tweeted about it, too."

Gage shook his head. "You never should've given her your password."

Ethan quirked a brow.

"Right," Gage muttered. He knew better. His aunt had ways of sniffing out information. He probably should put her on the payroll.

"You might want to warn Madison that Harrison wasn't happy to hear she's leading the opposition. And Gage, he's arriving on the twenty-third to launch a counterattack. Gotta go." He held up his bag, the smell of fries and burgers wafting past Gage's nostrils.

Up until then, Gage had been starving. He walked into the diner. Sheena sat in the booth at the far corner of the room holding court, while Lily and Annie, sitting on the bench across from her, looked dejected. A few days ago, he'd sat in the same booth with Madison and his daughters. They'd looked a whole lot happier and relaxed then.

"There he is. Gage, honey." Sheena waved him over.

For Lily and Annie's sake, he unclenched his jaw and smiled. The disheartened expression on Annie's face surprised him. She'd been asking Santa to bring her mother home for Christmas since she was four. Lily smiled up at him, but it wasn't her usual smile, the one that lit up her whole face.

As he said hello to the men crowded around Sheena, Gage caught sight of Dane sitting two tables over and made a mental note to speak to him before he left the diner. Gage was beginning to wonder just how deep in Harrison Hartwell's pocket Rick was.

Sheena patted the bench. "Sit here."

Gage didn't have much choice but to do as she asked. If he refused like he wanted to, she'd pout and make a scene. And there was already enough attention on their table as it was. The men scattered when Gage parked his butt on the edge of the bench.

"How did practice go?" Annie's shoulders went up around her ears at his question, and Lily shot a wary look from him to his ex.

Sheena stirred her coffee, then sharply tapped the spoon on the rim of the white mug. "I'll tell you how it went. Madison Lane shouldn't be allowed anywhere near children, let alone teaching them to sing. I'm going to speak to the ladies' auxiliary or whoever it was that put her in charge."

"Hold up there, Sheena. Madison's great with the kids and—"

"Great?" she sputtered. "The woman sings like a cat in heat and had the nerve to kick *me* out of the practice." The husky quality in her voice took on a shrill edge.

Annie looked like she wanted to crawl under the table

whereas Lily appeared ready to give her mother a piece of her mind.

"You're sure she kicked you out? Maybe you misunderstood." He knew Madison was feeling insecure, but he didn't think she'd take it this far. Then again, it was Madison—an emotional and hurt Madison.

"I did not misunderstand her. She threatened me and had those women forcibly remove me from the hall. I've never been so humiliated in my life, and all because that woman is jealous of me."

"I like when Maddie sings. She's fun. She doesn't make us—" Annie elbowed Lily. "That hurt," Lily complained, blinking her eyes. She looked down at her half-eaten pizza, then back up at Gage. "Daddy, I want to go home."

"Sure, sweetpea, just as soon as Annie—"

Annie pushed her plate away. "I want to go home, too."

Before Gage could ask what the hell was going on, Rick Dane sauntered over. "Don't want to interrupt your family reunion, but"—he held up his camera—"I'd appreciate a picture for tomorrow's edition. You have a lot of fans here in Christmas, Mrs. McBride."

"Yes, yes, of course." Sheena preened. "Why don't you take a family picture, Mr. Dane?"

Gage was about to bow out when he saw Annie's eyes light up. Sheena slid across the bench and wrapped an arm around her. "Lily, you go sit beside your daddy. Gage?" Sheena patted the spot beside her.

Reluctantly, he moved closer, drawing Lily with him. Just before the flash went off, Sheena cupped his chin and kissed him full on the lips.

Gage cursed inwardly. He should've known what she was up to.

Dane checked the screen. "Great shot. Folks will be pleased as punch to see the McBride family together again. Might even be good enough to get me picked up on the wire."

Gage hoped to hell not. It was bad enough people in Christmas would see it. And there was one person he knew who wouldn't be pleased as punch. From the smug smile Dane shot him, he knew it, too. But Gage didn't have time to deal with Rick now. He had to get his daughters and ex out of there before Sheena did any more damage.

*   *   *

Gage gave up questioning his youngest about the practice. He'd get his answers from Madison. Tucking Lily beneath her pink quilt, he stretched out beside her and retrieved her favorite book, *The Polar Express,* from the bedside table.

"Daddy," she whispered. "Santa wouldn't bring the present I asked for before Christmas, would he?"

From the worried look on her face, he went with no.

She shot him a relieved smile. "I didn't think so."

"Did you send your letter to Santa already?" With everything going on, it was just one more thing Gage hadn't gotten around to. But he had a good idea what his daughters wanted. They'd started making their lists, complete with pictures, the day after Halloween. He'd ordered most of what they'd asked for by the following week, but Lily had been known to change her mind at the last minute.

She wrinkled her nose. "Daddy, there's only three more sleeps till Christmas Eve. Me and Maddie mailed out the letter a long time ago."

God, he loved that woman. "So what did you ask Santa for this year?" He breathed a little easier when she rhymed off the contents of the wrapped presents locked away in his closet.

Until she got to the last item on the list, and he stopped breathing all together. "A mommy. A *new* mommy," she clarified, in case he wasn't quick on the uptake. And if that wasn't clear enough, she added, "Maddie'd make a good mommy. She likes us, and she's fun, and makes us laugh, and..." She continued to tick off Madison's mommy attributes on her fingers. All of which Gage agreed with, even though they were nowhere near that place in their relationship. Lily looked up at him expectantly.

He knew her well enough to word his response carefully. "You love Madison, don't you?"

She nodded. "Do you?"

Smart kid. "It'd be pretty hard for anyone not to love her. But you know, sweetpea, Madison lives in New York and—"

"I know. I asked Santa to get her a job here."

"Oh. Uh, Lily, did Madison help you write the letter?"

"Yep." She smiled. "I think she was hormonals 'cause she cried, but she said they were happy tears."

Gage decided it was time to end the conversation and opened the book. It worked. By the time he got to the second page, Lily started to nod off. He placed the book on her bedside table, shut off the lamp, and leaned over to kiss her forehead. "I love you, sweetpea."

"Daddy," she called out sleepily before he closed her door. "Maybe if you asked Santa for a new mommy for us, it'd help."

She was as tenacious as Nell. "I'll see what I can do."

He walked down the hall, tapped on the Keep Out sign, then eased the door open. "Annie?"

"Yeah," she said, her voice muffled.

She tucked whatever she'd held in her hand under her yellow happy face comforter. Like most girls Annie's age, her walls were plastered with posters. But instead of Justin Bieber's face staring out at him, it was Sheena's. He sat on the edge of her bed and brushed Annie's dark hair from her eyes. "You okay?"

She shrugged, her gaze flitting away from his.

There was something going on with her, and he wished she'd talk to him about it. Madison would've been able to get her to open up. Well, a week ago she would have. "You know I love you, right?"

"Yeah, Dad, I know."

He smiled at her you're-so-lame tone of voice. "Good. So you know you can ask or tell me anything, and I won't get mad, right?"

He wanted to know what went on with her mother. Because the more he thought about it, about Lily's comments and Annie's reaction, he was sure Sheena had somehow managed to upset her. That alone would explain why Madison kicked her out of the practice. He didn't always agree with how she went about it, but Madison was fiercely protective of those she cared about, and she cared about his daughter.

Annie nodded. Obviously, he wasn't going to get anything out of her tonight.

He tucked the covers under her chin and smiled when she rolled her eyes. "I'm glad you got your Christmas wish." He kissed her forehead, then went to turn off the light.

"I thought it was your Christmas wish, too," she mumbled.

Aw, hell. He turned. "No, sweetheart. Your mom's and my relationship was over a long time ago." Now he wanted one with a beautiful, brainy blonde whose mouth got her in trouble. But he wasn't sure Annie was ready to hear that.

"Last Valentine's…" She trailed off, her cheeks flushed.

"Was a mistake. I'm sorry if we confused you, Annie. I never meant for that to happen."

She twisted her hands in her comforter. "I'm sorry I hurt Maddie's feelings."

His first reaction, because she'd obviously had a tough day, was to let her off the hook. But he'd raised his girls to be aware of other people's feelings, and over the last couple of days, he'd let Annie get away with hurting Madison's.

"It's not me you owe the apology to. Madison's been nothing but good to you, and you've been pretty hard on her lately. Why don't you give her a call tomorrow? I'm sure she'd like to hear from you."

She reached under her comforter and held up the phone he'd given her to use when she went out with friends. "Can I text her?"

"Sure," he said, as he went to leave.

"Dad?"

"Yeah," he said slowly, wondering if she was going to ask him about his and Madison's relationship. He wasn't exactly sure what to say if she did.

"I…" She shook her head. "Nothing."

"You sure?"

"Sure."

"Okay then. Good night, Annie. See you in the morning." He closed the door, relieved to have dodged the relationship bullet.

Walking past Sheena's room on the way to his, a familiar tension pulled in his chest. He debated whether or not to deal with her now and decided against it. Tomorrow morning would be soon enough.

He opened his bedroom door. His jaw dropped. Sheena lay on his bed in a seductive pose wearing a red velvet bustier trimmed in white fur, a red lace G-string, and a pair of thigh-high black leather boots.

"What the hell do you think you're doing?" He grabbed his robe from the hook on the back of his door and tossed it at her.

She sat up, narrowing her perfectly made-up eyes at him. "When did you become such a prude?"

All he needed was for Annie to walk in on them. He closed the door and locked it.

"I always loved this room, this bed." She stroked the duvet cover, looking at him. "You."

"Cut it out." He rubbed the back of his neck. "You're worried about your career, and you're looking for something to hang on to. I'm sorry, Sheena, but I'm not interested."

She stabbed her arms into his white terry-cloth robe. "This is because of her, isn't it?"

"Yes and no." He leaned against the door. "I told you I was involved with Madison. You know me better than to think—"

"Big deal," she interrupted him. "So you're sleeping with her. A man has his needs, I understand that."

"Hold it right there. You're talking about the woman I'm in love with."

"You're in love with her? But I thought...Last February we—"

"—were lonely," he finished for her. "We had a good time together." He walked to the bed and sat down. "But it was a mistake. Now, why don't you tell me what this is really about?"

Her brown eyes filled. "I don't have anyone in my life, Gage. I'm thirty-four, and I've put all my energy into my career. Now it's over."

She looked lost, and he put an arm around her. "Who says it's over?"

"My doctor." She sniffed, leaning against him.

"Did you get a second opinion?"

"No." She shook her head. "I just—"

"—panicked." He lived with her long enough to know how she'd react to the news. "Tomorrow, you'll go see my dad and Matt. Between the two of them, they'll know someone to recommend you to."

"You always took such good care of me, Gage." Before he realized what she was up to, she climbed onto his lap, wrapping her arms around his neck.

"I'm serious, Sheena. I'm not interested." He unwound her arms and nudged her off his lap. "You're going to be fine," he said, as he stood up.

"You don't understand. I've had time to think about what I've given up. My career won't last forever. I want another chance with you and the girls. They need me."

"We're done, Sheena. As for the girls, I don't want you discussing your plans with them until you're sure what they are." He raked his hand through his hair. "We need to make other arrangements for when you visit. Having you stay here is confusing Lily and Annie."

Her eyes widened. "You're kicking me out of my own home?"

"It was never your home, Sheena. It was just one more compromise in a long list of them to get you to stay. Only you left before I finished the house."

"You're angry and hurt. I get that, and I'm sorry. I have a lot to make up for. I know that."

He shook his head. There was no reasoning with her. "I doubt we'd find anywhere for you to stay at this late date, but next time you won't be staying here." As soon as the words were out of his mouth, a weight lifted off his shoulders. For the girls' sakes, he'd put it off longer than he should have. He didn't think Lily would be a problem, and he'd have time after the holidays to ease Annie into the idea. "I'm going to the station. When I get back, I don't want to find you in my room."

"This is all Madison Lane's fault. If it wasn't for her, you wouldn't be kicking me out of my home. And don't think I don't know where you're going."

"It stopped being your business what I do and who I do it with a long time ago. This is between you and me. Leave Madison out of it."

She muttered something under her breath.

"What did you say?"

"Nothing."

But he knew better, and just to be sure he didn't fuel the fire, he said, "If the girls need me, I'll be at the station." Hopefully she believed him.

*   *   *

By the time Gage cleaned up some paperwork at the office and walked to his aunt's—he'd left the Suburban at the station to avoid Nell's nosy neighbors gossiping about his visit—it was close to midnight. He went to put in his key in the door, but the knob turned under his hand. Gage gave his head a frustrated shake. He couldn't believe Madison had left the door unlocked.

Christmas might be a small town with a low crime rate, but she needed to be more careful. A lot of people were unhappy the resort was being put to a vote. With Nell in the hospital, it was Madison who was the face of the campaign. And if the citizens of Christmas felt she was putting their opportunity for jobs at risk, they might do something stupid.

"Madison," he called out, doing a quick scan of the kitchen and upper hall as he toed off his boots. He glanced into the living room. She was asleep under the blinking red lights of the Christmas tree, its spindly limbs weighed down with thick mounds of fake snow and what looked to be Fruit Loops strung from its branches. His worried frustration gave way to a chest-tightening tenderness.

She opened her eyes when he crouched beside her. "Hi," she said with a sleepy smile.

"Hi." He kissed her warm, pliant mouth, then pulled back, licking his lips. "Peppermint?"

She wrinkled her nose. "Hailey brought peppermint schnapps. I like candy cane shooters better, but Brandi had to go home early."

"Hailey and Brandi were here?"

She nodded. Wrapped in a red wool blanket, she sat up. "Holly, Sophia, Jill, Autumn, and Grace, too. They decided I needed some support with your ex home for the holidays."

"Did it help?" he asked as he came to his feet.

With a tight grip on her blanket, she took the hand he held out to her. "It was fun. They had some suggestions for my presentation on Monday, and Hailey offered to give Sheena food poisoning. Jill said she'd shoot her, if I wanted her to." She bit her lip." I probably shouldn't have told you that, but don't worry, they were just kidding around."

"Good to know." And he thought men were more prone to violence.

She hadn't let go of the blanket yet, and he frowned. He placed the palm of his hand on her flushed cheek. "Are you coming down with something?"

"No, it's just…" She sighed. "Unlike Jill and Hailey, Sophia advocates the seduction route and brought me this." She let go of the blanket. It puddled at her feet, revealing the exact same outfit Sheena had worn earlier, only…

Trying hard not to laugh, he said, "I don't think she meant for you to wear Nell's Rudolph sweater with it, honey."

She looked down at herself and shrugged out of the sweater, letting it fall to the floor. "I was cold."

He practically swallowed his tongue. Compared to Madison, Sheena looked like a boy. His entranced gaze took in every delectable inch of her centerfold curves, traveling down her long, toned legs to…the fuzzy red slippers on her feet.

He rubbed his hand along his jaw. "Aren't you supposed to wear thigh-high leather boots with it?"

Her eyes narrowed. "How'd you know?"

Oh, no, he wasn't that stupid. "Educated guess."

She snorted. "I don't want to know." Then waved her hand at a shoe box under the tree. "Men must design those things. They suck women into thinking they have to wear boots that'll kill their feet, and break their damn necks if they're not careful, just to get a man's attention, to seduce him. Can you see a man doing that?" She tugged up the plunging fur-trimmed neckline. "Seriously, if we have to stuff ourselves into outfits like this just to—"

"You don't." He drew her into his arms. "You could seduce me wearing a paper bag."

She sighed, wrapping her arms around his waist. "Sorry," she murmured against his neck. "Vivi joined our little party via Skype. I guess her man-hating rant rubbed off on me."

He leaned back to stroke her cheek. "Trust me, it's you and only you I want."

"I do. I'm not going to let Vivi get to me again."

Taking her hand, he turned off the lights. "Good to hear. Come on, it's time to go to bed. I'm beat."

At the bottom of the stairs, she turned to him with a frown. "You want to go to bed and . . . sleep?"

"Yeah, aren't you tired?" He fought back a grin.

"Well, sort of, but I thought—"

He tossed her over his shoulder, smacking her lightly on the butt as he headed up the stairs. "You should've worn the boots."

Chapter Twenty-four

Madison wriggled backward beneath the covers, seeking the comforting weight that had been keeping her warm only a short time ago. Half-asleep, she reached behind her to pat the cold sheets and empty mattress.

The bed dipped. "Looking for me?" Gage asked, his deep voice warm with amusement.

"Um-hmm." She rolled onto her back, the comforter sliding down as she reached for him.

Stretching out beside her, his white teeth flashed in the still-dark room. "You make it tough to leave." He swallowed her "Good" in a minty-flavored kiss.

Fingers tangling in his damp hair, she deepened the kiss as he went to pull away. He groaned, resting his forehead against hers. "What am I going to do with you, Ms. Lane?"

"I can think of a few things." She drew him closer, bringing her mouth to his ear to tell him exactly what she wanted him to do. Something she'd never done before. She'd never been overly comfortable with her body and had been pretty inhibited in the bedroom. But after last night, her breasts no longer felt too large or her hips too round. He'd told her, not only with words, but with his every look, his every touch, that she was perfect, perfect for him.

A smile curved his firm lips when she finished whispering her request in his ear. Moving his large hand over her body in a slow and deliberate caress, he murmured, "I think I can manage that."

He gave her a toe-curling kiss before nipping and kissing his way down her neck while his strong fingers stroked her body. Small bursts of sensation exploded under her skin as he moved lower, tormenting and teasing her with his touch along the way. She arched beneath his hand, feeling wild and wanton, and felt his lips curve against her stomach, the muscles clenching in response to the caress of his warm breath. Within minutes he had her writhing, an abandoned cry escaping her parted lips as he made good on his promise, fulfilling her every demand. He lifted his head, watching her as she shattered.

It felt like she was having an out-of-body experience and it took her several minutes to recover. While she lay there in a dreamy state, he kissed his way back up her body. "Bet Mr. Rabbit never did that for you."

She wheezed out a laugh. "Mr. Rabbit is officially retired." When she lifted her hand to stroke the impressive bulge in his jeans, his laugh turned into a groan. She tilted her head. "What about you?"

He brought her hand to his mouth, brushing his lips over her knuckles. "Don't worry about me. It's cold out, and I have a thirty-minute walk to the station."

Frowning, she followed him off the bed. "Why? Did something happen to your truck?"

"No." Tucking his chambray shirt into his well-worn jeans, he walked to the small en suite bathroom. "I left it at the station last night. Didn't want to give the neighbors anything to talk about." He turned on the tap.

Her blissful contentment washed away at his admission. Slowly she lifted the pink velour robe off the hook behind the bedroom door. She was tying the belt when Gage came out of the bathroom, drying his hands on a towel.

"Madison?"

She fiddled with the knot, avoiding his eyes. "Um-hmm."

He tossed the towel on the bed, walked over to put his hands on her shoulders, then ducked to look her in the eyes. "What's wrong?"

"Nothing." But a tinge of anger mixed with her disappointment. "I thought we were done sneaking around."

His hands slid from her arms and into his pockets. "I don't like it any more than you do, but trust me, it's for the best. It won't be for much longer."

Did he honestly believe it was as hard on him as it was on her? He was a smart man, a caring man, so why did he not seem to understand how difficult this was for her?

"Gage, I don't think you understand how hard this is on me. My mother spent a lot of time sneaking around, being someone's dirty little secret."

He went to interrupt her, and she raised her hand. "Let me finish. Admittedly my mother had reason to sneak around and feel ashamed, but I don't, and I won't be made to feel like I do."

A muscle ticked in his jaw. "That sounds like an ultimatum."

Her stomach knotted. "I guess it is." Her drawl was as thick as if she'd left the Deep South only days ago and not ten years.

His gaze softened. "I won't lose you over this. We're not sneaking around, and you have nothing to be ashamed of. Keeping our relationship quiet is more for your benefit than mine. I'm trying to protect you."

"From what?"

He rubbed the back of his neck, glanced at his watch and grimaced. "Look, I really do have to get going. Lily's up at the crack of dawn, and I wanna be home before then. Can we talk about this later?"

Once again he'd chosen his family over her—at least that was how it felt. "Sure. I guess it would be awkward for your ex to catch you sneaking in after spending the night with your girlfriend. I would be considered a girlfriend, right? Not your mistress? You are legally divorced, aren't you? Because the way your ex was acting, you wouldn't know it."

His gaze narrowed and his jaw clenched. He was angry, but she didn't care. She wasn't doing anything wrong, and she was tired of being made to feel like she was. For God's sake, he'd walked thirty minutes in the freezing cold just so the neighbors... Her gaze shot to his. "Wait a minute. You won't feel awkward at all, will you? Because you lied to Sheena, and she thinks you're at work."

"Are you finished?" he asked tightly.

She'd disapproved of her mother's choices. Never understood how Jenny Mae Lane had allowed herself to be taken advantage of like she did, but Madison wasn't feeling so superior now. Love really was blind. "Yeah, I am, and so are we."

He looked like she'd hauled off and socked him in the gut. Good, because that was exactly how she felt. She stormed from the room and down the stairs to the front hall. Unlocking the door, she opened it.

She heard his heavy tread as he came after her, but she kept her eyes fixed on the snow-laden trees, determined not to cry. They looked like they'd been sprinkled with gold dust, sparkling under the yellow glow from the streetlamps. She welcomed the rush of cold air whipping the robe around her feet, rustling a copy of the *Chronicle* on the front porch. She picked up the paper, more to keep her mind off the man coming up behind her than anything else. Shaking off the snow, the front page headline caught her eye: Home for the Holidays or Home for Good? And below, a picture of the perfect family.

She really was a fool. A hot tear slid down her face, splashing onto Gage and his wife's locked lips.

He swore behind her, took her by the arm and jerked her back, scanning the street before he slammed the door.

"What do you think you're doing?" She shook off his hand and went to open the door. "I want you to leave. Now."

He splayed his palms above her head, holding the door shut. "What I'm trying to do is keep your picture off the front page of the paper, and I'm not leaving until you hear me out."

"Like you kept yours off the front page? Guess you don't mind a little PDA as long as it's with your wife. Here." She shoved the paper at his chest as she pushed by him. "I'm sure your family will want extra copies for their scrapbook."

"Oh no, you don't. You're going to listen to me if I have

to tie you up and gag you to get you to." He snagged her by the arm and locked the door.

Hauling her into the living room, he sat her down on the couch. "Don't move." He tossed the paper on the coffee table then walked to the front window to survey the street before closing the drapes, flipping on a light on his way back to the couch.

"Your guilty conscience has made you paranoid." She closed her eyes to keep the tears at bay and curled up on the couch, tucking her cold feet beneath her. The couch sagged, and she felt the weight of his gaze upon her. "I'm tired. I don't want to fight with you anymore."

"It takes two to fight, Madison, and it felt pretty one-sided to me. You know what your problem is?"

"Yeah—you."

"No, it's not me." She felt the heat of his body as he leaned close, his fingers gently wiping the tears from her face. "Your problem is you're confusing yourself with your mother."

She opened her eyes, slanting him a disdainful look. "You're wrong. I'm nothing like my mother. I've spent the last sixteen years making sure I wasn't."

"If that's true, then why do you believe you can be taken advantage of as easily as she was?"

"I don't. I'm not as gullible or as naïve as my mother. And I certainly don't need to depend on a man for my financial well-being."

"Yeah, well, I'm nothing like the men your mother was involved with, and you know it or you wouldn't be with me. I think you're scared that maybe you're more like your mother than you know." He took her hand. "I love you, Madison, and—"

"I'm sure the men who used my mother told her the same thing." She was grasping, she knew that, knew he wasn't like the men her mother had been involved with, but she was afraid. Afraid that maybe she'd fallen for him so hard, so fast, that'd she allowed herself to get involved with a man who would never be able to truly commit to her.

His eyes narrowed. "I'm going to let that slide because you're upset. But just so we're clear here, if all I wanted was a woman for a good time in bed, it wouldn't be you."

Perfect. Just as she realized she was being unfair to him, he decided he didn't want her in his bed. "Why, am I not—"

"You're a helluva lot of work. You're stubborn, and you speak your mind without thinking. You're strong and stand up for what you believe in. And you're loyal and sweet and so damn smart and beautiful you make my head spin. And I knew the moment I met you that one night with you would never be enough. I want you in my life for the long haul, and that means you're going to have to get used to the fact it's not always going to be easy. It's going to be messy and complicated. I'm a package deal, and no matter how much I love you, Lily's and Annie's well-being has to come first. And if you're not up for it, then maybe you're right, and we should end this now."

It was harder hearing the words than saying them, because deep down she knew hers had come from fear and hurt, but Gage's came from truth and honesty. She got that Lily and Annie had to be his priority. If she had children, she'd feel exactly the same way. Now she had to pull on her big-girl panties and decide whether she was going to let her insecurities and trust issues get in the way of having a relationship with the man she loved. Or she could head back to New York, find a job to devote every waking hour to, and her life would be pretty much the way it had been for the last five years. It was a no-brainer. "I can do messy and complicated."

Elbows on his knees, chin resting on his fisted hands, Gage closed his eyes. His broad shoulders rose on a deep inward breath. He leaned back against the couch, then slowly turned his head. "It took you long enough to decide."

"It's a big decision."

"I guess it is. I just thought we were on the same page a ways back."

"We were. We are. I love you and don't want to lose you because of my issues. I'll figure out a way to deal with your ex-wife." She rubbed his hand. "I'm sorry if I made you feel like I was comparing you to the men my mother dated. I wasn't."

He tugged her closer, wrapping an arm around her. "I'm sorry about the picture in the paper. I should've warned you. But if you look closely, you'll see I'm not a willing participant. And if it helps, I told Sheena I love you and that this is the last time she'll be staying at the house."

Madison worried her bottom lip between her teeth. "You told her that?"

"Yeah, I did." He tapped her nose. "Maybe next time, you'll give me a chance to get a word in."

"Umm." Embarrassed by the memory of her rant, she decided to move the conversation along. "Maybe you and Sheena could sit down with Annie and explain…" She stopped talking. He was rubbing the back of his neck again.

"Here's the thing. Sheena's afraid her throat problems

are going to end her singing career. She's not in a great place right now. She's alone and thinking about what she's given up and wants it back."

Madison winced. She sympathized until she realized what Gage said. "She wants *you* back?"

"Settle down, tiger. I've made it clear that's not going to happen. But Sheena's never been one to take no for an answer, and I wouldn't put it past her to stir the pot with Annie and…" He hesitated, then continued, "There are a lot of people in town who like the idea of a hometown boy being married to a celebrity, and when Sheena's here, it's like we never divorced."

"And because she stays with you, and you've maintained a good relationship for the girls' sakes…"

"Yeah. And if word gets out we're together, it could get ugly for you. That's why I want to keep our relationship on the down-low. I'm sorry, I know that's not what you want to hear."

She shook her head and tried to ignore the nervous flutter in her stomach. "No, it's not. But I understand where you're coming from now."

"Hey, look at me. We're not doing anything wrong, and the people who really matter know that. But with the vote on Monday, and everything else going on, it's for the best." He kissed the top of her head. "Maybe this will make you feel better. Annie feels bad about how she's been acting. You'll be hearing from her today with an apology."

"I'm glad. Thanks for telling me."

"You're welcome, and I'm going to get Sheena in to see my dad and Matt today. I'm sure one of them can recommend someone for a second opinion. She'll be out of here after the holidays. Trust me," he said when she went to contradict him. "I know Sheena. She'll only be able to handle life in Christmas for a couple of days. She's not a fan of small towns."

Madison didn't share his optimism. After all, who'd hated small towns more than she once did?

He reached for the paper. "And I'll deal with Rick."

"Good, because he's starting to get on my last nerve."

The corner of his mouth twitched. "Hate to tell you, honey, but I think the feeling's mutual. It's becoming obvious Dane wants you out of Christmas."

"Tell him to get in line." She tapped Rick's byline. "I'd wondered who was working with Harrison behind the scenes here. I should've realized it was Rick. He's the one who approached Hartwell about building a resort in Christmas, and it was Harrison he made contact with, not Joe, if I remember correctly."

"And he has the most to lose if the deal doesn't go through. He's drowning in debt."

"Not good."

"No, it's not, and it gets worse. Harrison tried to get Ethan to disallow the vote. We're pretty sure he paid Dane to hold back the announcement. He's flying into town tomorrow to counter your campaign."

"I can handle Harrison." She glanced at the paper and caught the headline beneath the McBride family picture. Her gaze shot to Gage. "I don't believe it. Did you know about this?

His brows drew together. "Know about what?"

She showed him the article. "It says here there's some obscure bylaw on the books, and we need five hundred signatures by tomorrow at five p.m. or they'll be able to table the vote on Monday."

"I never heard anything about it, but if it's true...I'm sorry, honey. I know you've put in a lot of hours on this."

She frowned. "You sound as if I should give up." And he didn't sound overly disappointed about it, either. "You want me to back out, don't you?" He grimaced. "Oh my God, you've wanted the deal with Hartwell to go through all along."

He held up his hands. "I don't care one way or another. What I do care about is you and this town, and this has shitshow written all over it."

"I'm sorry you feel that way, but I'll do whatever it takes to make sure Harrison doesn't win. And if you'd paid any attention at all to my presentation at the town hall, you'd understand why." Since he'd fallen asleep during the meeting, she recapped the problems and her findings. "So as you can see," she said fifteen minutes later, "the resort will go bankrupt within its first year. With Harrison at the helm, probably sooner. In the long run, my plan is better."

He gave his head a shake as if to clear it. "Oh, yeah, I got that. I also got that nothing I say will change your mind."

"No, it won't. I'm right about this. Now all I have to do is convince the citizens of Christmas."

"And that's exactly what I'm worried about. Remember, just because I love you doesn't mean I won't throw you in jail if you cause trouble."

"I swear, no trouble, Sheriff." But just in case, because when it came to Madison and the citizens of Christmas things tended to go awry, she crossed her fingers.

He scowled and tugged her hand from behind her back. "*Seriously?*"

Chapter Twenty-five

Dressed for another day of pounding the pavement in a puffy white snowsuit that made her look like the Michelin man, Madison stood in Nell's kitchen debating whether or not to pick up the phone. She couldn't shake the feeling that something was wrong. Gage hadn't shown up last night like he'd promised. But then again, he might have phoned to cancel, and she'd been comatose after spending ten hours running around Christmas trying to get enough signatures to get them on the ballot. And Nell didn't have an answering machine.

She picked up the phone, then put it down. She didn't want to come across as the annoying, needy girlfriend. She was being paranoid. Something probably came up with Annie and Lily. And with her big-girl panties firmly in place, Madison ignored the possibility that the something had to do with Sheena.

No doubt Madison would run into him downtown. She

was already late for the strategy session at Grace's. They were sixty-five names shy of the five hundred required to get them on the ballot tomorrow. And with her street team's friends and family tapped out, and a 5:00 p.m. deadline today, Madison didn't have time to waste.

As a blustery wind pushed her down the walkway to Nell's pickup, Stella waved her over. "This was delivered to me by mistake."

"Thanks," Madison said, accepting the package. It was addressed to her in Christmas, as if she actually lived there. Odd how something so small resonated. But somehow it made her feel like she belonged.

Waiting for the truck to warm up, she thought back to her interactions with the shop owners of Christmas the day before. They all seemed to think she'd set up a consulting business and were anxious for advice. Helping Joe build a successful business was the aspect Madison had enjoyed most about her job. And Lord knew if anyone needed her help, it was the citizens of Christmas.

A nervous laugh bubbled up her throat as she realized she was actually thinking of doing it, of moving to Christmas and setting up shop. The perfect excuse to get in touch with Gage without coming across as a stalker girlfriend, she decided.

She opened the package—careful not to rip the address—and pulled out the new phone she'd ordered. She sent off a quick text to Skye and Vivi, a little surprised when they didn't respond right away.

Erasing her first racier attempts to Gage, in case Annie or Lily would see the message, she settled on "Need to talk. Call me." She waited, fiddling with the radio stations to kill time. Then she checked the phone to see if it was working before trying again. "Everything ok?"

Busy, he's just busy, she told herself in response to the panicked uptick of her pulse. And if the guy on the radio was right—a storm system was expected to move in right about the time Harrison was scheduled to blow into town—she had to get busy, too. Pulling out of Nell's driveway, she headed downtown.

As Madison turned onto Main Street, she realized her instincts had been right after all. Dozens of placard-waving people held up traffic as they crossed the town square. She couldn't see what was on their signs or hear what they were protesting, but she didn't have to be a card-carrying member of Mensa to know it was about her. No wonder she hadn't heard from Gage. Probably better she hadn't. He'd have given her an I-told-you-so lecture.

She parked a safe distance away. Locking the truck, she took a quick look at her cell—no messages—before stuffing it in her pocket. She went to cross the road.

An older woman stood in front of Nell's pickup, wagging her cane at Madison. "You should be ashamed of yourself."

Before she could ask why, the teenager stuffing fliers under the windshield wipers of the parked cars shoved one into Madison's hand. He did a double take, gulped, and tried to snatch the paper back.

She jerked it away from him. Bile rose in her throat as she scanned the paper. There was a picture of Gage with Sheena and the girls, and beneath it, one from yesterday morning with Madison wearing the pink velour robe and Gage standing behind her. She looked like she'd just rolled out of bed. Printed above her head in bold black print were the words "Home wrecker." Gage hadn't been paranoid after all.

The protesters now marched around the decorated twenty-foot Douglas fir in the center of the town square, chanting, "Ho, ho, ho, go home. Home wreckers not welcome. Vote for Hartwell."

Madison's breath squeezed out of her. Faces blurred in front of her, their voices ringing in her ears. The town square melded into a schoolyard, kids circling, crowding, chanting, and shoving. A snowball hit her in the head, snapping her back to the here and now. Ted and Fred ran toward her, each taking an arm to drag her off the road.

Customers spilled from the shops onto the sidewalks as Jill, in uniform, a megaphone in hand, ran toward them. "Don't you dare listen to them," she said to Madison, then addressed Ted and Fred. "Help Ray keep them off the streets while I get Maddie out of here."

"Jill's right. Don't you pay them no mind," Ted said, as he gently brushed the snow from Madison's hair before turning to Jill. "Do we get badges and guns?"

"No! Get over there."

It was like everything was happening in slow motion, and Madison's feet were rooted to the cobblestone street. Jill took her by the hand, then glanced over her shoulder. "Brandi, Sophia, back off!" she yelled into the megaphone, waving the two women, who were defending Madison, away from the four older women who threatened them with their signs.

It was happening all over again, only this time it was Madison's fault, not her mother's. She wanted to run and hide. Get away from Christmas as fast as she could. "I'll go. I'll leave," she said in a strangled whisper, tugging her hand from Jill's.

"Okay. I'll…" A shout went up from the crowd. "Fred, Ted!" Jill bellowed, pointing to the decorations raining down on the protesters. "Move them back from the tree." She pinched the bridge of her nose. "We could use the sheriff's help right about now. Any idea where he is?"

Even with her emotions frozen in the past, Madison couldn't ignore the sick sense of worry building inside her. "No, I haven't been able to reach him this morning. Do you think something's wrong?"

Jill held the truck's door open. "No, I'm sure everything's fine. He's been putting in some long hours and probably slept in. I'll try him again."

The crowd now turned on Gage, calling for his resignation, slandering his character, his morals. Caught between wanting to defend him and getting out of there, Madison hesitated with one foot on the running board. She looked up to see Annie and Lily standing outside of Sophia's shop with their mother.

Madison wanted to yell at Sheena to get the girls back in the store. They shouldn't be hearing or seeing any of this. Annie and Lily, looking pale and scared, edged closer to their mother. A wave of protective anger rose up inside Madison, washing away her hurt and embarrassment. She'd had enough of small-minded bullies who didn't give a damn who they hurt.

She jumped off the running board and slammed the truck's door.

"Madison?" Jill said nervously.

She snatched the megaphone from Jill's hand. "Don't

worry. I'll handle this." Madison ran along the sidewalk to reach Ted and Fred's truck.

"Oh, no, Madison!" Jill cried, coming after her.

"Hey," Madison yelled into the megaphone. "Your problem's with me, not Gage McBride. You want me out of town?" She was heartened to hear about thirty *No*s beneath the roar of *Yes*es. "Fine, but first you'll hear me out. Ted and Fred, you mind if I stand on your truck?" she called out to the two men, making their way toward her.

They grinned when they reached her, giving her a boast onto the hood. "We were getting worried about you, girlie. Thought you might be listening to these idiots."

"Not anymore." She stood, looking out over the crowd who stamped their feet against the cold, blowing on their hands as they waited impatiently for her to speak.

"Do you people hear yourselves? What happened to being kind to strangers, loving your neighbors? Isn't that what all you good Christian folks preach? If you ask me, you're a bunch of hypocrites."

Rick Dane stood off to the side, looking furious as several people slowly lowered their signs. Sophia, Grace, and Autumn smiled up at her from where they now stood with Ted and Fred. Standing behind them, Brandi and Trent gave her the thumbs-up. "Tomorrow is Christmas Eve, a time for peace, goodwill toward men, a time for family, a time when little girls should be enjoying the excitement of the holiday and not listening to you slander their father. Did any of you happen to notice Gage's daughters standing there?" She pointed them out to the crowd, some of whom now looked ashamed. "Gage McBride is one of the most honorable men I've ever met, and he's done nothing to deserve this."

"He was till you came along," a man yelled.

"You should be ashamed of yourself, carrying on with a married man," an older woman in the front shouted.

Gage might not like what she was about to say, Lily and Annie might not, either, but it was about time Madison stood up for herself.

"If any of you knew me, you'd know the last thing I'd ever do is break up a family. Gage and Sheena divorced years ago. Something y'all have chosen to ignore. And I had nothing to do with that. I've done nothing to be ashamed of, but y'all have. I'm in love with Gage McBride . . . a-and he loves me, too." She hoped he still did after this. There were some grumbles of disbelief in the crowd, but at least half the protesters now lowered their signs.

"Lily, no," Sheena cried, as her daughter ran to the truck.

Fred chuckled, lifting Lily onto the hood beside Madison. The little girl leaned over and yelled into the megaphone Madison had lowered to her side. "My daddy does too love Maddie, and so do I." She wrapped her hands around the megaphone as if she had more to say, but Paul McBride pushed through the crowd with Nell and Liz trying to keep up with him, and said, "You let Grandpa have that for a minute, sweetpea." She did as he asked. Gage's dad looked up at Madison. "You okay, honey?"

He sounded just like his son. She gave him a watery smile and nodded. He turned to Ted and Fred. "Get Nell in the truck, boys."

Nell glowered at the crowd, then looked up at Madison. "You don't pay them no mind, you hear," she said before allowing Fred and Ted to help her into the truck.

Liz patted Madison's boot. "Don't you worry. Paul will take care of this."

"I just wish Gage were here."

"I know, dear. He probably went with Ethan to pick up Mr. Hartwell at the airport. Cell reception can be spotty on those roads."

Liz was right—that made perfect sense. Feeling like she could actually breathe again, Madison returned her attention to Gage's dad.

"Since my son is on the job, no doubt putting himself in harm's way like he does each and every day for you people, I'm going to speak for him. You should all be ashamed of yourselves. This woman is the best thing that has happened to my son in a long time. And if any of you say another word against her, you can find yourself a new doctor." There was a loud clatter as the rest of the signs were tossed on the ground.

One of the men at the front of the crowd rubbed his jaw. "Sorry, Doc, you're right. We were out of line. But I haven't worked in six months, and Ms. Lane here—"

"You owe Madison the apology, not me." Paul handed her the megaphone.

Madison looked at the man. "Believe me, I understand how scary it is to be out of work. I lost my job, too. But all I'm asking for is an opportunity to show you another way to turn things around in Christmas besides the resort. In the end, it will be up to all of you to decide."

Rick moved in. "Don't waste your energy, Ms. Lane. No one here wants an alternative to Hartwell, except maybe you."

"You're wrong, Rick. We do," her friends said.

He sneered. "Not enough of you to make a difference.

You'll never get five hundred signatures before the deadline today."

"Ha! That's where you're wrong, Dane." Hailey elbowed her way through the crowd with Holly at her heels. She held up two clipboards. "We did it, Maddie. Five hundred signatures!"

A cheer went up from below her. Madison joined in, feeling practically giddy with their success. Paul smiled up at her and helped both her and Lily down from the truck.

"Impossible! That's impossible," Rick yelled, a frantic look in his eyes. He grabbed the clipboards, scanning the names as he flipped through the pages. "Gage can't sign this. He's a member of the town council." Dane took a pen from inside his jacket pocket and furiously crossed out Gage's name.

With their goal achieved and Gage's family and her friends standing by her, Madison knew she'd made the right decision earlier. She was going to do it. She was going to move to Christmas to be with the man she loved and hang out her shingle. "No? But I can." She took Rick's pen from his hand and wrote her name.

Rick snatched the pen back. "You aren't a citizen of Christmas." He went to cross out her name.

She whipped the pen from his hand. "Yes I am, and I'll prove it." Everyone followed her to Nell's truck. She took out the cell phone box and handed it to Rick. "Can't argue with the U.S. postal service, now can you?" She smiled.

Despite the wind whipping down the road, the first flakes starting to fall, sweat beaded on Rick's forehead. "You haven't won yet." He looked her in the eyes, his voice low and rough. "And you won't. I'll make sure of that." Tossing the box at her, he stalked away. A group of men tried to talk to him, but he blew them off.

"Always was a sore loser," Nell said then smiled. "Guess I've got myself a roommate, Paul. You can release me from the hospital for good now."

"We'll see, Nell." He leaned into Madison. "Are you sure you know what you're getting yourself into?"

"Hey, I heard that," Nell said.

"Come on, everyone. We've got lots to celebrate. Hot chocolate's on me." Grace gestured them across the street to the bakery.

"No, my treat," Madison said. "Without all of your help, I probably would've had ten signatures tops. Thank you. All of you."

Brandi and Trent gave her a high five. Sophia, Autumn, Hailey, Holly, and Grace gave her a hug then headed for the bakery. Lily tugged on Madison's arm. "Can Mommy come, too?" she asked, as Sheena and Annie joined them.

"Sure. Of course she can." Even though it looked like Sheena would rather be anywhere else but there.

Madison touched Annie's arm as she went to follow her mother and sister. "Annie, I'm sorry if what I said about your dad and me upset you. I—"

Annie cut her off with a shake of her head. "No, it's okay. They were being really mean. I'm glad you stood up to them. I would've..." She trailed off, looking after her mother, then frowned. "Where's my dad?"

"Mrs. O'Connor thinks he went to pick up Mr. Hartwell." And Madison was trying hard to believe that.

Just then a black Escalade rolled down Main Street, pulling in behind Nell's truck. Ethan got out, a harried expression in his eyes. Madison could sympathize. She often felt like pulling her hair out when dealing with Harrison, either that or sticking a fork in his eye. But it wasn't Harrison who got out of the passenger side. It was a woman with curly, butterscotch-blonde hair. "Skye?" The back doors opened, and Harrison, in a mahogany mink coat, stepped out of one side, while a woman with long, chocolate-brown hair got out of the other side.

Madison frowned. "Vivi, Skye?" The women turned. Stunned, Madison jogged to the SUV. "I don't believe it. I thought I was imagining things." She threw herself into their open arms. "What are you two doing here?" she asked, pulling back from their group hug.

"We missed you, and Vivi's worried—" Skye began.

Vivi cut her off. "We'll get into that later. Right now—"

"Wait," Madison interrupted Vivi, scanning the group of people surrounding Harrison. "Ethan, where's Gage?"

He frowned. "I don't know. Why?"

"Come on, you've got to hear this." Vivi tugged on her hand, leading her to where Ethan and Harrison stood. "We sat behind the Snake on the flight from New York and overheard a very interesting conversation he was having with someone on the phone."

Madison was barely listening, her worry for Gage making it hard to concentrate on anything else. She was about to interrupt Vivi when she heard what she was saying, and her mouth fell open. Harrison didn't want the land in Christmas to build a resort. He wanted it for the gold Rick told him was there.

Madison had known all along there was more to Harrison's obsession with Christmas. She rounded on him. "You idiot! How could you lead these people on?"

The crowd grew as word spread that Harrison had

arrived. Coulter Dane came up beside Ethan. "What gold? Mine was tapped years ago."

"You're wrong." Harrison crouched to open his briefcase, pulling out a thick file. "Rick gave me samples of the soil and ore. I had a reputable geologist test them. It's a rich find, maybe one of the richest." The idiot had the nerve to look smug.

Coulter studied the papers, then shook his head. "Easy enough to salt the soil, and I suspect the samples of ore are the ones that went missing from my safe a few months back. They were my great-grandfather's from the first strike in the late 1900s. You've been had, boy."

Angry muttering broke out through the crowd, and Harrison glanced nervously around him. "I've done nothing illegal. If you're angry, blame Rick Dane. He's the one who approached me with this deal."

"Where's Rick?" Ethan asked, his jaw clenched.

"He peeled out of here about fifteen minutes ago," Fred said.

"I've got a bad feeling about this, Ethan." Madison's voice cracked with panic. "I haven't heard from or seen Gage since yesterday."

Ethan put a hand on her shoulder. "Okay, let's not jump to conclusions just yet. Paul?"

"No, same as Madison. Sheena." Paul waved her over.

Harrison slammed his briefcase closed and whipped out his phone, walking a safe distance from the crowd. He was furious, but kept his voice low so as not to be overheard. Madison figured his BFF was getting an earful. She didn't care. All she cared about was finding Gage.

"Sheena, when was the last time you saw Gage?" Paul asked.

The snow was falling harder now, and Sheena brushed the flakes from her hair before answering, "Shouldn't you ask Ms. Lane? I'm sure—"

"This is serious, Sheena. We're worried something has happened to Gage."

Her eyes widened. "Oh, I-I'm sorry. He, uh, he came home around eight last night to put Lily to bed and say good night to Annie. He left about an hour later to go back to work. He said he'd be home late. I thought he was with Ms. Lane."

Madison's knees buckled. It wasn't her imagination—something had happened to him. Vivi and Skye each put an arm around her waist.

Madison's cell rang. She fumbled the phone as she pulled it from her pocket. "It's Gage." She sagged against her friends. Relieved laughter greeted her announcement. "Where are—" She began.

"Where no one will find him, Ms. Lane," Rick cut her off. "So you better do as I say if you want to see him again."

Her gaze shot to Ethan and Paul. Ethan searched her face and held up a hand. "Quiet, everyone. Quiet," he said to the others. *Speaker,* he mouthed to Madison.

"Tonight, at midnight, you're going to be outside the church with two hundred and fifty grand in unmarked bills. No one else but you, Ms. Lane. Do you understand me?"

She focused on Ethan. She couldn't look at Nell, whom Fred and Ted supported, or Paul, whom Liz had wrapped her arms around. But most of all, she couldn't look at Lily and Annie, who stood beside their mother with tears streaming down their faces. "Yes . . . yes, I do, but that's a lot of money and it might take some time."

"Midnight tonight's all you got. And if anyone comes looking for us before then, he's dead."

"N-no one will. I'll get your money." Madison bit her lip, fighting back tears. "Why are you doing this?"

"Your boyfriend started putting things together. He was nosing around the *Chronicle* last night. The blood on the floor is his. He's alive...for now. You've got till midnight." The line went dead.

Closing her eyes, she tried to keep it together. Gage was alive. He needed her to stay strong, and so did Annie and Lily. Sheena was crying uncontrollably, upsetting them further.

Madison went to crouch in front of them. "Annie, Lily, you know how much your daddy loves you, don't you?" They nodded, sobs catching in their throats. She swallowed hard to hold back her own. "And you know how strong he is, how smart he is, and that he's doing everything he can to get back to you, right? Good," she said when they nodded. "You hang on to that. And we're going to do everything we can to help him." She wiped away their tears.

Annie took her sister's hand and nodded.

Madison had to do something. It was the only way she knew how to cope with her fear. She had to believe Rick wouldn't hurt Gage. He wanted the money, and they'd get it for him.

As she stood up, she saw Harrison's panicked gaze shift from her to his phone and knew exactly what he'd done. Beyond furious, she strode toward him. "It was you. You called Rick, didn't you? You told him you knew it was a scam. That we all knew."

"So what if I did? It's not my fault—"

She hauled off and punched him in the nose. He landed on his butt, blood splattering over the snow and his ridiculous coat. "Do something," he yelled at Jill, who'd come to stand beside her. "She assaulted me."

Jill lifted a shoulder. "I didn't see anything." She glanced over her shoulder. "Any of you see anything?"

"Nope, didn't see a thing," several people said.

"Ray, take Mr. Hartwell to the station and question him as to his involvement in Sherriff McBride's kidnapping," Ethan said.

Madison shook off the pain in her hand. "Coulter, you know your nephew. Is there any place you can think of that he might be holding Gage?"

He glanced at Nell, then nodded. "I have a couple of places in mind. If I had a better idea which way he was headed, I could narrow it down some, save time."

"Okay," she said, then walked to a bench in the town square. Vivi and Skye helped her onto it. She stood and lifted the megaphone to her lips. "If anyone saw Rick leaving Christmas between nine last night and when he left here at noon today, go on over to the bakery and give Fred and Ted your information." She glanced at the two older men. They nodded and headed across the street with Grace. "Everyone else, call your friends and family and ask them the same question. If you find anything out, let Ted and Fred know. They'll pass on the information to Jill."

Jill, talking on her phone, stopped pacing to nod.

"All right, folks, I know some of you are up against it financially, and the news that there was never going to be a resort was tough for you to hear. But I want you to know I have big plans for this town, and one way or another, we're going to turn it around. But right now, we have to come together, dig into our wallets, and bring Gage home." Madison would give every cent she had to bring him home safe. She'd transferred a hundred thousand dollars to the bank in Christmas a week ago to show the bank manager how much faith she had in her business plan for Grace's Sugar Plum Bakery. But she didn't know what he kept in the vault.

"We need to come up with a hundred and fifty thousand dollars by midnight tonight."

Vivi nudged her. "He said a quarter of a million."

"I know. I'm putting up a hundred thousand."

Vivi gave her a long look, then slowly nodded.

"If you're able to contribute, the ladies will keep track of whatever you put in." She gestured to Vivi, Skye, and her friends from Christmas, who helped her down from the bench.

Jill ran over. "Okay, we've located Gage's phone. It was out on Old Mill Road. Rick must've known it had GPS and tossed it after he called you."

"Does that help, Coulter?" Madison asked.

"Yep, narrows it down." He looked at the sky. "Storm's heading in. I'll have to take the dogs."

"I'm coming with you, Coulter," Ethan said.

"Shouldn't we call in—" Jill began.

"No." Ethan shook his head. "We don't want to spook Rick." He turned to Madison and put his hands on her shoulders. "My best friend is one hell've a lucky guy, and believe me, he knows it."

"Bring him home safe, Ethan."

"We will."

She had to believe that or she'd fall to pieces.

Chapter Twenty-six

Hands cuffed behind his back, Gage lay on the narrow cot trying to tighten his grip on the key slipping from his frozen fingers. He'd been half out of it from the hit he took to his head, lying facedown on the floor, when he realized Rick was going to cuff him. Gage had managed to get one of the keys off his belt before he did, sliding it into the back pocket of his jeans. If he'd known then how long it'd take to get the key out, he would've put it in his mouth.

Gage still had a hard time believing what Rick had done. It just went to prove that people would do anything if they were desperate enough. And if Gage had realized just how far Rick would go, he would've alerted his deputies to his suspicions—like the missing ore from Coulter's safe and the similarities between the Hartwell deal and a scam Rick had written an article about a year ago. But it was only once he began focusing on Rick and his relationship with Harrison Hartwell that Gage had started to put the pieces together, and he hadn't wanted to lose the element of surprise.

He lost his grip on the key and cursed. The bedsprings squeaked as he shifted. He bumped his head against the rough timber, sending a shower of cold white flakes onto his face. He lifted his eyes to the walls now coated in a thick frost. The fire in the woodstove had died an hour after Rick left.

Gage didn't have a choice. He had to get some heat in the place or risk succumbing to hypothermia. The smoke from the woodstove would alert Rick to the fact Gage had managed, using the sharp edge of the metal frame, to saw through the rope binding his feet, but hopefully he wouldn't turn tail and run. Then again, with Gage's gun in his pocket, Rick would be cocky enough to think he could handle him. That would be his downfall.

Because nothing was going to stop Gage from taking Rick out before he moved on to Plan B. Gage was betting Rick's Plan A—the one where Madison didn't get her five hundred signatures and Rick got his payoff from Hartwell and hit the road—would fail.

But if Rick got a chance to put his Plan B into action, Gage was worried just how far he'd go to get rid of Madison before the vote tomorrow.

Gage sat up, fighting against a wave of gut-churning light-headedness to push himself to his feet. Pain lanced through the back of his eyes at the movement. He rode it out before crossing to the far wall of the one-room cabin. With his back to the woodstove, he lowered to a squat and, with his cuffed hands, started to awkwardly feed logs into the mouth of the stove. Once he was finished, he managed to push himself upright and cross to the table.

He stared down at the pile of leaflets, at Madison looking so damn beautiful it was easy to miss the hurt in her eyes, the angry set of her lips. Given her past, he didn't want to think what seeing the leaflets and protesters had done to her.

He prayed to God someone stood up for her when he couldn't be there. His gaze shifted to Annie and Lily, then back to Madison. Rick really was insane if he didn't think Gage would do everything in his power to get back to them, to keep them safe.

By the time he crumpled the last flier and tossed it onto the logs, he could barely lift his arms. For Madison's and his daughters' sakes, he had to stay focused. He made his way to the shelf by the window where a metal container held matches.

Through the grime-smudged glass, he tried to get his bearings. But there was no chance of that with the blizzard raging outside. He listened for the whirr of the sled, but all he heard was the snow pelting the window and a lone wolf's howl joining the winds. With the storm, it would take Rick a couple of hours to get back with the blankets and supplies. At least the guy didn't want him dead, just out of the picture until he got his money.

Nudging the metal container off the shelf with his chin, he sent a shower of matches to the cabin floor. Awkwardly, he lowered himself to his knees and nearly fell on his face. He righted himself, scooping up a handful of matches. Unwilling to take the chance he'd fall, he made his way back to the woodstove on his knees.

Frustrated when seven of the nine matches snapped, he carefully lit the next. It sputtered out before it hit the paper. He clutched the last one in his hand. "Thank

Christ," he muttered, hearing the crackle of paper, the faint smell of wood smoke wafting past his nostrils.

He warmed himself by the fire until some feeling returned to his hands. Gritting his teeth, he came to his feet and moved to the edge of the mattress. He groped behind him for the key. His fingers closed around the cold metal at the same time he heard the distant whir of the sled. He fumbled the key. *You've got time. Focus.* He slowed his breathing.

The sound of the key sliding into the lock sent a rush of adrenaline through him, and he barely heard the snick of release or felt the cuffs fall open. He groaned as he brought his arms painfully forward, working out the aching numbness.

The sled came closer.

He picked up the poker resting against the woodstove and went to the window. Headlights bobbed up and down in the distance. Gage got into position behind the door. Several tension-filled minutes later, there was a loud screech of metal against metal and a heavy thud. Gage went back to the window. Thirty feet away, the lights at a sideways angle, the sled appeared to be suspended in mid-air. Rick's scream cut off Gage's curse. The stupid bastard must've hit a rock.

Gage threw open the door and headed out. He battled through the drifting snow to reach Rick, who lay beneath the overturned sled.

"Hurry! Get if off me. I think my leg's broken."

He dropped the poker by his feet and straddled Dane. Gage angled his shoulder to get better leverage. "How the hell did you not see the boulder, you moron?" he gritted out, as he attempted to push the machine over the rock.

"I saw it, but—" Rick's breath sawed in and out "—something ran out in front of me..." He let loose an anguished cry when Gage lifted the sled off his legs.

"I can't hold it for long, Dane. You're going to have to shimmy out from under it."

"I can't. I can't do it," Rick's voice came out a strangled sob.

Gage's arms started to buckle. He smoothed the sharp edge of anger from his voice. "Lever yourself up on your elbows and use them to pull yourself out. That's it. Keep going. Another six inches and you're good." Gage gave the sled one more hard push before he let go. Breathing hard, he sprawled across the leather seat.

"Gage...McBride...Sheriff," Rick's panicked whisper rose on each name.

"What?" Gage slowly turned his head to look down at Dane's bleached-white face.

A panicked look in his eyes, Rick's gaze darted from Gage to the cabin behind him. "Wolf."

With slow and careful movements, Gage eased himself off the sled to stand over Rick. "Where's my gun?" he said quietly.

"Somewhere, it fell out when..." Dane frantically swept his hands through the snow.

A low menacing growl came from behind.

"Stop. Now." Gage ordered, as he slowly lowered himself, reaching for the poker. The big and scary method would have to work. And he was feeling pretty damn big and scary at the moment. He turned to face down the wolf. Out of the corner of his eye, he spotted Coulter and Ethan coming up the far side of the cabin.

It was just one of Coulter's dogs.

Gage smothered a relieved laugh, and said, "Forget it. I'm not putting my life on the line for you, Dane." He tossed the poker and walked away to the sound of Dane screaming. After what he'd put Madison through, he deserved to suffer a bit.

*   *   *

Be at the church at midnight.

"Wait for us at the church. We'll be there at eight o'clock on the dot to pick you up. We're going to have a wonderful life, baby. I promise." Her mother smoothed Madison's hair from her face. "Mitch is going to be a real good daddy, you'll see." The sun's rays caught in her mother's long hair as she jogged to the side of the dusty road in her short black waitress's uniform to wait for her ride. She turned, blew Madison a kiss, and waved. "Love you to the moon and back, baby."

Be at the church at midnight. Rick's voice echoed in Madison's head as the bell tolled the hour. Unable to block the old memories, she sat on the stairs outside the church, trying to breathe past her fear.

The door creaked open behind her. "Any sign of them?" Nell asked gruffly.

"No, not yet, but it's just midnight. Rick probably didn't take the weather into account. Y'all be quiet now. I'm supposed to be alone here," Madison said, her gaze shifting from the road and parking lot to her left, the stand of trees and open field to her right. She'd been sitting on the steps for the last twenty minutes, watching in frustration as half the town snuck in through the back doors. She didn't blame them, but she didn't want to do anything that might put Gage in more danger.

"She's upset. She has a Southern drawl when she's upset," someone whispered.

"Well, of course she's upset—"

Madison sighed. "I'm fine. Now get...someone's coming." She clutched the black satchel to her chest as three shadows crept toward the church. Sliding along the step, she moved to peek through the rails. Fuzzy reindeer ears popped up in front of her. She screamed.

Jill burst through the doors, gun drawn.

Sheena jumped up. "Sorry...sorry," she yelped. "They snuck out of the house."

Madison stood on shaky legs, waving the three of them over. "It's okay. Come on, hurry up and get inside." Lily, in her reindeer hat, bounded up the stairs and threw herself at Madison. Annie, a black toque pulled low, hung back, gnawing on her bottom lip. Madison held out her hand. With a choked sob, Annie flew to her. She wrapped her arms around them both and held tight. "You two are just like your daddy, do you know that? Nothing could stop you from being here tonight, and nothing will stop him, either."

They nodded, sniffed, and clung a little tighter. Their mother, standing beside them, sniffed too. Madison dropped a kiss on Lily's and Annie's heads. "You go inside and wait. Grace brought hot chocolate and sugar cookies."

Lily gave her a watery smile. "It's like a party to welcome Daddy home." Taking her sister's hand, she followed Sheena inside.

As the door closed behind them, Madison sat back down on the steps. Haunted by the look of fear in Lily's and Annie's eyes, she buried her face in her hands and did something she hadn't done in a very long time. "Don't let them lose their dad, God. Not like this, not now. Please bring him back to us." She released a shuddered breath. "I can't do it. I can't go through this again. I'll do whatever you ask me to, God. But please, please, let him come home safe."

She felt a gentle hand on her back, the soft scent of roses teasing her senses. It was the same fragrance Madison's mother used to wear. Someone sat down beside her. Madison lifted her head.

"Sorry." Sheena winced, her gloved hands twisting in her lap. "I just wanted to apologize for encouraging Rick. I wasn't in a good place. I know it's no excuse, but I felt like I'd lost everything: my career, Gage, the girls, my home." She glanced over her shoulder. "They all pretty much hate me now."

You've got a real interesting sense of humor, Big Guy.

"They'll get over it. I have." It was true. Nothing mattered anymore, her worries over money, Sheena, what other people thought of her, nothing mattered but Gage coming home to them.

"I really do love him. But I'd rather know he was happy here with you than lose him forever." She took Madison's hand, her eyes bright with tears. "We can't lose him."

Madison squeezed her hand. "We won't."

Sheena nodded, brushing away her tears. "You'll make a great wife and mother, much better than me."

"Whoa, we're not getting married, at least not yet…I mean…" Lately Madison had let herself fantasize about being married to Gage, and it'd been an amazing fantasy. But it was a big step, and they hadn't known each other that long. Even if sometimes it felt like she'd known him forever.

"Maybe not right away, but you will."

"Whether we get married or not, Sheena, I want you to know I'll never try to take your place with Annie and Lily."

"Thanks." She grimaced. "But you're already more of a mother to them than me. I'm not what you'd call the motherly type."

Madison felt a pang of sympathy for the woman. "All they need to know is that you love them. That if they ever need you, you'll be there for them."

"I haven't been. Maybe you could help me with that."

"Sure, you bet."

She patted Madison's hand, then looked out over the parking lot. "I got a call from a specialist." She frowned. "I'm not sure how he found out about me. He wasn't the specialist Dr. McBride recommended. But he's treated cases similar to mine and is pretty sure he'll be able to help me. He's fitting me in at four today."

Madison knew exactly how he'd found her: Nell. But Madison had made a promise to help Sheena, and for Annie's sake she would. "Did you know that all Annie has ever wanted for Christmas was for you to come home?"

She looked stricken. "No...no one told me." She twisted her gloved hands in her lap.

Madison covered her hand with hers. "You should stay. I'm sure the doctor can fit you in after the holidays."

"I guess I could, but I thought you'd all be relieved to get rid of me."

"No. Christmas is a time for family, you should be here with yours."

"Thank you." Sheena hugged her.

Madison surreptitiously sniffed Sheena's fur collar. "Do you wear...I forget the name, but it's a perfume that smells like roses?" she asked when Sheena released her.

She shook her head. "No, I'm allergic to perfume."

In the distance, Madison heard what sounded like the jingle of bells. She straightened, peering through the falling snow. "Do you hear that?"

Sheena stood and cocked her head. "It sounds like bells." Her eyes widened. "Maybe it's Rick. I'll get inside." She opened the door. "Be careful, Madison."

She nodded as she stood to look beyond the open field.

The jingle of bells grew louder. "On Donner, On Blitzen..."

No, she must be hearing things.

"For chrissakes, Coulter," grumbled a familiar deep voice.

"Ho, ho, ho," someone chuckled.

Please let it be Gage, she thought, as she took off down the church steps. A white light shone through the frosted mist. Then a team of dogs cleared the trees with Coulter Dane, a Santa hat on his head, holding the reins. The light from the lantern swinging on the pole at the front of the sleigh illuminated his passenger. "Thank God," Madison cried, running through the snow.

As Coulter reined in the team in front of her, Gage flung back the furs he'd been wrapped in. He came to his feet, opening his arms in time to catch her.

"You're here. You're really here, and you're okay." Tears streaming down her cheeks, she rained kisses over his face. "When you weren't here at midnight, I-I thought it was happening all over again. I thought I was going to lose you, too." Her voice caught on a sob.

Gage's arms tightened around her before he pulled back to look down at her. "I'm sorry, honey. We had to rest the dogs, and Ethan couldn't get cell service." He framed her face with his hands, wiping away her tears with his thumbs. Beside them, Ethan reined in the sleigh carrying Rick Dane. Gage's expression hardened. "Don't worry, he'll pay for what he put you through tonight."

"It doesn't matter. All that matters is that you're home safe."

"You matter. I love you, Madison Lane," he said and lowered his head.

"Daddy, Daddy." Lily and Annie charged through the snow with half the town on their heels.

"Gage, *everyone's* here," she murmured against his lips.

"I don't care, it's about time they all know how I feel about you,"

"Umm, I kind of told them that already. I told them I love you too," she confessed.

"Good. Now be quiet and let me kiss you," he said, taking her lips in a passionate, possessive kiss.

She melted against him and looped her arms around his neck, stroking his hair.

He yelped, rearing back with a pained grimace.

She looked from her hand to him. "You're bleeding."

"Shh, keep it down. I'm fine. Hey, Lily, Annie." He knelt in the snow, wrapping the girls in his arms and reassuring them in his calm, steady voice that he was fine.

"You're not fine," Madison grumbled, then called out to his father, "Dr. McBride . . . Paul."

Gage slanted her an I-don't-believe-you look. "Really? You're telling my father on me?"

"Telling me what?" Paul walked toward them and helped his son to his feet. Nell, Sheena, Ted, Fred, and Liz crowded around him.

Ethan, wearing a black Ski-Doo suit, got off the sleigh

and said, "He's probably got a grade two concussion. He was out for a bit, he's dizzy and has a headache, mild case of hypothermia, too."

"Thanks a lot, pal." Gage muttered. "Remind me not to tell you anything again."

Ethan ignored him and, along with everyone else, glared at Rick. He whimpered and sank beneath the furs.

Madison turned to Dr. McBride. "I think we should get Gage to the hospital. He probably needs a CT scan."

Gage gave a frustrated shake of his head then shared a look with Coulter. "I'll take Gage and Madison to the hospital. Snow's letting up, turning into a nice night for a sleigh ride," the older man volunteered.

Paul hesitated, then nodded. "Okay, I'll take the girls and Sheena with me. Nell, you go with Ted and Fred."

Jill, carrying the black satchel, came over. "Good to have you home, Sheriff. You want me to bring Rick in?"

"Thanks, Jill. His leg's broken. I've got it in a splint. Probably just as easy to have Ethan take him over to the hospital on the sleigh."

"Okay. I'll have Ray meet them there and get this in the safe until morning." She held up the satchel and instructed the crowd to come at 9 a.m. to pick up their donations.

It took a while before they could get in the sleigh. Everyone wanted to shake Gage's hand and give Rick a talking-to.

Sheena reached up to kiss Gage's cheek. "I'm glad you're home. I was worried about you." She smiled at Madison, taking Annie and Lily by the hand. "Come on, girls. You'll see your dad at the hospital."

Ted and Fred slapped him on the back, and Nell patted his chest. "Don't be scaring me like that again, you hear?

Pretty near took ten years off my life." She rubbed Madison's arm, then looked at Coulter. "Thanks for bringing him home to us. You have yourself a merry Christmas, Coulter."

Something passed between them, like old hurts had been forgiven. "You too, Nellie."

Gage drew Madison into the sleigh with him. Once he'd settled her between his legs, he wrapped the furs around them.

"All right, folks, gotta get our boy to the hospital." Coulter slapped the reins, and the crowd parted, waving as they started across the field.

Above the church, a star appeared. Madison had never seen one quite so big or bright. "Look." She pointed it out.

"The Christmas star," Coulter said. "That's the same one that guided Gage's and Ethan's great-great-great-grandfathers and my great-grandfather to Christmas all those years ago. It's how the town got its name. Don't recall seeing it shining quite so bright in a good long while; you, Gage?"

Gage rested his chin on the top of her head, his arms wrapped around her under the furs. "Can't say I have, Coulter."

Something touched Madison's cheek. It felt like a kiss, the scent of roses wafting by her nose. As a deep sense of peace enveloped her, she realized her mother hadn't abandoned her after all. Madison had simply closed her heart and her mind to her presence. "Thank you," she whispered.

"Did you say something, honey?"

Snuggling into him, she lifted Gage's hand to her lips and kissed his palm. "Just grateful to have you home safe."

"I'm grateful to have you here in my arms. And just so you know, I don't plan on letting you go." He tipped her face up and kissed her.

Chapter Twenty-seven

Gage struggled to keep his emotions in check as he joined the citizens of Christmas in a standing ovation. He figured he'd eventually become accustomed to hearing Annie's incredible voice, and it wouldn't affect him as deeply as it did tonight.

"Bravo, bravo," Madison's friend Skye cheered beside him.

Gage held back a grin at the shell-shocked expression on his best friend's face. Ethan, who stood on the other side of her, mouthed, *She's nuts.*

But hot? Gage mouthed back. He'd seen the look on Ethan's face when she'd taken off her coat, revealing a pink knit dress that hugged her lithe, well-toned form—exactly the type of body that turned his best friend's crank.

Just like Madison's turned Gage's. He was counting down the minutes until he had her to himself. Up until a few hours ago, at his father's insistence, Gage had been in the hospital. With the citizens of Christmas sneaking in to check on him every five minutes and Madison's long to-do list, they'd barely had any time alone. Then his father had thrown a curve ball into his plans for the night, inviting friends and family to spend Christmas Eve at his place. Since Santa had a delivery to make and would require the services of his little helper—hopefully in costume— Gage and Madison would have at least a couple of hours of one-on-one time.

Before Gage got an answer to his question, Skye turned to Ethan as they took their seats. "You have the wonkiest aura I've ever seen. You're way too uptight. It's not healthy, you know. But I can help with that." She put her hand on Ethan's stomach. "Now just—"

"Hey, cut it out. We're in a church."

"She's right, honey. You are a little uptight," Liz said.

Skye put a hand on Ethan's thigh, leaning across him to talk to his mother. Ethan tipped his head back and closed his eyes. "Oh." She beamed at Liz and Gage's father. "You're perfect for each other. You've got matching auras."

"That's, um," Liz stammered, "oh, look, the children are coming back in to sing."

Gage's father was doing a good job at playing statue, eyes focused front and center.

"Maybe you should listen to her, Mom." Ethan grinned.

Skye smiled up at him, and his jaw dropped. He gave his head a slight shake. "Okay, you just sit there"—he removed her hand from his leg and put it in her lap—"and be quiet."

Her eyes narrowed. "You're a Republican, aren't you?"

"What the hell has that got to do with anything?"

Nell and the boys, along with the rest of the seniors in the row in front of them, turned to glare at Ethan. "Sorry. Heck," he said and glared at Skye.

She tossed her long, curly hair and moved closer to Gage.

"And I bet you're a bleeding-heart liberal," Ethan muttered.

Madison's friend Vivi slid in the pew beside Gage, a stack of papers bundled in her arms. "Did I miss anything?" she asked.

"The pageant, but they're going to finish up with a few carols," he said, as he watched Madison, wearing the red dress she'd worn at the Penalty Box, leading the kids back in.

Vivi looked at him and frowned. "Do you have a brother?"

He grinned as Madison threw up her hands when Hailey reorganized the kids in line, then reluctantly turned to answer Vivi. "Yeah, I have two of them—my older brother, Chance, and my younger brother, Easton."

"Do you have a picture of them?"

The expression on her face worried him. Not only did the bad guys shoot at his brothers, so did the women they'd left behind. They lived by a "love 'em and leave 'em" credo. He got his dad's attention. "You have a picture of Chance and Easton on you?" His father nodded and reached in his back pocket for his wallet.

"Whoa, and I thought you were hot," Skye said, looking at the photo Ethan passed to her. Ignoring Ethan's muttered "They're not that hot," she handed it to Vivi.

His aunt looked over her shoulder to check out what

was going on. Her gaze went from the photo to Vivi. Nell winced, a guilty expression on her face.

Gage leaned forward to whisper in his aunt's ear. "What did you do now?"

"Nothing." She whipped her head around.

He sat back and turned to Vivi. "You okay?"

Tight-lipped, she nodded and shoved the photo into his hand.

He wondered which one of his brothers had screwed her over, and how his aunt was involved—because no matter what she said, Nell *was* involved.

He'd have to solve the mystery later, because right then the choir began to sing. They sang all the old favorites, and just as he thought they were going to take a bow, the kids waved Madison onto the dais. She took her place between Lily and Annie, her face lighting up with her incredible smile when she opened her mouth to sing "Silent Night." None of the kids joined in. They watched her with goofy grins on their faces as she sang her heart out.

Vivi and Skye groaned, sinking down in the pew. Ted put his hand to his ear, turning off his hearing aid. "I wish I was deaf," Fred muttered.

The two men turned to look at Gage. "You're never going to have to worry about a talent scout stealing that one away from you."

Maybe not, but she was the one woman he'd follow anywhere.

As she hit the last discordant note, Gage stood, put two fingers between his lips, and whistled. Up and down the rows, people looked at him like he'd lost it. He didn't care and started to clap.

"I guess he really does love her," Skye said.

"Yeah, but I thought love was supposed to be blind, not deaf, too," Vivi said, as they stood up and clapped.

The choir held hands and started to sing "We Wish You a Merry Christmas," encouraging the audience to join in. As they were wrapping up, a phone rang, loudly. "Sorry...sorry." Madison waved, her face flushed. She slunk off to grab her purse from the floor beside the piano.

Not long after she answered her cell, whispers worked their way through the congregation. "It's Joe Hartwell. Probably trying to steal her away from us." A couple of people shushed them, the better to hear the conversation. It was one Gage wanted to hear, too.

He excused himself, discreetly making his way up the side aisle. So much for being discreet; he was like the Pied Piper with everyone following behind him.

"Yes, it was a shock." Madison nodded, looking to where Gage now stood below her. "I'll tell him. Really, that's a very generous offer, Joe. I appreciate your confidence in me." Her gaze swept over the people crowding in behind him, then back to Gage.

"We'll make it work," he said, pretty sure the offer was for her to take over Hartwell. "Accept if you want to."

"What the Sam Hill are you thinking?" his aunt snapped from behind him.

That he'd do whatever he had to to make Madison happy.

She smiled. "Joe, you gave me a piece of advice not too long ago, and I'm going to give the same to you. Now's the time for you to enjoy life, enjoy your time with Martha. Sell out to Ben at Triwest." She nodded. "Sure, I'll be happy to help you with the offer after the holidays. No, I appreciate it, but I've had a pretty good offer for a job here in Christmas." She glanced at Ethan. He nodded.

Gage frowned. "What's going on?"

"Merry Christmas, buddy." Ethan smiled.

"You remember the mayor, Ethan O'Connor? Well, he's been asked to throw his hat in the Senate race, and the town council has asked me to step in as interim mayor." She glanced at Gage and mouthed, *Good surprise?*

"Best ever," he said.

"Ethan, honey," Liz cried and hugged her son.

"What party would you be running for?" Skye asked, her voice saccharine sweet.

"Why, the Republican Party, of course," one of the old timers informed her, as he joined the crowd gathering around Ethan.

She snorted and walked away. Ethan's gaze followed her as he shook hands with his supporters.

No way, buddy, Gage thought, seeing a look he was familiar with in his best friend's eyes, *not in a million years.*

He tuned back in to Madison's conversation. "Merry Christmas, Joe, to both you and Martha. Yes, it seems to be the year for Christmas miracles. I'm so glad you got yours. Yes, I did, I got my Christmas miracle, too." Her gaze held Gage's.

"Back 'atcha." He smiled, then held out his hand to help her down when she disconnected. He drew her into his arms. "That was a pretty big secret to keep."

"It was, but I didn't have to keep it for very long. Ethan asked me this afternoon."

Half the town descended on them, wanting to congratulate Madison and give her advice. Gage gave up and decided to wait for her and his daughters by the entrance doors.

As he walked to the back of the church, Grace stopped him with a hand on his arm. "Merry Christmas, Gage." She smiled up at him. "I'm so glad Madison's moving here."

"Me too." He kissed her cheek. "Merry Christmas." He glanced at the tall blond man standing behind her with a sleepy Jack Junior in his arms. And for some reason, that bugged the hell out of Gage. Jack should be here with his wife and son, not Sawyer Anderson. The two men had been best friends growing up, and Gage knew Sawyer missed Jack as much as he did. But lately, he'd had the uncomfortable feeling that Sawyer wanted more than friendship from Grace.

Sawyer stuck out his hand. "Merry Christmas, Gage."

Aw hell, what was he thinking? It was Sawyer. He was a good guy. "Merry Christmas," Gage said, feeling like an idiot. Just because he was in love didn't mean everyone else was. They chatted for a couple of minutes as they headed to the entrance, then said good-bye. Gage ruffled Jack Junior's hair. "Hope Santa's good to you, buddy." The best gift the little boy could receive was his father, and Gage prayed Jack came home to him soon.

He walked to where Vivi and Skye were handing out copies of the *Chronicle* and snagged one of the papers from Skye. He'd heard Vivi had commandeered the paper for the day and now he knew why. On the front page, the headline read: The Grinch Who Saved Christmas, with a picture of Madison surrounded by a crowd of people, a megaphone at her lips.

Madison came up beside him, shrugging into her coat. "What's that?"

He grinned and handed her the paper.

"Aw, you guys," she said when she saw the headline, then groaned. "Couldn't you have found a better picture of me?"

Skye shrugged. "There weren't any. Face it, you're not very photogenic."

"I think you're beautiful," Gage said.

She kissed his cheek. "I think you're beautiful, too."

"Gross," Annie said, taking Madison's hand. "Come on, we gotta go. Grandpa said we can open a present tonight."

Lily smiled up at Gage, slipping her hand into his. "It's going to be the best Christmas ever."

"It already is," he said, taking Madison's other hand.

The four of them headed out into the lightly falling snow to the sound of church bells ringing and everyone wishing one another a Merry Christmas.

"I love Christmas," Madison said, her face lit up with a smile.

Looking down at the woman he loved, Gage decided that this time next year, he'd propose to her right here on the church steps.

If he could wait that long.

When an MIA soldier returns
from war, being home for the
holiday takes on a whole new
meaning...
Don't miss the next book in this
heartwarming series.

Please turn this page for a

preview of

Christmas in July

Chapter One

Till death do us part.

Grace Flaherty, owner of the Sugar Plum Bakery, tried to drown out the wedding vows she couldn't get out of her head by humming a song. Her breath hitched when she recognized the melody—"Amazed," her and Jack's song. It was as if he knew what she was going to do and tried to stop her. A warm, spring-scented breeze wafted through the screen door, and she closed her eyes, letting its soft caress soothe her aching heart.

Today was her husband's thirty-fifth birthday, and the day Grace said good-bye to him.

"I'm sorry, Jack. I can't do it anymore. I can't keep pretending you're coming home," she whispered, as she put the finishing touches on the cake, tying a yellow ribbon on the tiny, white picket fence that circled the pink-fondant house.

Since the day Jack's Black Hawk went down in Afghanistan and he'd been listed as MIA, she'd clung to the hope he'd come home to her and their two-year-old son. But where hope had once sustained her, now, seventeen months later, the spiderlike threads held her in limbo. The not knowing was making her crazy. She had to move on with her life and somehow heal her broken heart. The only way she knew how to do that was to let Jack go.

Kneeling on the stool beside her, her son Jack Junior dumped a bottle of blue sprinkles onto the stainless steel island instead of the cupcake she'd given him to decorate.

"Oh, Jack," she sighed, prying the bottle from his hand.

"Me do." Under a tumble of curly dark hair, a frown puckered the brow of his sweet face. "Mommy sad."

So sad that it hurt. "No, Mommy's happy." She gave him a reassuring hug, touching the tips of her fingers to her cheek to ensure there were no tears. For someone who'd been schooled at an early age to hide her feelings, it amazed Grace how easily her son picked up on her emotions. Then again, she could never hide her feelings from his father, either.

Forcing a smile, she handed him a miniature American flag. "Put it on your cupcake," she said, as she attached one to the Victorian's front porch. His hand darted in front of her. "No..." She swallowed a frustrated groan when he smashed the flag in the wildflower garden, taking out two poppies and a sunflower.

If she didn't hurry up, he'd destroy the cake. She darted to the refrigerator, retrieving the chocolate sugar plum she'd prepared earlier. Typically, the sugar plum contained an engagement ring or a wish. This one held Jack's wedding band, a good-bye note, and a wish for her future. A man's man, her husband didn't wear jewelry and had worn the ring only on their wedding day. Their life had been filled with such promise then, promises and dreams, like the house on her cake. But while her dreams with Jack might be over, she was determined to create new ones for herself and her son. Different dreams, but just as bright.

Instead of hiding the sugar plum in the cake like she always did, she placed it beneath the house. She couldn't risk someone else finding it, but she needed the sugar plum to be there. It wouldn't be her signature cake without it. And lately she'd been receiving letters from people whose sugar plum wishes had come true. Something her silent business partner and friend—not that Madison McBride knew what the word *silent* meant—had been happily exploiting. Grace didn't believe there was anything magical about her cakes, but if there was a chance . . .

The stool wobbled as Jack Junior tried to get down. "Me go to party," he said, referring to the gathering Jack's friends had organized to celebrate his birthday at the Penalty Box tonight.

After putting in twelve hours before picking up her son at the sitter—two of her employees had called in sick that morning—the last thing Grace wanted to do was spend an emotional evening with the citizens of the small town of Christmas, Colorado, who believed with all their hearts that their hometown hero would one day come home. It wasn't as if she could plead a headache or heartache and drop her cake off and leave. They expected her there, as upbeat and as naïvely positive as they were.

At the thought, Grace wearily scooped her son into her arms. "As soon as Mommy's cleaned up the kitchen, we'll go."

"No. Go now." Wriggling in her arms, he tried to break free.

She couldn't handle his Flaherty temper right now, but she couldn't leave the bakery in a mess, either. With a firm grip on his hand, she put him down and reached for the broom. "Here." She handed him the dustbin. "Let's play catch the sprinkles."

After a frustrating five minutes, even though the black-and-white tiles were clear of sprinkles, Grace reached for the mop, then stopped herself. She was being ridiculous. Searching for something to occupy her precocious son while she cleaned off the island, she latched on to the cupcake liners he'd dumped on the counter. Handing him the container and liners, she sat him on the floor at her feet. "Can you put these back in the tube for Mommy?"

He nodded and picked up the container. She ruffled his baby-soft hair then turned to clean up the mess. The crushed flowers called to her. She needed the last cake she made for Jack to be perfect. When a quick, over-the-shoulder glance revealed her son to be engrossed in his task, she reached for the pastry bag and rose nail.

Ten minutes later, she replaced the last of the three flowers in the garden and turned to her son. "Jack..." He was gone. Panic threatened to overwhelm her as the memory of another child who'd gone missing on her watch came back to haunt her. She pushed the thought from her mind, her gaze darting to the narrow spaces between the industrial ovens and refrigerator.

"Jack, it's time to go to the party," she cajoled as she knelt to look under the island. At the sound of a shuddering crash from the front of the bakery, she shot to her feet and tore through the double doors. "Jack!"

Chunks of wet plaster had knocked over a round bistro table as water gushed from a hole in the ceiling above. In one breath she was thanking God her baby hadn't been hiding under the table, while in the next she was crying out his name, her voice ragged with fear.

"I've got him, Grace," a deep male voice called from the kitchen. Sawyer Anderson, Jack's childhood best friend and owner of the Penalty Box, came through the swinging doors with her son in his arms. The former captain of the Colorado Flurries, a professional hockey team, he had been there for Grace since the day Jack went missing. Incredibly good-looking and laid-back, he was the one person she'd been able to share her fears with. The one person who understood why she couldn't keep pretending Jack was coming home. His support made it easy to be with him. Only lately, it'd been too easy.

She reached for Jack Junior, who wrapped his small arms around Sawyer's neck. She laid a palm on her son's back; the rise and fall of his breath and the warm body beneath his blue T-shirt calmed the panicked gallop of her heart. It took a moment before she could get the words out. "Where did you find him?"

"Back alley. I was coming to check on you..."

She closed her eyes. The screen door.

Sawyer rubbed her arm. "He's fine, Grace."

"Only because you were there. If you..." She shook her head, trying not to think of what could've happened. Of what had happened that long-ago summer. "Thank you."

From beneath the ball cap pulled low on his dark blond hair, he scanned her face, then lifted his gaze to the ceiling. "Shit," he muttered.

"Shit," said her son.

Grace shot Sawyer a don't-you-dare look as he fought back a laugh. "Jackson Flaherty, what did I tell you about using the S-word?" Grace's sweetly innocent child had been spouting expletives with an alarming frequency, and now it seemed she'd discovered the reason why.

"Me no say *shit*, Mama, me say *shh*." He grinned at Sawyer, who'd lost his battle with laughter.

She narrowed her eyes at the two of them. Sawyer winced. "Okay, buddy, I'll make you a deal. No more S-words this week, and Mommy'll bring you to the bar for a root beer float on the weekend." He raised a brow at her.

"Bribery?"

He shrugged. "Worked for me."

Obviously it worked for her son, too. He nodded. "Me like beer."

"I'm sure that's just what your mother wanted to hear," Sawyer said, handing Jack to her. "We need to do something about the leak."

Distracted by her son's safe return, she'd forgotten about the gaping hole in the ceiling. She wished she could ignore it completely and the dent it was going to put in her meager bank account.

Leaning over the table, she called to their tenant, "Stu, are you up there?"

"Stu up there?" her son echoed.

"He's not there, Grace. Get me the keys."

"How can you be..." She caught the sympathetic look in Sawyer's eyes. "You think he skipped out on us, don't you?" She groaned. "Jill's going to kill me. She wanted to put him out when he didn't pay last month's rent, but I thought..." She gave a disgusted shake of her head. "Jill's right. I'm a sucker."

Hefting Jack Junior higher on her hip, Grace rounded the display case and opened the cash register drawer.

"You're not a sucker," Sawyer said, as he followed her. He took the key she retrieved from under the tray and held on to her hand until she looked at him. "You were just trying to give the guy a break. Nothing wrong with that."

There wouldn't be if she could afford to, but she couldn't, at least not yet. Stu, a recent divorcé whose wife had had an affair and got both their home and their children in the settlement, had easily garnered Grace's sympathy. She hated the thought she'd been played.

"I could be wrong. Maybe he didn't skip out on you. Give me a couple of minutes upstairs and—"

She shut the register drawer and locked it. "I'll go with you."

"You sure? He might have left the place in a mess."

"Oh, I didn't think of that." Going into the apartment was hard at the best of times, and this was not the best of times. There were too many memories of Jack there. It was one of the reasons Grace had moved in with her sister-in-law a year ago, the other being the extra income from the rental.

"Me go, Da. Me go you." Jack Junior held out his arms to Sawyer.

Sawyer bowed his head, then lifted his eyes to hers. "I wish, buddy," he murmured as he rubbed her son's head and held her gaze.

Grace clutched the fabric at her throat. "Oh, Sawyer, I can't—"

He lifted his hand from her son's head to caress her cheek. "Yeah, I know. It's too soon. But—"

"What the hell's going on here?" Jill, Grace's sister-in-law, snapped, keys jangling in her clenched fist as she strode through the front door. Eyes the same vibrant blue as her brother's were dangerously narrowed beneath her dark hair, her blade-sharp cheekbones flushed with Flaherty temper.

Grace went to take a guilty step back. But Sawyer, with a gentle yet firm grip on her shoulder, held her in place. He gestured to the plaster-ridden table. "There was an accident. I'm going up to see what I can do."

Jill's gaze shot to Grace and her nephew. "Are you guys okay?"

"We're fine," Grace quickly reassured her. She knew how important she and her son were to her sister-in-law. They were the only family she had left.

Jill looked up at the ceiling. "Son of a—"

"Jill," Grace interrupted her in an exasperated tone.

"Sorry." Hands on the hips of her tan uniform pants, Jill's lips flattened. "So Stu decided to leave us a good-bye present when he skipped out, did he? Wait till I get hold of the little pri—"

Sawyer cut her off. "I'll take care of it. Help Grace get the cake and Jack Junior to the party." The look in his eyes dared her to argue.

Grace breathed a sigh of relief when her son broke their silent standoff. "Me go party."

"Right." As quick as Jill's anger flared, it dissolved with one word from her nephew. "Are you going to show me the cake you and Mommy made for your daddy?"

Jack Junior nodded as Jill took him from Grace's arms and headed for the kitchen. He looked back at Sawyer and opened his mouth.

Don't say it, Grace prayed, *don't call him Da.* Jill would never understand that it was normal for a little boy without a father to be looking for one. She'd blame Grace for spending too much time with Sawyer. Given what he'd just said to her, maybe she'd be right.

"See you at the party, buddy. Save me a piece of cake."

Jack Junior grinned. "Me have beer."

Jill shook her head. "Nice, Sawyer. Now you're corrupting my nephew."

"Don't listen to her," Grace said, as the doors swung closed behind them. She went to drag the garbage pail over to clean up the mess.

"I'll take care of it." Sawyer stopped her with a hand on her arm. "Don't let her get to you, Grace. You're not doing anything wrong."

"I know. It's just…" She shrugged, then looked up at him with a smile. "Thanks for everything."

"It's not your thanks I want," he said before he headed for the door.

*   *   *

With the cake in her arms, Grace walked the half block along Main Street with Jill and her son. Jack Junior giggled as his aunt swung him up the street by his hands.

"No wonder he'd rather walk with you than me," Grace said, as though it didn't bother her how often her son chose her sister-in-law and Sawyer over her.

Jill laughed. "Mommies aren't supposed to be fun."

"Thanks." Grace wasn't fun; she was boring and overprotective. She used to wonder what it was about her that her adventure-loving husband had fallen in love with.

Jill cast her a sidelong glance. "I was teasing. You're a great mom." She stopped, lifting a protesting Jack Junior into her arms. "Are you okay?"

No, I've just said good-bye to the man I loved with all my heart, and if you ever found out, you'd never forgive me. "Just tired. It's been a long day. Not to mention the ceiling caving in and Stu skipping out on the rent." Grace sighed. "I'm sorry. I should've listened to you."

"I'm sorry too, about earlier, with Sawyer. It's just seeing the two of you…" Jill held the door to the bar open with her shoulder. "Jack's coming home, Grace. You still believe that, don't you?"

I wish I did. "Of course I do," she said, smiling in response to the greetings their friends called out. It seemed like half the town had crowded into the rustic-looking bar with its exposed log walls and wood-planked floors. Jack Junior reached for one of the hundred yellow balloons that were tied to the chairs and bar stools.

Gage McBride, Christmas's sheriff, came over. "Hey, Grace, Jill." He kissed both their cheeks and took the cake from Grace, setting it on a nearby table. His wife, Madison, who was not only Grace's partner and friend but also the town's mayor, took Jack Junior from Jill and untied a balloon from the back of a chair. "Here you go, sugar."

Madison smiled at Grace then rolled her eyes when Nell McBride, Gage's great-aunt, sauntered over with her best friends, Ted and Fred, in tow. "Here we go," Madison sighed.

Gage, standing behind his wife, grinned. "You'd better give me little Jack."

Madison handed him off to her husband and took a seat, holding up her hands in surrender. "I'm sitting, okay?"

Ted pulled out a chair, and Fred plunked Madison's pink-sandaled feet on it. "Now you stay put, girlie," Nell ordered.

The three of them shared a few memories of Jack before moving off to join their friends at a large table near the jukebox.

"Gage, you have to talk to them. I can't take five more months of this," Madison complained, rubbing the barely noticeable baby bump beneath her floral sundress.

He leaned over and kissed her. "I'll give it my best shot, honey. But the three of them are almost as stubborn as you are when you set your mind on something."

"Hey, I'm not stubborn."

Gage snorted. "Come on, buddy," he said to little Jack, "let's go play some air hockey."

Grace felt a sharp twinge of longing. In the beginning, she and Jack had been as head over heels in love as Gage and Madison. Grace missed the feeling, missed being loved, being in love, having a man's arms around her. She wondered if she'd ever have that again. Just thinking the thought made her feel horribly disloyal. But who was she trying to kid? The citizens of Christmas, especially Jill, would never forgive her if she moved on with someone else. And it wasn't as if she'd ever leave town. Her father's military career had taken them all over the world, and Christmas was the only place that had ever felt like home.

"I'll be right back," Jill said.

Madison held out a hand. "Come sit with me."

Grace took a seat. "How are you feeling?"

Madison groaned. "Not you, too. I'm fine." She looked at her closely. "But you're not. Do you wanna talk about it?"

"We had a minicatastrophe at the bakery. There was a leak in the apartment and part of the ceiling came down. Sawyer's—What's wrong?"

"Nothing."

Grace arched a brow.

Madison grimaced. "It's Gage. He's worried Sawyer—"

She was right. They'd never be able to let her move on. "We're friends, that's all. And I couldn't ask for a better one."

"Forget I said anything. And don't worry about the leak. Your insurance will cover the damages. Plus, I have an idea that's going to make us rich." Grace's skepticism must've shown, because Madison said, "I'm serious. I've been thinking about all those letters. We're going to create a story about a Sugar Plum Fairy being the one who granted their wishes. We'll sell T-shirts, and books, and wands... Anything you can think of, we can sell."

Grace could almost see the dollar signs flashing in her business partner's blue eyes. She didn't want to be a downer, but she had to ask, "Umm, won't there be an issue with copyright? There's a Sugar Plum Fairy in *The Nutcracker*?"

"Fine." Madison gave a dismissive wave of her hand. "The Sugar Plum Cake Fairy, then. My friend Vivi can write the stories, and you can do the illustrations. Oh my God, this is brilliant. Are you excited?"

It was hard not to be. Madison's excitement was contagious. "Of course I am. It's a fantastic idea." She just didn't know where she'd find the time, but it was exactly what she needed right now. The perfect way for her to move on with her life.

Madison glanced at the door and reached for her hand. "Okay, just breathe."

"What..." She followed Madison's gaze and swallowed, hard.

Jill followed behind their friends—the twins Holly and Hailey, and Sophia and her sister-in-law, Autumn—with a life-sized cutout of Jack tucked beneath her arm.

A warm hand gently squeezed Grace's shoulder. Brandi, one of Sawyer's waitresses and another of Grace's friends, set a drink in front of her. "This'll help. It's the Hero. Sawyer named it after Jack."

"Thanks, Brandi," Grace murmured, wrapping her fingers around the cold, frosted glass.

"What do you think?" Jill asked, setting up the cardboard likeness beside Grace as the other women took their seats around the table. They placed their orders with Brandi while commenting on the lifelike Jack in his desert camouflage fatigues and Kevlar vest, a helmet tucked under his arm, his sexy grin flashing perfect white teeth in his deeply tanned face.

"Good Lord, there's nothing hotter than a man in uniform. And Jack Flaherty was—" Autumn, the owner of Sugar and Spice, and the woman who made Grace's chocolate sugar plums, quickly corrected herself "—*is*, hands down the hottest man I've ever seen."

He was. And looking at him now, Grace felt the same heart-stopping punch of attraction she did on the night he strode into the Washington ballroom to receive his Medal of Honor.

Sophia, owner of the high-end clothing store Naughty and Nice, pointed at Jack. "Yes, and he is coming home with me tonight," she said in her heavily accented voice.

"Grace?" Jill said, looking hurt.

She took Jill's hand. "It was a great idea. It's like he's here with us."

Jill smiled, her eyes bright with unshed tears. Brandi

came back with their drinks, and they lifted their glasses. "To Jack."

Everyone in the bar followed suit, and then, one after another, they stood to share their stories about Jack and their prayers for his safe return. By the time they were finished, Grace had downed two Heroes.

Jill clapped her hands. "Okay, time for cake."

They cleared the table and placed the cake in front of Grace. She stood, relieved that her emotional torture would soon be over. Gage, with Jack Junior in his arms, took his place behind Madison.

Sawyer moved in behind Grace and whispered, "Hang in there. Not much longer."

Before Grace could turn to ask how it went at the apartment, Jack Junior yelled, "Da, Da." And put his arms out.

Grace's breath seized in her chest.

Several people said, "Aw." While her friends quietly sniffed. "He'll be home soon, buddy," Jill said, swiping at her eyes.

Grace wheezed out a relieved breath. Thank God, no one seemed to realize he'd meant Sawyer.

But Sawyer did. "How about that root beer float I promised you, buddy?" He went to take Jack Junior from Gage, who gave him a hard look before passing him over. Of course Gage would notice, Grace thought miserably.

"Yeah, me want beer."

Everyone laughed as Sawyer carried her son to the bar. After they sang "Happy Birthday" to Jack, Grace cut the cake while Jill handed out the pieces.

She reached across Grace, bumping into her. "Sorry," she said when Grace stumbled.

The knife jerked and hit the house and it toppled over, revealing the chocolate sugar plum underneath.

"Hey, no fair, it's supposed to be hidden in the cake," someone yelled.

Grace sucked in a panicked breath and dove for the sugar plum. Jill beat her to it.

Her sister-in-law laughed. "Finally, I got a sugar plum."

As she opened it, Grace wished the floor would crack open and swallow her whole. Jill's laughter faded on a choked sob. She stared at Grace. "How could you? How could you give up on him?" she said in a strangled whisper.

"Jill, let me explain," Grace called after her as she strode to the door.

From behind the bar came a shrill whistle. "Everyone quiet," Sawyer yelled, directing their attention to the big screen behind the bar, where a newscaster was announcing breaking news. Sawyer turned up the volume.

"We have just received unconfirmed reports that the four crew members of the Black Hawk that went down in the mountains of Afghanistan seventeen months ago have been recovered...alive."

THE DISH

♥ ♥ ♥ ♥ ♥ ♥ ♥ ♥ ♥ ♥ ♥ ♥ ♥ ♥ ♥

From the desk of Jennifer Delamere

Dear Reader,

One reason I love writing historical fiction is that I find fascinating facts during my research that I can use to add spice to my novels.

For Tom Poole's story in A LADY MOST LOVELY, I was particularly inspired by an intriguing tidbit I found while researching shipwrecks off the southern coast of Australia. In describing the wreck of a steamer called *Champion* in the 1850s, the article included this one line: "A racehorse aboard *Champion* broke loose, swam seven miles to the shore, and raced again in the Western District." Isn't that amazing!? Not only that the horse could make it to land, but that it remained healthy enough to continue racing.

Although I was unable to find out any more details about the racehorse, as a writer this little piece of information was really all I needed. I knew it would be a wonderful way to introduce the animal that would come to mean so much to Tom Poole. Tom and the stallion are the only survivors of a terrible shipwreck that left them washed up on the coast near Melbourne, Australia, in early 1851. Tom was aboard that ship in the first place because he was chasing after the man who had murdered his best friend. By the time he meets Margaret Vaughn in A LADY MOST LOVELY, Tom has been involved in two other real-life events as well: a massive wildfire near Melbourne, and the gold rush that would ultimately make him a wealthy man.

As you may have guessed by now, Tom Poole is a man of action. This aspect of his nature certainly leads him into some interesting adventures! However, when he arrives in London and meets the beguiling but elusive Miss Margaret Vaughn, he's going to discover that affairs of the heart require an entirely different set of skills, but no less determination.

Jennifer Delamere

♥ ♥ ♥ ♥ ♥ ♥ ♥ ♥ ♥ ♥ ♥ ♥ ♥ ♥ ♥ ♥

From the desk of Erin Kern

Dear Reader,

There are two things in this world that I love almost as much as dark chocolate. One of them is a striking pair of blue eyes framed by thick black lashes, with equally dark hair just long enough for a woman's fingers to run through... Excuse me for a moment while I compose myself.

And the other is fried pie.

Okay, I just threw that last part in as an FYI. But what I'm really doing is tucking that useless tidbit away for a future project. That's just how my weird mind works, folks.

But in all seriousness, while I really do love a blue-eyed man, even more than that I love a wounded soul. Because I love to fix things. In my books. In real life I kind of suck at it.

Way back when I first started writing the Trouble series, as was kicked off with *Looking for Trouble*, I had an atypical wounded soul already forming in the cavernous recesses of my mind. I just needed to find a home for her.

Yes, I'm talking about a wounded heroine. I know that sounds kind of strange. Most romance readers love a scarred hero who gets his butt kicked into shape by some head-strong Miss Fix-It. Not that I don't love that also. But I also knew *Looking for Trouble* wasn't the place for her.

Lacy Taylor needed her own story with her own hero. And not only her own hero, but one with an extra tough brand of love that could break through her well-built defense mechanisms.

But make no mistake. Lacy Taylor isn't as much of a tough cookie as she'd like everyone to think. Oh, no. She has a much softer side that only Chase McDermott could bring to the surface. Of course, she tries to keep Chase at arm's length like everyone else in her life. But he's too good for her defenses. Too good-looking. Too loose-hipped. Too quick with his melt-your-bones smile. Not to mention his blue eyes. Gotta have those baby blues.

But Chase underestimates Lacy's power. And I'm not talking about her tough-girl attitude. Never in Chase's years as an adult would he have expected Lacy Taylor to get under his skin so quickly. Not only that, but nothing could have prepared him for his reaction to it.

Or to her.

You see, Chase and Lacy have known each other for a long time. And that's another one of my weaknesses—childhood crushes turned steamy love stories. And Chase and Lacy can cook up steam faster than a drop of water on hot pavement. But it wasn't always like that for these two. You see, Lacy blew out of Trouble years earlier, and after that Chase hardly gave the tough blonde a second thought.

But then she comes back. Now *that's* when things get interesting.

Mostly because Lacy had to all but beg Chase for a job, which, in Lacy's opinion, was almost as painful as a bikini wax. So then they're working together. Seeing each other often. Subtle brushes here and there…you get the picture.

It gets hot. *Real* hot.

But the most fun part is seeing how these two wear each other down. Lacy thinks she's so tough, and Chase thinks he can charm the habit off a nun. Well, actually he probably could.

Needless to say, heads butt, tempers flare, and the clothes, they go a-flying.

But which of these comes first? It's all in HERE COMES TROUBLE. Because every woman needs some Trouble in her life.

Especially the blue-eyed kind.

Steamy readin',

Erin Kern

♥ ♥ ♥ ♥ ♥ ♥ ♥ ♥ ♥ ♥ ♥ ♥ ♥ ♥ ♥ ♥

From the desk of Lily Dalton

Dear Reader,

History has always been my thing.

Boring? Never! I've always viewed the subject as a colorful, dynamic puzzle of moving pieces, fascinating to analyze and relive, in whatever way possible. I used to have a history professor who often raised the question, "What if?"

For example, what if Ragnar Lodbrok and his naughty horde of Vikings had decided that they adored farming, so instead of setting off to maraud the coast of England in search adventure and riches, they had just stayed home? How might that omission from history have changed the face of England?

And jumping forward a few centuries: What if historical bad boy Henry VIII had not had such poor impulse control, and had instead just behaved himself? What if he'd tried harder to be faithful to Catherine? What if he'd never taken a shine to Anne Boleyn? There wouldn't have been an Elizabeth I. How might this have changed the path of history?

At the heart of history, of course, are people and personalities and motivations. *Characters.* They weren't flat, dusty words in black and white on the pages of a textbook. Instead, they lived in a vivid, colorful, and dangerous world. They had hearts and feelings and suffered agonies and joy.

Just like Vane Barwick, the Duke of Claxton, and his

estranged wife, the duchess Sophia, who stand on the precipice of a forever sort of good-bye. Though the earlier days of their marriage were marked by passion and bliss, so much has happened since, and on this cold, dark night, understanding and forgiveness seem impossible.

Of course, in NEVER DESIRE A DUKE, the "what if?" is a much simpler question, in that the outcome will not change the course of nations.

What if there hadn't been a snow storm that night?

Hmm. Now that I've forced that difficult question upon us, I realize I don't want to imagine such an alternate ending to Vane and Sophia's love story. Being snowbound with someone gorgeous and intriguing and desirable and, yes, provoking, is such a delicious fantasy.

If there hadn't been a snow storm that night. . .

Well . . . thankfully, dear reader, there was!

Hugs and Happy Reading,

Lily Dalton

www.lilydalton.com
Twitter@LilyDalton
Facebook.com

♥ ♥   ♥   ♥   ♥

From the desk of Debbie Mason

Dear Reader,

So there I was, sitting in my office in the middle of a heat wave, staring at a blank page waiting for inspiration to strike. I typed Chapter One. Nothing. Nada.

And the problem wasn't that I was writing a Christmas story in the middle of July. I had the air conditioner cranked up, holiday music playing in the background, a pine-scented candle burning, and a supply of Hammond's chocolate-filled peppermint candy canes on my desk. FYI, best candy canes ever!

No, the problem was my heroine, Madison Lane. I didn't get her, and honestly, I was afraid I wasn't going to like her very much. Because really, who doesn't love Christmas and small towns? At that point, I was thinking of changing the title from *The Trouble with Christmas* to *The Trouble with Madison Lane*.

It took a couple of hours of staring at her picture on my wall before Madison finally opened up to me. Okay, so I may have thrown a few darts at her, drawn devil horns on her head, and given her an impressive mustache before she did. But she won me over. Once I found out what had happened to her in that small Southern town all those years ago, I fell in love with Madison. She's strong, incredibly smart, and loyal, and after what she suffered as a little girl, she deserves a happily-ever-after more than most.

Now all I needed was a man who was up for the challenge. Enter Gage McBride, the gorgeous small-town sheriff and single father of two young girls. A born protector, Gage is strong enough to deal with Madison and smart enough to see the sweet and vulnerable woman beneath her tough, take-no-prisoners attitude. But just because these two are a perfect match doesn't mean their journey to a happily-ever-after is an easy one. The title of the book is THE TROUBLE WITH CHRISTMAS, after all.

I hope you have as much fun reading Gage and Madison's story as I did writing it. And I hope, like Gage and Madison, that this holiday season finds you surrounded by the love of family and friends.

Wishing you much joy and laughter!

Debbie Mason